MEMORIES OF THE
OTHERWORLD

Vol. I: Prelude of Darkness

ZACK ABSHERE

*"The most dangerous foe we could ever face is
the one that lies within."*

SILVERSMITH
PRESS

Published by Silversmith Press–Houston, Texas
www.silversmithpress.com

ISBN 978-1-961093-61-4 (Hardcover Book)
ISBN 978-1-961093-57-7 (Softcover Book)
ISBN 978-1-961093-58-4 (eBook)

CONTENTS

Dedicated to my sister Emily
who helped make this book possible.

PROLOGUE

Fate cannot be erased, only changed.
One life ends, and another begins.
Two paths. One leads to darkness and the other to uncertainty.
For fate to be altered, a choice must be made.
But no choice comes without consequence.

There's nothing.
No reason.
No purpose.
No point.

A feeling of anguish followed by hopelessness. A world full of cruelty that will never change. To be rid of a curse that has no end, only one thing can be done.

It all ends somewhere—or perhaps, begins.

The sound of a gunshot snapped Isaac Wolfe awake.

He was in someplace he couldn't recognize. The darkness that surrounded him showed little more than his own hands.

"Brave soul who does not fear death," a voice echoed from the abyss. "Heed our call."

Isaac glanced around but couldn't see anything, or anyone, beyond the veil of darkness.

"We draw you from across the endless sea."

"Who are you?" he called out.

"There is much to be done, and yet, very little to do."

He took a few steps, but the darkness remained ever thick. "What is this place?" he asked out loud.

"It is your time to awaken," the darkness spoke. "Come forth and fulfill your desire."

Isaac frowned in confusion. "My ... desire?" He tried to remember how he had come to this mysterious place.

"Yes, the desire you've held deep within," the darkness replied. "Take hold and embrace destiny."

Memories of the past came rushing to his head. The anger. The fear. The pain. The sound of a gunshot.

"No ... don't ..." another voice echoed from the beyond. "Don't ... listen ..."

"Who's there?" Isaac called out.

"You are the beginning of the end," the first voice told him. "Step forward and invoke your true potential."

He clenched his fist at the darkness. "I don't want this!" he shouted. "Leave me alone!"

"Do not be afraid." As the voice spoke, there was the sound of wind blowing all around him. "You are the final piece toward salvation."

Isaac tried to back away, but an unseen force held him in place. "Just let me be at peace!" he yelled.

"Do not be afraid," the voice repeated.

As the darkness thickened, he felt his body growing heavy.

"Isaac!" the second voice called out to him, and he looked up in time to see a faint light descend upon him.

Then there was nothing.

PART I
A NEW WORLD

Endless night, no end in sight.
Darkness seeps and brings terrible fright,
a plague upon the souls of the righteous, corrupting all it touches.
Once trusted, the traitor now shows his true colors.
Who can stand against this foe, when light no longer lingers?
Cast aside, no hope remains, abandoned by the authors of our fate,
darkness engulfs me as I grow weak where I lay,
I feel the hands of a beast lift me up and take me away.
But it is not malice I sense from the one who carries me.
No, it is gentleness and comfort as he sets me free.

—Aurelia

CHAPTER 1

REFLECTION

"IsAaC!"

The horrific sound echoed down the hallway of the subway station as Isaac made his way toward the junction.

"I just need to transfer here!" he told himself as he entered the station.

"ThEre'S nO uSe HiDing!"

The creature pursuing him was getting closer.

"C'mon, dammit!" He slammed his hand on the call button. Glancing back, he saw a shadow form in the dim hallway.

In the distance, a metallic screeching sound could be heard. The subway was coming.

"I kNoW yOu'RE iN here!" The creature, a tall, lanky, old hag staggered into the station. Its black hair was ragged, covering thin, long bones. "wE NeEd you!"

Isaac quickly ducked behind a large container as the thing entered the vicinity. In the distance, the train was getting closer.

"StoP rUnNinG!"

His heart was beating fast, but Isaac tried to keep his breath silent as the train pulled into the station.

"tRyiNG tO esCApE, aRe wE!?"

As the train's doors opened, Isaac quickly dashed through, and he slammed his hand onto the panel to force them closed.

"NOOO!" The creature lunged at the doors.

Isaac quickly ran to the driver controls and flipped the lever. The train immediately began moving. The creature hit the side of the subway and was pushed away.

11

Taking a deep breath, he grabbed his arm, which had several gashes on it. *I gotta stop the bleeding*, he thought. Looking around, he spotted a first aid kit. He grabbed it and began using the gauze to wrap his arm. *Why the hell does that thing keep following me?* he wondered.

Eventually the train pulled into the next station, and Isaac cautiously stepped out. Looking around, the area was empty.

He spotted the location. Central Station.

He knew he was close.

He held his arm as pain shot through it. The medication and bandage from the first aid did little to help. "I just need to get out of here, but which way?" He made his way up a few flights of stairs and eventually found himself in a large terminal. "Where the hell is the exit?"

The place was dead; the lights were dim and eerie. It was like being in a horror film.

"Goddammit! Does this place have no end?" He made his way down the long terminal when he heard another noise.

A whisper.

"Shit!" he mumbled to himself. "Not again ..."

Even though he couldn't make out the words, the soft sound of whispering could be heard close by.

I have to hit the alarm, he thought. *That's the only way to stop it, to activate the fire system.* He slowly made his way toward what looked like an alarm panel.

The whispering increased. He was being too loud.

Carefully, Isaac tiptoed as he tried his best to be silent. *Please be a fire alarm, please.*

The whispering was growing closer.

As he approached the panel, to his dismay, it was a handicap button for a door.

Dammit! He crouched down as the whispering grew closer and closer, eventually passing him down the terminal.

That was close ...

He could barely see with the lights off, but the emergency lamps lit just enough for him to spy a red panel a reasonable distance away. That was definitely a fire switch. He crouched and slowly made his way toward it. The whispering was still in the area. It knew he was there.

CHAPTER 1: REFLECTION

Trying to steady his breathing, Isaac closed in on the panel. As he approached, he felt something brush his leg, and he tripped. Holding his hand out to stop the fall, it gave a loud *SLAP* as it hit the ground. The thing that had brushed his leg was what he was trying to avoid.

A trill echoed in the air, and Isaac knew he'd been discovered. He quickly jumped up, grabbed the red lever, and pulled.

The alarm system blared, and the fire suppression kicked in. A strong mist enveloped the area.

"Dammit!" He used the sound as cover and raced down the terminal, a loud trilling sound following him. Thankfully the voice system for the subway station kicked in to mask his sound.

"Attention! Emergency! All personnel must evacuate to a safe location!"

The hazard lights began to spin, lighting up the area. Isaac made his way to the exit signs, the trilling growing softer behind him. *I'm losing that thing,* he thought. As he rounded a corner, there was a dim light in the distance shining behind the cracks of a door with the final exit sign.

There!

Isaac rushed his way toward it, but as he came upon an intersection, a giant creature with multiple legs crawled into the center and hissed at him.

He stopped and began to back away. The creature was huge, filling most of the intersection, its vicious mandibles clicking menacingly.

"Are you kidding me!?" Isaac turned and sprinted down another path as the creature pursued him.

There's no way out of here! He stopped as the hallway seemed to have ended. There was no exit.

Turning, Isaac faced the insect-like creature.

I'm dead ...

It hissed, and its mandibles stretched out to devour him.

Suddenly there was a flash of light, and he was engulfed in a brilliant prism.

As the light faded away, he looked around and realized that he was now standing inside a prison. The monster was gone.

"What ... the hell?" he whispered.

"Are you okay?" There was a young woman with beautiful, long, black hair standing before him. "I didn't think I would make it in time." She smiled at him.

"Lucia?" Isaac stared at her in surprise. "How did you ... I thought I was done for."

"But your will kept you here, huh?" She beckoned to him. "Please, it will be safer over here."

The woman led him down a narrow hallway filled with prison cells. Eventually, they reached a door.

"Come inside, there's much to discuss." She opened the door, and Isaac entered.

It was an interrogation room. In the center was a table with two chairs on either side.

"Please, have a seat." She sat at one end and motioned for him to sit on the opposite side. He did so and stared cautiously at the woman as she sat across from him.

"That got pretty dicey there for moment, didn't it?" She smiled secretively to him.

"Uh, yeah." He narrowed his eyes at her. "But what are you doing here?"

"Whatever do you mean?" She put her hand on her cheek mischievously. "I've been with you for a while now, couldn't you tell?"

"What do you mean?" He studied the woman who sat in front of him. Even though he recognized her, her personality was nothing like the woman he knew.

"We can get to that later." She giggled playfully. "First, we need to talk about how you got here."

"My memory's a little fuzzy." He frowned despairingly. "But I know that I hurt people."

"That is one way to put it." She nodded solemnly. "Can you remember what it was that pushed you into this reality?"

"This ... reality?" He gave her a puzzled expression. "Am I trapped?"

"Unfortunately, yes," she answered sadly. "You used too much dark power, and now it's taken you over."

He looked down in dismay. "I guess I ended up becoming a monster after all."

"That's not true." She reached over and took his hand in hers. "We all fall at some point in our lives, but there's always a chance to make things right."

He could feel the warmth from her hand, and for a moment he felt at ease. "Your touch is the same as hers, but you're not really her, are you?"

"Who I am is not important right now." She looked at him sweetly. "You've just been through a lot, and you must be confused."

"This isn't like those other times." He sighed. "I was able to escape before, but now ..."

"Now comes the hard part," she told him with a hint of worry. "You need to heal your wounded heart and reflect on your reason for being here."

He shrugged in defeat. "There is no reason. I tried to avoid becoming that ... thing ... but I failed." He gave a soft chuckle while trying to hold back tears. "I just wanted to see Senko again, but instead I ended up attacking my friends."

"The darkness takes the worst of us and makes it manifest." She gave his hand a light squeeze before letting go and leaning back in her chair. "The fact that you're still here is testament to your strong will."

"I'm not strong." He shook his head.

"You're a lot stronger than you think." She smiled knowingly. "You need to piece together the memories of your journey, and the answers you seek will present themselves."

"I'm not sure where to begin," he said, looking hopelessly into her eyes.

"Just start from the beginning." Her eyes twinkled back at him. "From the moment you first appeared on Terra, and we'll go from there."

"I don't know how I got there." He frowned thoughtfully. "But I do remember having a nightmare."

CHAPTER 2
A FATEFUL MEETING

Isaac looked around the food court of New Meadows Mall noticing all the people enjoying life like there wasn't a care in the world. People were smiling, laughing, and kids were running around.

It was a beautiful Saturday afternoon, yet he couldn't feel the energies that went through here that everyone else could; all he felt was emptiness as he sat in the corner of the food court watching all the families and couples enjoying each other's company.

Isaac, however, was alone.

A couple walked past the table where he was sitting, and he overheard a few words that were said.

"So, what do you wanna do tonight?"

"Whatever you want, baby."

Isaac grimaced. Why did that always bother him?

He stood up and made his way to the front of the food court where the exit was when he began to hear music coming from somewhere behind him. With the activity that was going on, he could strangely make out the music over all the noise.

Overcome with curiosity he decided to go investigate.

Got nothing better to do, he thought, as he made his way past all the people toward the sound of the music.

As he got nearer, he realized that this melody sounded quite familiar, but oddly, it was a tune he thought he'd heard from when he was a child.

Yes, that was it.

Isaac had heard this tune because his parents had listened to it a lot. The music was an old classic from the early forties. Why would a modern-day shop be playing old music like that?

He looked around as he kept moving toward the melody. Did nobody notice, or did they not care that this music was so loud? Whatever. He didn't like this music. It reminded him of bad memories. He had to shut it off.

Straight ahead of him, the music was coming from a shop at the far end of a dead ended part of the mall. How could they have their music turned up this loud from way back there and still nobody noticed? He pushed past all the people and eventually reached the shop.

Now the music was so loud he couldn't hear anything else. Isaac entered the shop and realized it was practically empty. A record player was sitting on a desk in the middle of the shop. The shelves were lined with an odd assortment of dolls and records. He made his way to the desk and took the needle off the spinning record.

As the music stopped, he gave a sigh of relief. He hated that music.

Exiting the shop, he noticed that everything was silent. Not a sound could be heard. All the people that had been having lively conversations with each other had stopped talking completely; they stood where they were, completely motionless. It was as if stopping the music had stopped all life itself.

What the hell? What's going on?

Walking over to an old lady sitting on one of the nearby benches, Isaac looked at her as she sat there staring into space, ever so still. Everyone was the same. No one was looking at anything in particular, just simply staring.

Cautiously, he began moving back toward the food court, watching as everyone around him remained stationary. He didn't dare touch any of them as this could be an elaborate hoax and he was the victim. But then how could these parents make their babies stop crying? It was dead silent.

Isaac's heart began to race as he jerked his head to peer behind him. Something had moved. He was sure of it.

Just keep going, he told himself. *Just gotta reach the exit.*

He pressed forward.

As he came up to the food court, something caught his eye. It was fast. It moved between all the people, and he couldn't get a very good look at it, but the sound wasn't footsteps. No. More like claws on tile floor. A dog?

He began to move toward the thing when it stopped behind a group of women. What was it? He felt that whatever it was, was watching him.

"Isaac ..."

He turned around at the voice, but no one was there. Turning back, his heart sank. The thing behind the women was gone.

Screw this, Isaac thought. *I'm getting out of here.* He continued toward the exit.

He reached the center of the food court and froze. Everyone had turned their heads toward him and were staring at him.

No. Not at him.

At something behind him.

Isaac felt something breathe on his neck; he turned around in time to see a shadowy creature lunge at him.

Isaac jolted awake. *Another weird dream*, he thought. He looked at the crystal hung up on the wall. It shone a quiet blue.

Too early.

Swinging a leg over, he sat on the edge of his cot, looking around at the other men sleeping in their own. He stood up and headed for a glass door. He opened it and stood out on a balcony overlooking a city. The full moon gave an ominous shine as it reflected off the darkened windows of the houses below.

Adamas. That was the name of the city. Isaac had traveled from Earth to another planet called Terra. It had only been a few days, but he had already learned a lot about the different oddities on this new planet. To his surprise, everyone here spoke English and they had advanced technologies such as vehicles and devices similar to cellphones. After talking to a few people, he immediately signed up for a local tournament in order to earn some money since he didn't have any. Food and shelter were provided for tournament participants, so this was really a good start for him to go on.

This was a team-based survival tournament, and everyone who entered was a skilled fighter of sorts. Isaac was a little nervous, but how tough could these guys be anyway? He had passed the entry test with ease so this shouldn't be too hard, right?

As the sun rose above the mountains, people started to move around, going about their daily business and bringing the city to life. When the crystal on the wall shone a faint green, Isaac, along with all the other combatants, began to dress, preparing for the beginning of the tournament. He was ready before everyone else and headed down the stairs toward the initiation room.

Inside the large room were rows of benches and tables. He looked around, noticing there were already a few people from the other dorms talking amongst each other. He walked over to a bench in the upper right corner of the room and sat down.

"So whaddya say you and me be on the same team? It'll be fun, I promise!"

A young blond-haired boy around the age of twenty was near the middle of the room talking to a girl sitting down.

Giggling, the girl replied to the boy, "I dunno, are we even allowed to pick?"

"Of course we are! Just leave it to me!" The boy gave a wide grin as he hit his chest with his fist. "As for what we're gonna do, well, that's a surprise!"

Isaac furrowed his brow as he tried to ignore them.

Soon, all the other tournament participants entered the room and filled the benches.

"Alright, settle down!" A middle-aged man walked into the room followed by three other men. "You are all here because you passed the entry exam and have been accepted into this annual tournament. After a brief introduction, we will put you all into teams. But first, allow me to introduce myself. I am Bart Seros, Commander of the Adamas Royal Guard. You have all been given a great opportunity to be here, for this year we have new events planned."

Bart scanned the room, looking at all the candidates. "There seems to be quite a few of you. I won't be able to learn all your names, but that's the least of my concern." He looked over at one of the men standing behind him. "Have they all signed the form?"

"Yes, sir."

"Good." Bart smiled, looking back at the candidates. "For those who need clarification on that form you signed yesterday, it was a liability waiver. Basically, if you die, we aren't responsible." Bart laughed out loud at this.

Everyone in the room began whispering nervously to each other.

Why are they so surprised? Isaac thought. It stated clearly that this was a no-holds-barred combat tournament designed to pick the strongest participant.

"This is a no-holds-barred freestyle combat tournament designed to bring out the strongest candidate in this room."

See?

"That means you will be allowed the use of any abilities you possess, which also means you have the potential of being killed by other participants." Bart leaned over and whispered something in one of his assistant's ears. The assistant drew a scroll from his vest and handed it to Bart. "I have a list here of all the candidates and the teams you are assigned to. But, before I get into that, now that you all understand the rules, if you wish, you may drop out of the tournament at this time. You will not be given another chance."

After a short pause, someone in the crowd stood up and proceeded to the exit, followed by another, then another until little more than half the room was empty.

Bart waited till the last person left then looked at the remaining candidates.

Only about thirty remained.

"A shame; I was hoping for more people than this, but I like to give everyone a chance to reconsider giving up their lives if they feel they aren't skilled enough." Bart smiled and nodded. "Let me go over the full set of rules and events that we have planned before we put you all together into teams."

"Excuse me, sir." A man walked in and whispered something to Bart.

CHAPTER 2: A FATEFUL MEETING

"My apologies," Bart said to the candidates. "But I need to leave for a minute. Stay here till I return." With that, he turned and left with his assistants.

Isaac listened as everyone began talking to each other.

"Can you believe they changed the rules this year?"

"Never would have guessed they would allow lethal force."

"I could end up fighting any of you. Maybe we should all agree not to kill each other."

"No way I'm gonna agree to that. I'll kill anyone who brandishes an aural blade at me."

"But this is still a tournament, right?"

Isaac thought about that last comment. Still a tournament? Seems more like a test to him, but it did say they were trying to find the best candidate. Could they be looking for someone?

After a few minutes, Bart and his followers came back into the room.

"Again, I apologize for that interruption," Bart said. "It appears the tournament has been postponed. It will take place thirty days from now."

Turning to one of his assistants, Bart took a parchment from him. "I do, however, have the new list of teams here that we will organize you all into. But first, the rules and events."

Something was obviously going on. Now they were setting the tournament back? Who did Bart talk to, and what was it about?

"First off, the rules are simple. As each event takes place, you will be given an objective. Teams will compete against each other in order to achieve said objective. As stated before, you are given free use of your powers, so use them to your advantage. Be warned though as the opposing teams will use theirs, and if a battle ensues, one or more of you could be killed depending on the determination of the individuals. So, if you don't want to die, I suggest you just give up and let the opponent win if you think you're losing, but, seeing as you are all still here, I don't think any of you are going to just 'give up.'"

Bart looked at the parchment. "Before I tell you the first event, I will announce the teams. Stand up as I say your name so your teammates can recognize you."

All the candidates in the room straightened in anticipation. Bart began naming individuals in sets of three. One team Isaac noticed was all female, one of which was the girl that blond-haired boy was flirting with. He saw the boy's face show disappointment.

"Next team ..." Isaac stood up as he heard his name. "Team five, Isaac Wolfe, Drake Hardy ..." Isaac watched as a fairly big guy with brown, spiky hair stood up. "... and Vin Astor." Oh crap ... it was him. The blond-haired boy. Vin must have been thinking the same thing because he stood up with a disappointed look as he stared at Isaac and Drake.

After the rest of the teams were called out, Bart rolled the scroll back up and handed it to his assistant.

"Alright, now that you've all been put into teams, I shall reveal the first two events, which will take place at the Adamas Coliseum. First will be a one-on-one duel, so be sure to select the best fighter on your team. Second will be a monster slaying competition. Two teams of two will compete to take down a beast in the quickest time possible. And last will be a test of teamwork. It will involve solving several puzzles which require three people to initiate. That is why you have been put into teams of three, because you will require all the strength each of your comrades possesses. Without a good grasp on teamwork, there will be no victory."

Isaac couldn't believe this. He figured this would be cake if he just completed the tasks he was given. He glanced at Drake and Vin. If one of them were to mess up, they all messed up.

"Meet at the Coliseum thirty days from now. There, we will begin the start of the tournament. Take this time to get to know your teammates and learn their skills so you can achieve victory. Dismissed!" With that, Bart and his assistants left the room as with the rest of the candidates as they grouped into their teams.

"I'm Drake." Isaac shook Drake's hand as he introduced himself. "You're Isaac, right? Good to meet you."

"Sure," Isaac replied, folding his arms.

"Where's that other guy?" Drake looked around.

"Over there, flirting with those girls." Isaac motioned toward Vin, who was talking to the all-female team.

"Man, looks like he's gonna be the problem on this team." Drake started toward the group. "Let's go pry him away so we can get to training."

Isaac and Drake made their way to Vin. As they approached, the three girls acknowledged them. "Hey, I think your team-mates are here," said the girl with purple hair.

Vin turned to look at Isaac and Drake. "Oh, hey guys!" he said with a sarcastic tone. "This'll only take a sec."

"Let's go, hotshot. We should get started with training," Drake told him.

"Oh, come on," Vin pleaded. "We have thirty whole days. This will only take a minute."

"I dunno, Vinny," said the girl with brown hair. "They seem to be in a hurry."

"That's because they're over excited," Vin explained. "They just need to relax and realize that we're gonna have a lot of time to spend." Vin looked at Isaac and Drake. "Oh, by the way, this is Natalie." Vin pointed to the girl with brown hair. "This is Yuri," he pointed to the girl with purple hair, "and this is Tara." He pointed to the last girl who had teal-colored hair.

"You have really big muscles; do you work out?" Yuri asked Drake with a giggle as she felt his biceps.

"Well, I, uhhh ..." Drake's face turned pink.

Yuri ran her hand down his arm. "Oh, you must be a power wielder, would explain why you're so big."

Drake blushed deeper.

"Hey, this is great!" Vin clapped his hands together. "We could all go on a triple date!"

"Not interested." Isaac turned and headed for the door. "I'll be at the forest battle grounds when you're actually ready to train."

Vin was taken aback. "Well ..."

"We really should be going though," Drake explained. "Sorry ladies, but this will have to wait." Gently taking Yuri's hand off his, he turned around and proceeded to catch up with Isaac.

"Ahh, hell!" Vin sulked. "Just my luck to be stuck with those two." He turned to the girls. "Guess I better catch up with them. See you later!"

As Vin ran to catch up with Isaac and Drake, the three girls watched them leave.

"Well, HE'S not gonna be a problem," Natalie said. "And I'm not sure about that Drake character; he seems like he isn't very smart, that one belongs to you Yuri."

"But about that third one, Isaac," Yuri mused. "He seems a little too focused."

"He was also kinda weird." Natalie frowned. "His aura was different. For a moment I thought I detected two auras, but for the most part I believe he uses energy. We'll leave him to you, Tara."

Tara remained silent as she watched the three boys walk out of the building.

"Hey! You gonna stop daydreaming and show me what you got or what?"

Isaac gave Vin an annoyed look. "Whatever ..."

Isaac, Drake, and Vin stood within a forest clearing near the outskirts of Adamas.

Isaac stood about twenty yards away facing Vin.

"You drag me out here away from some cute girls just to say 'whatever'?" Vin folded his arms. "You better show me something impressive."

"Maybe we should start by telling each other what our abilities are," Drake suggested.

"Or we could figure it out through combat," Vin replied with a grin.

Drake shook his head. "We're supposed to be a team, not try to kill each other. If we understand what our powers are now, we can figure out how to spar with each other in order to improve our teamwork."

"Well, then, why don't you start?" Vin said with a hint of sarcasm.

"Alright." Drake beamed with confidence. "As you can see, I'm a power wielder. My weapon is an axe, and I specialize in shockwaves."

"Oh yeah, totally cool." Vin seemed unimpressed. "Well, let's see what you can do then."

"Very well!" Vin's eyes shone with enthusiasm. "I possess speed!" He turned toward a nearby tree, and in a very quick movement, ran up the tree and stood on one of its sturdy branches. Holding his hand out, a yellow dagger, about sixteen inches long, appeared in his hand. "There isn't anyone in this tournament faster than me!"

Isaac gave a loud yawn. "Good job. You qualify for the monkey fair. Now all you need is a tail."

Vin descended the tree, bouncing from trunk to trunk on his way down. "You make that all up on your own?" He pointed his dagger at Isaac. "What can you do, Mr. Serious?"

Honestly, Isaac didn't really know that answer. Compared to Earth, since coming to Terra, he could run faster, lift heavy things he couldn't before, and even levitate objects with telekinesis. When going through the initial orientation for the tournament, the people there told him he was a gifted mage, so ...

"Energy. I'm an Energy wielder."

"That's what I figured," Drake said, rubbing his chin curiously. "They made our team with all three primaries in order to compensate for each other's weaknesses."

"So, you're a mage, huh?" Vin stared at Isaac. Waving his hand, the yellow aural blade vanished. "Unfortunately, you will never be able to touch me. See, I'm way too fast for your magic to keep up." Vin chuckled out loud, placing both his hands behind his head.

"Is that a challenge?" Isaac gave Vin an uninterested look.

"Hells ya that was a challenge!" Vin replied with confidence.

"Hold on, guys! Don't go ripping each other's faces off just yet!" Drake moved to stand in between Isaac and Vin, holding his arms up. "We should set up a proper way to spar rather than have death matches. We're trying to train, not kill each other."

"Ya ya, you said that already," Vin said with disappointment, dropping his hands back to his side.

Drake looked at Isaac. "What kind of magic are we talkin' about here?"

Isaac stared blankly at Drake. "Just a few wind spells and telekinesis techniques."

Vin laughed loudly as he began to pace in a circle.

Drake looked solemnly at Isaac. "I don't mean to sound rude, but do you know any fire or ice magics?"

"I don't."

Vin laughed loudly again.

"You got a problem?" Isaac stared coldly at Vin, anger glistening in his eyes.

"Sorry, it's just you act all serious and quiet, and yet, you are starting to sound like a weakling." Vin laughed at the idea as he continued to pace.

"You do realize that if you are correct, then this could have a negative effect on our team, right?" Drake replied to Vin.

What did he say!? Isaac was uneasy at Drake's statement. Was he really that weak?

"You don't have to worry about me. I can handle myself," Isaac said straight to Vin.

"At least he's confident." Vin stopped pacing. "Anyway, what kinda training you got for us Drake?"

Drake paused to think. Placing his hand on his chin, he thought to himself. "Well, to be honest, I don't know."

Vin gave a confused look. "Wait—what!? You were just telling us how we need to train, and yet you don't have a plan?"

A sheepish grin spread across Drake's face. "Well, I kind of thought that we could just sorta practice fighting on each other."

"I see ..." Vin put his hand to his chin in thought.

"I suppose I'll just head into town and find myself a library then," Isaac said while heading toward the gate.

"I've got it!" Vin clapped his hands together.

Isaac stopped and stared at Vin. "What?"

"I know a place where we can train!" Vin gave a wide smile.

Drake looked curious. "What do you mean?"

"Well ..." Vin started, waving his hands in the air. "There's this place I go to that is strictly for aura training. It's where I learned everything I know."

Isaac was annoyed. He folded his arms and stared dumbfounded at Vin. "Why didn't we just go there to begin with, genius?"

"Well, as a matter of fact!" Vin replied sternly, pointing his finger at Isaac. "They don't just let anyone in."

"Then how are you gonna get us in?"

"I told you, I've been training there for a while, and I know the people that run it."

"That's great!" Drake said with satisfaction. "What are we waiting for? Let's go!"

"Alright! Just follow me!" Vin said, turning, heading toward Adamas' main gates.

Isaac shook his head in disbelief.

"NO WAY!"

The trio stood at the doors to Adamas Castle. A young woman stood guarding the entrance. She had majestic, long, blue hair that appeared mesmerizing with her deep blue eyes and an air of allure about her.

"You realize you're asking me to let two complete strangers into the castle so you can train for some silly competition!?"

Vin gave a look of surprise as he motioned playfully at her. "Oh, come on Raine, you know I wouldn't let them do anything outrageous!"

"Oh please! Like that last fellow you brought in here?" Raine gave Vin a mocking stare. "And don't get me started on that bird of yours!"

Vin gasped dramatically, putting both his hands on his chest. "That incident was not my fault! And please leave Ulrix out of this; that poor bird gets enough crap from the maids."

"Ah, the maids. While we're on that subject, might I remind you that they have a job to do, and if you keep fraternizing with them, I will have you removed from the premises permanently."

"Raine, you know I only do a little casual flirting with them every now and then."

"Oh really?" Raine stared Vin down with an icy, cold glare. "Saying vulgar remarks and touching them inappropriately is 'casual' flirting? I don't know how many complaints I've had from those poor girls begging me to just burn you to a crisp!"

Vin leaned toward Drake with his hand up to his mouth and whispered loudly, "That could be hot!"

Raine scoffed, putting her hands on her hips. She glowered at Vin. "This conversation is over; take your friends somewhere else."

As she walked away, Vin quickly took a few steps toward her with his arms outstretched in a pleading manner. "Okay, okay! You're right, I do flirt a little aggressively, but if you let us into the training room, I swear to you that we won't be doing anything else but training."

"This isn't up for debate," Raine replied as she held up her hand to stop Vin from proceeding. "Unless you've got some kind of celebrity or king with you, strangers aren't permitted inside these walls."

"Well, what if these guys WERE celebrities?" Vin said confidently, glowing with pride as he placed his hands on his hips in a heroic manner.

Raine rolled her eyes. "Really? You're gonna try and tell me that this muscle head power wielder ..." She looked uninterested at Drake, who nervously waved and smiled at her. "And this ..."

Raine's words cut short as she stared at Isaac.

Isaac looked blankly at Raine.

For a moment time stood still as Isaac felt Raine look him up and down.

Vin looked back and forth from Raine to Isaac. "Uhh, hehe, whatcha doin'?"

"Who are you?" Raine's voice sounded calm and gentle.

"He's nobody!" Vin interrupted, stepping between the two. "Just another tourney goer like myself, hehe!"

"I wasn't asking you!" Raine hissed as she forced Vin aside.

Isaac looked Raine in the eyes. "I'm Isaac."

"Isaac ..." Raine repeated his name with curiosity. Turning her head, she looked at Vin. "You all may enter. But you better be on your best behavior. We go to see the queen."

"WHA!?" Vin stammered in disbelief.

The castle was huge.

Everywhere Isaac looked, there were paintings of beautiful scenery on the walls, and the carpets were maroon with gold décor imbedded in them. Chandeliers hung from the ceiling, and there were more of those glowing crystals that kept track of the day. Assortments of furniture were scattered along the hallways, and there were people in fancy dresses and suits sitting and chatting amongst them. Everything seemed so colorful compared to the town. Isaac felt a little out of place considering he had never been around such nobility.

After a stroll through the long and wide hallways, Raine led the three to a large set of double doors. Through the doors they stood at the botton of a grand staircase.

"Alright." Raine stopped, turning to face the three. "When we get up there, you will remain quiet and respectful." Vin started to reply when Raine held up her hand to silence him. "Especially you, Vin. If you mess this up, I will make you wish you were never born. You got me? Just nod your head."

Vin looked at Raine with innocence in his eyes as he nodded to her.

"Alright. Let's go. And not a single word!"

As they reached the top of the grand staircase, Isaac could see a huge area about the size of half a football field, the maroon carpet running straight down the center toward the far end, which had around twenty people or so engaged in conversation.

As they approached the group, Isaac could make out two big chairs with a young woman sitting in the smaller one. The queen. She was a beautiful woman with fair skin and long, black hair with dark brown eyes, wearing an elegant silver dress.

Raine stopped them about twenty feet from the group of people conversing with the queen. Isaac spied one of those people to be the commander of the royal guard, Bart Seros.

"Your Majesty," Bart said with respect in his voice. "At the time being, we do not know what Rubens is planning against Esmeraldas, but we have sent scouts to determine what countermeasures can be done in case of an attack."

Another gentleman turned his attention toward Bart. "Sir, how do you know that Rubens is even planning something as drastic as an attack on our allied nation? That is absurd!"

Bart turned toward the gentleman. "Because our intelligence has uncovered the fact that they are building a huge army and fortifying their defenses."

"But isn't that what we do? Strengthen our numbers for the case of an emergency?"

"Not like this, though. They do it in secret and quickly. Even if we were to assume this was just a military exercise, the timing would be too perfect, especially after the tornado hit Esmeraldas and the tree lost many of its limbs. The mages there are still doing their best to regrow the ancient tree's branches, but these things take time."

"Not to mention the power and precision with which that tornado hit," another person added, nodding toward Bart. "The way it hit has left Esmeraldas with quite a weak spot for Rubens to send in their units. One could say that they themselves caused this tornado in order to get the tactical advantage."

"Do not assume anything until we have viable proof!" the gentleman stated angrily, hitting his left palm with the back of his right hand. "We cannot jump to conclusions and start a war!"

"Then what do you propose we do, Frederick?" The queen spoke with a soft but firm voice.

"Milady, the council has assured us that all must be taken into consideration before we start accusing those of acts of treason," Frederick explained pleadingly.

The queen paused for a moment before replying, "Does the council have a plan?"

"They are working out a peaceful negotiation to determine if Rubens is planning to start a war."

"We are running out of time, Frederick." She sighed. "If the council doesn't come through with a plan by the end of the month, I will have no choice but to take action."

"Milady—"

"With or without the council's consent," she declared. "I will not let the people of this kingdom, or that of Esmeraldas, be harmed by a nation that may want to start a war." She turned to Bart. "Sir, please keep an eye on Rubens before we are able to determine the proper action in keeping our allied nation safe."

"Milady," Bart acknowledged with a nod.

She turned back to Frederick. "Let the council know they have one month to make peaceful resolutions. Dismissed."

Isaac could see slight frustration hidden on the gentleman's face as he walked past the four waiting patiently.

The queen motioned for Raine to approach.

"You three wait here," Raine whispered to them as she proceeded toward the throne.

Isaac watched as Raine whispered something in her ear. The queen whispered something back and then immediately looked at him. Some of the people standing in front of the throne looked curiously at the three.

Isaac felt a little nervous being stared at by all the men and women in fancy clothing, and he could feel the other two were thinking the same.

Finally, Raine called the three over to the throne.

"You stand before Lucia, Queen of Adamas," Raine said with pride. "Kneel and show your proper respects."

"I am Drake, Your Majesty." Drake kneeled politely as he bowed his head.

Lucia nodded in approval. "Nice to meet you, Drake."

"Ah, my queen!" Vin kneeled with a sly smile on his face as he looked at Lucia.

There was a slight grin on Lucia's face as she replied, "Hello, Vin."

Raine rolled her eyes.

Isaac felt everyone watching him as he slowly bent down on one knee.

"What is your name?" Lucia asked him with a sweet tone.

"It's Isaac."

"You may all stand. No need to dirty your trousers," the queen said merrily.

Trousers? A part of Isaac wanted to laugh but held it in without notice.

"You are all here for the tournament, correct?" the queen asked them, placing her hands gently on her lap.

Vin gave a broad grin. "That's right! And I'm the leader!" He motioned to himself.

"Since when did you become the leader?" Drake scoffed, slightly elbowing Vin in his arm.

"Since I'm obviously the strongest of us three!" Vin said, puffing his chest out with confidence.

Raine laughed loudly at Vin's remark.

"What!?" Vin looked insulted.

"What makes you think you are the strongest?" Raine asked with sarcasm, folding her arms and staring at Vin. "It better not be your ego."

Vin gave Raine a sly wink. "Well, considering what I do for a living ..."

"Court jester?" Isaac asked blankly.

Lucia chuckled.

Vin gave Isaac an uninterested look.

"Well, in any case, I believe you three were here to use the training facility?" Raine turned to look at Lucia.

"Yes, ma'am," Drake replied respectfully. "If that is alright with you."

Lucia nodded. "I will allow it as long as you have an escort." She turned to Raine. "Would you kindly see to it?"

"I knew you were going to say that." Raine sighed.

"Looks like I'll be able to show you my super cool moves after all," Vin said to Raine with a sheepish grin.

She wasn't paying attention; she was looking at Isaac.

"So, this room can restrict our aura completely?"

The four stood in a rather large room that had a lot of practice equipment in it, including training dummies, obstacles, and an assortment of weapons.

"That's right; in here we can practice by limiting our own powers," Vin said confidently.

"And this helps us how?" Drake inquired.

Vin walked over to a nearby training dummy. "If we practice with limited power during training," he explained as he punched the dummy a few times, "then when we get into a real fight, using our full potential will be a whole lot easier." He slammed into the dummy with full force, causing it to rock heavily back and forth. "Of course, you'll be able to hit this thing a lot harder, I suppose," Vin finished, looking at Drake.

"That's right," Raine interrupted. "While you are here, you are not to destroy the equipment, simply use it to practice."

"No worries here, ma'am," Drake replied sincerely.

Raine turned to a set of nearby benches. "Good." She moved toward them and sat down, opening a book she had brought with her and began to read.

"There's also a practice area off to the side here where we can spar," Vin continued. "I suppose we could start by restricting the amount of our powers to twenty-five percent." He handed Drake and Isaac each a belt that had three tiny knobs on them. "Each knob corresponds to an aura; you can limit your power by the amount you turn each knob."

"Pretty cool!" Drake said, turning the red knob on his belt till the meter read: 25%.

Isaac did the same, only with the blue knob on his belt.

"Alright, I'm set here; you two good?" Vin asked, looking from Drake to Isaac.

They both nodded.

"Alright then, let's get started!"

Two hours went by as the three practiced fighting techniques and drills. Isaac wasn't feeling any different than what he'd always been used to since gaining his powers. As the other two were starting to get tired, Isaac felt just as good as when he started.

Raine quietly sat on her bench reading her book.

"HIYAAA!" Vin was upside down on a set of monkey bars about fifteen feet off the ground, as he twisted his body to lunge toward a second set of monkey bars directly ahead and below him. He caught the bar and swung, arching his body till his legs hooked over another bar on the same set. "Whew! This is getting pretty tiring." He dismounted, tumbling till he landed on the ground.

Drake was doing weapon drills with a battle axe he had taken from the weapon stock. "I've never trained by restricting my aura like this. I wonder how it will feel once we take off the belt."

"Don't just yet," Vin said, sitting down on a nearby chair. "Just one more drill before we call it a day."

Isaac had been training with targets that were set up on the wall; he was practicing his accuracy by hurling objects with telekinesis.

"Hey, mage! Let's see what you've got!" Vin said, looking directly at Isaac.

Isaac stopped and turned to look at Vin. "What?"

Vin stood up, wiping some sweat off his forehead with a towel. "Let's spar, you and me."

"I'm assuming we keep the belts on, right?" Isaac replied.

"Of course," Vin stated. "We wouldn't want a certain someone to get mad because of my amazing abilities."

"This will be interesting," Raine said from across the room, her eyes never leaving her book.

I'm going to crush this guy, Isaac thought as he made his way over to the sparring area.

"Put these on." Vin tossed Isaac a bag; inside were a pair of gloves, head gear, and body protection. "Select whatever training weapon you desire."

After Isaac had put on all his gear, he went over to the weapon rack and selected a standard straight sword that appeared to be made out of bamboo. Walking back, he stood on one side of the sparring area facing Vin, who already had his gear on and was wielding a pair of wooden daggers.

"Don't kill each other, you got that?" Drake said as he sat down on one of the nearby chairs to spectate. "This is training, not a death match."

"Don't worry," Vin replied with confidence. "He's not gonna know what hit him."

Raine chuckled from across the room.

Isaac gave a grim look. *How dare they make fun of me?*

"See, even Raine agrees?" Vin laughed, twirling his daggers with his fingers.

"Actually," Raine explained, still reading her book, "I was laughing because you're probably gonna lose."

Isaac and Vin both looked at her with surprise.

"Really?" Vin said with annoyance. "We'll see about that. You ready?" He looked at Isaac.

"Let's go!" Isaac crouched in a defensive stance.

Vin twirled one of his daggers before getting into his own stance. "Winner takes all!"

Isaac watched as Vin bounded across the room at him. With only twenty-five percent aura, Vin was a lot slower than before, and Isaac readied his sword for a defensive strike.

CHAPTER 2: A FATEFUL MEETING

Vin darted from side to side as he approached Isaac, ready to deal a swift blow to his left. Isaac saw the attack and moved to counter, but the attack never came.

A feint.

Vin twisted his body around to deal a strike to Isaac's now unguarded right side. As the dagger sliced through the air, Isaac swiftly moved his sword back to his right side by bending his wrist. Vin gave a shocked look as his blade was blocked by Isaac's sword. Bringing his left hand up swiftly, Isaac sent a small blast of wind into Vin's chest, causing him to be thrown backward.

"What the hell!?" Vin was sitting on the ground.

Isaac smirked. "That it?"

Vin got up and readied himself. "You got lucky!" He hurled himself back at Isaac, only this time he unleashed a flurry of dagger strikes aiming for his chest.

Isaac saw the incoming attack and moved his body, arching in and out, avoiding all the attacks. Using his telekinesis, he was able to snag one of Vin's daggers and pull it from his hand; when this happened, Vin let out a yell and threw a spinning back kick toward his face, which Isaac dodged easily.

Isaac thrust his sword toward Vin's chest as he completed his spinning kick, which, again, knocked Vin to the ground.

Drake laughed. "Haha! Isaac is a defensive fighter, but he barely uses any magic at all!"

"It is rather strange, actually," Raine commented. "Your hand-to-hand is exceptional, but you seem to have no magic abilities whatsoever."

Isaac watched as she closed her book, stood up, and made her way over to him. "This fight is over. You lose, Vin," she declared, looking at Vin, who was still sitting on the ground.

"I don't get it!" Vin said in disbelief. "Aren't you supposed to be a mage?" he asked, looking at Isaac.

"Oh, quit whining!" Raine chuckled, facing Isaac. "Isaac, can I speak to you over there?"

He looked at her curiously. "Okay."

"Whatcha talkin' about?" Vin asked while rising to his feet.

"None of your business!" Raine snapped back at him.

Isaac and Raine made their way to the back of the training room.

"You think maybe she's gonna ask him on a date?" Drake asked Vin playfully.

Vin jerked his head toward Drake. "Are you kidding? Look at that guy! He's a shrimp! There's no way Raine would go for a guy like that!"

"Well, I don't think he's all that bad. A little weird, sure, but not bad." Drake used a nearby towel to wipe sweat off his forehead. "Plus, he DID beat you."

"Whatever," Vin grumbled.

Raine stood with Isaac out of earshot of the other two.

He saw her face change to a friendly, yet almost humorous expression.

"You haven't told them, have you?" she questioned him.

Isaac looked confused. "Told them what?"

Raine rolled her eyes. "You can't fool me. I know."

He was genuinely confused. "Know WHAT?"

She stood back a little. "You really don't know?" Her face was serious now.

"I'm not sure what you're asking me."

Raine watched Isaac for a moment before replying, "I see."

"Is there something wrong?" He tried to sound polite.

"No, but I'm curious now," she explained. "They said you were a mage, but you barely use any magic, yet they make you take an entrance exam before entering the tournament."

"So?"

"So, I mean, how can you be a mage if you don't use magic?" Raine looked questioningly at Isaac.

He stared blankly at her. "But I CAN use magic. You saw me."

"Tufts of wind and moving objects isn't exactly magic."

He folded his arms. "What are you saying?"

She nodded thoughtfully. "I would be willing to teach you how to use magic properly, if—" she gave him a serious look, "—you are willing to move into the castle."

WHAT!?

Isaac was seriously shocked. *What did she just say?* "I thought you said you didn't want us here to begin with."

"I did." She gave him a half smile. "But I can't stand seeing you struggle like this. If you move into the castle, you won't have to sleep in the same room with a bunch of smelly guys. You'll have your own room. Plus, I will be able to help teach you proper magic use while still being able to perform my duties to the queen."

Isaac looked Raine in the eyes. "What do you care? I'm just a regular guy. What do you get out of this?"

"Perhaps there's something about you that sparks my interest," she replied, punching him playfully in the arm.

Sparked her interest? She wasn't attracted to him, that's for sure, Isaac thought. So, what could it be?

"Deal?" She held out her hand.

He paused before accepting. "Alright.

After training, the three went to a bar called Ruby's, owned by an incredible woman by the same name.

Vin studied Isaac from across the table. "I don't get it," he said in disbelief. "Why would she ask you to stay in the castle and not Drake? He's much better looking than you."

Isaac gave him a wry look.

"I don't think it's about the looks." Drake took a drink from his mug. "Clearly she sees something in you that's for sure."

"Huh, still boggles my mind," Vin stated.

Isaac peered at Vin from across the table. "Why? Because she's taken an interest in me instead of you?"

Vin looked back, an expression of annoyance on his face. "No, because she doesn't take interest in anyone so fast, that's why."

The three looked up as a middle-aged woman approached the table with plates of food in her arms.

"Afternoon, boys!" the woman said in a southern accent, surprising Isaac.

"Ruby!" Vin said playfully. "You're lookin' beautiful as ever!"

Ruby wore a sheepish grin. "Oh Vin, you're such a flatterer!" She laid the plates down on the table and handed Vin three forks. "How ya been, hun?"

Vin gave Isaac and Drake each a fork. "Well, I've entered into the tournament, and these guys are my partners."

"Well, hi there!" Ruby leaned over to shake Isaac and Drake's hands. "I'm Ruby; a friend of Vin's is a friend of mine!"

"We're only teammates, nothing more," Isaac said.

Vin sighed. "Don't mind him, he's ... different."

Isaac started to get agitated. *Just calm down*, he thought, *don't say anything.*

Ruby gave Isaac a warm smile. "Well, then hows about we just be friends for the fun of it?"

Isaac nodded quietly as he shook her hand.

"Well, anyways, I best get back to work," Ruby said as she noticed another customer motioning to her. "It was nice meetin' you two."

After she was out of earshot, Vin turned to Isaac. "You could be a little nicer, ya know."

"That was kind of rude," Drake agreed.

Isaac stood up. "Whatever, I don't need this." He turned and started for the door.

"You aren't even gonna finish your food?" Drake inquired.

"Lost my appetite. I'm going to bed." Isaac walked out of the bar.

Vin scoffed. "Seriously, what is his problem?"

Drake let out a long sigh. "Maybe he's just got a lot on his mind."

"I still can't believe Raine asked him to stay in the castle!"

"You still on about that?" Drake began to eat his food.

Vin leaned closer to him. "Look, I've known Raine for years, and not once has she ever let anyone just stay in the castle. Also, she rarely takes any interest in men, and I've never seen her with a steady boyfriend."

Drake scratched his chin. "So, she's not interested in hooking up with him?"

"Exactly," Vin explained. "Raine has an uncanny gift with aura, and I'm betting she sees some kind of potential in him."

"Well, he did beat you in practice today." Drake chuckled.

"Shut up!"

"You entered the tournament. Was there a reason?" the black-haired woman asked Isaac.

"I needed money. After all, I was new to this world. I couldn't very well just go about being homeless, and they offered shelter and food to participants."

"Is that so?" She cocked her head to the side. "There wasn't another reason?"

"Other reason?" He looked at her.

"Yes. There must have been another reason you decided to join. You didn't even know if you'd win."

Isaac thought about it. Was there another reason? "I can't remember."

"I see." She sighed. "But that's when you met your two teammates. You didn't seem to like them at first."

He remained silent.

"You aren't really a people person, or was there something else bothering you?"

Isaac frowned. "I just ... didn't know what to do. It's not like I could be their friend."

"Why not?"

He let out a long sigh. "It doesn't matter."

"Either way, you found yourself at the castle gates."

"Yeah." He nodded. "I was really surprised."

"Raine gave you entrance to the castle, and even the queen accepted you," the black-haired woman said. "Seems kind of sudden for a first meeting."

Isaac nodded again. "Yeah, I was shocked as well."

"But you know now why they did, right?"

"Yeah, it's because I'm special."

She laughed. "Special, huh? Whatever do you mean?"

"They called me a guardian. Like I even really know what that is ..."

The woman looked at him thoughtfully. "A guardian? I'm afraid that term means nothing to me. Are you supposed to be some kind of hero?"

"I'm definitely not a hero," he dismissed her. "I'm just a regular guy."

"Heroes are overrated." She grinned deviously at him. "Either way, whatever it was that they thought of you, it conveniently allowed you access to the castle and your first interaction with her."

He smiled fondly as he remembered his first meeting with Lucia. "I didn't know it then, but she turned out to be someone important to me."

"An otherworldly traveler and the queen of Adamas." The woman hummed. "What are the odds of that happening?"

"Oh, it gets weirder." Isaac chuckled. "Much weirder."

CHAPTER 3
A RISKY PLAN

Isaac woke up in his new room inside the castle. It was large with lots of fancy paintings on the walls, and there were several pieces of high-quality wooden furniture in various spots of the room. The bed was a little bigger than a standard king size, and the blankets were extremely comfortable. This was definitely a room fit for a royal castle.

Dressing quickly, Isaac went to the training room to meet with Raine. As he walked in, she was seated patiently on the training benches reading a book.

"You're a late riser," she said, closing her book and standing up. "The crystal's almost turned completely yellow."

That's almost ten in the morning, he thought. "Sorry, I guess I slept in."

Raine took off the dress robe she was wearing, revealing a set of tighter, more elegant clothes underneath. "Today was rather slow anyway. I can be patient, but not for very long. You're lucky I'm in a good mood today."

He shuffled nervously as he looked at her. She was quite beautiful.

After placing her robe on a wall hook, she turned to him. "Okay, let's begin." She guided him toward the center of the training court. "Today I'm only going to teach you the basics. Seeing as how you can't properly perform any magic, I'm going to assume you don't even know how to control aura."

He remained silent and listened intently.

41

"Vin tells me you're quite the charmer," she said abruptly.

He gave her an annoyed expression. "Let's just say we don't really agree on things."

"It's alright." She chuckled. "I don't really agree with him either. He can be quite the pain."

Isaac rolled his eyes.

"Just don't let your emotions get the better of you," she told him sincerely. "Aura is mostly influenced by our emotions. If you lose control, it can be devastating, not only to everyone around you, but also to yourself." She reached out and took his hand, holding it palm up. "Firstly, we need to get you to understand the idea of aura control. I want you to make static electricity pulse from your fingertips. To do this, you will need to imagine power coursing through your body into the tips of your fingers, almost like when you rub your feet on carpet."

Isaac stared at his palm but couldn't feel any energy.

"When you feel the energy, release it through your fingers," Raine explained. "Just be careful not to release too much or you could shock yourself."

He tried to focus as best as he could, but nothing happened. "It's not working; I don't even know what I'm supposed to be feeling here."

She looked puzzled. "They should have taught you this in school at least. What nation do you come from?"

He started to stammer. "Well, uhh ..."

She shook her head. "It doesn't really matter. Here ..." She stepped around behind him and placed her hand gently under his right elbow with his palm still facing up and placed her left hand on Isaac's shoulder. "I'm going to help you by forcing the aura from your arm."

He felt the warmth of her touch on his shoulder and shuddered slightly.

"This might sting a little, but it will help you get the idea of what I'm talking about." With that, he could feel a sudden rush through his arm like it was struck by lightning, and from his fingertips came an electrostatic burst. He let out a yell as he jerked away from Raine and grabbed his arm. "WHAAAAA!"

She started laughing. "Feels good, huh?"

Even though it hurt, the pain quickly went away. "I was not expecting that!" he told her. "I think it startled me more than anything."

"Haha, you should've seen when I did that to Vin for snooping around in my room while I wasn't there. Thought he was going to have a heart attack!" Still laughing, she shook her head. "He doesn't have energy aura, so it hurt him like ten times as much."

"Well, I think I actually got an idea of how it works." Isaac refocused. Concentrating on the feeling he had, he attempted to make static again, but still nothing happened.

"Hmm, you're worse off than I had thought," Raine said, looking him up and down. "I thought giving you a little jolt would kickstart your aura flow, but nothing has happened."

"What do you mean?" he asked.

"Well, you see, according to your aura, you've never used magic, not once, therefore your body has no knowledge of working it, so it's shut it off completely."

He looked questioningly at her. "How do you know that?"

"Well," she explained, "I have an ability that allows me to see what types of aura people possess. By looking at you, I can see the type and color of your abilities as well as if you are active with using it."

"So, what do you see about me?"

"Well, I can see that you haven't ever used proper magic, but also, your aura is ... different," she explained.

"Different?" He frowned. "What do you mean?"

"Well, for someone claiming to be a mage, your aura sure doesn't reflect it."

He narrowed his eyes are her in confusion.

"You act as if you hadn't known this," Raine commented.

"There's a lot I don't know, so what?" Isaac replied defensively.

"I didn't mean anything by it, just curious is all." She stepped up behind him again. "Here, I have an idea." She placed her hands again on his elbow and his shoulder. "I'm going to do it again, but this time I'm only gonna throw a little at you, and I'm gonna keep it constant. Your arm might go numb, just pull away if it gets too much to bear."

He braced himself as he felt the energy current flow through his arm again, this time not as painful.

"Try to focus as much as you can on keeping the static at a constant flow," she said as static burst from his hand. "I'll keep the electricity going, you just concentrate on controlling it."

He could feel his arm starting to go numb from the energy but did his best to concentrate on the spark. Trying to keep the static from jumping all over the place was a lot harder than he had imagined. After about thirty seconds, he pulled his arm away. "It isn't working."

"It's all in your mind," she assured him. "Try to imagine strands of thread flowing in all directions, and you need to grab and focus each strand into one."

He rubbed his arm as the tingling started to fade. "Give me a second and we can start again."

After a minute, he was ready.

When the static began to pulse, it looked like a bunch of hair jumping around his fingers.

"There, don't lose it!" she said when she saw the sparks crackling.

Isaac focused all his thoughts into "pulling" each electrified strand together, but as he started to focus the fourth one, the electricity began to arc, causing random bursts.

"You're pulling the strands too hard; you need to be gentle," she said calmly.

He tried to let up a little, but the static arced and struck him in the forearm.

"Ow, ow, ow!" He shook his arm as the bolt shot to his elbow. "Dammit!"

Chuckling, she gently took his hand in her own. "Here."

He could feel a cooling sensation easing the numbness throughout his arm as small ice crystals began to form on Raine's hand and his own.

"Why can't I start out with something less dangerous, like ice?" he asked in frustration.

She paused. "Less *dangerous*?" She started laughing.

"What?"

"Ice magic is an advanced form of magic. You can't even make something as simple as lightning; if you attempt to make ice at this point, you will do far more *permanent* damage to yourself than any static could."

"How so?"

"Well for one," she explained, "you could freeze your whole hand solid, and the only cure is amputation. When playing with ice, you have the potential of freezing your own blood, and perhaps a brain cell or two, which would cause severe brain damage."

"Then why not start out learning fire?" He shrugged.

"Do you want to burn yourself, or possibly burn the castle down?"

"Oh, I didn't think about that."

"You just have to focus on channeling lighting like a conduit. Think of a pulley: When you pull the rope, it just goes in a circle. The line is connected on both ends, but when pulled, it can raise a door or a bridge. You just need to imagine a circle of lightning that can roll with itself."

A pulley, huh, Isaac thought. With this idea, he started imagining a constant flowing current within his arm and tried to focus on making that current stronger till power erupted from his hand.

After about an hour of training, he was able to form several hairy strands of electricity from his fingertips without Raine's help.

She looked up at the orange crystal hanging on the wall. "I gotta run; keep practicing on controlling it and focusing the strands into one. We'll start again tomorrow."

He watched as she put on her robe and picked up her book. "Uhh, thanks for the help."

She paused. "You're a fast learner, and you have lots of potential. Just try to keep your emotions in check. They can really harm you if you have too many negative feelings." With that, she turned and walked out of the training room.

Lots of potential. Negative feelings. Was she trying to tell him something?

The midday sun shone through the windowpanes, and the light reflected along the walls of the great hall of castle Adamas. All was quiet except for the soft footsteps that lightly echoed down the hall.

Raine made her way toward the queen's living quarters, passing maids who were busy dusting paintings, sweeping floors, and cleaning staircases. Eventually she reached a door with gold embroidery along its edges. Shortly after knocking, a woman's voice beckoned her into the room.

"Milady," she said politely as she entered the room. "It's pretty quiet today."

Queen Lucia, who was seated at her desk, welcomed Raine as she entered. "Isn't that a good thing?"

She frowned slightly. "I don't know. It was only a few days ago that Esmeraldas was hit, and now it's gone completely quiet. I just ... have a bad feeling is all."

"You're right," Lucia agreed. "I feel the same, though there is naught we can do about it for the moment." She stood up, walking over to Raine with an envelope in her hand. "Here, I would appreciate it if you gave this to Bart."

She accepted the note. "Is this about the reinforcements?"

"Not exactly." Lucia glanced toward her bedroom window. "I fear something bad is heading our way. We need an alternative in case our plan fails." Glancing back at her, she wore a worried expression. "We need hope."

Raine looked down at the envelope. "You mean, the guardian?"

"I mean, Isaac."

"Are you sure that's a wise decision?" Raine sounded shaky. "I mean, he's not exactly gifted. I don't think we can count on him ..."

Lucia smiled at her. "I remember a young girl whose whole world was turned upside down, and she had felt there was no reason left for her to live."

Raine became silent.

"In the end, she became a fine woman, and despite countless failures, become a grand sorceress." Putting her hand on Raine's shoulder, Lucia looked her deep in the eyes. "Even the smallest light can outshine the deepest darkness; it just needs a chance to grow."

Raine looked away, "I ... guess, you're right." She put the envelope in her robe pocket. "I'll deliver this immediately."

"Have faith in him." Lucia smiled warmly. "No one starts out perfect."

"I'll try." She nodded to her then left the room.

On her way back down the hall, she saw Vin and instantly detected trouble.

"What are you doing?" she asked him suspiciously.

"Uhh," Vin stammered. "Nothing ..."

Raine stared back sarcastically. "Really? You have the look of a culprit written all over you!" She shook her head. "What did you do?"

He wore the expression of innocence. "I didn't do anything!"

"Aren't you supposed to be preparing for your dumb tournament?"

"Well, it just so happens that I'm already prepared," he replied smugly.

"Then what are you doing here?"

He wrinkled his nose. "Sheesh, what are you so angry about?"

"Why aren't you answering my question?" she countered with a hint of sarcastic playfulness.

"Well ... uhh ..." Vin started, but then let out a sigh when he saw Raine's eyes grow questioningly wide. "Dang it, Raine! You're so nosey!"

She folded her arms.

"Okay! Okay ..." Vin gave in. "Ulrix may have gotten into the courtyard ..."

"Vin," she began softly. "You know that bird isn't allowed within the castle walls during the council's meetings."

"I know, I know, but he just sorta flew off like he was chasing something."

Raine turned and headed back down the hall toward the courtyard. "Let's just hurry and get him!"

Outside, the sun shone through a cloudless sky. Down below, the open courtyard was lined with a garden of flowers and beautiful plants. In the center was a large, stone table with nine stone chairs. At the head, a larger, tenth chair sat apart from the rest. In each chair sat a person, and they were all deep in conversation.

Raine and Vin poked their heads out and began to scan the area for Ulrix.

"There he is," he whispered.

Sitting on the top of the outer wall was a hawk the size of four horses put together. Ulrix was well hidden behind a tree that reached above the inside of the courtyard wall. He sat, staring unblinking at the group of councilmen down below.

"Good, they haven't seen him," Raine whispered to Vin with a sigh of relief. "Let's just get him out of here quietly."

The two made their way around the garden path, staying as low as possible. When they reached the spot under Ulrix, Vin tried to motion to him.

"Why isn't he moving?" He tried to throw a rock up the wall, but it hit about halfway and fell back to the ground.

"What are you doing?" Raine hissed. "If we get caught interrupting the council's meeting, we'll get into some serious trouble!"

He peeked over at the ten figures still in conversation. They hadn't heard the rock.

"He's never ignored me like this." He looked up at the huge bird, still gazing upon the council.

"I'm going up." He reached back into one of the many pouches he had on his belt and produced a thin rope and some gloves.

"Are you crazy!?" Raine grabbed his arm.

Vin grinned back at her. "Just use some of your magic and help me get up. Once I'm up there, I'll ride Ulrix down the other side, away from the meeting."

After putting the gloves on, he waved his hand and a yellow aural bow appeared. Drawing the magical string back, an arrow appeared already notched and ready to fly. Using his left index finger, he held the arrow drawn back slightly so that it wouldn't disappear, and he tied the rope to the shaft of the arrow.

Taking a quick peek to make sure the council was still conversing, he aimed his shot at the top of the tree directly in front of Ulrix and fired.

The arrow flew swiftly to its mark and dug deep into the wood.

"Cover me."

Using the rope and the wall, Vin scaled upward rather swiftly, while Raine produced a magical chameleon-type spell on him to conceal him from the council.

Reaching the top of the wall, he stood next to Ulrix. "Hey! What the heck are ya doin'?"

The large bird slightly acknowledged him and continued to stare downward at the meeting.

Raine's voice sounded within his head. *Well?*

"Ugh! I hate when you do that!" he whispered.

With her magic, Raine was able to use telepathy to communicate, and she could hear incredibly well, even a quiet whisper.

Oh, yeah, what am I supposed to do, shout so everyone can hear me? she replied telepathically. *You gonna get him down or not?*

He peered down and shrugged. "I dunno what his deal is; he just keeps staring at them."

Raine looked up toward Ulrix, then followed his gaze to the council. She did this a few more times. *Oh geez! He's eyeballing Vetis' cat!*

Sitting on the table in front of one of the councilmen was a black cat with a white patch on its chest. It was sitting obediently and alert.

Vin gave Ulrix a sour look. "Dude, you don't even like cats!" No response. "Alright, no more games!" Jumping onto his back, he pulled on the bird's feathers, causing him to lose his balance on the wall. This action made Ulrix flap his wings in order to regain stability, and he and Vin fell backward onto the roof of a nearby building opposite the courtyard. Ulrix flapped his wings repeatedly, trying to maintain his balance as Vin guided him along the roof toward the outside of the castle.

"Come on, Ulrix! Stop messing around!" Vin pulled hard on his feathers, and the two rose into the air as Ulrix took flight.

Soaring above the rooftops, the giant bird flew to the castle's main gates.

The two safely landed on the open ground in front of the castle's main entrance. Vin hopped off Ulrix and looked him in the eyes. "What the heck, dude? You know you aren't supposed to be in there!"

Ulrix gave a soft squawk in reply.

On the council side of the wall, Raine quietly made her way back around the garden and into the castle without being noticed. She swiftly went through the hall and out the door toward the front of the castle.

Outside, she approached Vin scolding Ulrix.

"Now that we have that settled," she began. "You know the rules ..."

"Yeah, I know!" Vin stopped her. "But seriously, I have never seen Ulrix act like this. He always listens to me."

She folded her arms. "Apparently, he still needs some training. Just don't cause any more trouble today!"

He stared back at her with annoyance. "Yeah, I got it, thanks. You know, I don't just do these things on purpose."

"Look ..." She stood close to him. "I'm sorry if I seem overreactive. Everyone's on edge with the recent attack on Esmeraldas."

Vin let out a sigh. "I know. Sorry." Looking up at Ulrix, he wore a thoughtful expression. "That was really weird though. Why would Ulrix be so interested in a cat? He eats fish and rodents."

Raine looked at the giant bird. "Who knows what goes on in the minds of animals? Anyway, I really need to be off."

He watched as she started for the castle gates. "Any word from the queen?"

"Still figuring that out. Gotta wait till after the tournament," she replied as she walked past the castle walls.

"Come on, Ulrix." Vin took the bird to the castle reserve.

Lucia was entering the training room when she heard a crackling noise followed by a loud bang. Isaac had unleashed a bolt of lightning into a nearby training dummy, causing it to shatter into tiny bits of wood.

"Wow! That was quite impressive!"

Isaac, realizing someone had walked in, looked over at her. "Woops! Didn't know anyone else was here." Looking back at what was left of the dummy, his expression was shamefaced. "Uhh, I didn't mean to do that ..."

"It's quite alright." Lucia's voice was cheerful. "That's what they're there for, after all." She smiled warmly at him. "I believe we did not get a chance to talk when we first met."

"You seemed pretty busy at the time," he replied.

"You aren't from around here, are you?"

Isaac hesitated before answering. "Why do you say that?"

"Because you're really laid back around the queen," she replied with a giggle. "But worry not, I prefer it this way."

There was something charming about this woman, Isaac thought. She seemed genuinely kind. Just being around her, he felt very trusting, which was incredibly rare.

"Lucia Elnur." She held out her hand.

Accepting, he returned the greeting. "Isaac Wolfe."

"Well met, Isaac." Lucia beamed. "Where are you from?"

"Well ..." *How do you tell someone you're from another world?* "Nowhere at the moment. I sorta come and go."

"The adventuring sort, eh?" She looked curiously into his eyes. "I hope Raine hasn't been hard on you. She's usually rough with new folks."

"She's been fairly good, oddly enough," he said with curiousness in his voice. "Which reminds me. It wasn't Raine who wanted me in the castle; it was you, wasn't it?"

A smile spread across Lucia's face as if a great secret had been revealed. "You are quite observant, aren't you?" She put her finger up to her cheek.

"But why me and not Vin or Drake?"

"Vin already lives in the castle," she replied. "But unfortunately, I don't know who Drake is or if I can trust him." Her face wore a quiet calm. "But I feel that having you here keeps my mind at ease."

Umm ... what? What is she talking about? Isaac thought. *If she doesn't know Drake, she* definitely *doesn't know me!* "But we've only just met. How could you possibly put your trust in me since we don't really know each other?"

"I have a knack for knowing these things," she replied with a grin. "Maybe I can see something in you that even you yourself cannot see." She pushed some of her black hair away from her face.

"What do you mean?"

"I sense a certain determination in you." Her answer sounded hopeful. "Whether you believe it or not, I feel I can trust you more than most right now. This world is full of enemies who would seek to destroy it, and even now, I know there are some within these walls." Lucia's face turned bleak. "The future of this world, I fear, is not good. A terrible darkness is coming. I can feel it." She looked at him with hope in her eyes. "We need heroes like you. I believe that the strength of those willing to stand up against evil is what will save us."

Isaac was quizzical. "I think you've got me all wrong. I'm not a hero." He looked at the ground. "I'm just ... I'm just a nobody."

Lucia looked at him with sincerity. "Well, I believe in you. And I know Raine does as well. She may seem tough at first, but there is naught but kindness in her heart." She smiled warmly. "Perhaps you are the one that needs to believe."

He looked into her eyes. "I don't know what you want from me. Why you let me into the castle. Why you told Raine to train me. I don't know."

"I see." She paused a moment before giving a very coy smile. "Well, then maybe I will let you figure that out. I know how stale that sounds, but it's probably best if someone else tells you aside from myself." She took a step backward, hinting at the intention to leave. "It was certainly great to finally meet you, Isaac Wolfe, but I must leave now. I will be cheering you on at the tournament. Please remember what I have said; I really am counting on you."

Isaac watched as Lucia turned toward the door, still very quizzical to what she had said.

"Oh, by the way ..." She stopped in the doorway and turned back to him. "Do you know what the wolf truly stands for?" She smiled meaningfully before turning and leaving the training room.

What was she trying to tell him?

Raine entered the royal guardhouse. Peering around, all the soldiers who were busy paused a moment to look at her; some had awe in their expressions. She gave them a sour look and marched past them into the commander's office.

Bart Seros sat at his desk going over some documents. He looked up when Raine stepped in.

"Ah, good evening Ms. Beria. How can I assist you?" He looked intently at her as she handed him a sealed envelope.

"This is from the queen," she told him.

"Let's see ..." He opened the letter and began to read.

Raine was a little curious. "She said it was urgent and that it pertained to the tournament."

"Well ... yes and no." Bart started mumbling as he continued to read the letter. "Secret team ... elite fighters ... covert operations ... and ..." He paused, holding the letter up high. "More incense." He laughed. "She knows that most of the council hates that stuff. Hmm, perhaps she uses it as joke to them." Still chuckling, he looked up at Raine. "Well, it seems I've got work to do. This tournament is gonna be pretty crazy, I can tell you that."

"Why exactly have we posted this tournament?" she asked suddenly. "With the recent attack on Esmeraldas, shouldn't we have bigger things to consider instead of playing games?"

"I guess the queen hasn't told you, then." He leaned back in his chair and motioned toward the door. "This is private."

Raine turned and with a soft wave of her hand, the door shut on its own with telekinesis. "What exactly is going on?"

"This doesn't leave the room," Bart began. "This 'tournament' is designed to reveal a few suspicions the queen and I have on some individuals. Vin, being our highest informant, has entered on my order to gather information on some of the participants."

She looked stern. "Why wasn't I informed of this?"

"Because the queen didn't want you getting involved. She knew that had you known of this, you would have entered the tournament regardless of duty. Besides, as much as you would hate to hear this, Vin is the perfect choice for this kind of operation."

"My job is to protect the queen! How can I do that if you keep information like this from me?"

"Because this mission doesn't directly put the queen in harm's way. And besides, we need you at her side should anything happen." Bart leaned forward. "I know how powerful you are. If you entered this tournament, every participant would be obliterated by you. I know this. But we need someone who can gather evidence from the other participants and keep a low profile. *That* is Vin's strength."

She let out a deep breath. "Fine! I get your point. I'm guessing Isaac wasn't a mistake either, was he?"

A smile crept along Bart's face. "You are correct. Our entrance officials spotted him right away, and we made sure to pair Vin with him so that we could get him into the castle."

Everything is starting to make sense now, Raine thought. "And this is why the queen told me specifically to 'help' Vin with his new guests ..." She started to simmer down as she began to understand. "I see. Had I known this, I would have informed Vetis. You think he's a spy?"

He nodded. "Have you seen his cat?"

She peered back at him. "What about it?"

"It's strange, but that cat has been seen acting very uncatlike," he explained. "For instance, the queen woke up the other night, and she said she saw it on her windowsill, just staring at her. When it noticed she was looking back at it, it jumped out quickly, as if to avoid detection."

"But that doesn't prove anything."

Bart nodded again. "Right, but that's why we need to keep an eye on Vetis, because this isn't the only incident where someone has seen that cat doing weird things."

Raine looked puzzled. "But how will this tournament reveal any suspicions?"

"Many participants come from all over the land to participate. That being said, if the enemy would want to attack, they would first send in spies to assess the threat."

She was shocked. "That's ridiculous! Why would you open up a possibility for an enemy invasion, less invite them in?"

He put his hand up to silence her. "Ms. Beria, understand, we would not do this unless we felt it necessary. After talking with the officials from Esmeraldas after they were attacked, they informed us that no one had entered the city for two weeks, and yet, the attack happened from inside, with no warning."

"So, what does that mean?"

"Think about it. No one entered for two weeks, and an attack still happened. What does that tell you?"

She stared blankly back at him. "That a spy was already inside and had been there for a while. This can happen at any time, though."

Bart looked stern. "Exactly, that you can guarantee there is at least one spy here, in this city, right now."

Both just sat there for a moment, before Raine spoke. "So, Vin is trying to find out who the spy could be?"

"Yes. Only four people know that Vin works for us: you, the queen, myself, and Anwir."

"But Anwir is the head of the council. Would it not be safe to assume that the rest of them, including Vetis, would know about this?" she inquired.

"There are many secrets that only Anwir knows that he keeps from the rest of the councilmen. We have made sure, especially, that he keeps Vin's identity from all."

"What's this 'team' I heard you muttering to yourself while you read that letter?" she implored.

"That ..." Bart began. "I don't even know. It just says to expect changes after the tournament. It seems the queen has a plan. She wants to put together some kind of team to do a special mission. Only the best are going to be allowed to join."

"Interesting." Raine thought out loud. "Well, I hope you're right about this. About sending Vin to try and figure out who our spy is."

"Trust me," he said confidently. "Vin has never failed a covert mission. When it comes to spying, he's the best."

The black-haired woman looked over at Isaac. "You trained under Raine for a while. Eventually you were able to perfect some lightning spells."

Isaac nodded. "Yeah. She was good at explaining everything; it only took me a few days to figure out how to cast lightning bolts."

"You two bonded during this time. It seemed like Raine had high hopes for you."

"But in the end, I failed her ..." He lowered his gaze.

The black-haired woman frowned. "Are you going to give up?"

"I don't know ... maybe."

"You could end it all here, if you wanted."

Isaac looked at her. "Perhaps that would be best, right?"

"Is that what you want?" She cocked her head slightly. He remained silent.

"I think you should recall the rest before making your decision." She leaned forward. "You and Vin didn't seem to get along all that well."

"It was rough at first," he explained. "We didn't really see eye to eye."

"Perhaps it was a difference in personalities."

Isaac shrugged. "Maybe. We ended up fighting, and in the process, we discovered some weird place in the nearby mountains."

"An interesting turn of events." She smiled with interest. "What happened?"

"Well, what had started as a nice day turned into a fight for our lives when this demon showed up."

CHAPTER 4

TRIALS AND TRIBULATIONS

The sun shone through the canopy of an endless sea of trees. The atmosphere was ominous and quiet. The ambient sound of crickets, bees, flies, as well as scores of other insects could be heard through the forest. The air was warm, and there wasn't any wind to sweep away the smell of rotting tree bark.

Isaac peered at his surroundings, trying to make out where he was. The dense forest showed no signs of any way to go, as if he was sucked into a paradox of which he could never escape. A nearby screech sent chills down his spine as he jerked his head in time to see a crow flying from a nearby tree branch.

Where could everyone be? he thought. Why did they leave him here alone? Should he try and find them? What if they come back and he was gone? So many questions ran through his head, and he started to hallucinate.

He heard footsteps to his right, and Isaac looked over with hope. *Is that them?* But when he looked in the direction of the noise, there was nothing, and the footsteps were gone.

Panic began to set in, and he started to get angry. Why would they just leave? Didn't they care? So many emotions began to set in, and for a moment, he felt tears welling up inside. *How could they do this to me? How long have they even been gone? Minutes? Hours?* He began to pace as if he was searching for an answer that could never be found. *What happened before I got here?*

We were camping.

That's right.

Everyone was laughing. A campfire. There were games. *Wait. I don't remember any games*, he thought. No, there weren't any games, only conversations. Conversations he wasn't invited to. *I remember now, I think.* Everyone was talking and laughing. But he wasn't laughing. At least, he couldn't remember if he was or not.

The light through the trees began to darken as a cloud moved in front of the sun. But was it a cloud, or something else? Isaac began to question his own thoughts. As he searched for an answer, he thought he could hear someone breathing a few feet behind him. But when he turned to look, there was no one there.

Anger. Hatred. Fear. Pain.

These were the emotions that raced through his mind as he continued to pace, abandoned in the middle of an endless forest.

That's it! I don't need them! I don't need ANY of them! Isaac stopped pacing and began to search around. If he was to be stuck here, he might as well start walking; at least that was better than doing nothing. But which way should he go? The sun rises in the east and sets in the west; but he couldn't see the sun. In fact, now that he thought about it, he couldn't even see the sky through the dense trees.

Can't think. Didn't a cloud or something cover the sun? It felt as if a dark shadow was watching him.

It's coming from behind, he thought, *so I will move away from it.* He began to walk in the direction opposite this "darkness," and soon found himself running. *Why am I running, and from what?* It didn't matter; the suffocating trees were too much, and he started to panic. For a moment, he hoped that whatever this darkness was, hallucination or imagination, had hurt or killed the others. This thought made him feel slightly better. *I hope they have suffered for what they did, leaving me here by myself without even telling me they were leaving.*

He hated them.

As the negative thoughts entered his mind, a swift move-ment to his left caught his attention. As he peered over, he saw it. This darkness wasn't imaginary. It was real. And it was watching him, as he kept running, keeping pace with his own speed. As this shadow moved closer to him, the light in the forest dimmed, and the evil took shape into a humanoid creature with long arms, legs, and fingers. Its face wore hol-low eyes and razor-sharp teeth. As this thing chased him, its footsteps weren't normal, but scraping, like the sound of claws dragging along rocks and wood. It gave off a kind of trilling, clicking sound and tried to reach out and grab him. Its fingers seemed to grow a few inches as they reached for his back.

In the distance, an opening in the forest appeared. As Isaac neared the opening, he noticed that it was divided by a large chasm. There was a bridge extended across, but it had been broken, and now there was about an eight-meter gap between the two halves.

I just gotta build up enough speed, and I can make this, he thought. *Then this demon will be stuck over here, and I will be safe!*

As the distance between Isaac and the chasm began to close, he could feel the creature's breath on his neck. Sprinting across the first part of the bridge, he jumped as high as he could at the edge, reaching for the other side. He grabbed at the ledge as he barely reached the other end and started to climb onto the walkway. *I made it!* he thought as he pulled himself up, but his victory was celebrated too early. The stones that made up the bridge began to give way where he was hanging, and when his section broke off, he plummeted into the dark chasm.

Isaac snapped awake as he felt himself hit the floor. Sit-ting there, he noticed he had fallen off his bed. It was those dreams again, the ones he'd been having recently. They felt so real, as if he was being sucked into a different reality. He looked over at the crystal sitting on his nightstand which shone a quiet blue. Still early.

He rose to his feet, allowing the blanket which had followed him when he fell out of the bed to gently pool on the ground. Still in his pajamas, he walked to the bedroom door and stepped out into the castle hallway.

Walking slowly down the empty hall, he simply stared into space, not even looking at the decorations or paintings, just walking and thinking. *I've never had these dreams, so realistic, and terrifying. What were they?* A part of him thought about Earth and everything he had left behind. It didn't matter. There was nothing in that world for him. Not anymore.

Isaac eventually found himself going through a side door into the courtyard. Outside, the stars could be seen covering the sky. He stopped and stared up at them. Where was Earth mixed in between all those tiny lights? He thought about this, but soon his thoughts turned to negativity, and he pushed those memories away. *Who cares? Maybe this world will offer more.* He walked to the center of the courtyard and sat in the big chair of the council's meeting table.

Memories of his encounter with Lucia began to flow through his mind. What did she mean by 'hero'? He was definitely no hero. Both Raine and Lucia had been acting weird toward him. Why did Raine invite him into the castle, and why did Lucia arrange for him to stay there? Queens didn't give their trust to just anyone like that. At least, Isaac only knew what he had read in old history books when he went through school on Earth. This world was very similar to Earth, although there were many advanced technologies here because of the abilities that aura gave. But why would Raine and Lucia want him around? Was he special? *No way*, he dismissed the thought. *I'm nothing special.*

He noticed movement in the corner of his eye and glanced up. Sitting on the far end of the table was a black cat with a white spot on its chest. It stared back at him with big, yellow eyes. Isaac remained silent as he stared at this creature who seemed to be watching him with intelligent interest. This cat seemed familiar, as if he had seen it before, watching him from time to time through his training. Its tail began to sway back and forth in a whip-like motion as its mouth seemed to turn to a slight grin. He stared it blankly in the eyes as if to challenge it. The hair on its back could be seen visibly standing straight, indicating a threat.

Isaac stood up and began to approach this mystery cat; as he got closer, it reared up and paused, still watching him intently. He made a quick motion as if he were going to chase this sinister cat down, and as predicted, the cat quickly turned and jumped off the table, sprinting across the grass toward a gate at the back of the courtyard.

Before it squeezed itself through the gate's metal bars, it peered back at Isaac with what seemed to be a hint of hatred. After a couple of seconds, the cat disappeared through the gate and out of sight.

Dumb cat.

He made his way back into the castle, and as he stepped into the hallway, he was met by Raine.

"What were you doing?" she demanded.

Isaac looked at her quizzically. "Umm, nothing ... why?"

She folded her arms, and her gaze went to the ground thoughtfully. "I felt a wave of darkness a little bit ago. I've been looking around for it, and you're the only one I have seen so far." She looked up and down the hallway.

"Shouldn't you warn the guards?" he suggested casually.

She looked at him, pulling her night robe a little tighter against the slight chill that crept through the doorway. "Honestly, I don't know. I've never felt this energy before." She gave him a look of interest. "So, what were you doing outside this early?"

Isaac began walking back toward his room, and Raine followed next to him. "I was just thinking about a few things," he told her, stuffing his hands into his pajama pockets. "Then this weird cat just came out of nowhere, so I scared it off."

"Weird ..." She put her hand on her chin thoughtfully.

"Is something wrong?"

Shaking her head, she peered down the long hallway. "No, nothing."

He stared back at her suspiciously. "Well, either way, I won't be able to go back to sleep. I'm gonna go get breakfast at the dining hall." He turned as they came up to his room.

"Isaac." Raine paused. "Why did you come here?"

He turned back toward her. "What do you mean?"

She stared at him with a slight look of hope in her eyes. "You're here for a reason, aren't you? Because you're the Sotér? I mean, why else would you be here?"

"I don't know what you're talking about. What's Sotér?"

"You don't know about that either?" Raine sounded dumbfounded.

"I told you. There's a lot I don't know."

"But everyone knows what the Sotér is!"

Isaac turned back to his bedroom door. "Look. I come from a place very far away. I don't know much about anything that happens here, or what you all expect me to be; but where I'm from, people don't look to me for anything. In fact, they usually try to avoid me." He looked over his shoulder at her. "To answer your question, I didn't want to live in that world anymore, so I left and ended up here in hopes of finding a new life, something worth living for, I guess. But so far, nothing has changed. It's already been close to a month since I've been here, and people still treat me the same." Isaac paused for a moment. "Well, everyone except you and the queen." He leaned against the doorframe and looked questioningly at her. "You never told me why you allowed me into the castle."

Raine's reply was very calm, as if she was starting to understand him a little. "It's because of your aura. It's different than anyone else's." She smiled warmly at him. "Have you seen the city yet?"

He noticed her change in topic but accepted it. "I've only been to a few places so far, but I haven't been through all of it."

"How about we get breakfast together and I'll show you around?" she asked him casually. "I know a good place that's better than the dining hall."

"But what about training?"

"It's my day off, and I'd rather not spend it working."

Isaac thought about this for a moment. A part of him wanted to refuse this offer. "Aren't you supposed to be with the queen?"

"I'm not required to monitor her all day every day, you know. I still get to have my personal time as well," Raine answered, her hands on her hips. "I figured we could talk a little, ya know, get to know each other."

"That sounds like a date," he said with a slightly flirtatious tone.

"Don't get any ideas." Her voice was stern. "This is simply because you've piqued my curiosity with how little you know of this place, that's all."

"I see," he said nonchalantly. He wasn't sure if he actually wanted to go with her, but after a brief thought, he acquiesced. "Alright. I'll meet you at the gate in ten minutes."

It was twilight outside when Isaac met with Raine. The light from the sky reflected slightly off his brown hair and Raine's seemed to glow dark blue.

"So is your hair naturally that color?" he asked.

She ran her hand through her long hair. "Yes, it is. You like it?"

He gave a half smile. "I do. Where I'm from, you would never see anyone with natural hair that color."

"Is that so? Well, I would certainly like to hear more about this place you come from, but for now, come on." She beckoned to him. "Let's talk some more over breakfast. I'm starving."

The two made their way through the town toward Ruby's bar.

"I've been here before," Isaac said as the two walked in.

The bar was quiet, and only two other people were there. They sat at a table near the back. She leaned her elbow on the table and rested her chin on her hand. "This is the place we usually hang out at," she told him as Ruby approached to take their order.

"Well, hey there, Raine!" Ruby greeted with that southern accent of hers. "I see ya brought a guest." She looked at Isaac, her eyes beaming with delight. "Oh, hi there! It's good to see you again, Isaac!"

"Hi Ruby, I was just taking Isaac to see the city. Thought we'd stop in for some breakfast," Raine replied cheerfully.

"Oh, really? Sounds like you two are gettin' along well, then," Ruby said.

"It's not like that," Raine explained. "Isaac is staying in the castle, and I figured, since I'm training him, I might as well show him around since he's never been here."

Ruby looked at her suspiciously. "Well, I don't mean to pry, darlin', but you never just 'show' anyone around. What makes him special, huh?"

Raine folded her arms. "Maybe I just like his personality." She playfully looked over at Isaac, who had been sitting there in silence the whole time.

"Oh, jeez! Here we are talkin' 'bout him, and he's been just sittin' here takin' it." Ruby laughed as she playfully jabbed Isaac in the arm. "How you been, hun? You didn't stay very long last time you was here."

Isaac looked at Ruby sheepishly. "I was a little tired last time, so I went to bed early."

"Well, I hope you stay a little longer this time around, huh?" She smiled as she placed her hand on his shoulder.

Isaac felt a little uncomfortable with her touching him but refrained from expressing it. He forced a smile back at her as he replied, "For you, I guess I'll make an effort."

Ruby smiled back at him. "Well, before I go and talk your ear off, what can I get you two to eat?"

For about forty or so minutes, the three sat there making conversation. Isaac learned that Ruby had opened shop for over ten years, and that Vin and Raine—as well as many others—frequented her place. Apparently, Ruby, as the owner, was also the peacekeeper of the place; if anyone were to cause trouble, she was the one to deal with them. She had a cook by the name of Marcus who happened to be an excellent chef. On the side, along with the bar, she also owned a mini theatre, which she had plays scheduled for each month. She had offered if Isaac would like to audition for one of them, but he refused immediately.

After Isaac and Raine were finished eating, the two left the bar, giving Ruby proper farewells.

"Every time I see you smile, it's always forced," Raine told him suddenly. "What's with that?"

How does she know these things? Isaac wondered. "Just trying to be polite, is all."

She frowned. "Well, I don't wanna pry, but if you wanna talk about it …"

He remained silent.

"Alright," she said, looking away. "Touchy subject." She pointed ahead. "The start of the city is right up ahead."

In the distance, there were buildings on buildings, as if a second city were on top of the lower one. The morning was starting to pick up as people were moving about their daily business.

"This little area is the Adamas Castle central district. Most of the places here you travel through are on foot, but we're gonna hit up one of the transit hubs," she said, pointing to a building with odd-looking machines in it. "You ever seen a sylphid?"

"Can't say I have," he told her.

"Wait till you ride one," she said with excitement. "You'd think they would be kinda bumpy the way they work, but because of aura, we can make them very stable."

As they moved through the residential district, Isaac noticed that the architecture was similar to that of Earth's early civilization but seemed more durable and precise with a higher quality of technology.

She guided him into the transit hub where a bunch of people were waiting to catch rides to other districts.

The sylphids themselves were rather sleek and compact. About the size of a van with twin turbines underneath them. One in front and one in the back.

After people boarded the sylphids, they would be launched upward and the machine's twin aural turbines would kick in, allowing the craft to fly, taking the passengers to their requested districts.

"We're up," Raine told Isaac as the next sylphid pulled up to the onramp. The two stepped into the aircraft.

"Where to?" the pilot asked.

"The Market District," she told him.

The sylphid began to hum as the door shut, and after a few moments, the craft shot straight up out of the building, and, to Isaac's surprise, he didn't feel the sudden rush of gravity he expected. The turbines activated, and they took off through the air toward the market district.

"Pretty impressive, huh?" Raine asked him joyfully.

He was looking out the window as he replied, "I've definitely never experienced anything like it. Why didn't we feel any rush when we were launched?"

"Because the aura pulses into the cab and makes the air match the momentum of the craft so we don't feel the sudden change in gravity." She pointed to the large buildings they were headed toward. "That's the capitol of Adamas; that's where all the shops are."

"I don't have much cash." He shrugged.

"Don't worry, we're only gonna look around," she replied. "Which reminds me, what do you do for money?"

"Nothing at the moment. I'm hoping this tournament could pay well enough for me to start on."

"I see." She looked out the window at the city, which was now very close. "We'll see if we can get you something to do to earn a few aurums back at the castle."

Isaac watched as the sylphid made its way into the city, weaving between the buildings. Some of the structures were linked together near the top, and going under them was like going through a tunnel. With the light shining through each break between the skyscrapers, it seemed majestic.

"We're here," the pilot announced as he landed the craft onto a platform in line with other sylphids.

Raine and Isaac stepped out onto the walkway, which was about thirty stories above ground.

"We don't have to pay?" he asked.

"Nope. Aura is constantly renewing, so it really costs us nothing to run these aircrafts." She guided him toward the many buildings lining the walkway. "This walkway we are on is called the Lower Skyway, and that upper one there ..." She pointed up about fifty stories higher. "Is the Upper Skyway. Both of these walkways wrap all the way around the entire city!"

The city was full of activity. There were people all over the place, shopping, eating, or just talking. This place was full of energy the likes Isaac had never seen. Raine took him to many shops: clothes shops, toy shops, book shops, even a beauty shop. If there was ever a time you needed anything, you could find it here. The Lower Skyway was awesome, but once she took him to the Upper Skyway, he saw a completely different world. Sylphids could be seen flying between the buildings, the city looked so small from above, and the skyway was higher than the connecting structures, so the sky was clearly visible.

"I've never seen anything like this!" Isaac said in amazement.

Raine peered over the skyway railing at the city below. "I love coming up here. I feel like I'm on top of the world!"

It was funny. Isaac had never felt this excited before. Even though it wasn't an overwhelming amount of excitement, it was still more than he'd ever felt, and that was saying a lot. He also knew it was because he was able to share this wonderment with someone.

"Hey ... uhh," he began as Raine turned to look at him. "I just wanted to say thanks. For showing me around and all."

She smiled warmly at him. "Of course. Isn't that what friends are for?" She turned back to peer down below. "We'll have to do this often. Especially after the tournament."

Isaac looked at her, surprised. "After? I thought once the tournament was over, we were gonna go our separate ways." He looked sad, but only slightly.

Still looking down, she reassured him, "After these few weeks of training, I think we've become pretty good friends, don'tcha think? And friends stick together no matter what, right?" She gave a little chuckle. "At least, that's what I think." She turned and started to head toward one of the shops. "Hey, I wanna show you something!"

Isaac followed her. They entered a pet shop, and he could see there were several different animals roaming about in separate fenced off areas.

"Aww, look at this cute ferret!" Raine leaned over the fence to pet one of the many ferrets looking up at her. "Come on, Isaac, come pet him!"

He leaned down and pet the brown ferret; after the third pet, it began to scamper away in a playful manner, staring back at him curiously.

Raine laughed. "Haha, he wants to play."

He stared back at the little creature; there was no denying that it was adorable. It hopped around as it looked at him intently.

Back then, he *always used to stare at me the same way,* Isaac thought. On Earth, there were those who said that animals had no souls, but he knew that wasn't true; they could argue it all day, but in the end, looking into those eyes, there was more soul in there than most humans he had ever met.

Isaac felt a sudden rush welling in his chest, and then the feeling of tears hit him. He quickly turned away from Raine and averted his attention to a tank of odd-looking fish as he casually wiped his eyes before she could notice.

"Aww, I really like animals!" she said as she came to stand next to him. "I could stay here all day!" She smiled at him. "But I guess it's getting late. We should head back."

Isaac looked at her, forcing a smile to cloak his thoughts. "Yeah, I think Vin and Drake wanted to meet for some kind of training this evening."

The two began to make their way to the elevator down to the lower skyway.

"So, what's your favorite animal?" she asked him as they stepped into the elevator. She watched him curiously as he answered.

"Huh? Oh, wolves, I guess."

"A wolf, huh?" She chuckled. "Kinda like your name?"

"Not exactly." Isaac was a little embarrassed. "My name has nothing to do with my fondness for wolves."

"Hmm." Raine stared thoughtfully back at him. "Isaac Wolfe ... has a nice ring to it though."

He looked back at her with a slight smile. "What about you?"

They stepped out of the elevator and headed toward the transit hub.

"I like cats," she told him.

Isaac gave half a chuckle. "Crazy cat lady, huh?"

She stared back curiously. "I don't get it."

"Never mind," he said, changing the subject. "Why cats, though?"

"Cats remind me of what it means to be free without restrictions."

"That's not a bad way to look at it," he replied.

As they arrived at one of the transit hubs, a sylphid pulled into the station and the two boarded.

"To the castle," Raine told the pilot.

"Today was actually pretty fun," Isaac said. "Not often do I get to actually say that."

"I enjoyed it too." She beamed. "You're a little quiet, but I don't think you're such a bad guy."

"Uhh, thanks?"

After a few minutes, the sylphid pulled up to the transit hub near the castle, and they both got out.

As they were walking up the path to the gates, they saw Vin and Drake waiting for them.

"We've been waiting for ages, Isaac. Where've you been?" Vin asked, slightly annoyed.

"Raine was showing me around the city," Isaac answered.

"Is there a problem?" Raine looked at Vin with her usual bossy stare.

Vin grinned back at her. "You could've told me you two were dating. It's just I didn't know why Isaac was late. He seems to be late for almost everything, but now I know why."

Raine leered at him. "We aren't dating. And maybe you should learn to keep your nose where it belongs." She was back to her usual self.

"Hey, hey!" Drake intervened. "I don't want an argument. Let's just go train, alright?"

Vin relaxed. "Hey, I wasn't trying to start anything."

Raine turned to Isaac. "I'll catch you later." She headed off toward the castle.

He watched her leave briefly before turning to the others.

"We've decided to climb up the peak today for training," Drake told Isaac. "We figured it would be nice to get out of the castle for a change, and no one would really care if we blew up a few things out there." He smiled at that last part.

Vin looked eager as he started toward the transit hub. "Come on! We've wasted enough time as it is."

The three were making their way up a rather steep mountain path. Drake was leading the way, and Vin was just ahead of Isaac.

"So, you and Raine, huh?" Vin said jokingly. "I never thought it was possible, Raine actually dating someone."

Isaac was irritated. "It's not what you think. We're just friends."

Vin laughed. "You're probably right. Raine doesn't usually go out anyway."

"What's that supposed to mean!?" Isaac snapped back.

Vin half glanced back at Isaac. "It means she doesn't usually spend her time with little boys."

"Let's just keep going, you two," Drake called back. "Look. We're almost at the top."

Ahead, the sun glistened off a beautifully carved mountainside. The peak of the mountain rose so high that looking back down, Isaac could see the majority of Adamas. They called this path Mortuus Mons, which stood for: Dead Mountain.

"Apparently," Drake said as they continued hiking, "people have mysteriously vanished up here on this mountain. Some have wound up mysteriously dead."

"Maybe there's a secret glade with a bunch of beautiful naked women, and the ones who died were because their hearts stopped at the gorgeous sight. And the ones who disappeared were accepted by all the women for ... activities." Vin chuckled to himself after saying this in a dreamlike manner.

Just the idea of this guy being so simple-minded irritated Isaac even more than before. "Is that the only thing you ever think of—naked women?" he said angrily. "Maybe you could learn a bit of decency!"

"I'm a guy," Vin replied with a tone of arrogance. "I like beautiful women, so what? Maybe if you weren't such a snob, you'd get more ladies."

"You're the snob! Continually talking as if you're the hottest shit, when really, you're the biggest dick!"

Vin laughed. "You're right, I do have the biggest dick, especially compared to yours!"

Isaac extended his arm out toward him, causing a blast of wind to spin him around. "Maybe you should look at the person you're insulting!" He gave Vin an icy stare.

Vin took a step forward, his eyes flaring angrily. "You'd better be careful who you fight. You might just regret it."

Isaac clenched his fist. "I'm not too worried, considering I beat you so easily before!"

"There's no restriction this time, Wolfe." Vin moved his hand as if he were going to draw a weapon.

Drake came racing back to the two about ready to kill each other. "Stop, we're supposed to be a team here!" He stood before them, trying to calm them down. "You've been going at it since our team was formed. If we can't just talk this over, we're never gonna win the tournament."

"Tell that to mister stuck up over here," Vin snarled. "He thinks he's so much wiser than us, maybe he should learn to keep his mouth shut!"

"Coming from a dumbass who only thinks with his dick!" Isaac retorted. "You've done nothing but act like an arrogant jerk. You're the one who needs to shape up!"

Vin scoffed. "Oh yeah! I'm the jerk! Do you even hear yourself? I've tried my best to be nice to you, and not once have you even tried to be nice to me!"

"You guys!" Drake called desperately, but he could already see the aura starting to pulse from them. This was getting ugly.

"You're just jealous because Raine hangs out with me and not you," Isaac sneered. "Maybe if you had any manners, she might actually look at you without wanting to rip your face off!" He gave a slight grin.

Yellow, translucent daggers appeared in both of Vin's hands. "Raine only hangs out with you because she feels sorry for you!"

"Oh?" Isaac challenged. "I guess that insecurity you carry around turns you into a beta bitch."

That had done it. Vin snapped. He lunged at Isaac with his daggers, aiming for his mid-section.

Isaac saw Vin come at him, though much faster than the last time they'd fought. He quickly rolled backward to dodge Vin's strike to his chest. As he came up, he used telekinesis to grab two small rocks and hurled them at Vin's face.

Vin used his aura to see the rocks being hurled at him and brought his left dagger up to deflect one rock and his right dagger up to deflect the other as he rushed in toward Isaac.

"STOP IT!" Drake shouted at them. "What is wrong with you guys?" He moved toward them, trying to break them up, but as he got within arm's reach, Vin, after nimbly dodging Isaac's backhand, went for a low kick and took Isaac's feet out from under him, causing him to slip down the side of the steep hill. As Isaac started to fall, he reached out and grabbed Vin's ankle, pulling him down with him, and the two rolled toward the bottom of the mountain at an accelerated rate.

Drake could only watch as his would-be teammates descended out of view into the thick trees covering the mountainside.

As they rolled, Isaac and Vin tried to avoid trees by bounding off them as best they could, although their attempts at slowing down ended in failure. The two continued to descend until finally, about a hundred yards down the mountain, they dropped straight into a giant hole.

"Agh!" Isaac yelled as he hit the ground with a loud thud.

"Oof!" Vin fell right behind him.

The two stood up, still furious from their previous confrontation.

"Ugh! You idiot!" Isaac growled at Vin; he looked up at the hole they had fallen into. The walls were about twenty feet high and made of some kind of dark stone.

Vin glared at Isaac. "I'm the idiot? You started all of this!"

"Well, I wasn't the one who pushed you down a hill!"

Vin grabbed his head in frustration. "That was an accident!"

Isaac was about to reply, but the area was suddenly filled with an orange light. The light came from the ground, and the two noticed that it was forming in a circular pattern.

"What is this?" Isaac questioned Vin.

"How am I supposed to know!?" he replied nastily.

The light began to pulse, and then the ground started to move ... downward.

CHAPTER 4: TRIALS AND TRIBULATIONS

"What did you do?" Isaac asked.

Vin stared back dumbfounded. "I didn't!"

Isaac realized that they were on some kind of elevator that was leading them downward to the unknown. After a while, the elevator stopped.

"Uhh, okay," Vin said warily as the two found themselves staring down a long, dark hallway.

"Now what?"

"I don't know what this is," Vin stated. "I've never seen this before."

They stepped out into the hallway, and as they did, the platform's lights went out and it began to rise back up.

"Ahh crap!" Vin quickly jumped and grabbed the edge of the platform, but it didn't stop, and he had to let go so he didn't get his fingers smashed by the ceiling.

"Seems we're finding another way out," Isaac said blankly.

The hallway began to light up as if some kind of mechanism was triggered. Crystals along the wall glowed yellow and orange, revealing the path.

They made their way through and soon entered a large, circular chamber with many weird statues circling around the wall.

"What are these?" Vin asked rhetorically. "I don't remember anything about this in any kind of text."

The statues included images of a giant, winged serpent, a three-headed dog, a half woman half bird, a hulking humanoid creature with horns, a skeleton horse, a steel behemoth, a dragon, a golem, and a beautiful woman with four arms.

Isaac and Vin stood in the center of the room staring at the statues.

"I recognize the images these statues represent," Isaac said. "They're well-known demons."

"Demons?" Vin gasped. "How do you know this?"

"Because where I'm from, I've studied these," Isaac explained. "You sure you haven't read anything about them? See, there's Cerberus, a Nightmare, a Siren ..."

"We need to find a way out of here," Vin said impatiently with a hint of fear. "This place doesn't feel right."

Isaac searched around and noticed there were three doors separate from the one they entered. "Why? Are you scared?" he stated as he stared at the glyphs drawn upon the ground.

"Are you serious right now?" Vin looked over at Isaac. "This isn't the time to be arguing, for once. We need to get out of here first, then we can fight."

"Or you can just say what you're thinking right now and be done with it." Isaac stared blankly.

Vin stepped closely to Isaac till they were less than two feet away. "What is your freaking problem?"

Isaac gritted his teeth and was about to retaliate when they both froze.

A large, raspy roar could be heard from down one of the three corridors.

Isaac and Vin slowly turned their heads as the sound of large, cracking footsteps could be heard from the corridor to the right.

In the darkness of the doorway, a large set of yellow eyes could be seen staring back at them; and then after a moment, a set of razor-sharp teeth connected to a hideous face poked its way through the dark veil. The creature had two twisted horns coming out of its head, and as it stepped out into the chamber, Isaac could see its body was scaly with red skin, and it stood on two hoofed legs, a long spear-like tail protruding from its backside.

The thing towered over them, and after a moment, it reared its head back as a burst of fire emitted from its mouth and the creature's body seemed to ignite in flames.

"Run!" Vin shouted as he turned and raced for the doorway to the left.

Isaac followed him, and with swift movement, the creature gave chase.

Vin, incredibly fast due to his speed aura, was surprised to see Isaac keeping pace with him. The creature, however, was faster, and it gained on them with every stride.

Crystals were lighting up the path as they raced onward.

"The hell is that thing!?" Vin shouted.

"I think it's an efreet!" Isaac said, swiftly dodging a blast of fire the creature threw at him.

"A what??"

Isaac quickly did a hop and spun himself, using an air blast to block an incoming fireball. "It's a demon!" He landed and continued fleeing.

The efreet was within ten yards of them as they came into another room, an open door on the other side. As they approached it, the efreet waved its hand and the doorway magically sealed itself.

Isaac and Vin halted in front of the seal.

"Oh boy." Vin spun around. The efreet bounded into the room, sealing the doorway behind him, and continued to charge at the two.

They both dodged in opposite directions as the efreet crashed into the seal.

"Now what?" Isaac moved to the opposite side of the room, trying to keep his distance from the demon.

"Up there!" Vin pointed at a bridge about twenty feet above them.

The efreet had recovered and was making his way toward them.

"And how do you suppose we get up there?" Isaac inquired as he dodged the two slashes the efreet made at him. On the third swipe, Isaac did a dodge roll to the side and shot a lightning bolt at the demon's arm. The efreet briefly grabbed its arm but recovered quickly.

Vin was looking around the room, trying to find a way up to the bridge. "There's no way up!"

Isaac was circling around the room as the demon stalked after him. "We've got to fight this thing then!" He shot a blast of air at an incoming fireball but was too slow at dodging the following jab, and Isaac flew across the room, rolling along the ground as he landed.

A pair of yellow daggers appeared in Vin's hands, and he jumped onto the efreet's back as it was making its way toward Isaac, who was scrambling to get on his feet. Driving one dagger into the demon's back as anchorage, Vin started slashing with the other dagger, ripping apart scales but barely penetrating the demon's flesh.

The efreet gave a loud roar, and its body burst into flame. Vin quickly dismounted as he started to get burned. "Agh!"

As the efreet began to simmer, Isaac shot a bolt of lightning into the demon's face, causing it to stagger backward. "Quick! I'll throw you up to the bridge!"

Vin quickly ran toward Isaac, who was kneeled with his hands cupped waiting for him; as he got his foot in place, Vin was surprised at how much force Isaac was able to throw him with, but as he launched toward the bridge, he came short and fell back down.

"I need more height!"

The efreet was recovering and beginning to turn its attention back to Isaac. "Well, that's the best I've got!" He began to circle the room again, but at a faster pace, flames erupting from its hands, scoring the area.

Vin held his hand up, and a yellow bow appeared, and he began firing arrows, but they barely dug into the scales of the demon and fell to the floor. "This thing is too tough; we need a solution!" He did a cartwheel as a fireball smashed into the floor where he was previously standing.

As the demon turned its attention to Vin, Isaac took the brief moment to come up with a way out.

The bridge is twenty feet up, and I was able to throw Vin about fourteen feet, he thought, *but I need to figure out how to get him the extra six.*

Vin dodged like crazy as the efreet tried to grab him, flames spouting in all directions.

"I've got it!" Isaac moved to the side of the room, directly to the left under the bridge. "Bring him over here to the side of the room!"

Vin dove, rolling back to his feet as the efreet lunged at him; he repositioned himself over to where Isaac was standing. "Now what?"

Isaac pushed Vin behind him. "Get ready to jump!" He waited for the demon to begin running at him before acting.

As the demon bounded up, Isaac jumped backward and shot lightning again into the efreet's face, which caused the demon to briefly stagger, and it began to grab at its face.

As the efreet stood there attempting to recover, Isaac swiftly scaled onto the demon's back. Standing on its shoulders, he turned to face Vin. "NOW!"

CHAPTER 4: TRIALS AND TRIBULATIONS

Amazed, Vin followed up the demon toward Isaac and was again launched upward. With the extra eight or so feet, he was able to grab the edge of the bridge and pulled himself up. "Here!" He pulled a rope from his small pack that he kept with him and tossed the coil down below while holding onto the other end.

Isaac jumped off the efreet's head and grabbed hold of the rope while the demon began to recover. He began to climb up at an incredible speed, and soon, Vin helped him up onto the bridge.

Down below, the efreet tried to jump up to them, but it couldn't find enough momentum and fell short; it waved its hand to release the seals on both doors and vanished through one of them.

"It's probably trying to find a way up to us," Vin said. "Let's find a way out."

The two turned to look down the path they were on. Another hallway extended before them, and they could make out a large room thirty or so feet ahead. In the opposite direction was just a veil of darkness.

"I vote fairly lit room," Vin said sarcastically.

Inside the room there were rows of chairs. "Doesn't seem like anyone has been here for quite some time," he muttered.

Isaac examined a painting on the wall; it showed what seemed to be the sky, only it was covered in some kind of black fog, and in the center was a giant, red dome, kind of like the eye on a hurricane. There were other similar paintings, but most of these reflected the statues they had seen earlier. "I know what this is," he said to Vin, who was peering down a hallway. "At least, I think I know what this is."

"Oh yeah?" Vin said, barely paying attention as he scanned the room and listened for the efreet.

Isaac made his way toward him. "I think this is some kind of organization room. You know, like a religion or cult."

"Well, it doesn't seem familiar to me," Vin replied. "By the way, you surprised me down there. Was that magic you used to throw me up to the bridge?"

"What?" Isaac muttered back to him, distracted by the paintings.

Vin stood between the chairs at the center of the room. Crystal chandeliers were lit up and hanging from the ceiling, revealing the large room. It had the appearance of a Catholic church.

"Raine must be teaching you how to control your magic well for you to be able to throw me up that high."

Isaac turned to look at Vin. "I'm not sure what you're talking about. You were simply light enough that I had no trouble lifting you."

Vin stared back dumbfounded. "You mean you didn't use magic?"

"No." Isaac began to search around the room.

"Weird ..." Vin turned to look down the room at the double doors that seemed to be the only way out, aside from the way they came. "I guess the only way to go is this way."

Isaac was standing up at the pedestal mounted ahead of the chairs, almost like a stage. "Why does this place seem so familiar ...?" As he glanced around room, his vision started to get hazy, and images began to flash in his mind.

Brave soul who does not fear death, heed our call.

In the vison, he could see the chairs were filled with several people in black cloaks, their hoods covering their faces.

"Come forth and fulfill your desire," he heard a voice echo out to him.

In his blurry eyesight, he looked down as he tried to push himself up off the ground. His hands were covered in darkness, but his fingers weren't normal; they were claws like a monster.

"You are the final piece," the voice echoed again.

His vision flashed briefly in the light, and he saw his hands changing back to normal.

"What was that?" the voice sneered.

"Someone is interfering with the summoning," another voice replied.

Isaac shook his head as his vision started to return and the images faded.

"We might be able to find an exit through these doors," Vin said as he headed for the double doors.

"What ..." Isaac glanced around in confusion, "was that?" He was back in the dark chapel with Vin.

As Vin came up to the doors, they burst open, throwing him backward.

The efreet stood, hulking in the doorway, fire pulsing from its body.

Vin landed in between all the chairs and was struggling to get up as he lay within all the broken wood. "I'm stuck!"

The demon leaped over the rows of chairs and stood above Vin, its claws raised, ready to strike.

"Isaac, I could use some help!" Vin pleaded as he watched the efreet slashing through the air.

All time seemed to stand still for a moment as Vin watched his life being ripped in half; but he never felt the claws strike him.

In a flash, Isaac stood above him, a radiant white longsword in his hands, blocking the efreet's claws.

"What ...?" Vin lay there, staring at the aural blade in Isaac's hand.

The efreet was drawing its other hand back to strike at Isaac. "Move!" he yelled down at Vin, who simply laid there in shock. The efreet's other hand began to swipe through the air, and Isaac acted quickly. Waving his hand, Isaac made a chair slide across the ground, pushing Vin backward and away from himself and the efreet. As the claws reached Isaac, he swiftly spun himself horizontally through the air, barely dodging the attack, using his momentum to slide his sword across the demon's hand, causing a fair cut on its palm.

Vin, being pushed clear of the chairs, was able to get on his feet. As the efreet grabbed its hand in pain, Isaac leaped at it, placing his feet on its chest and made a slashing motion with his sword as he kicked away from it, leaving a light cut across its neck, but not enough to draw any blood.

Vin recovered and had his daggers drawn. "I can see light through that door!" He pointed past the double doors, down yet another long hallway; a faint light, not cast from any crystal, could be seen reflecting on the wall at the end.

Isaac made for the exit. "Then come on!"

The efreet was standing between them and the door. Isaac threw a blast of air at its face and vaulted over it, while Vin came in behind and slid between its open feet; it spun around and bounded after them, roaring in anger.

Down the hallway, they ran past a set of stairs. Around the corner at the end of the hallway, however, Isaac and Vin saw a gate with light peering through a small hole on the far side.

"It's a dead end!" Vin said, panicked.

Isaac saw a lever just ahead on their side of the gate. "Maybe that lever will open the gate!"

As they neared it, the efreet slid around the corner.

Vin pulled the lever, and the gate began to slowly rise. "Come on! Can't this thing go any faster!?"

The efreet was getting closer. Isaac tried to delay it by hurling several lightning bolts at its feet, which seemed to work, but just barely. Vin joined in by firing arrows at its face, which caused it to hold its hand up to block them. They were able to slow down the demon long enough for the gate to rise just enough for them to slide under.

On the other side, Isaac used telekinesis to push the lever back the other way, making the gate lower back down, and with a swift tug, broke the lever at the base in order to prevent the demon from re-opening it. The efreet grabbed the bottom of the gate and began to lift it up.

"Are you fucking kidding me!?" Vin yelled.

Isaac pulled on Vin's arm. "Let's just go!"

There was a stone door blocking the path. A light could be seen through a six-inch hole.

"This leads to the outside!" Vin said, as trees could be seen through the tiny window.

As they came up to the door, it lit up, and a mechanism next to it activated. The stone wall began to swiftly rise.

"Let's go!"

As Isaac and Vin moved under the heavy, stone door, they looked back and saw the efreet had made it past the gate and was sprinting toward them.

"This guy doesn't quit, does he?"

The stone wall had to have been at least ten feet wide, and Isaac and Vin were about halfway through when they heard the sound of creaking metal as the mechanism gave way to rust and aging.

CHAPTER 4: TRIALS AND TRIBULATIONS

The stone wall came crashing down, about to squash the two, when Isaac thrust his sword sideways against the edge of the stone wall, causing it to halt the door's decent.

The white sword, being made of pure aura, was able to hold the door long enough for the two to leap out of harm's way, outside.

The sword disappeared, allowing the stone to close completely, locking the efreet within.

"Holy shit!" Vin sighed in relief. "That was crazy!" He laughed.

"That was way too close!" Isaac replied.

The exit they had gone through a second ago had magically disappeared, blending in with the surrounding forest.

"Everything makes sense about you now," Vin told Isaac.

"What do you mean?"

Vin stared at Isaac as if he'd just found out a big secret. "You're a guardian!"

The black-haired woman looked questioningly at Isaac. "You and Raine seemed to get along."

"Yeah, she was really kind," he replied.

"That must have seemed new to you."

Isaac remained silent.

"But you and Vin, however." She chuckled. "You two always fought."

"I think that was my fault," Isaac explained. "I provoked him when I shouldn't have."

"Why did you?"

"I don't know. Maybe I was jealous of how laid back he was when I'm so ..." He trailed off.

"Miserable?"

He just stared at the table between them. "Yeah ..."

"But you two ended up bonding over this ordeal, right? So, in the end, maybe it was for the best?" She smiled warmly.

"I guess."

"What did you make of that place? It seemed strange that you recognized most of the things in there and Vin did not," the woman questioned.

Isaac held his chin in thought. "Yeah, I was surprised he didn't know what those statues were of. I've seen them many times on Earth, but he had no idea about them. Does this have something to do with where I'm from?"

"I wonder ..." She stared blankly. "Maybe your coming here wasn't a mere coincidence."

"I've thought about that, but then, who brought me here, and why?"

"I'm sure you'll find the answer to that question in time." She shrugged. "But the fact is, you're here, and maybe it has something to do with that aura of yours."

"What do you mean?" He frowned.

"Oh, it's nothing." She laughed. "It just seems people apparently think you're special."

"I'm not, though."

She nodded. "We both know that much, at least. Please continue, though. I feel this is only the beginning."

Isaac took a deep breath. "The tournament was just around the corner ..."

CHAPTER 5

THE FIRST ROUND

"So why didn't you tell us?" Vin asked Isaac as the two made their way through the forest, trying to find their way back to Adamas.

Isaac shrugged. "I don't even know what a guardian is."

Vin paused. "How can you not know?"

"C'mon! I'm not from around here, alright?"

Vin looked at Isaac sincerely. "Hey, I'm not meaning anything by it. It's just everyone here knows what a guardian is ... sorry." He glanced around at the foliage, trying to figure out their location. "But don't go telling everyone what you are. People might freak out, and we'll probably get banned from the tournament."

They continued through the forest.

"So, what exactly is a guardian?" Isaac asked.

Vin pushed two branches out of his way as he spoke. "A guardian is a hero of legend, said to have a mastery over all powers. In the ancient texts we've learned from, here at our schools, a guardian is supposed to appear during a time of great darkness."

"And how, exactly, do you know that I'm one of them?" Isaac narrowed his eyes.

"It's your sword that gives it away," Vin explained. "No one has an aural weapon that's pure white light. The three colors are red, blue, and yellow. Only guardians wield white blades. Why didn't you ever use it before?"

Isaac shrugged. "I never really found a need to until this recent fight."

"Well, I wouldn't use it until we at least finish the tournament. Maybe this is why Queen Lucia wanted you to stay in the castle." Vin stopped walking and looked at Isaac. "Wow! It all makes sense now. Raine saw what you were, that's why she let us into the castle!"

Isaac chuckled sarcastically. "You think the queen knows about me?"

"Definitely. Raine doesn't keep any secrets from Her Majesty."

"Well, I guess you don't have to be jealous of me and Raine then." Isaac chuckled.

Vin began to shake his head dramatically. "Geez. You and Drake really jump to conclusions. I'm not interested in Raine what-so-ever."

"Really ..." Isaac replied with doubt.

"I guess I just couldn't figure out why Raine was so nice to you from the beginning."

"I'm that bad, huh?" Isaac seemed both angry and hurt.

"No, no. I mean, Raine isn't that nice from the get-go," Vin explained. "She's kinda rude to everyone until she gets to know them."

So, she was only kind to him because of his power. This thought didn't sit right with Isaac. "So, that's why people have been so nice to me? Because I have this power? I see ..."

"Hey, I didn't mean it like that," Vin tried to console. "Look, if my hunch is right, and it usually is, I'd say Raine only told the queen about you, which would mean the three of us are the only ones who know."

Nobody likes you. Face it.

"But the way Her Majesty sees you, I can honestly say she genuinely likes you. Anytime she's in the room with you, her eyes light up."

"She's like that with everyone," Isaac said halfheartedly.

"No, she isn't," Vin said seriously. "I have to work missions under her often, and she's usually very serious to others. But you, she always seems excited just to hear your name."

"That's because I have these powers."

"Dude, I'm telling you, if that were the case, she would be polite, but serious."

Isaac paused. "I didn't want these powers, you know." He glanced into the distance. "I just wish you guys would stop treating me like a hero and maybe act like you truly want me around."

Vin put his hand on Isaac's shoulder. "Hey man, I'm sorry about that. I guess I crossed some lines I shouldn't have."

Isaac sighed. "I'm just trying to get used to this place, and it's really frustrating not knowing what's going on."

"How's about I fill you in on the things that you don't know about?" Vin suggested.

"Like what?"

"Like anything. If you have any questions, just ask. Like for instance, have you met any of the council members?"

Isaac scratched his head thoughtfully. "What is this council? I've heard a lot about them, but I haven't really seen them."

"The council is the central point of all five kingdoms," Vin explained. "They maintain balance and order, and essentially rule overall."

"Then why are there even royalty?" Isaac asked. "If the council has that much power, then there would be no point."

"Not true. While the council maintains order for the five kingdoms as a whole, kings and queens still maintain order for the individual kingdoms."

"Lucia is younger than me, and yet she leads an entire kingdom?" Isaac inquired.

"That's right, and she does a damn good job of it too!"

"I see. So does she have any authority over the council, or does she have to do whatever they say?"

"Well, the council has most of the authority when it comes to decisions that affect all the nations, but in some cases, a king or queen could overrule them."

"Seems like they have too much power to me," Isaac stated.

"And there are some who also believe that, but ever since they were organized, we've actually been much better off."

Isaac shrugged. "If you say so."

"So now I have a question for you," Vin said suddenly.

Let me guess, Isaac thought, *he wants to know about my 'gift', this power he calls being a guardian.*

"Why are you so introverted?"

Isaac didn't expect that. "What do you mean?"

Vin stuffed his hands into his pockets casually and said, with a calm, almost apologetic voice, "You're very reserved. I was just curious. You don't really talk much, and when you do, it's usually cold and indignant."

Isaac looked down at the dirt. What do you say to something like that? He shrugged and looked up at Vin. "I guess that's just how I am."

Vin nodded thoughtfully. "Maybe when we get back, we'll have to get a few drinks at Ruby's." He gave Isaac a knowing look. "What do you think? Will you stick around this time and hang out with us?"

"Alright." Isaac shrugged. "But what's this all of a sudden?"

"This'll be my way of thanks for what happened back there. I'd be a goner if you didn't block that demon, so thanks, man."

"I should also apologize," Isaac said. "I don't know why I got so annoyed with you up on the mountain. I didn't mean what I said."

"I guess we both got carried away, huh?" Vin replied. "Well, let's start over, then. I feel like that battle taught me a lot about you. You're pretty brave to jump in front of that monster without thinking."

Isaac shrugged. "I guess I just sorta moved."

"Well, I'm glad you're on the team." Vin smiled. "We'll win this tournament for sure!" He gave a thumbs up.

Isaac nodded. "Yeah, you're pretty good yourself. I think we can win easily."

"By the way, how did you become a guardian?"

Isaac thought for a moment. "I'm not sure."

"So, you've always had this power?"

Isaac shook his head. "No, I grew up without any of this. I didn't get these powers until I came here."

"And you've only been here for a month?"

Isaac nodded.

"So that explains the reason for you not knowing any magic."

"Where I'm from, magic doesn't exist," Isaac replied.

Vin stared at Isaac as if trying to rip info out of him. "Where *are* you from?"

"It doesn't matter. I left, and I have no intention of going back."

"Okay, I won't pry."

"Sorry about how I've acted," Isaac said. "It's just really frustrating with everyone looking at me like I'm supposed to be their hero or whatever."

Vin chuckled. "Look man, it's okay. Let's both do our best to be better, eh?" He jabbed Isaac in the arm. "I guess we both have our faults, don't we?"

"You can have these powers if you'd like," Isaac attempted to joke. "They don't really fit me."

"Shit, dude, I think I'll pass. Too much pressure, ya know." Vin laughed. "Besides, I thought you looked pretty cool fighting that demon back there."

The two continued to chat and joke about their encounter as they made their way back to Adamas.

"They should be somewhere over here!"

Drake was frantic. He walked through the woods with two guards. It had been a few hours since Isaac and Vin had fallen down the mountain, and Drake was worried.

"Are you sure they fell this way?" one of the guards asked.

"I'm positive." Drake sounded forceful.

After about twenty more minutes, Drake heard talking coming from deeper in the forest. "HEY, ISAAC, VIN, IS THAT YOU!?"

In the distance, Drake could see two figures appear out of the brush: Isaac and Vin. But to his surprise, they were laughing.

"Oh hey, Drake!" Vin shouted. "You missed the party!"

"Where the hell have you guys been!? It's been hours!"

Isaac stared blankly at Drake. "What? Were you lonely?"

"I was worried!"

"Well, we're fine now." Vin shrugged.

"I guess the training was a success?" Isaac chuckled.

"If you think about it, yeah, I guess it was." Vin scratched his chin thoughtfully.

Drake just stared dumbfounded at Vin and Isaac. "You guys were trying to rip each other's heads off, and now you're all buddy-buddy?"

Vin gave a cocky smile as he nodded. "We kinda had some trouble. First there was this creepy tomb, or whatever that place was—"

"A church," Isaac helped him.

"Yeah, that's it. Then we ran into some kinda fire monster—"

"An efreet."

"Yeah, that thing. Then we were running for our lives—"

"It was crazy!"

"Yeah, it was!"

"Whoa, whoa, whoa!" Drake held his hands up. "What happened!?"

Isaac sighed and shook his head. "I'm gonna need a drink if we're gonna go over this whole thing."

Vin nodded his approval. "Good idea. Let's go to Ruby's and chat. I'm sure Raine will want to hear this as well."

Isaac, Vin, Drake, and Raine sat at a table inside Ruby's bar. Isaac and Vin relayed everything they had experienced in the underground church to the two sitting before them.

"I have never heard of anything like this," Raine said. "How did you two just 'fall' into a hole that we have never discovered? And better yet, encounter a demon from religious texts which shouldn't exist?"

Vin started to explain. "We just fell into it; how're we supposed to know where it came from?"

"How do you know about efreets being a religious demon?" Isaac interrupted.

"They're referenced in our religious texts," Raine replied. "But they aren't frequently mentioned, so most people don't really know about them."

"But what was with that church—" Vin began, but Isaac again interrupted him.

"What do you mean? What religious texts?"

Raine stared at Isaac suspiciously. "You know, the church? Of God? What's gotten into you?"

Isaac noticed everyone looking at him and started to feel a little nervous. "Nothing, I'm still just a little excited from the incident." He took a long drink from his mug.

Raine looked at Vin. "Well, from what I understand, you two were acting irrational before this ever happened."

Vin looked surprised. "We were almost killed by a fire breathing psycho monster, and you're worried about our relationship?"

"Let me handle the creepy dungeon," Raine said. "You two need to worry about the tournament. You only have four days till it starts."

Vin, Drake, and Isaac looked at each other.

"I'll talk with the castle scientists, and we'll do a search for your hidden church," Raine reassured. "In the meantime, you three need to focus on winning that tournament."

"Aww, she does care!" Vin said cheekily.

Raine stared at Vin, uninterested. "I only care that my time spent helping Isaac wasn't a complete waste."

"Hey, Drake." Vin turned to the big man. "Could you go ask Ruby for another round? I'm buyin'."

Drake's eyes lit up. "If it's on you, sure!" He stood up and headed to the bar.

After Drake was out of ear shot, Vin leaned closer to Raine and Isaac. "Look, Raine, I know that Isaac is a guardian."

Raine was slightly taken aback. "How'd you find out?"

Isaac supplied the answer. "It was during our fight with the efreet. It seems my sword is white instead of one of the basic three colors."

"You seem a little surprised yourself," Raine observed.

"I am," Isaac replied. "Considering I don't even know what a guardian truly is."

Raine let out a calm sigh. "It's because you possess every aural ability. You're extremely unique."

"Yeah, I was really surprised at how easily you were able to keep up with me during training," Vin said. "Since I was under the impression you could only use magic, it was a little confusing to see you reacting as fast as you could."

Isaac shrugged. "It's hard to explain, but since coming here, this power seems to come naturally to me."

Drake approached with four mugs of spirits.

"Let's talk about this later." Raine told them.

"Hey, gang, here we are!" Drake gave each of them a mug and sat down next to Raine. "Ruby said she's real glad you both came back unharmed."

"Oh, where is she?" Vin perked up, looking around.

"She said she had things to take care of and didn't have the time to chat," Drake explained. "Said it was very urgent."

Vin looked sad. "Aww, I guess I'll just have to see her next time."

After about an hour, the group decided to head out.

It was close to midnight, and there was a slight chill in the air. Isaac, Vin, and Raine bid farewell to Drake as they started toward the castle.

"So, why do I need to keep my powers a secret?" Isaac asked Raine.

"Because a lot of people might freak out. You are, after all, the reincarnation of a being who once saved the world."

"Really." Isaac wasn't convinced.

"Actually," Vin began, "people would probably either worship you or want you dead."

"What!?" Isaac almost laughed. "That just sounds ridiculous. What if I'm actually a bad person with evil intentions? People would worship that?"

Vin shook his head. "No, it's because the historical archives tell of stories about one being who saved the world from great evil. And apparently it has happened several times."

"Granted those times span over the last few millennia," Raine stated. "In the religious teachings, it was declared that these beings were guardians of our planet and would come to save us in a time of darkness."

"Hold up," Isaac interrupted. "How come you two aren't freaking out, then?"

"Oh, we aren't religious," Vin answered confidently. "I personally don't believe that you are some reincarnation of a god or whatever."

Raine smiled. "Especially since you can barely cast any magic."

CHAPTER 5: THE FIRST ROUND

Isaac nodded. "Well, I'm definitely glad you guys aren't annoying fanatics. There must be a good reason for me having these powers."

"That's what we think too," Raine said.

The three approached the castle gates, and the guard let them in. Vin waved farewell to Isaac and Raine and headed toward the other side of the castle where his room was. Raine and Isaac continued through the main entrance.

"By the way," Raine told Isaac, "only the queen, Bart, Vin, and I know of your identity. It's best if we keep it that way for now."

"Bart? From the tournament?"

"Yes. He knew what you were from your entry exam."

"I see."

The moonlight created an ominous atmosphere. They went down the hallway in silence, keeping to their own thoughts until they finally reached Isaac's room.

"Hey, Isaac," Raine began, a hint of concern in her eyes. "Take care of Lucia, alright?"

Isaac peered back curiously. "Umm ...?"

"It's just, I feel something bad is going to happen, and if it does, I may not be able to do much to stop it." Raine paused. Isaac could see she was worried about something.

"Raine—"

"I know you'll be there," Raine said suddenly. "Guardian aside, I think you're pretty great. If something bad happens, I know I can count on you." She stared at Isaac for a brief moment, then turned and continued down the hall alone.

Isaac just stared. *What was that about? Great? Me? I'm nothing like that. Even if I wanted to, I couldn't even hope to be that. Raine acted as if I was some kind of hero.*

I'm not a hero. Not even close.

He turned and opened his door. The moon lit up his room like a dark prison. The power of aura gave Isaac a keen sight, and that's why he was able to clearly see the shadowy figure in the far corner of his room.

"She is mistaken, you know," a raspy, evil voice came from the darkness where the figure stood. "In time, she will learn to fear you, even hate you."

91

Isaac gritted his teeth.

"You think they care, but they only want what you can give them. You're just an object of their salvation."

A sound came from the hallway behind Isaac, and he quickly looked to see what it was. There was nothing there. When he turned back, the shadowy figure was gone.

The tournament had begun, and the Adamas coliseum was packed. There were a lot of people, and it was incredibly loud.

Isaac felt nervous knowing that everyone would be watching him when it was his turn to go out there. Vin was trying to psych him up, and Drake just sort of stared into the crowd.

"Hey, Vin." Isaac leaned close so only Vin could hear. "Didn't you say something about a spy being planted in the tournament?"

Vin nodded quietly. "Yeah, remember those three girls we met?"

Isaac thought for a moment. "Oh yeah! At the orientation."

"Yup, those ones. I went out with them a few times because I thought they were suspicious. Turns out, they entered the tournament to win, so they could get a chance to assassinate the queen."

Vin explained it all to Isaac. The winner of this competition would be given the award from the queen herself. The idea was that if anyone wanted to harm this kingdom, they would use this opportunity to do so, and that would give the Adamas Intelligence Division a lead on who was planning these attacks. Vin was one of the few agents assigned to the AID and had been tasked with finding the spy who had entered the tournament. It was a risky mission, but Bart Seros, the director of the AID, had been informed of these women and had set up a chance for Isaac, Vin, and Drake to fight them for the championship; they just had to get past the first few rounds.

"Why wouldn't they let Raine into the competition?" Isaac inquired.

"Are you kidding? She's the queen's right hand. Everyone would automatically suspect something. Nobody knows about me because that's how we keep it. And even better—we found *you*, so that's a bonus." Vin patted Isaac on the shoulder. "We got this, you an' me!"

"What about Drake?" Isaac motioned to Drake, who was still looking out into the crowd.

"Unfortunately, he's still a regular civilian, and therefore can't be fully trusted. But he got high ratings on the entrance exam, so he'll at least be good in a fight. Bart made sure of that."

"Why didn't Bart just have these girls arrested?" Isaac inquired.

"Because we have no proof that they're here to kill Lucia."

"Don't you have a tape recorder or something so that you could have gotten evidence?"

Vin shook his head. "They didn't tell me straight out, but after poking around, I discovered a strong reason to believe they're the ones." He looked at Isaac and winked. "I'm never wrong about these things."

Isaac could hear the announcer calling out the different teams. This made him even more nervous.

"We got you set up for the one-on-one match," Vin said suddenly. "It's gonna be cake, so don't sweat it. Just make sure not to overdo it, because we don't want people knowing about you yet."

What? That's the first match! Now Isaac was REALLY nervous. "Who is it against?"

"Some power user; apparently he's all brawn and no brains."

"Do you know all the matches set up for this whole thing?"

Vin scratched his head. "Naw, only the first match. We can't determine the rest since we don't know who'll win on the other teams. But our chance of winning against all of them is pretty high."

"So why don't you compete in the first match?" Isaac asked.

"I need to keep watch in case Bart gives an order." Vin stared at Isaac and chuckled. "Are you nervous?"

"A little."

"Trust me, you're gonna be fine."

Drake glanced over at his two teammates. "They're announcing the first part of the competition."

At a podium set high above the circular arena stood the announcer. The whole setup was like that of a football stadium. He spoke into what looked to be a microphone.

"Ladies and gentlemen." His voice boomed over the entire arena. "Welcome to the Adamas Grand Tournament where many warriors across the land have come to face off in the ultimate test of power and skill."

Vin chuckled and leaned closer to Isaac so only he could hear. "That's bullshit."

"I present to you, our own royal majesty, Queen Lucia!"

The announcer waved his hand toward a central viewpoint where Lucia, Raine, and several others sat overlooking the arena.

"The winner of this tournament will be presented the Grand Champion Trophy as well as a large sum of aurums, received from the queen herself!"

Lucia stood up and gave a courteous wave as the crowd cheered even louder.

"This tournament is a one loss elimination style. If a team loses any match, it's game over, so give it your all. First up, we have one member from each team competing in one versus one combat!"

Isaac wasn't too fond of being the central point of attention, and this announcement only fueled his anxiety.

"In this match, a single member from each team will face off against another member from a different team. There are no restrictions, so please exercise caution as serious injury is a possibility, even death." The announcer held up a parchment. "The rules are simple: One person will get a choice for arena style, and the other will get the choice for victory conditions. This will be available for each match. We shall start with the first two fighters."

Isaac held his breath.

"Kaito Nishimura and Vektor Sano."

He gave a quiet sigh.

The two called contenders entered the center of the arena. A man who looked like a referee walked over to them. After briefly talking with them, he turned toward the stadium, his voice echoing loudly. "Arena will be labyrinth, and victory will be orb collecting."

Isaac turned to Vin. "What the hell?"

"Basically, each fighter needs to find and collect more orbs than the other before time expires."

"What? I thought this was a fighting competition."

"This is a tournament; fighting isn't going to be the only event."

The announcer's voice thundered across the playing field. "Combatants take your places!"

Kaito and Vektor both separated from each other to the opposite ends of the arena. After they were in position, the arena exploded with activity as large walls began to rise from the ground.

"We get to choose the battle arena we fight in?" Isaac questioned Vin.

Beaming back, Vin replied, "Yeah! This arena is made from aural magic, so it can transform into anything."

The arena seemed to be only filled with sand but had now transformed as if the sand had gathered into a maze of walls throughout the stadium.

"Contenders, get ready! The arena will be filled with a set number of orbs that you two will have to compete in collecting," the announcer stated. "You will have five minutes to collect as many as you can. Be warned that fighting is allowed, so watch for the other fighter. When the time is over, whoever has the most orbs wins."

Bright lights began to fill the maze as glowing orbs appeared all over the arena between the twisting and winding hallways.

"Orbs are in place. Contenders, on your marks. GO!"

Vektor and Kaito began to run through the twisting hallways of the maze, searching for glowing orbs. Vektor was much faster than Kaito as he began to collect orb after orb. Each time he ran through one of the glowing balls, it would vanish in a puff of mist, and he would gain an additional point under his name on the scoreboard high above the arena. Kaito, however, seemed to be avoiding all the orbs he came into contact with and would occasionally run his hand along the maze wall.

"What is he doing?" Isaac asked Vin.

"Not sure." Vin shrugged.

Kaito's movements were unorthodox. He would occasionally circle around a part of the maze or just stop completely, never once touching an orb. After about two minutes, Vektor had obtained over twenty orbs, and Kaito had zero.

Vin pointed at the area of orbs that remained. "That guy seems to be keeping a specific area untouched, like he's waiting for that other guy to show up."

It was a rather wide area, but the orbs that remained seemed to be in a specific block of the labyrinth, which Vektor was beginning to close in on. Kaito began to circle around near the backside of one of the walls where the other guy was approaching. He crouched down to mitigate his sound, and as he did, he placed his hand on the wall and waited.

Vektor ran through the maze quickly trying to obtain orbs, and he didn't notice the sigil that had been place along the wall nearby. Feeling his presence, Kaito snapped his fingers as the man approached the sigil. An explosion went off, and the man was thrown against the wall behind him.

Kaito jumped up and darted around the corner of the wall, throwing his arm out. A spike with a cord attached to it shot from under his sleeve, wrapping around Vektor's leg and pulling him to the ground.

The man quickly waved his hand, and a yellow shortsword appeared, which he used to cut the cable. Bounding up, Kaito ran along the wall, spewing a torrent of flame from his hand, causing the ground to heat up. Vektor quickly jumped to his feet and ran the opposite way. Pulling several throwing knives from his pocket, he hurled them at the assassin, who swiftly hopped from the wall he was on to the one across the way.

Darting around the corner, Vektor broke into a full sprint as the hallway behind him burst into flame and the attacker sprang from the fire, landing behind him. Kaito was much slower than the other man and could not catch him; instead he waited. The fleeing man reached the end of the long hallway and began to round the corner when another explosion went off, this time burning his left arm and causing his head to spin. Kaito pulled a small canister from his pocket and held his arm out. The old canister that fired a compact spike cord fell from his sleeve, and he reloaded it with the new one.

CHAPTER 5: THE FIRST ROUND

"One minute remains!" the announcer's voice boomed over the stadium.

Vektor had barley recovered when the other man ran up on him. He quickly held his sword at the ready, trying to ignore his injured arm. Kaito jumped at the nearby wall, vaulting off it to kick at the other man swinging his sword at him. He connected and sent the man's sword flying from his hand, following up with a palm strike to his chest, forcing him back to the wall.

Vektor threw a small pellet from his pocket which caused a blinding flash, temporarily stunning Kaito. He made his sword appear in his hand again and lunged. The assassin, still dazed, waved his hand into the air, causing the sand from the ground to fly up as he covered his eyes and retreated a few steps. Vektor was caught off guard from the sand and began to scratch at his eyes while still going after Kaito. As he approached, he swung his sword down, aiming for the assassin's left arm.

There was a clicking sound, and an eight-inch hidden blade appeared from Kaito's sleeve, blocking the incoming sword. Fully recovered, he kicked the man away from him and shot the spike cord, grabbing the man's leg yet again and pulling him to the ground. He quickly vaulted on top of him and punched him in the face. After a few hits, the man lay motionless on the ground.

"Winner by K.O.," the announcer shouted. "Kaito Nishimaru!"

The crowd cheered as the walls lowered back into the ground. A medic team rushed out to retrieve the unconscious man.

"Huh." Vin sat back. "He built a trap."

"What do you mean?" Isaac inquired.

"He knew he couldn't beat him in a race, so he set a trap in order to beat him by default, which is to simply beat up your opponent."

Isaac thought for a moment. "Then it doesn't matter what victory conditions you pick?"

"Well, it also depends on what the conditions are. For instance, if you chose something that would force you to fight your opponent, then that rule would be the condition for winning. Orbs were chosen for this one, so it was the primary way to win, but if you become incapacitated and are unable to continue, then you lose by default. Make sense?"

"I think so."

A few more rounds cycled through, and then, on one of them, Vin sat up. "Here we go."

The announcer held up his list and called out the next fighters.

"Kino Dern and Natalie Calvor."

Isaac looked at Vin. "That's the girl you were talking about."

"Yep."

The two combatants approached the announcer. After a brief moment, he turned to the audience. "Arena will be pillars, and victory will be flag retrieval."

The arena burst into life as the sand shifted into several pillars throughout.

"She's a speed user, that's why she picked capture the flag." Vin snorted.

"Combatants, take your places!"

Natalie had this stupid grin on her face the entire time, like this whole match was a joke. Isaac already didn't like her.

"Flag is in place. It will move every thirty seconds," the announcer explained. "On your marks. GO!"

The two contenders began to make their way through the pillars. Atop one of the pillars in the center of the arena was a glowing flag.

Natalie waved her hand, and a few yellow shuriken appeared between her fingers. She dashed up the side of a nearby pillar and spotted the flag several pillars ahead. Kino had taken a lower approach and sprinted toward the base of the glowing flag, a yellow ninja blade in his left hand.

Chuckling, Natalie was hopping from pillar to pillar toward the flag when the crowd began to chant. "Three, two, one!" As she bounded up, the flag disappeared. On the opposite end of the pillar, Kino appeared and took a swift slash at her with his blade. She quickly pushed away from the pillar and threw her shuriken at him, which he rapidly blocked with his weapon.

CHAPTER 5: THE FIRST ROUND

The flag reappeared about ten pillars behind Kino. He threw his blade at Natalie and made his way toward the flag. Natalie dodged the incoming sword and reached into a pouch she had strapped to her thigh and produced an object the size and shape of a quarter. Hurling the small disk at Kino, she quickly darted to the side of a nearby pillar, attaching to it, and then began hopping from pillar to pillar toward Kino. The flying disk hit the side of the platform in front if the man and burst into a cloud of electricity. Unable to stop, he hit the cloud, and his body seized up. As he plummeted toward the ground, he fought to regain his composure and was barely able to land on his feet, finishing in a roll.

Natalie threw a few more shuriken at him and vaulted toward the flag.

"Three, two ..." the crowd began as she reached her hand for the glowing fabric. "One!" The flag vanished as she reached the pillar.

"Damn!" she said as she looked around, waiting for it to reappear.

Kino had recovered and was making his way to the center of the arena, anticipating where the flag would appear.

After a few seconds, it appeared on the far end of the arena where Natalie and Kino were situated.

Natalie began throwing shuriken at Kino, who was, again, closer to the flag. While moving between the pillars, Kino dodged shuriken left and right. Eventually one of them made it through and hit him on the right shoulder. "Gahh!" It was enough to slow him down a bit, and Natalie took the lead, bounding on top of the pillars. "See ya, sucker!" She laughed down at him.

As she came up to the flag, the crowd began to chant yet again. "Three ... two ..." She bounded upon the final pillar. Her victory, however, was cut short. A bola had wrapped itself around her unsuspecting legs, causing her to trip. "One!" The flag vanished yet again, and Natalie found herself lying on the ground at the bottom of the pillars.

"Nice try, missy!" Kino laughed at her as he swung a second bola from his hand.

Natalie cut the bola off and scoffed. "Lucky shot. Won't happen again!"

Vin held back a laugh. "She's way too cocky. She doesn't pay attention to her surroundings."

The flag reappeared, this time off to the left part of the arena where the two combatants stood.

Kino made his way toward it, but Natalie had a better idea. She threw several shuriken and another disk toward the man, who dodged the shuriken but stopped as another electric cloud blocked his path. He was about to start climbing a nearby pillar when Natalie lunged at him. She latched onto his back with a thin cord between her hands in an attempt to choke Kino. He swiftly threw her off and broke her cord with his ninja blade. Natalie threw a small pellet on the ground, which caused a large cloud of smoke.

The crowd chanted that the flag had disappeared, but Natalie wasn't concerned ... yet.

Kino coughed from the smoke, but waved his hand, causing a blast of wind to clear the air. The nimble woman had left a few presents for him, however. As he started toward Natalie, he tripped a wire that triggered a fire blast nearby. He barely made it out with a few burns and saw that the would-be trickster was heading toward the reappeared flag.

Kino produced another bola and threw it at Natalie, who quickly spun around and hurled a shuriken, cutting the rope in half, making his bola useless. "Hahaha, nice try, fella!" She cackled as she raced off toward the flag.

The scoreboard showed five seconds left, and the two players were within a few seconds of the flag.

Natalie darted up a nearby pillar as Kino did the same. When she reached the top, she flung a final volley of shuriken at him and lunged for the flag. Kino, in a mad attempt to reach the flag, was caught by the volley of projectiles and hit the edge of his pillar, attempting to pull himself up.

"We have a winner!" the announcer shouted. "Natalie Calvor!"

The yellow shuriken in Kino's arm vanished as he grumbled, "Dammit!"

Natalie laughed at him. "Too bad, sweetheart. Maybe next time." She gave a cocky smile. "Oh, right, there *isn't* a next time. Haha!"

CHAPTER 5: THE FIRST ROUND

The crowd cheered as the pillars lowered back into the arena.

"Tsk, tsk." Vin shook his head. "She was holding back a little. But she actually almost lost because of it."

Isaac just watched as she left the arena, her arms held wide for the crowd. He didn't like her attitude, and he couldn't wait to face her team in the coming matches.

The crowd simmered down as the arena was reset.

"The next round!" the announcer's voice boomed out. "Garoth Daku and Isaac Wolfe!"

"I guess this is it ..." Isaac said as he stood up.

Vin gave him a pat on the back. "You'll be fine, just remember, magic only."

"Right ..."

Stepping out onto the field made Isaac very nervous. The stadium thundered with the cheers of its audience. Up high, sitting above the crowd, Isaac could see Raine and Lucia. They both gave him an encouraging smile. As he came up to the referee, Garoth also approached. Vin wasn't lying when he said this guy was big. Towering at what seemed to be well over six feet and two hundred and fifty pounds of raw muscle, this guy was a beast.

Garoth laughed arrogantly. *"You're* my opponent!? HAHAHA! What luck! This is gonna be easy!"

Isaac just stared at him in disbelief, his anxiety fading, being replaced by anger. "What's that supposed to mean?"

"Well, just *look* at you!" Garoth snorted.

Yeah, Isaac only weighed about a hundred and fifty pounds at five foot ten, and wasn't the best-looking guy, but that didn't give this muscle head the right to make fun of him, especially right before their match.

In the audience, Isaac could hear laughter and several comments about his size compared to Garoth's. He looked up at them and noticed a few people pointing at him, followed by laughter.

The referee looked at Garoth. "What do you choose for the arena style?"

"Easy!" Garoth spat. "Cage."

"Seriously!?" Isaac growled.

"I don't want you running away."

Isaac was pissed, but his face didn't show it; instead, his face was taunting. "I'll give you a chance to take it back."

Garoth laughed egotistically. "No way, little man, I'm gonna knock you the hell out, and you won't even know what hit you!"

The referee looked at Isaac. "What do you choose for victory conditions?"

All he could hear was the crowd laughing at him and this big man mocking him. Why were they laughing? They didn't know him. "Last chance," Isaac said, his nervousness completely gone. "Change the arena."

Garoth stared back at him defiantly. "No."

"C'mon, man, I'm giving you a chance here. Don't be an idiot," Isaac pleaded with Garoth.

He could see an arrogant smile forming across Garoth's face. Swallowing hard as to not lose his cool, he turned to the referee to give him his answer.

The crowd watched patiently as Isaac talked with the referee. After a few seconds, the referee's face changed to that of shock. He stood there for a few seconds before talking with Isaac some more.

"What's taking so long?" Raine muttered rhetorically to herself. After almost another minute, she had her answer.

The referee turned toward the stadium, hesitation in his voice as Garoth also seemed a little shaken up. "The arena will be a cage match; the victory conditions will be ... death."

The whole stadium fell silent for a moment until quiet whispers could be heard from the audience.

"No one has ever chosen that!" seemed to be the conversations going around.

Raine glanced over at Lucia, who looked back at her. "What the hell is he thinking!?"

Lucia tilted her head and grimaced. "It's in the rules ..."

The arena shook as the sand formed into a fence-like structure that surrounded the two combatants.

"You can't be serious," Garoth said, his composure a little rattled.

CHAPTER 5: THE FIRST ROUND

Isaac only stared back at him with murder in his eyes. "I gave you a chance, you threw it away in your arrogance."

The cage was finally finished, which included a roof. With only about twenty feet of space in all directions, there was no escape.

Drake swiftly looked over at Vin. "He won't actually kill him, will he?"

"Well, he has to now." Vin had his chin resting on both his hands as he tapped his foot nervously.

Garoth's face twisted into that of anger. "Well, I hope you're ready to die, then, because you don't have a chance of beating me, much less *killing* me!"

Isaac's sadistic facial expression didn't change, and he remained silent, his gaze never leaving Garoth. From the corner of his eye, he could see the referee raise his whistle, about to start the match.

Isaac, despite what was happening, was very calm; even as the whistle sounded, indicating the match had begun, he continued watching Garoth for any sign of movement.

Garoth roared as he thundered across the gap between them, his fists now covered in what seemed to be red gauntlets; Isaac patiently waited for him to approach.

As Garoth came up, he swung his fist, aiming for Isaac's face, who, out of instinct, quickly ducked away and delivered a powerful left jab square into the big man's face.

Garoth staggered backward in utter disbelief as blood ran from his nose.

Magic, Isaac! Only use magic! Raine's voice echoed in Isaac's head. Whoops, he had been so distracted with killing this guy that he had forgotten about his handicap.

Garoth recovered and this time began walking up to Isaac cautiously, his fists raised defensively. Isaac waited until the giant was about a foot away before swiftly taking a step back as Garoth attacked. Shoving his hand forward, a blast of wind pulsed from Isaac's palm, slamming into Garoth's gauntlets, causing him to lose balance. As he bounded up, hoping for another quick blast, Isaac had to change his tactics as Garoth had recovered quickly and was already taking another swing at him.

Ducking out of the way, Isaac rolled to safety a few feet to Garoth's left.

"Slippery, little shit!" Garoth said as he changed stances.

Isaac shot a bolt of lightning at him in an attempt to taunt him. It worked. The big man dashed up to him, trying to grab him in a vice. Isaac easily pushed him back, hit him with a blast of wind, then swiftly reached down, grabbed a handful of sand, and threw it into Garoth's eyes.

Garoth yelled in rage as he scratched at his face, his eyes burning from the sand. Isaac quickly bounded up and threw his whole weight into him, causing him to slam into the cage wall. A steady stream of lightning pulsed from Isaac's hand, continually electrocuting Garoth as he lay pressed against the cage.

"You thought I would be locked in with you," Isaac said maliciously. "But it is actually *you* who is locked in here with *me*." It was subtle, but Isaac's blue eyes began to darken, changing to solid black.

Garoth struggled as the lightning coursed through his body. Focusing all his strength, he gritted his teeth and pulled himself off the cage.

Isaac simply watched as the fool in front of him struggled for his life, approaching him with the remaining strength he had left. Garoth gave a mighty roar as he threw himself at Isaac in a desperate last attempt to get at him, however, the smaller, nimbler fighter swiftly sidestepped him and kicked him in the stomach. As Garoth barreled over, Isaac brought his palm into his chest, blasting wind, which propelled him upward. As the big man hit the roof of the cage, three more consecutive blasts of wind slammed into him, each one with the strength of a stone hammer, causing bones to break and flesh to rip. As Garoth fell to the ground, Isaac did an acrobatic flip out of the way of the falling body, and before it could hit the ground, he thrust both hands forward, blasting a concussive shockwave into Garoth, snuffing out what little life there was left. The man was dead before he slammed into the side of the cage; whiplash had taken its toll with the already fractured spine.

A hush fell over the stadium. The referee stared at the lifeless body that now lay crumpled to the ground. After a moment, the referee spoke, swallowing hard. "The winner is Isaac Wolfe."

As the cage disassembled and sunk back into the ground, there were no cheers. The audience had witnessed a brutal killing, and all eyes now rested on Isaac. Turning to leave, he paid no attention to the crowed. *That will teach you to laugh at me!* The thought echoed in his head.

Whispers arose as he left the arena, and a subtle smile spread across his face as his eyes turned back to normal.

"So, you killed your opponent." The black-hair woman stared blankly at Isaac from across the table.

He nodded. "Yes, I did."

"Why do that, especially in front of a crowd?"

"They were making fun of me. He just wanted to humiliate me in front of everyone."

The woman narrowed her eyes. "Is that the only reason?"

"What do you mean?"

She smiled mischievously. "Being made fun of doesn't usually bother you *that* badly."

Isaac remained silent.

"You must have had a strong feeling toward him to make you hate him as such."

He thought for a moment before replying. "Somehow, I just felt, deep down, 'this guy is evil.' That's the best I can describe it."

The black-haired woman leaned back in her chair as if she received the answer she was looking for. "Fascinating." Her voice was secretive. "And this hunch of yours, was it correct?"

"Yeah," he replied halfheartedly. "It turned out he was one of the spies we didn't know about. They told me in a report later on."

"And you just happened to eliminate him." She seemed amused. "I think there's more to you than you're letting on."

"I assure you there's not."

"And who are you trying to convince of that?" She grinned satirically. "Because I'm not fooled."

"I'm not what you think I am." He narrowed his eyes at her.

"Oh, I'm sure." She hummed. "Tell me more, then, of who you really are."

CHAPTER 6

THE SECOND ROUND

"You gonna tell me what that was about?"

Isaac was in a waiting room with Vin, Drake, and Raine.

"What?" Isaac shrugged.

"No one has ever chosen that victory. It was totally unnecessary!" Raine frowned at him.

"Look." Isaac's eyes narrowed. "I gave him a chance. He chose this outcome, plus, it was always a part of the rules. Just because it hadn't been done before doesn't make it wrong."

"No, it makes it immoral."

"Really ... so, the whole crowd makes fun of me and then I do something about it and I'm the one who's wrong?"

Raine looked confused. "What are you talking about? They weren't making fun of you."

Isaac scoffed. "Oh? They started laughing at me the second I walked out onto that field, and that meathead tried to belittle me. I'd say I was justified."

"Justified? Isaac, you killed someone!"

"So, what, people die all the time. I didn't do it for pleasure, I did it because that shitbag was trying to humiliate me."

"Isaac ..." Vin spoke up. "No one was laughing at you."

Isaac stared at Vin, his face puzzled. "Of course they were! They even pointed at me!"

Drake shook his head. "Dude, no one was doing that. I was watching the stands the entire time. I promise you; no one was laughing."

Isaac stood silent and stared at the floor as if searching for something.

"I need a minute alone," Raine said. "Vin, Drake ..."

Vin glanced at Drake and nodded. The two left the room.

"Raine ..." Isaac began, "I swear, I saw everyone laughing and pointing at me. It hurt, just like back then."

"When you were down there, something formed inside of you," Raine said softly. "Something dark."

"What do you mean?"

Raine looked a little shaken. "I don't want to jump to conclusions, but I saw a dark aura pulse from you. It was the same feeling I had that morning the other day."

Isaac stared blankly at Raine. "I don't know what that is. I didn't feel any different out there."

"You said you saw things no one else did?" Raine inquired. "How did you feel?"

"Angry, of course. It pisses me off when people laugh at me just by looking at me. I just wanted to teach them all a lesson." He clenched his fists. "It just infuriates me!"

"Isaac, you can't let those kinds of things get to you. That darkness, it eats away at you, turning you into something you're not." Her voice grew solemn. "You could lose yourself. I don't know much about it, but in the past, I believe it was told that dark aura destroys the soul." She put her hands on his shoulders. "Please, Isaac, we don't have time to investigate this, so I beg you, just don't let go of your emotions. Until we can figure this out, please just be careful."

Isaac stared back at her. "You act as if I'm a monster."

"I'm worried about you, okay? You caused a lot of commotion out there. A lot of people are afraid of you now. Just please don't do anything crazy. You're our only chance here." She stepped back. "Look, I need to get back. We're counting on you, all of us." Turning away, she left the room, signaling that Vin and Drake could go back in.

Why should I care if they're afraid of me? Isaac thought. *It's only because I'm your so-called guardian that you keep me around.*

After the short break, everyone returned to the coliseum. Vin and Drake were going to compete in the next match. Vin told Isaac that he felt it would be best if he sat out this round.

"Get ready for round two!" The announcer's voice boomed out. "For this round, each team will only fight with two of their members!"

Vin was bouncing back and forth from left foot to right as if he was getting ready for a boxing match. "You ready, Drake?" He jabbed at the big man. "I've got a feeling we're up first!"

Drake looked nervous. "Yeah, I'm ready."

"You seem on edge, just relax."

"For this round," the announcer continued, "two teams shall compete against each other to take down a dangerous beast!"

"Huh, not what I expected," Drake said. He seemed a bit more confident.

Vin stretched. "We got this."

"The arena will be divided into two. Each team will take place on either side. First team to slay their monster will be the winner," the announcer declared.

The sands shifted throughout the arena until there was a large wall that formed in the center, dividing the field in two.

First up, teams five and eight!" the announcer declared. "Combatants, take your positions!"

Vin and Drake appeared onto the field from one side of the wall. Two other combatants appeared on the other side.

"Here we go, big guy!" Vin did a little 360 step-spin on the field with a little hop skip; seemed he enjoyed being in the limelight.

Isaac watched from the sideline. *Please don't screw this up,* he thought.

The crowd cheered as the match was about to begin.

"Feast your eyes on the monsters we have in store for these unfortunate fighters," the announcer boomed. All eyes turned as two gates appeared on either side of the center wall; deep snarling could now be heard from behind them. "We present a creature created from our own mystic laboratories in representation to the creature from myth." The bars on the gates began to slowly rise. "Combatants, may luck be with you as you face off against the deadly lesser chimera!"

Two large creatures appeared from their cages. They both had the body and head of a lion, a second head which was a goat, a snake for a tail, and stood about eight feet tall, probably weighing close to a ton.

"Did NOT expect that!" Drake said as his red battle axe appeared in his hand. "This has to be a joke!"

"Nope," Vin replied nonchalantly. "Not a joke." His yellow bow appeared in his hand. "Let's just do this with no mess-ups."

The lesser chimera roared as it charged from across the arena toward them.

"Take point, I'll cover from a distance and get close when I see any openings!" Vin called to Drake while moving away.

"You gotta be shitting me!" Drake mumbled while readying his axe.

The chimera came in hard and attempted to tackle Drake, who brought his axe blade upward at the beast, catching it across the lion's cheek as he was thrown to the ground. Blood ran from the open wound on the lion, and its eyes flashed with anger.

Drake picked himself off the ground and quickly backed off defensively. "This thing's hide is tough!" he called to Vin, who fired an arrow at the goat head, barely piercing its neck.

"I'm mostly worried about the snake," Vin replied. "I don't think they would give that thing venom ... probably."

The chimera made biting attacks at Drake, who blocked most of them. As the last attack was blocked, the beast reared up and made to claw at him, but a corded line launched by Vin snagged its paw, forcing it off-balance as Vin pulled with what strength he could. Drake seized the opportunity and slammed his whole body into the creature, rolling it onto its side. As the monster lay there for a brief second, Drake's red axe came slamming down into the beast's side, causing a deep gash. The big man dragged the axe blade downward as he ripped the blade free from the chimera.

In an instant, the goat head opened its mouth and spewed a torrent of flame at Drake, who threw himself backward, parts of his body aflame. "What the hell!?" he yelled as he rolled to put out the flames. "Goats can't breathe fire!"

"But a chimera can!" Vin said. "We'll have to focus on taking out each individual animal part if we are to bring this thing down!"

The chimera was back on its feet, seeming unfazed by its wound. The snake began to hiss and rear back. Vin moved up to a closer attack position. "Maybe we can start with the snake. I will try and distract the goat; you keep an eye on an opening," Vin called instruction. "We'll have to switch tactics for this one." He fired a few arrows at the goat which buried themselves into the base of its neck, causing slight wounds. The chimera turned toward Vin and began to charge; as it did so, the goat spewed more fire from its mouth.

Vin swiftly dodged about as globs of molten flame fell his way. The beast came up on him, and he did a handspring out of the way as it charged past. The snake lashed out, barely missing its target before it was jerked away by the main chimera body.

"Jeez!" Vin panted as he readied himself. "Get ready, I'm going in!" He sprinted toward the monster as it was read-justing from its onslaught. Drake moved in as Vin engaged the snake head. He ducked as the snake head shot toward him, and before it could retreat, Vin's dagger appeared in his hand and he used it to grab the open mouth of the viper. Twisting himself through the air, he vaulted onto the back of the chi-mera. His other dagger appeared in his other hand, and he drove that into the back of the monster's tough skin.

Vin was now anchored to the back of the beast with the snake thrashing to get free from the bite of his blade. "Get ready, Drake!" The chimera jumped about, trying to throw Vin off, and the goat head couldn't turn to attack him either. He allowed the dagger holding the snake to disappear, and as it did, the snake immediately reared back and attacked.

Anticipating the attack, Vin swiftly vaulted in the air and conjured his bow. The snake drove its fangs into the back of the goat, and before it could un-attach itself, three arrows found their way through the snake's head and into the goat's back, pinning the head of the viper to the goat.

"Now, Drake, do it *now!*" Vin cried as he landed on the ground.

Drake bounded up with his battle axe in hand. He gave a mighty cry as he arced the blade through the air toward the base of the snake that connected to the chimera. The beast noticed the burly warrior at the last second, but it was too late. Drake's axe cleaved through the snake, severing it from the main body in a spray of blood. The chimera roared in pain and batted Drake several feet across the field. With the fangs still buried in the back of the goat, the dead snake body flailed about as the chimera danced around in a fury.

Vin rushed to help Drake up. "Well done!"

"Ouch ..." Drake replied sarcastically. "I wonder how they're doing on the other side."

"Oh, don't worry, I've got a way to buy us some time." An arrow appeared on Vin's bow, and he reached into one of his pouches secured to his belt and produced what looked to be a firecracker. "Not that we need it." He chuckled as he attached the object to his arrow. "Don't stare at this. Look away." He aimed his bow over the top of the wall in the center of the arena and let the arrow loose. A loud whistling sound could be heard from the missile as it soared over the wall to the other side. After a moment, there was a loud popping noise as the arrow emitted a blinding flash of light, and both Drake and Vin could hear two frustrated yells from the other side.

"Hahaha! Oh shit, watch out!" Vin laughed as the chimera bounded up to them. The two quickly dodged out of the way and turned to face the now bloody chimera.

"What was that?" Drake asked.

"Just a stun bomb. It blinds anyone who looks at it for a bit."

The beast whirled around, hatred in its eyes, and began to approach the two.

"Split up, don't let it focus on one area," Vin said as he made to circle around it.

The chimera lunged and swiped with its claws, left, then right, then left again. Vin and Drake dodged helter-skelter as the chimera began its rampage. The goat head was spewing molten flame into the air, causing fireballs to rain down to the ground.

"We *really* pissed this thing off!" Drake yelled as fire dropped around him.

"We need to take out that goat head!"

"See if you can distract it!"

Vin tossed a few explosives from his pouch at the ground where the chimera was prancing around, causing it to stagger from the blasts. Taking the moment, he moved in, avoiding falling fireballs, and shot an arrow point-blank at the lion's head. As the chimera moved to attack Vin, Drake came up and swung his axe, snagging the left eye of the goat head with the corner of his blade. Straining with effort, Drake viciously yanked on his axe, ripping out the eye out of the goat, and causing a long gash along the side of its head. The effort in pulling his axe also caused the chimera to keel over, and it now lay on its side, kicking and flailing.

Drake wasted no time. He grabbed the lifeless form of the snake, and with its fangs still embedded into the back of the goat, he pulled on it with all his might, tearing open a large wound.

"Yuck!" he said as he threw the snake's body away from him.

The chimera was now almost completely covered in blood and looked to be in very bad shape as it rose from the ground.

"Damn, almost had him!" The chimera swiftly advanced toward Drake with startling speed and knocked him to the ground. The big man held up his axe defensively as the beast began ripping at him with its claws.

"Vin!" Drake cried.

Vin was already on it. He quickly attached an explosive to a notched arrow and sprinted up to the monster. "Hey, dumbass!" he yelled at the chimera as he fired the arrow at the gaping wound in the side of the beast's body. The explosion caused the chimera to stagger long enough for Vin to rush in and fire another arrow into the lion head's eye. Reaching down, he grabbed Drake's hand and quickly helped pull him away in time as the goat blasted the ground with fire.

"Ugh!" Drake grumbled. "Dammit!"

"Don't relax yet, this is the home stretch!"

The yellow arrow had dissipated, and the chimera was furiously rubbing its head into the sandy ground in pain.

"Now is our chance!" Vin fired several arrows at the goat head as it focused its fire at him. He circled around the beast, bringing its attention away from Drake, who jumped up, driving his axe into the back of the goat where its heavy wound was. As the axe blade hit the goat, it was followed by a concussive blast, ripping chucks of flesh from the beat.

The goat's head hung limp next to the body of the lion, dead.

"Time to finish it!"

The chimera laid on the ground weakly trying to climb to its feet, but Vin gave it no chance and was quickly standing on the back of the lion. He made his daggers appear and, reaching around the neck of the beast, he drove his daggers in deep and brought them upward, carving two deep gashes on the weak skin of the beast's neck, ending its life.

There was a loud cheer as, from the other side of the wall, several people ran to restrain the chimera the other team had failed to kill in time.

"Winner!" the announcer yelled. "Team five, Vin Astor and Drake Hardy!"

"You alright, my man?" Vin asked Drake.

"I think I'll make it," he replied.

"You took a few hits there. Almost had me worried."

Aside from several cuts and a few bruises, Drake didn't seem hurt.

On the other side of the wall, a man was yelling at a nearby referee. "They cheated!"

"Sir, you are allowed to interfere with your opponent. It's part of the rules," the referee replied.

"Bullshit! They should have been disqualified!"

"Aww, don't be a sour sport!" Vin yelled out as he and Drake moved to sit up in the benches with Isaac. "Maybe next time, pal!"

The man's face turned red with anger, and Vin chuckled to himself.

"And you said I shouldn't be rude," Isaac told Vin sarcastically. "Well done."

"Holy crap! Was that a compliment?" Vin asked.

"I think it was." Drake smiled.

Isaac shrugged.

"Well, we might as well rest up for next round," Vin said. "Next round is the finals. We made it, guys, but next round will be the most difficult."

Drake rubbed healing ointment on his injuries. "Should be fun."

CHAPTER 7

THE THIRD ROUND

Only three teams remained for the final round, but it was decided that the third team would face off against the winning team from this round. For this round, it would be Isaac's team against the three women who were thought to be spies.

"This is it," Vin said to Isaac and Drake.

The three were on a sylphid heading for a distant mountaintop.

"This round we'll be sent through several trials." Even though Vin was speaking to both of his teammates, his gaze was strictly on Isaac. "Failure is not an option."

"Well," Isaac said, pulling a flask from his jacket. "We should fill our buddy in on what's happening." He took a drink as he stared at Drake.

"What?" Drake asked.

Vin stared back from Isaac to Drake.

"You tell him, or I will," Isaac pushed. "He's made it this far with us, I think it'll be okay. Besides, we need him on board with your little plan." He stared at Vin seriously as he tapped his finger on the metal flask impatiently.

"Fine," Vin replied, giving Isaac somewhat of a glare.

After a few minutes, Vin had relayed the whole story about the three spies.

Drake sat back and remained silent for a moment before speaking. "I don't know what to say. If you really believe the queen is in danger, then I will do whatever it takes to protect her, even if I must die."

"Might be stretching it a little," Vin replied humorously. "But we really need your help on this one."

"Why didn't you just send more of your own men into this tournament?" Drake asked. "Why depend on a stranger?"

Vin stared at the floor of sylphid. "Because I was the only one in the royal guard who thought the queen could be in danger," he explained. "I tried to tell Bart, but he said I was being paranoid, but I knew. I knew something was up, the number of 'tourists' increasing in the town. The subtle whispers coming from people in the bar." He clenched his fist. "I'm a spy myself, you know. When I start to see behavior similar to some of the things I have been trained for, I can't help but get suspicious."

"So, you found the proof to convince Bart?" Isaac asked.

"Yeah," Vin said. "It was a message I had intercepted. It explained about a set up at Esmeraldas and that Adamas was next."

"Who do you think is behind it?" Drake asked.

Vin shrugged. "Rubens, maybe."

"They've denied all accusations regarding Esmeraldas."

Isaac scoffed. "Wow. A criminal denying he did anything wrong." He shook his head in disappointment. "What would you expect them to say? 'It was me! I did it!'" He chuckled.

"Either way, this is an opportunity to find out who's behind this," Vin stated. "It's up to us."

"What about the queen?" Isaac asked. "What if she's attacked while everyone is distracted by this little 'game'?"

"I'm not worried."

"Why is that?"

"Because," Vin smiled, "Raine is with her."

Yeah, Isaac thought. *Raine could probably take on an army single-handedly.*

"We aren't the only ones in on this scheme now," Vin reassured. "Bart has many people on watch; it's just our mission to get info from these women."

"Sir!" the pilot of the craft called out. "We are coming up to the final round's entry point. The camera will be rolling in ten minutes."

"We're still in a tournament, guys, so act like it," Vin told them. "I know the layout of this dungeon we are to go through, but we need to act like nothing is wrong." He gave a confident grin. "Let's do this!"

Back at the arena, Raine spoke privately to Lucia.

"Everything is prepared. Are you sure the council will approve?"

Lucia smiled slyly. "I told Bart to make sure they didn't know about our plans."

Raine shrugged. "I hope you know what you're doing."

"This is my kingdom, not theirs. I'll do what I must to protect it."

"Let's just hope those three can win against the spies."

"They will," Lucia replied confidently.

Isaac, Vin, and Drake stood at the entrance to the dungeon. It was at the mid-point of an inactive volcano about eighty miles from Adamas. A giant, steel gate barred their path.

"Here, take these." Vin handed his companions each a radio earpiece. "This way we can communicate with each other when we get separated."

"We won't stick together?" Drake asked.

"There are parts that require us to split up in order to proceed."

"Sir!" the pilot called out. "Two minutes until the round begins!"

"Alrighty, get ready and put on a good show."

After a few moments, sound could be heard from a speaker near the entrance to the volcano.

"Here we go!" the announcer's voice could be heard. "At the entrance to the once deadly Raqash Volcano, we have team five! And at the rear entry, we have team three!"

Cheering was audible from the speakers.

"They love us, they really love us!" Vin joked.

"Hooray," Isaac replied, drinking the last bit of booze from his flask.

"You shouldn't drink on the job." Vin nudged him.

Isaac ignored him.

The voice of the announcer thundered loudly from the entrance. "The round starts in three, two, one, GOOOOO!"

The iron gates lifted, and the three companions entered the dungeon.

Outside of the arena, in the town area, was subtle activity. Three figures approached each other.

"Is it ready?"

"Yeah, all personnel are in position."

"Good. If our assets fail, we need to move. Too many have already failed, and one was killed."

"Garoth was an accident, some other player eliminated him."

"Odd, considering he was one of our best."

"That same player is against our final assets."

"Natalie can handle it. Let's just do our part and retrieve the artifact."

"What about the queen?"

"It's not time yet. Zagaan made it clear we are to stage the attack as if we are after her, but our ultimate goal is that artifact."

"Hehe, this will be fun!"

"Hail Zagaan!"

Inside the dungeon was a wide-open cavern. Several meters high and wide, the cave glowed with giant, magical crystals and lava.

"Stay focused, guys," Vin said. "This place is crawling with nasties."

Moving forward, the three came up to a large archway near the back of the cavern. The path ahead split into three ways, the center being barred by a giant, stone door.

"Our goal is through that door," Vin explained. "We just need to get past the traps from the other two paths and activate the switches at the end of each."

"Which way do we go first?" Drake asked.

"Doesn't matter."

"Then let's go left," Isaac suggested.

The three began down the path. As they rounded a corner, a stone wall slammed down behind them.

"Uh oh." Vin conjured his daggers.

A minotaur appeared at the far end of the hallway. A loud, scraping noise could be heard from the stone wall, and it began to move toward the group. Behind the minotaur at the far end was a closed gate.

"We need to kill this bastard or we'll be crushed!" Vin said, dashing toward the beast.

Drake bounded up behind Vin as Isaac took the rear. The monster flashed its sharp claws at the three as it charged. Vin quickly ducked under the minotaur's attack and slashed at its legs with his daggers. Drake came in with his axe, driving it into the beast's hand as it swiped at him.

The minotaur fell to one knee as Vin's dagger cut through its calf. Isaac unleashed a lightning bolt he had charged up, blasting the beast through the head. Falling to the ground, Drake dealt a mighty blow, killing the monster where it lay.

"Hurry, get through the gate," Vin shouted as the gate began to rise. The stone wall behind them was inching closer at an increasing speed.

The three hurled themselves through. On the other side was another large cavern.

"Okay, we gotta split up for this one," Vin explained.

"But it's one large room," Drake stated, looking around.

"Yes, but we need to stand on separate plates. C'mon, I'll show you."

The three walked down a flight of stairs and into a circular area. At the far left and right, about twenty yards apart, were two glowing platforms; the third was farther ahead down the center, between the left and right plate.

"I'll take the center one, you two take the sides."

"We just need to stand on them?" Isaac asked.

"Yep."

The three quickly ran to their plates. As they each stood on top of them, they began to glow. Once all three were standing on their respective platforms, the entire cavern began to glow.

Suddenly, the ground shuddered and broke apart, and the platforms moved upward. Below the broken ground was a pool of lava.

"Get ready!" Vin said. "We're gonna have to work together to get to the opened door over there." He pointed at the far end of the cavern where a gate had just opened.

"How do we do that?" Drake asked. As he did, his platform began to move in a circle around the area. "Jeez!"

"Just hang on. Isaac, you see that rock floating nearby to your left?"

Isaac looked over. "Yeah."

"You need to jump to that and the other rocks around that one to the glowing rock beyond that."

Isaac stared around. The cavern was now filled with other floating platforms, only a few were glowing, but the one Vin pointed out was the only one Isaac could reach. Carefully he jumped from one rock to another.

"Please hurry," Drake pleaded. "I get motion sickness."

Isaac held back a chuckle. Heh, motion sickness.

"You just gotta stand on it," Vin explained as Isaac jumped onto the glowing platform.

Drake began to slow down to stop near another cluster of floating rocks.

"Okay, Drake, your turn. Just reach that glowing rock like Isaac did, and we're almost there."

"Okay, ugh, I'll try," Drake gasped. He leaped and was barely able to make it over. After a few more jumps, Drake was on his glowing rock. "Now what?"

"I gotta get to that gate and pull a switch," Vin replied as he jumped from several rocks that had moved close together. With ease, Vin made it to the gate. "There's a lever inside the gateway here," he said as he pulled it.

There was an audible click and the gate crashed down, locking Vin out from Isaac and Drake.

"What did you do?" Isaac shouted at Vin.

"Woops. Forgot about this part, haha," Vin chuckled wryly.

The rocks Isaac and Drake were on began to move upward.

"Ugh ..." Drake moaned as he lay flat on the rock.

"It's okay," Vin called to them. "They are gonna carry you to other pathways. We split up from here—see you back at the entrance."

Isaac watched as he approached a hole in the wall where his rock was taking him. Jumping through, he then found himself in a long corridor. "Great," he said to himself. "More hallways." He ran down the path.

In the arena, Raine watched the giant monitor that showed the two teams' progress. She leaned close to Lucia and whispered suspicion. "Milady, it makes sense that Vin could lead them through quickly, but the other team is also moving at the same pace. How could they know the layout of this trial?"

Lucia stared at the monitor. "Yeah, I know what you mean." The other team practically mirrored Isaac's team, as if they knew where to go and what to do. Lucia frowned.

"This means there are more spies within our walls," Raine said. "Some who might be high in rank."

Lucia clenched her fists. "So, it would seem."

Isaac, Vin, and Drake finally made it back to the entrance.

"Well, that was fun," Vin said cheerfully.

"Not really," Isaac replied. "It was boring. Just had to climb a few ledges and jump over pits."

"Really?" Drake motioned angrily. "Well, I had to fight off a pack of rabid beasts!"

Vin shook his head. "We made it, nonetheless. Let's hurry up and get the other path done so we can get through the big door." He pointed to the right pathway.

The three entered, and ahead of them were three doorways. There were closed gates at each one and a glowing pad in front of each as well.

"We'll have to split up from here," Vin explained. "I don't think there are any beasts through this path, but we will have to work together at the end to figure out a puzzle. Shouldn't be too hard."

"Guess I'll take the left," Isaac said as he stepped onto the left pad.

"I'll take middle," replied Drake.

Vin stepped onto the right. "I've got the right then. Good luck guys." As soon as they were all on their pads, gates closed behind each of them, and the gates in front opened.

CHAPTER 7: THE THIRD ROUND

As Isaac walked down a winding corridor, the light began to dim. After a bit more, there was barely any light. "Great," Isaac muttered. "More hallways and now no light to see in."

Eventually there was barely any trace of light, and only a few torches on the walls lit up the pathway.

"Hey," Isaac tried to talk to Vin over his radio. "You could've told me about the dark corridors. We could have brought gear to help us see."

There was no reply.

"Wow, thanks buddy," Isaac said angrily. "Just ignore me, then." It reminded him of being back on Earth when he was out with a few of the students from school and they all decided to ditch him as a prank. "Why am I thinking of that now?" he muttered out loud. The thought only angered him more. Grumbling to himself, he held his hand out, intending to use his own magic to make a light source.

Nothing happened.

"What ...?"

He tried again, but still nothing. He couldn't even feel his own aura flowing at all.

That was when he heard it.

"She's coming for you," an eerie voice said out of the darkness.

"What?" Isaac whispered as he started to shiver. "Who?"

"You know who ..."

A high-pitched shrill of a voice echoed from down the corridor where Isaac had just come from.

"IsAaC!"

He felt a shiver run down his spine as he heard footsteps getting closer. The sound of bare feet scraping along the ground was noticeable. Running, Isaac quickly made his way through the corridor to try and distance himself from whatever it was that was after him. With only the random torches along the walls as light, he eventually made his way into an open chamber. The chamber was rather dark, but he could make out large boulders scattered around, and an exit that seemed to be at the end, giving off a dim light.

Before he could do anything further, he heard the voice again, this time closer than before.

"wHerE aRe YoU, IsAaC?"

Quickly ducking behind a nearby boulder, Isaac attempted to hide as the thing came out into the chamber.

A long, boney arm reached out of the darkness and was followed by a sunken, grisly face resembling what remained of an old woman. Its hair was caked in blood and matted to its head as the disgusting strands flowed down its sickly thin body. The creature emerged into the chamber, standing about seven feet tall in a tattered, white, bloodstained dress.

"It'S BeEN sO LoNg, IsAaC!"

Its movement was unnatural. Sporadic. Its head always tilted to the side, and a raspy breathing came from its grinning, pale mouth. The thing shook with each step as if it could collapse at a moment's notice.

"I kNoW yOu'Re HeRe, IsAaC! yOU caN CoMe OuT!"

Isaac held his breath as the creature slinked its way past the boulder he was hiding behind. *I've got to get past this thing and get to the exit over there*, Isaac thought to himself, trying to calm his nerves.

"YoU DoN't HaVe tO hIDe!"

After it had gone enough distance, he decided to try and sneak his way around this sinister being. Without any of his abilities, he wouldn't be able to fight it. Making himself as quiet as possible, Isaac swiftly moved to hide behind another boulder close by. He would just have to inch his way to the exit. Still no powers, and still not a word from Vin or Drake. What kind of trial was this? Vin had said there weren't any monsters this way. *I'm gonna kill him*, Isaac angrily thought.

The creature suddenly crouched down on all fours and bolted across the room in an unnatural, snake-like way similar to a millipede. It grabbed a boulder and threw it several yards into a wall where it smashed to pieces with a loud bang.

"NO MORE GAMES!" it snarled. "wE oNLy WanT WhAt'S beST fOr YOu!"

Isaac held his breath, anxiety starting to take over. He began to shiver even more. He could feel this *thing* giving off a dark presence. It felt as if the air around him was going to suck him in. *I can't stay in one spot*, he thought, *the air is getting thicker.* He slowly moved farther along, keeping behind any boulders or rubble that could hide him from the creature. The thing in question was still searching the area, and it was fast. If Isaac didn't keep pressing forward, it would find him quickly.

"tHe ONly rEAsoN tO hIDe iS FroM sHaMe. I cAn MaKe EVeRythINg bEtTEr, iT's whAT wE wAnT iSn'T IT!?" It threw itself into a rock pile, sending pieces flying in every direction. "SO, STOP MESSING AROUND, YOU LITTLE SHIT, AND SHOW YOURSELF!" Its voice echoed through the entire chamber.

Focus. Focus. His anxiety was increasing. This was no ordinary creature, and somehow Isaac felt as if it was sapping his soul the longer he was near it. Moving helped to keep ahead of the swallowing darkness, which seemed to thicken around him. A part of him wanted to cry out for help but knew the creature would get to him before anyone else.

He was on his own.

Outside, in the stadium, there were six large holographic displays that showed the progress of each player going through the volcano dungeon; however, one display had turned to static once the player had entered one of the split paths.

"Have they figured out what's causing the malfunction?" Lucia asked Raine, who had been on a communicator keeping up to date on the repair team working to fix it. "Not yet," was the reply. "There doesn't seem to be any issues with the system. It should be working."

"Perhaps it could be an issue from the camera within."

Raine shook her head. "That's the thing, the camera inside the volcano is linked to the others. If one goes down, the others do as well. But if all the others are working, then I'm not sure how one could mess up." Raine stared at the static screen. "Unless a large dispersal of aura was unleashed. However, no reports of conflict have been reported by the on-site emergency teams."

Lucia shifted worriedly in her seat. "Isaac ..."

Isaac continued making his way slowly toward what he thought was the exit. Each step, each breath, he felt only the slightest noise would bring the attention of this creature. The darkness around him felt heavy, and the room seemed to get darker with every moment. If he stood still for too long, he would start to feel lightheaded as if the dark was sapping his strength. *What kind of monster is this?* he thought. *And why would they put it in a tournament?* Were they trying to get him killed? Isaac knew that one mistake would mean his death. His powers hadn't come back to him; in fact, he felt weaker than normal. He moved as cautiously and quietly as he could, but it was tiring. He struggled to keep his breath steady, and his hands were shaking. But he had to ignore it as best as he could.

"WhY dO YoU hIdE, IsAaC? wE DoN't WanT tO hUrT yOu ... MuCh!" The gangly hag continued searching for her prey. Long, boney fingers gripped at the air, as if imagining the feel of its target. "YoU BeLoNg tO Us!"

Isaac rounded another boulder in the room and was finally able to spy the exit in the distance. Maybe twenty yards. He could try to make a run for it, but he didn't know if he would be fast enough. The creature was less than ten yards away from him but faced away.

Stepping out of cover, he moved forward as quietly as he could, always keeping an eye on the hag. It shifted sporadically from side to side, then suddenly stopped. Isaac stopped as well, his heart racing. Did it hear him? The silence seemed to stagnate as he watched the hideous monster.

After a moment, he heard it.

The crying.

IT was crying.

A cold, heartless, wailing came from the monster. "wE nEeD yOu. We NeEd YoU," it kept repeating. "sO ... WHY WOULD YOU LEAVE US!?"

Isaac's heart briefly stopped at what he saw next: The creature, still facing away, bent backward till its head touched the ground ... to stare at him standing between it and the exit. Its mouth twisted in anger and eyes hollow, yet seeing, it screamed and lurched toward him.

"fOuNd YoU!"

Panic set in. Isaac immediately turned and sprinted toward the shallow light. As he ran, he could hear the scratching of the monster's feet as it raced after him.

C'mon, c'mon! he thought, as fear overtook him. The exit was so close, but he could feel the creature even closer. Its raspy breathing echoed in his ears.

Almost there. Almost there!

Isaac burst through the doorway and out of the open chamber. A short way in, he spied a button on a pedestal near a closed gate. That's it! he thought. *That will take me to the others.* At least that's what he hoped. Running up, he slammed on the button. Nothing happened. He pushed it again and again. The screech of the creature echoed around him, and when he thought it would get him, the gate opened.

Isaac threw himself through the doorway and fell onto the ground outside.

"Dude, what the hell happened?"

It was Vin's voice.

Looking around, Isaac saw Vin and Drake standing near him.

"We were waiting forever!" Vin said. "Why didn't you answer your radio?"

Through the door he had just come from, the darkness was gone. So was the creature.

"Th-there was ... I mean—I ..." Isaac stammered. He wiped sweat off his brow as his nerves started to calm. "There was a ... a thing."

"What are you talking about?"

"A creature. It was tall and lanky. And ..."

"Isaac, you drinking too much? There weren't any creatures for this part."

"Yeah," Drake jumped in. "We had to solve some weird riddles. Didn't you have to do a puzzle or something?"

What? A puzzle? Isaac stared back at them in confusion.

"Are ... you okay?" Vin stared at him with concern.

Isaac quickly collected his thoughts and his composure. "Yeah. Maybe that last shot of whiskey was too much," he said with a half-hearted sarcastic tone. "Let's just keep going."

Vin frowned at him. "Sure, if you're okay, then yeah, let's finish this. Just one last trial to go and we win."

"What's that?" Drake asked.

"Just gotta get to the big door at the entrance and retrieve the prize."

The three started for their destination. Isaac stopped and glanced back. What was that thing?

The monitor was back on, and Raine watched as Isaac's team reached the big gate at the entrance. "Looks like the other team is at their gate also." The all-female team had also reached their big gate and was about to head in. "Let's hope our guys can beat them."

"Don't worry," Lucia said confidently. "They'll win. For now, let's focus on the more pressing matter."

"It's already done. I must say, this is way too risky and reckless."

"There's a reason we are doing this. Trust in me."

Raine looked out at the crowd watching the tournament; the people were oblivious to what was about to happen. "I trust you."

The large gate slowly opened as the three stood before it.

"Hold up ..." Vin stopped. "Something's not right."

"What now?" Drake asked. "We just gotta go in, right?"

"Yeah, but ... be ready, I think they actually made it on their side as well."

"How do you figure?" Isaac frowned.

"I can use my aura to feel shifts in the air, and something is moving about up ahead."

"What? You can do that?"

"Yeah, part of my job is knowing my surroundings." Vin smirked.

"Let's just kick their asses, then," Isaac replied.

"Don't underestimate them."

"Yeah, yeah."

The three stepped up through the open gate and proceeded down a corridor eventually leading into an open room. At the center was an altar with a small chest on top. As they approached it, a door opened on the opposite side of the room, and three figures stepped through it.

It was them.

"What? They're here too!?" Natalie snapped.

Vin shot across the room toward the chest at an incredible speed. As he reached for it, a cage appeared, covering the chest, and in an instant the altar sank into the ground, disappearing from sight.

"It looks like we have a sudden death, team battle on our hands!" the voice of the announcer boomed out in the chamber. "Only the last team standing will get the prize!"

Natalie motioned toward her companions. "Yuri, Tara, you know which ones to take."

Vin gave a cheeky grin. "Oh, I hope I get the cutest one!"

Isaac shot a lightning bolt at Natalie, but Tara stepped in front of her and created a barrier that easily blocked it. Yuri rushed Drake with a giant, red club held in both hands.

As the battle started, the walls of the chamber crumbled apart, revealing that the six were situated in a large cavern with twists and turns and a few pools of lava.

"I guess it's time for our date, Vinny!" Natalie said sinisterly as she charged Vin.

"Nice, looks like I did get the cutest one!" Vin winked at her as he deflected one of her shurikens with his aural daggers as he hopped down into the cavern with Natalie in pursuit.

I guess that leaves her to me, Isaac thought, focusing on Tara. She stared blankly back at him. *What's with this girl?* He shot several blasts of lightning at her, but she deflected each of them.

Jumping into the cavern, Isaac grumbled. This was going to be a pain.

A few minutes into the battle, the fighters were already starting to tire out.

Vin and Natalie were about even, and Drake was slowly overpowering Yuri. Isaac, on the other hand, was losing. Badly.

Isaac dodged another blast of fire and ducked around a corner for cover. "This is bullshit!" he yelled.

"Isaac, hang in there. Once we take care of these two, we will help you, but you have to use only magic."

GOD, I KNOW! Isaac was getting frustrated. Every magical shot Tara would just deflect. Every chance of getting close, she would push him away with magic. Isaac couldn't beat her. Not with magic. If only he wasn't trying to conceal his abilities, he could beat her into the ground.

"Shit!" Isaac broke from his cover as the wall he was crouched behind shattered as a magic blast hit it.

This wasn't good. Raine watched as Isaac was struggling to fight. *He's going to lose control again!*

"What's wrong?" Lucia asked her.

"It's Isaac. I sensed a darkness in him," Raine explained. "I fear it might take over."

Lucia stared at the giant screen silently.

"What if we—" Raine was cut short.

"I believe in him. He won't lose control," Lucia said.

"But—"

"He WON'T!" Lucia stared at Raine seriously. She had never seen Lucia so adamant.

"Okay. I believe you."

Vin fired several arrows in succession at Natalie as she dashed around. She used the terrain as cover from his relentless attacks as she planned her own counter offensive. Bounding off the wall, she hurled several shuriken at him, forcing him to duck out of the way as they flew past him.

She took the brief opportunity to conjure a pair of sais as she rushed in. Vin's bow disappeared, and he conjured his daggers as Natalie swung at him with her sais. Their blades connected as they clashed, Vin pushing her back.

"Ya know, I think we really have a connection here!" he told her humorously. "Some real chemistry!"

Spinning her sais in her hands, she continued her attack, swinging wildly at him as their blades bounced off each other.

"Aww, really, Vinny?" she replied sarcastically. "Then be a dear and handle the check!"

She threw one of her electric shock devices at him. Vin quickly used a burst of speed and lunged out of the way as the area he had just been in was covered in electricity.

"Oh, come on!" He quickly conjured his bow and fired an arrow at her, which she narrowly dodged. "We can at least go halfsies?"

Farther away, Drake was fighting Yuri. He spun, swinging his battle axe at her as she held up her large club to defend herself. His weapon connected with hers, causing her to reel backward. She quickly recovered and brought her club down hard as it smashed into the ground, breaking apart the rock floor in a spray of shrapnel.

Drake was able to jump out of the way as he rolled to his feet.

"Hey, stop moving!" She yanked her club out of the ground and leered at him. "Do you always run away from every girl you meet?"

"Only the one's trying to crush me!" he replied as he charged her.

She swung her large club as he came bounding in. He blocked the attack, shoving her club aside, and then followed up with his own downward swing. As his axe struck the ground, it sent a shockwave blasting out, forcing Yuri off balance. Drake then dropped his shoulder and slammed into her, throwing her to the ground.

"Owie!" she whined loudly as she sat there looking up at him with watery eyes. "You big brute! Is this how you treat women, by beating on them?"

He paused and looked at her in surprise. "Wh-what??" he stammered. "I don't ... I mean ... that's just ..."

"You meanie!" she cried. "How despicable and cruel. Jerk. Bully!"

"Hold on, now!" he pleaded. "I don't beat on women! And I'm certainly not a bully!"

As he stood there baffled, Yuri suddenly jumped to her feet, reconjured her large club, and swung it. Drake was barely able to jump out of the way.

"You dirty—" He readied himself as she came in for a follow up attack.

Isaac continued to struggle against Tara. He used a lightning bolt to shoot down a fireball she had thrown.

This was impossible, and he was furious.

"Where the hell are you guys!?" he yelled through his earpiece. "I'm getting my ass kicked here!"

"Just hang in there, I've almost got mine down," Drake replied.

Several fiery blasts erupted near Isaac, singeing him slightly.

"SCREW THIS!" Isaac charged Tara, using his aura to move at a superhuman speed.

Tara levitated some of the lava, forming it as a shield as she made several fireballs appear above her head. Isaac vaulted over a few boulders, attempting to gain a higher ground over his foe. The fireballs were launched, and as they flew toward their mark, Isaac used his force blasts to push them away where they exploded into nearby walls.

Outside, Raine could hear the crowd making remarks.

"I thought he was a magic wielder, how come he's able to move like that?"

"How is that guy so fast? That's impossible!"

Dammit Isaac, you're going to give away your abilities, she thought to herself.

Bounding off the cavern walls around him, Isaac approached Tara. *Screw this,* he thought, rage filling him. *I'm not gonna look like a loser.* He pushed more fireballs away, and as he approached the shield of lava, Isaac's sword appeared in his hand. He swung, and adding a bit of wind to it, he was able to cleave the lava as the wind force blasted it aside, giving him a direct shot at Tara.

He took it.

She tried to create more magic, but Isaac didn't give her the chance. Using air to blast her off balance, he came in for a sword swipe.

She quickly conjured a blue staff which she used to block Isaac's attack.

"Stupid bitch!" He brought his left hand to punch her in the face, then when she stumbled, he yanked the weapon from her hand and slammed the hilt of his sword into her gut. Tara crumpled to the ground, grabbing her stomach in pain as she looked up at Isaac in shock.

CHAPTER 7: THE THIRD ROUND

Time seemed to have stopped. Because Isaac just realized what he had done.

Across the cavern, both Natalie and Yuri stared over at Isaac, as did Vin and Drake.

The glowing, white longsword sat in Isaac's hand.

"You idiot ..." Vin muttered.

CHAPTER 8

UNDER SIEGE

The crowd was silent. The radiant, white blade was directly on the screen.

"Oh no ..." Raine and Lucia both stared, slightly panicked. "This is bad."

Already, the crowd was becoming confused.

"I'm calling Bart!" Raine turned and went for her phone.

"Good idea," Lucia replied as she stared at Isaac.

Natalie was shocked. "You're a ... a ... GUARDIAN!?"

Vin took no hesitation. He had some kind of glove on one hand, and he quickly grabbed Natalie by the back of her neck as electricity crackled from his glove.

She let out a sharp cry before crumbling to the ground, unconscious.

"Drake, quickly subdue her!" Vin shouted to his companion.

Drake turned as Yuri was recovering. He swung his axe with the flat side aimed at her. It slammed into her club and forced it aside as he quickly grabbed her and pushed her face-first to the ground.

Yuri struggled under his grip as he put his weight on her.

"I've got her pinned!" Drake shouted.

Vin came dashing up. "Hold her down!" He reached out with his gloved hand and grabbed her by the back of the neck, knocking her out with a shock.

"Whew, she was feisty." Drake sighed in relief.

"Isaac, you got her?" Vin called out.

Isaac frowned as he looked down at Tara who was sitting on the ground, glancing around in confusion.

Vin appeared next to him. "What's wrong?"

"She seems confused," Isaac said. "But I don't sense any hostility now. It's weird."

She looked at Vin then Isaac. "Who ... are you?" Before they could answer, she looked at Isaac's blade. Instantly, she started to shake. "You're the guardian!"

Isaac stared at her. It was odd, she seemed completely different from before, and this was also the first time he had heard her speak.

"Did you ... did you save me?" Tara looked as if she was going to cry.

"Uhh ..." He didn't know how to respond.

"She must have been mind-controlled," Vin said. "I thought something was odd about her."

"Can you stand?" Isaac reached his hand out to her.

"I—I think so." She took his hand and rose to her feet. She took a few steps and stumbled, but Isaac caught her and kept her steady. "Sorry, I'm just a little dizzy."

"I hope I didn't hurt you too badly." He gave her a kind look as she leaned against him.

"I'm okay." She smiled weakly. "My head's just a little fuzzy."

"Sir, we've got a problem," a voice crackled over the radio. "The tournament is called off. We need you to return to the city."

"We need emergency medical services in here," Vin spoke over the radio. "We've got two unconscious women and one injured."

"Medics are on their way," the voice spoke to them. "We've got a couple of sylphids prepped to take you all back to the city."

"Understood." Vin glanced over at Natalie, who was still motionless on the ground. "We'll bring the suspects to the landing pad."

"Roger that."

Motioning to Drake, Vin walked over to Natalie. "We can't just leave them in this heat. You grab that other one." He bent down and grabbed her arm, carefully hoisting her over his shoulder.

Drake easily picked up Yuri and turned to his companions. "Let's get out of here."

Isaac helped Tara as they all headed out of the volcano.

The figures skulking about Adamas town saw the screen. Saw the guardian.

"It's time."

They raised their hands, and soon several dark creatures began to appear in the town.

"Find the artifact. Kill anyone who stands in our way."

"Hail Zagaan."

The demonic creatures dispersed, scattering in multiple directions.

The invasion had begun.

It wasn't long before they got to the medical team waiting for them on the landing pad.

"Be sure to keep them sedated until we can question them," Vin told the staff as he and Drake placed both women on stretchers.

"What about her?" One of them motioned to Tara.

"She may have been mind-controlled," Vin explained. "She'll need a checkup. Take her back with the other two."

"No!" Tara quickly stepped behind Isaac. "I can help!"

"You need to rest up, mind control isn't something you can just shake off."

"I feel fine now, honest!" She looked at Isaac. "Please, let me help. I'm okay now, really."

Isaac looked her in the eyes. Was this a trick? No, she seemed genuine. "Okay, just stay close."

"Isaac?" Vin looked at him curiously.

"Let's give her a chance to redeem herself. Besides, she's really good at magic, we could use her help." Isaac smiled at Tara.

"I don't like this, but we can't waste time arguing," Vin gave in. "Fine. Let's go help secure the city."

It wasn't long before Isaac, Vin, Drake, and now Tara made their way to the main capitol of Adamas on a sylphid.

"I just got confirmation from Bart. There's fighting going on in the streets; they have pulled the entirety of the guard to defend the city, but we need to get back and assist."

"I'm sorry. This is my fault," Isaac told Vin.

"Actually, we were anticipating this, so it isn't. We just didn't want it to happen so soon." Vin patted Isaac on the back. "It's okay. Now all we can do is back up the defense. Let's get in there and give 'em hell."

The sylphid landed near the central square.

"Let's go!" Vin and Drake hopped out and looked around.

Isaac jumped out and helped Tara. "Will you be okay?"

She took his hand and nodded. "Yes, thank you for believing in me."

The four of them headed toward the battle.

There were monsters everywhere. For the most part, Raine had no issue killing them. "C'mon, let's get to the throne room, milady!" She guided Lucia toward the main gates, taking out any demon that dared stray too close. The master sorceress was a devastating force to be reckoned with. She was bodyguard to the queen for a reason.

"We're almost there!" Raine said as she slayed several other demons who attempted an ambush. She had the ability to see through walls and detect life around her, so there was no chance anyone could sneak up on them.

They entered the castle, and Raine put a barrier on the main door. "This should hold them for a bit. Let's get up to the main hall." The two took off down the hall, issuing anyone they saw to stay in their rooms and lock the doors.

"What about Isaac and the others?" Lucia asked.

"They can take care of themselves. We've prepared for this, so casualties should be minimal," Raine replied, however, she did not feel very confident in those words. She had just recently found out about this plan, and she didn't like it.

At the top of the throne room, they stood at the end where the queen's chair was.

"Now we wait," Lucia said. "If anyone comes in, please do your thing."

Raine bowed. "You have my word." She waited. Defensively.

Isaac approached the main square. The Adamas guards were fending off hordes of horrifying creatures.

"What are those things!?" Isaac asked.

"Demons," Vin replied. "Minions of the darkness that threatens this world. Don't hesitate to put them down. C'mon!" Vin made off to help assist the guards.

"Isaac, you think we should split up?" Drake asked.

Why is he asking me? Isaac thought.

"Probably not. We should pair up," he replied. "Tara, can you assist Vin?"

"O-okay!" She began to chase after him.

"C'mon, we'll go that way, Drake!" Isaac and Drake took off in a different direction than Vin and Tara.

Entering the right part of the square, Isaac could see that the guards had already evacuated and put barricades in place to block the demons from entering other areas of the town. The two leaped into the fray, Isaac cutting down one demon, and Drake another.

"How can we help?" Drake asked one of the guards.

"Who the hell are you guys?" the guard replied. He glanced at Isaac's sword. "Wait a minute ..."

"We're here to help," Isaac said. "Is there a place that needs a couple more fighters?"

After a brief hesitation, the guard replied, "Uh, yeah, over at the east battlements. It seems the main force is coming from there. Any help would be much appreciated."

"Alright," Drake responded. "We'll head right over. You can count on us."

On their way to the battlement, Drake spied a panicked young woman on the outside corner of a building, huddled up. "Hey!" He stopped. "We have to help her!"

Isaac nodded. "Alright, but we should hurry. Who knows how many of those things are out here?"

Drake knelt down next to her. "Hey, it's going to be okay." He held out his hand. "I'll take you somewhere safe."

She looked at him, shaking. "I was scared ..." she said in a quiet voice.

"I know." Drake took her hand gently. "You're safe now." He helped her to stand.

Without warning, a demon leapt out from behind him. He didn't have time to react.

"Shit!" Isaac plunged his blade into the demon's neck before it could reach his companion, savagely throwing it to the ground and stomping its head into a bloody paste. As it died, its body burnt up into ash. "That was close!"

"Thanks, man." Drake took the woman's hand. "Come on, let's get you somewhere safe."

"I thought I saw a garrison a short way back," Isaac suggested, pointing down the path they had come from. "We should take her there."

After the two had escorted the woman to the safety of nearby guards, they continued toward their destination.

"This is not good," Drake said. "I've only heard of demons from stories and churches; never have I seen a full-blown invasion of the bastards!"

"Same," Isaac agreed. "Where I'm from, this kind of shit never happens. We need to hurry!"

They approached the east battlement. There were definitely a lot more demons here than anywhere else, and it was all the guards could do to keep most of them from finding their way past and into the city.

"Isaac!" Vin's voice came from the earpiece he still wore. "We're making our way to the east battlement; we'll meet you there!"

"We're already here," Isaac replied.

"Oh good—see you soon."

They wasted no time. Demons approached from all sides of the defense, and the two took up their arms.

As Vin and Tara arrived, Isaac and Drake were finishing with their last batch of monsters. The two were partially covered in blood.

"You two look like shit," Vin said sarcastically.

"Looks like you missed the party," Isaac responded blankly.

"How did you two fair?" Drake asked.

"Well, Tara and I didn't get all that much action. Actually, it seems most of the demons are on this side and trickling into the center square."

"Not much of an attack," Isaac said.

"It seems more like a diversion," Vin replied. "I've already informed Commander Bart, and he agrees."

"So, what now?"

"We just maintain this area and protect the town; he'll look into any matters of subterfuge."

After a short while of dealing with demons, they started to thin out.

"Looks like we're winning!" Vin said as a fiery symbol about twelve feet in diameter appeared near them on top of the battlement.

"What's that?" Drake asked.

In an instant, a giant, ten-foot, fiery demon appeared in the center of the symbol.

"Isaac!" Vin shouted. "It's *him*!"

There, with its body covered in flames, stood the efreet.

Isaac moved closer to Vin. "We can beat him this time!" he assured his companion. "There are four of us now! You guys!" he shouted to several guards who had noticed the efreet. "We'll take care of the big guy; you take care of the little ones and keep them off our backs while we deal with him."

The guards saluted. "Aye aye, guardian, sir!"

What the hell was that? Isaac was taken aback by their response. It felt weird to him. "Tara, he uses fire attacks, can you deflect them?"

Tara nodded. "Yes, I believe I can."

"Drake, watch out for his claws; this guy is no joke!" Vin shouted.

"You've fought him before!?" Drake was on edge.

"Yeah, right after Isaac and I had our disagreement. We'll tell you later, here he comes!" Vin readied himself.

The efreet leapt toward Isaac and Vin, who dodged quickly as it slammed the ground, causing flames to erupt around it. Tara waved her hands, and the flames receded. Drake came rushing in, axe in hand. He went for an overhead blow, but

the efreet grabbed the hilt of his blade. Before it could counterattack, Isaac lunged, stabbing the demon in the shoulder. It
growled at him but was silenced with a few arrows to its face,
which barely scratched it.

"Geez, my arrows just can't hurt this guy!" Vin said as
Drake released his axe, pulling away from the demon. "Guess
I'll have to try something else." His daggers appeared in
his hands.

The efreet jumped at Tara, surely to prevent her from
repressing its fire, but in an instant, Isaac quickly pushed her
out of the way as he brought his blade up to block the incoming attack. The demon grabbed him and hurled him across
the battlement. He went flying and fell into a pack of demons
with a thud. "Gahh!" It hurt, but he had to quickly recover
himself because now those demons were turning toward him.
"Oh shit ..."

Vin leapt onto the efreet, swinging his blades with deadly
grace. Each slice seemed to do a little more damage than his
arrows but were still quite underwhelming. Still, Vin kept up
his onslaught, maneuvering around the giant demon to dodge
its attacks. "Drake!" he yelled. "Get him while I distract it!"

Drake spared no hesitation. His axe appeared, and he lunged
at the efreet. "Back me up, Tara!" He swung his axe at the
demon's back.

"A-alright!" Tara approached. Her blue staff in hand, she
spun it around, and a blue light began to circle the efreet.
With a flick of her weapon, the demon was bound within the
blue light, struggling to get its arms free.

Drake brought his axe crashing into the back of the demon,
burrowed deep. The efreet roared as he ripped the blade from
its hide.

Vin hopped off the demon and retreated to stand in front of
Tara. "Nice one. This gives us a bit of a breather, but that seal
won't hold him for long."

Nearby, Isaac had smashed the last demon's head into a
nearby wall, killing it instantly. He looked over to where his
allies were fighting the large demon. *Damn, I gotta get over
there,* he thought. As he moved toward the battle, he stopped.
Above, on a battlement tower near the efreet, was a loose

stone the size of a car. If he could push it loose, they could send it crashing down on the demon.

"Vin!" Isaac shouted.

Vin looked over. "Where've you been, eh?"

"I'm gonna push that stone loose, make sure it hits the efreet!"

Vin saw the spot Isaac was pointing at. "Sounds crazy! I like it!"

Isaac quickly made his way to the tower, cutting a few demons down in the process. At the top, he could see that the efreet had broken loose from its magical bonds. As he approached the broken part of the wall, Isaac could see the battle below. *Just gotta kick this free in the right direction*, he thought as he plunged his sword between the break in the stone. "Vin, you guys ready?" he yelled into his radio.

"Tara's about to pin him again. Go for it! Drake's standing by!" Vin replied.

Isaac delivered a mighty kick to his weapon's hilt, sending the chunk of stone toward the efreet. Down below, Tara had suppressed the demon once again, and as the boulder fell to the earth, it was slightly off its mark, but Drake leapt high into the air and with his axe, he snagged the stone and pulled hard, driving it down on the efreet, crushing it entirely.

"HELL YEAH!" Drake shouted.

"We did it!" Tara exclaimed.

A moment later, Isaac made his way off the tower and to the bottom of the battlements where his companions stood.

"That was rough, but we did it!" Vin said encouragingly.

"So, what now?" Isaac asked.

Suddenly, a giant shadow flew across the ground.

"You had to ask?" Vin replied, looking up.

"Shit ..." Drake frowned at their next foe.

"I see you don't really care for hiding."

A sinister-looking man in a black cloak stood before Raine and Lucia in the throne room.

"That's because there's no need to," Raine replied. "You have no business here."

The man smirked. "Oh, but I do." He pointed a finger at Lucia. "You have no right being on that throne. You are a sham, and one I plan to make an example of."

"I'd like to see you try!" Raine sneered, her eyes glowing a vibrant blue.

The man laughed. "If you only knew, my dear child. This world doesn't have much longer."

"What do you mean by that!?" Lucia demanded.

"You know very well, or at least you *should*," he replied. "How's your 'ol pal guardian coming along, eh?" He laughed again.

"Enough with your babble!" A tense mist began to swirl around Raine. "Are you just going to stand there and monologue?"

The man gave a wicked grin. "I guess I could test you before we actually meet face to face." He pulled the hood of his cloak back, revealing solid black eyes. "This should be entertaining."

Raine stood defensively.

A black sickle with an attached chain and weighted ball appeared in his hands.

"A black weapon??" Lucia's eyes went wide.

"Stay behind me, milady." Raine watched the man intently.

"Please be careful, Raine."

The man laughed yet again. "Oh yes, *please* be careful. I wouldn't want you to disappoint me now." He lunged at Raine but was met by an intense wall of flaming spikes. He backed off and hurled the weighted ball at her, but it was easily blocked by a magical shield.

"You never should have come here!" Raine spat as she waved her hands. A massive lightning ball formed above the man's head and came crashing down. He was barely able to dodge it.

"You certainly know what you're doing." He waved his hand, and the air around Raine began to thicken and she could feel a crushing force pushing down on her.

She stood her ground and simply waved away the spell the man had cast. "Your magic is weak." She fired torrents of flame from her hand, and as the man went to dodge them, she used her other hand to cause an instant bolt of lightning to hit him where he moved. The man was struck and staggered back.

"Oh YEAH!" he growled. "This is what I'm talking about!" He smiled as if he enjoyed the pain.

What's with this guy? Raine thought as she readied her next spell.

"I guess I'll stop going easy on you." He chuckled as he vanished in a cloud of black mist. In an instant, he was standing next to Raine. He grabbed her by the neck, but he couldn't tighten his grip as an invisible force field covered her.

"You shouldn't get so close to me," Raine told him confidently. A blast of flames exploded from her body, devouring the man. Once the smoke had cleared, only pieces of the man's cloak remained.

"Thank goodness you're okay," Lucia said with a sigh.

Raine remained silent.

"We should check on Bart and see if—" Lucia's words were cut short. The man had appeared behind her. As he brought his weapon up to deliver a killing blow, his body froze.

"Your invisibility cannot fool me." Raine stood next to the man, her hand held out and a giant, blue, magic hand holding him in place.

"Impressive," the man said. "I definitely underestimated you."

With a single clench of her fist, the magic hand crushed the mysterious man, and he crumpled to the ground.

"Hehe," he laughed as he died. "We'll meet again, sweetheart." The pitch-black eyes faded, and only dead, brown eyes remained.

"Who was that? And how does he mean to 'see you again'?" Lucia stammered.

Raine stared blankly at the dead body. "I don't know, but there was darkness in him." She turned. "We need to check on the others."

Outside, Isaac and the others had grouped near the main battlement at the front gate. High up in the sky was a hellkite, a demon wyvern that was flying around and breathing fire.

Unlike usual dragons, this one's wings were attached to its front arms.

"How the hell are we going to bring that thing down?" Drake asked, dumbfounded.

"I have an idea," Vin replied. "Hey you!" he shouted at a nearby guard. "Do you have any ballista we can tie a rope to?"

"Uhh, like a harpoon?" the guard asked.

"Yeah!"

"I don't think so, but I believe we can rig something up!"

"Okay." Vin turned to Isaac. "I'm going to help him get something together. Can you and Tara use magic to distract it while we prepare? We need to ground that thing, and fast!"

"Yeah." Isaac looked at Tara. "You up for this?"

She nodded. "Yes, I believe so."

The two of them made off for the creature.

"What can I do?" Drake asked Vin.

"You need to get ready. Once we get this thing grounded, that's when you rush it with all you've got."

Other guards who were adept at magic were already casting spells into the air.

"We need to keep it within the area of this battlement, don't let up!" one guard yelled orders to the others.

"Let's follow their lead," Isaac told Tara.

Isaac cast the only spells he really knew, which were all lightning based, but Tara was able to cast all sorts of abilities. She threw out waves of condensed air that seemed to block the hellkite from the direction it tried to fly; she even was able to snag a magic chain to its leg for a brief moment.

"You're really good at this." Isaac watched her.

"Years of training," she explained.

They kept up the assault, making sure to keep the creature within the main battlement. A few times it would descend and shower the area with flames, which took all the guard mages to deflect.

"What's the status?" Isaac asked Vin.

"Almost ready, return to us when you can."

Isaac turned to Tara. "Will you be okay helping out here while I go back? You seem to be better at this than the rest of the guards—even myself."

"Y-yeah, I can manage," she replied with a smile.

He turned to leave, but she stopped him. "I'm ... sorry for attacking you earlier."

"It's fine." Isaac put his hand on her shoulder. "You weren't yourself."

"I ..." She looked at him with gratitude. "Th-thank you! I won't let you down, Isaac!"

She looked at him with such admiration that he was taken aback. "Don't, uh, sweat it." He smiled at her. "I'm counting on you!"

She watched him head off toward the others and turned back to the hellkite. *I don't want to be thought of as a villain*, she thought to herself.

"So, you're sure this will be able to pull that thing down?" Isaac asked Vin at the main battlement guard shack.

"Yeah, but with it flying around out there, getting an accurate hit will be tough." Vin had rigged a ballista to shoot an arrow with a long rope attached to the base. "I'll need you to fire the arrow, Isaac. With your aura, you should have no problem if we can slow it down enough."

"Okay, and how will you slow it down?"

"I'm going to scale that beast and guide it lower to the ground." Vin grinned with confidence.

"How so?" Isaac frowned. "You'll need to get up there, first."

"No problem." Vin stepped out of the shack and gave a sharp whistle. After a few moments, the air shifted around them, and a giant bird came to land next to him.

"This is Ulrix, my partner."

The bird cheeped cheerfully.

"I didn't know you had a giant hawk!" Isaac stated.

"I tend to keep that on the down low, you know, for job secrecy." Vin hopped onto Ulrix's back. "Be ready. Once I'm up there, it'll be up to you to fire the arrow. Take the best shot you can. We're counting on you!" With that, they took off to the skies.

Isaac watched as the bird flew toward the hellkite. "Let's get in position. Like Vin said, once that thing hits the ground, you hit it with everything."

"I've got it," Drake said, readying his axe.

Isaac went over to the ballista and felt the weight and aim of it. "Nothing like fighting a dragon in another world, eh? Totally normal."

Vin ascended on Ulrix, making their way toward the hellkite. "C'mon, buddy, let's show 'em how it's done!" They veered near the beast, and he stood up, ready to make the leap. "Just a bit closer!" The hellkite noticed them and turned to face them. "Watch out!" As the wyvern attempted to torch them, a magic chain lassoed onto the hellkite's foot, pulling it offset.

"Nice one, Tara!" Vin shouted as he took the opportunity to leap onto the demon's back. "Go, Ulrix, get back to land!" The bird descended, leaving Vin on the back of the winged creature.

The hellkite dipped through the sky in an attempt to throw him off, but Vin held his ground and grabbed a long, thin cord from his side pouch. "You aren't going anywhere." Each end of the cord had a hook. Carefully climbing up to the demon's head, he skillfully threw one end of the cord toward the head of the beast. The hook sunk into the side of its mouth. Vin did the same to the other side. Now he had a reigns-like tether to the hellkite.

"Yeah, attaboy!" Vin laughed as he yanked left and right on the cord. "Gotcha now!" He kicked at the hellkite's head, causing the demon to drop in altitude. A few tugs here and there and a couple of kicks brought the monster to ballista level. "C'mon, Isaac, this is your chance!" Vin shouted.

Down below, Isaac stood with the ballista aimed at the ready. "It's low enough, I should be able to hit it!"

"Take the shot, then!" Drake said.

Time slowed for Isaac as he concentrated on using his power. *This is it.*

He fired.

The giant arrow flew toward its prey, finding its mark a little off but still burrowed in the right wing of the hellkite.

"Got it!" Isaac hit the pulley switch, and it started to reel the demon downward.

"Alright!" Vin could be heard yelling from on top of the hellkite.

CRASH! The wyvern hit the battlement and tumbled toward the courtyard.

"Go, Drake!" Isaac told his companion.

"Got it!" Drake bounded down the battlement steps and hurled himself at the hellkite, axe in hand. He got a good hit in and forced a blast to erupt from his weapon, knocking the demon onto its side.

Vin vaulted off the creature and was firing arrows at it. "Keep it up, big man!"

Drake readied another blow, but the hellkite reached out with its arm and grabbed Drake, a claw through his belly.

"AGGHH!" Drake cried out as blood ran from his injury.

The demon was about to crush Drake, but Isaac appeared and cut one of its talons off. It released Drake and pulled its arm back.

"Drake!" Isaac rushed to his ally. "You okay!?"

Drake didn't look too good. "Ah, shit!" He coughed as blood oozed from where the claw had stabbed him.

"Hang in there!" Isaac glanced around. "We need a medic!"

Tara came over to them. "I can mend him, but it will take a bit." She held her hand over his wound. "Take care of the monster, I'll help him."

"Okay," Isaac said, standing and facing the battle. "He's in your hands."

Vin was dodging left and right. The demon had regained its posture and was attacking anything near it in a fury. "This isn't good!" he said as Isaac approached. "This thing is way worse than that efreet."

"Well, we have to try!" Isaac moved toward the hellkite, sword in hand. He brought the blade down at its unguarded wing, slicing through it. This caused the wyvern to turn around and attack. Isaac blocked the onslaught but soon had to retreat.

"I don't think it'll fly anytime soon, so at least there's that," Isaac said to Vin.

"Good job. The best we can do now is—" Vin started, but then there was a flash and a man appeared above the hellkite's head with a red spear in hand.

The mysterious stranger delivered a sharp yet powerful blow to the hellkite's head. It died almost instantly.

"YEAH!" the guards cheered. "The hero is here!"

"Sorry I took so long," the man stated. "There were other areas that needed clearing, but it looks like this was the last one." He looked at Isaac. "Ah! You're that guardian fellow, right?"

"Uhh." Isaac stared at the mystery man. "I guess. And you are?"

"Name's Xander." The man held out his hand. "You must be Isaac."

Isaac didn't shake his hand. "If you say so. We had this under control."

"Hey, I don't doubt that," Xander replied. "I'm just glad to help out."

"Yeah, whatev—" Before Isaac could finish, Xander had turned and was calling out to people.

"Hey! That man needs help. Let's get this rubble off this soldier!" He ran off, assisting with damage control.

"We should help too," Vin said. "Let's check on Drake. We have a lot to talk about with the queen."

Isaac didn't say anything; he just stared after Xander. *We do the work, but he takes the credit? I don't like him*, he thought to himself.

"It's kind of strange." The woman with black hair grinned knowingly. "Why didn't you kill that girl?"

"She was innocent," Isaac replied.

"And how did you know that?"

"I didn't know at the time, but I could sense she wasn't evil." He shrugged.

"Like a sixth sense, huh?" The woman tapped her fingers on the table. "But that invasion, now that was unexpected."

"Yeah." Isaac nodded. "I got so frustrated when fighting Tara that I lost control. Everyone saw me conjure my weapon."

"It's not like the attack was your fault, you know." She smiled at him.

"That's what they told me." He shrugged. "But even still, there were some people that put the blame on me. That if I hadn't shown up, none of it would have happened."

"Some people are quick to point their finger."

"It didn't matter what they thought," he scoffed. "We stopped the invasion, that's what matters."

"But now people knew about you." She looked at him thoughtfully. "A person who wields a blade of pure light. Things changed after this, didn't they?"

"A lot of people started to treat me differently," he explained. "And yet, there were still a few who treated me the same. Vin and Raine being two of them."

"What about her?" the woman asked.

"You mean Lucia?" Isaac had a fond expression as he thought about her. "She was always kind to me, but after the invasion, it was almost like she was even happier to have me around. But I don't think it was because of my power."

"Perhaps she could see the side of you that you do not?"

"It's not like she really knew me." He laughed. "But maybe you're right. She always had this sense about her, like there was something she wasn't telling me."

"After the invasion, did you talk to her?"

"Yeah, she asked me to join them," he explained. "I don't know what brought that on, but she requested my help with a special mission."

"That's what brings us to your journey, isn't it?" She leaned back and stared at him intently. "We are one step closer to finding out the truth—how you got here."

"I never expected what would happen, or the people I would meet." He sighed. "But this was where everything really began."

PART II
DARKNESS EMERGES

Fate takes hold and hope fades.
A betrayal foreseen by shadowy shades.
As death looms ever nearer, evil takes form in many guises,
but upon the souls of those who are wicked, a shadow casts its wrath,
and from the depths of despair, one born from darkness rises,
unexpected and unrelenting, the beast carves a new path.
Fate changes and hope returns.
Upon the fangs of vengeance, evil burns.
Heed this warning, traitor, before encroaching.
Beware, for he is the storm that is approaching!

—Aurelia

CHAPTER 9

THE QUEEN'S QUEST

The air was thick, the silence deafening.

Isaac stood in an empty school, alone. The lights flickered, crackling.

Why am I here? This place, I remember it, he thought to himself as he walked down the hallway. Not a single soul was around, yet he didn't feel truly alone.

I hope I'm not late for class again. Wait, what am I thinking? I don't go to school anymore. He was confused, not thinking straight. *I should just leave.*

He rounded a corner to where he remembered an exit, however, there was only a dead end. A solid wall leading nowhere blocked his path. *That's weird.* He turned back around, and this time, the hallway was gone. Instead, he was in the cafeteria.

He frantically looked back, but the dead ended hallway was also gone; he was somehow in the center of the cafeteria.

What the ...? He scanned the area; the lights had grown dim, and he couldn't see the whole place. He felt like he was being watched.

Cautiously, he walked toward the front of the cafeteria that led to the main common area. *If only I could use my powers*, he thought as his aura had left him once again.

He neared the end of the area when he heard the sound of utensils hitting the ground. Isaac jerked his head around to look back as the sound of swift footsteps could be heard. The light was too dim for him to make anything out, and instead of calling out to it, he quickly moved into the common area

153

and positioned himself behind one of the many pillars in the large open area.

He waited for a few minutes, listening.

Nothing. Not a damn thing.

He peeked around the pillar, but the cafeteria was gone. Instead, across the way was a single door, half cracked open, with an ominous light shining out.

He started to back up, but his back hit a wall. Turning, he was now blocked off. The common area was gone, and turning back toward the door, he now stood in a hallway.

This isn't good ... Only one way to go.

He slowly inched toward the door. Where was this place leading him?

As he approached, he leaned left and right, trying to get a look into the room. It looked to be a classroom, but he couldn't see if anyone was in there. He looked back, but it was still a dead end. Taking a deep breath, he entered the classroom.

He saw chairs and desks, but what caught Isaac's attention was the old lady standing at the teacher's desk, her back turned.

"Back again, I see." She didn't turn around, and her voice was different, as if it belonged to someone else. "Nowhere else to go? Nowhere else to run?" Slowly, she turned her head. It looked as if her eyes had been gouged out, and only empty, bloody sockets remained. "Abandoned by the ones who you called 'friend'?" Her voice now sounded demonic. "You can stay here. We would love if you joined us." Her skin began to darken, and a black liquid ran from her eyeless sockets. "wE'll bE yOur nEW fRienDS!"

The old woman hunched over and let out an ear-piercing scream. Isaac clapped his hands to his ears in pain. The old lady, without moving her legs, floated toward him. Flinching with pain, he forced himself to run out the door, and to his surprise, he was in a long hallway with no dead end.

"Running again!?" The old lady laughed. "Run, run, RUN!"

Isaac bolted down the hallway away from the hovering banshee. *How do I get out of here?* He saw another door at the end of the hallway and slammed through it, quickly locking it.

"I see you've finally made it ..."

Isaac jolted at the sinister voice. He turned, and there, standing in the center of the room, was a dark, shadowy figure.

"It's about time we had a chat."

"Who are you?" Isaac's voice was shaky.

The figure didn't move. He stood in the darkness, barely visible in the dim lighting, though Isaac realized there weren't any lightbulbs, just an ominous haze lingering in the air.

"You will know in due time," the figure replied. "But tell me, do you really trust them?"

Isaac stared back, not daring to go near this demon. "Who are you talking about?"

"Oh, you know who."

Isaac thought for a moment then scanned the room for an exit.

"You know they don't really care about you," the figure stated. "Only what you can do for them. Once you've catered to their will, they'll forget you in an instant." He held one hand up. "It starts with one thing." He raised his other hand. "Then another. Once you've played into their hands, it'll be all over." He clapped his hands together. "You aren't what they want. It's your power they crave. To use as they wish."

Isaac spied a doorway. "Why are you telling me this?"

"You know it to be true. Why would they accept you so willingly and easily?" the figure sneered. "The blond idiot instantly became your friend when he saw what you were, the blue haired bitch invited you into the castle once she saw what you were. Even that naïve queen thinks highly of you."

"Leave her out of this," Isaac growled.

"She doesn't care about you, only the power you possess. Don't be fooled."

Isaac glared back at the dark figure. "Maybe you're right, but I don't exactly trust you either."

The figure took a single step toward him. "I'm the only one that can grant you what you desire!" He held his hands out. "I know you and what you truly want. An escape from this torturous life. I can grant that, just accept me, and all will be given."

For a moment, Isaac pondered the offer.

In the distance, he heard a dog barking. The figure reeled in dismay. Isaac took the opportunity to bolt for the door.

"NO!" the figure shouted, taking chase.

Isaac ran through several hallways with the sinister being hot on his heels.

"Always running!" it shouted.

Isaac turned a corner and saw a glass door with daylight beaming through it.

Gotta make it!

He flung himself through the door as light absorbed him.

Isaac woke with a jolt. *These nightmares are getting worse*, he thought in frustration. It felt so real. What was that thing? He shifted to get out of bed.

Getting dressed, he glanced out the window. Below, the city had taken some damage in the attack, but overall, everyone was okay. The guards had acted quickly, and with everyone's help, they were able to take down the worst of it before it got out of control.

In the castle hallway, he saw a few of the maids. Upon seeing him, they quickly turned and bowed, looking at him in awe. What was wrong with them? They'd never treated him like this before. He continued till he came to a large room with quite a few people in it. One of those people was Raine.

"I'm here," Isaac said to her.

Everyone in the room stopped and looked at him.

Well, this is awkward, he thought as he stared back at them. "The hell are you all looking at?"

"Please don't mind him." Raine quickly stepped in. "He's uhh ... kinda new to our city, haha." She chuckled nervously. Turning to Isaac, she widened her eyes at him. "Please be polite," she whispered. "These are some of the top leaders in the world here, and on top of that, the head of the council is present." She motioned to a middle-aged man. "His name is Anwir. You should go introduce yourself, but please be polite."

He stared blankly at her. "Is this whole guardian thing really a big deal? I mean, people have been treating me differently since the invasion."

"Yes, Isaac, it really is," she replied. "You are this world's hope, so please conduct yourself appropriately."

"Raine, I don't even know what a guardian is. I'm not the hope this world wants, okay?" he told her with a frown. "I'm just a regular guy, nothing more."

Raine pulled Isaac away from everyone. "Look, I know it's a lot to take in, but you are the guardian of light, your weapon proves it." She grabbed Isaac's hand. "No one else has a weapon with the white color yours has. There's only you, so please just bear with us for a bit and you'll see."

He shrugged, unconvinced. "Just because my blade gives a different shine doesn't mean I'm better. You know it was some guy named Xander who killed the dragon, right?"

"That's what they told me, yes."

"So, if I was this great hero, or whatever everyone thinks I am, wouldn't it make sense that I should have been powerful enough to kill it myself?"

"I know what you're saying, but please, you've made an impression on everyone, so don't make it more difficult for the queen," she pleaded.

Isaac paused. "What do you mean? Lucia has nothing to do with this."

"Actually," she stated, "Her Majesty has already told everyone about you, that's kind of why everyone is eager to meet you, because she's given her approval."

He remained silent. *Why would she tell them something like that? I'm nothing. No one. She's mistaken, and yet ...*

"So please, you also represent her as well, you see?" she pleaded again.

"Fine," he replied. "I'll do my best."

Raine was taken aback. "Th-that's good to hear." She motioned again to the head councilman. "Let's introduce you to the council." She guided him toward the middle-aged man.

"You must be Isaac." Anwir, the head of the council, held his hand out. Isaac shook it. "I've heard quite a bit about you," he said with a chuckle. "And I saw you in the tournament."

"It's good to meet you, uhh, Anw-err ..." Isaac started.

"Just call me Anwir." He beamed.

"Uhh, right, my apologies, uhh, Anwir." Isaac wasn't used to giving courtesy.

Anwir laughed. "He's very modest! I see why the queen likes you. Where is she, by the way?"

"She should be here any moment, councilman," Raine replied.

"So, Isaac, what exactly can you do, if I may ask?" Anwir said. "Being a guardian has to be an amazing gift."

Isaac glanced at Raine.

Just tell him you can do all sorts of things. I don't know! she told him telepathically.

"Uhh, well, I can do magic and stuff. I'm not sure what to tell you."

"Well, we haven't had a guardian in a long time, so I'm not sure what to expect." Anwir laughed. "But I have high hopes for you."

The air in the room livened up as a particular figure entered.

"Sorry if I am late." The statement came from a radiant source. The queen.

"Actually, you are just on time," Anwir stated as he approached Lucia. "I just met this guardian you've talked about; he's an odd fellow."

I'm right here, you bastard, Isaac thought.

"Oh! Isaac is here?" Lucia looked at him. "It is great to see you again!" She hurried over, smiling brightly. "I hope you're doing okay after the incident."

"I'm fine," Isaac replied sheepishly.

"You know you can call on me anytime," Lucia told him with a smile.

What the hell is going on? Suddenly everyone wants to be my friend. But ... Lucia was always this nice to me even before the chaos. She must be this nice to everyone, I guess.

"Uhh, thanks," Isaac said as he averted his eyes.

"So, what did I miss?"

"We were just talking about the invasion and the artifact that was stolen." Raine explained.

"The whole thing was just a diversion!" yelled a man named Frederick. "Maybe if the guard had been more competent, they would have known to protect it!"

"Excuse me!?" Bart shouted. "Don't you dare ever insult my men or myself like that! It's because of us your dumbass is still alive while you hid in your room like a coward!"

"Gentlemen, please!" Anwir said. "This bickering will get us nowhere."

"I agree," Lucia stepped in. "We must assemble a scouting force to find where they went, to work on retrieving what was taken."

"I'm sorry, milady, but the council cannot allow that," Anwir said sadly. "We don't know what the enemy has plans for next, and we must make sure all available resources are ready to defend the city in case of another attack."

Lucia furrowed her brow. "They've fled, Anwir. They got what they wanted, and they won't be coming back. We need to act now before they get too far from our border."

"I'm sorry. I truly am. I thought the same, but after a long meeting, the vote was unanimous. We need to remain cautious and not make any rash decisions." He sighed. "We will make preparations for a counterattack after we have fortified our city and contacted Esmeraldas on the situation."

"That could take weeks!" Lucia pushed back. "The longer we take to act, the more difficult this will become."

"I understand how you feel," Anwir replied in a comforting tone, "but we have to follow the vote of the council."

Lucia didn't reply, but she was clearly angry.

"Our first steps should be to focus on the damage the city incurred during the attack, make sure everyone is okay, and see to the injured," Anwir explained to the group. "Bart, we'll need your men to make sure to direct the response teams on this."

"Understood, councilman," Bart replied.

"Let's at least get our own city in order before coming up with a way forward." Even though he was looking at everyone, it seemed Anwir was speaking to Lucia. "Once we clean up the town, we can talk about retaliation."

The meeting had ended, but Lucia, Isaac, Raine, and Bart stayed behind.

Lucia narrowed her eyes in frustration.

"Milady, we just have to hold out until we recompose our city," Raine reassured her.

"We cannot wait any longer, Raine." Lucia shook her head. "The artifact must be reclaimed. If it's used improperly, people could die! Innocent people!"

"Uhh ..." Isaac hesitantly spoke up. "What is this artifact?"

Lucia gave Isaac a pleading look and spoke gently to him. "It's an amulet—my mother's, to be exact. The sentiment is the least of my worries. It harnesses incredible power."

"Oh."

"Raine, please get Vin and meet me in my quarters at noon. Bart, Isaac, will you please also be there?"

"Yes, ma'am." Bart bowed.

"Uhh, sure?" Isaac was confused why he had been invited.

Five of them stood inside Lucia's quarters.

"I called you all here because I've been coming up with a plan," Lucia explained to them. "I've been talking with Bart, and I want to form a team to go out and seek the stolen artifact as well as find out why Esmeraldas was attacked."

Isaac frowned. He didn't like where this was going.

"What kind of team?" Raine asked.

"A secretive one. One that could operate outside of the council."

"Uhh, you mean behind their back?" Vin asked in surprise.

"Yes, Vin, that is exactly what I'm implying," Lucia replied sternly. "The council doesn't seem to understand the seriousness of the situation. If that amulet gets into the wrong hands, it could spell disaster."

"So, who would be on this team?" Raine asked. That was the question Isaac was waiting to hear the answer to.

"Well, that's why I called you all here," Lucia explained. "Bart, you are someone I can trust, so I want you to foresee this operation. As for who, I think an expert operative as well as a master mage would make a formidable force. And let's not forget there's him." She smiled at Isaac.

"Hold on!" Isaac interrupted. "I knew this was where that was going." Everyone looked at him as he slowly backed away. "Look, I appreciate everything you've all done for me, but I'm not looking to participate in any wars."

Lucia's expression saddened. "What are you saying?"

"I'm sorry, but I don't want any part of this," he explained. "I'm just new to this place and needed some money to support myself. I only came here to participate in the tournament. I didn't know all this stuff was gonna happen."

"Isaac, I'm not fully sure what's going on myself, but would you at least reconsider?" Raine attempted to convince him.

"Yeah, man, we haven't even heard all the details," Vin spoke up. "Hell, I'm sure you would be paid for this as well if that's what you're worried about."

"This isn't about money!" Isaac said. "I just knew I was decent at fighting, and I needed a quick buck. Look, I didn't want these powers, I just want to live a quiet life, okay? Fighting wars, causing conflict, I don't want that. Hell, I barely even know all of you and suddenly you want me to join you on some top-secret mission?"

"But Isaac—" Raine began.

"My mind's made up."

Silence filled the room. Lucia looked distraught.

"Hey—" Vin started but was interrupted by Lucia.

"Leave him be. He's right," she spoke. "I'm sorry to have pushed this on you so suddenly, Isaac." She gave him an apologetic smile. "It was wrong of me. I'll make sure you get paid for your victory in the tournament. After that, I really do wish you well."

"Thanks ..." Isaac gave a polite bow.

"Just please take care of yourself, okay?"

"I ... I will." Isaac turned to the door.

"Talk to the guard near the castle gate. Tell him I sent you to collect the tournament prize," Bart told him.

"Thanks," Isaac replied as he left.

They watched him leave and then turned to Lucia.

"I guess we'll have to find someone else." Raine shrugged.

"Not necessarily." Lucia gave her a secretive look. "Have faith."

After talking with the guard, Isaac made his way to Ruby's bar. He wouldn't be able to collect till later, so he figured he'd grab a drink or two.

As he walked down the city road, there were people cleaning up the mess the attack had made. Some people noticed him and ushered their children inside, while some looked at him in awe. Isaac did his best to ignore them, but overall, he felt everyone was watching him.

"That's him," he heard someone say.

"He's the one from the tournament with the blade of light!"

No one approached, but the feelings were mixed. Finally, he arrived at the bar.

"Well, hi there!" Ruby said as he sat down. "Haven't seen your face in a while."

"Yeah, uhh, I was busy."

"So, I saw," she drawled. "You did pretty darn good in that tourn'ment, I must say."

"Uhh, thanks." He shrugged. "I didn't do much."

"Well, you sure as hell scared a lot of people."

"What?"

"You being the guardian and all. Hell, you sure fool'd me."

Isaac looked at Ruby dejectedly. "Oh right. That."

"Shit, I don't care if you're a guardian or a donkey's ass. As long as you don't cause any trouble, we can be friends." She chuckled.

"Works for me."

"So, what'll you have, darlin'?"

"I'll take your highest percent of whiskey with ice."

She narrowed her eyes. "Rough day?"

He gave a halfhearted chuckle. "Yeah, something like that."

"Alright, I'll bring it over in a moment." She headed back to the counter.

As he waited, he thought about Lucia. *Why would she want me? I don't really know her. Vin told me she has some fascination toward me and swears it isn't because of my powers. Goddammit, I wish I didn't have them. I just want to live in peace.*

Just then, two men walked into the bar, and as they passed Isaac, one of them paused.

"Hey, isn't that the dude who caused the attack?"

"Who, that wimpy-lookin' guy?"

One of the men walked over to where Isaac was sitting. "Hey man, weren't you in the tournament?"

"Yeah, what of it?" Isaac cautiously replied.

"It seems all this bullshit started when you appeared."

Isaac glared at the man. "I had nothing to do with it."

"Well," the man replied, "it seems that since you showed your hand, this shit happened. I would say that ain't no coincidence."

"Seems your logic is misplaced. I didn't cause any of this."

"You think you're some kind of guardian; I think you're a fraud."

"Whatever, stop bothering me." Isaac kept his guard up. A part of him wanted the fight. Yearned for it, even.

"I think you should pay for what you've done!" The man leaned closer to Isaac. "We don't need no guardians or monsters or whatever!"

Ruby approached the table. "Here's your drink, darlin'." She purposefully nudged the man out of the way and placed Isaac's whiskey in front of him. "Are these men botherin' you?"

Isaac thought for a moment. *I don't want to trouble Ruby, but yeah, they are bothering me. Maybe she has some bouncers that can handle them. As much as I would like to fight them, it's probably a bad idea.* "Yeah, they are bothering me," he replied.

"Is that so?" Ruby eyed the two bullies. "If you have any problems, you'll take it up with me."

"This guy's a traitor!" the man said angrily. "We all saw the TV."

"First off, he was nowhere near the attack," Ruby growled. "Second, ain't none of ya'll better start anything here or I'll throw ya out!"

The man looked at her stubbornly. "Oh, I'm sure you will, little lady." He chuckled and moved toward her.

Isaac was about to get up and confront the two troublemakers but instead was surprised to see Ruby fiercely grab the man's wrist as he went to touch her leg. Twisting his arm and raising it up, Ruby easily held him there, and the man yelped in pain.

"How dare you!" She threw a punch with her other hand into the man's gut, and he bowled over. The other man moved to attack her, but she quickly grabbed him by the throat and slammed him on the ground.

All the patrons in the bar looked on in shock as Ruby dragged the two toward the exit.

"Ya'll come 'ere into mah bar and b'have this way!?"

Isaac just stared wide-eyed as she easily grabbed one man by his leg and forcefully threw him out the open door, then grabbed the other and hurled him as well.

"And stay out, ya shit eatin' weasels!"

The two men, coughing, got up and ran off.

Ruby made her way back to Isaac, fixing her now slightly messy hair. "Sorry 'bout that, darlin'." She gave him a wink, and he saw a slight spark of red aura from her eyes.

Isaac took a sip of his whiskey, still startled by what he'd just witnessed.

"Don't let those buffoons get to ya." she consoled him. "Lotsa people are jus' scared by the incident." She sat across from him. "Ya'll did a great job helpin' out here during the attack. Saved a lotta lives." She smiled. "I may not be a believer in guardians or whatever, but I think you're an okay fella."

"Uhh ..." Isaac hesitated. "Thanks."

"If you have any problems, you're always welcome here, hun." She got up as new customers walked in. "I know you'll do great." She winked again and approached the newcomers.

Great at what? Isaac thought. *I don't want to fight more people or participate in any wars. I just wanna be left in peace.*

A woman approached Isaac. "Um, hello, sir."

He stared back at her curiously. "Uhh, hi."

"I'm sorry to bother you, it's just, uhh, I saw you in the attack. You're the guardian, right?"

"So, I'm told," he replied halfheartedly.

"I just wanted to say thank you. You may not have noticed, but you saved my life that night." She smiled at him timidly. "I was hiding from some demons on the battlement, and they would have found me if you hadn't come jumping into the midst of them. They turned their attention to you, and I was able to get away. I can't express how thankful I am. Thank you so much!" She bowed her head and left.

I saved her? Isaac remembered the instance she was talking about. It was when the efreet threw him into that group of demons. He thought about the look in her eyes. She looked at him with gratitude. Not many people had ever looked at him that way before. It ... felt good.

After Isaac finished his drink, he bid farewell to Ruby and left the bar. After returning to the castle and receiving his tournament reward, he headed toward the outskirts of the main city. The money he had received for the tournament was substantial enough to last him a good while till he could figure out where to live in quiet.

Where are you going? A voice in his head spoke to him.

Not sure, Isaac thought. Guess I'll figure it out eventually.

What are you going do when you get there? You don't really know this world.

I'll catch on.

What about the others?

I'm sure they'll figure something out. It's not like they need me. I'm no hero.

He stopped at the edge of the city and looked out onto the small, rural area.

You can't do it, can you?

He just stared dejectedly into the distance.

You can't turn your back on them when they're asking for help. That's not who you are.

Isaac stared down at his hand. It was slightly shaking. That woman, he thought, she said she was thankful.

She would have died if it weren't for you.

It wasn't intentional.

A lot of people will die if that amulet gets used.

...

She called on you specifically, with that same look in her eyes.

Lucia ...

What if something bad happens to her?

Isaac reached into his pocket and pulled out a photo. It was of a large, black dog. The hand holding the picture slightly shook as he stared at it.

You want to remember that feeling, don't you?
He looked back into the distance.
You won't find it out there.
I know. He turned back and glanced at the city. The highest tower of the castle could be seen.
She looked sad when you turned down her offer. I think she was really looking forward to having you with her.
He put the picture back in his pocket.
Your mind's made up?
Yeah ...
Then what are you waiting for?

"Be sure to send help over to the business district."

"Yes, milady."

Lucia and Raine were organizing the cleanup. They were instructing several members of the guard and emergency crew.

"Make sure we use supplies from the castle storehouse. You have my permission," Lucia told them.

"I think Vin should be ready with that matter you requested," Raine told her. "I'll go check on him."

"Very well."

Raine made her way toward the special ops post inside the castle.

"Ah, Lady Raine!" One of the maids stopped her. "Please tell that vile urchin to leave us alone. We have our hands busy cleaning up the mess around the castle, we don't need him bothering us as well."

"Oh geez ..." Raine shook her head. "I'll make sure to give him a proper scolding!"

"But that other one," a different maid commented. "I don't mind if he talks to me." She blushed slightly.

"He's so quiet, though," a third chimed in. "He's kinda cute, I guess."

"I know, right? He's so mysterious!" the blushing maid said. "I like that! I tried to talk to him a minute ago, but he just said 'hello' and left." She looked disappointed.

"Hold on," Raine interrupted. "This guy, was he in the tournament?"

"Why, yes, actually. He was on the same team as that wretch!" she explained.

"Maria's got a crush on the Sotēr." The first maid giggled.

"Do not!"

"You JUST saw him!?" Raine stammered.

"Uhh, that's right."

"Where did he go?"

"Lady Raine must have a crush as well!" The maids all giggled.

"That's not what I mean! I don't like him like that!"

"We're just kidding!" They laughed. "He went that way, toward the north end." They pointed.

"Thank you!" Raine took off down the hall, leaving the maids to their gossip.

Isaac was looking at a painting of a grassy field when Raine approached.

"Fancy seeing you here," she greeted him. "I thought you had left."

"Hey ..." He gave a thoughtful shrug. "Guess I may have been a little hasty in my decision."

She smiled. "Does this mean ...?"

"Yeah, I'll join you."

"I'm relieved you changed your mind!" She beamed. "And I promise you won't regret it!"

"Where's the queen?"

"Oh, she's in the throne room. Let's go tell her!" She started to turn. "Oh, wait! I need to see Vin first. Let's go talk to him, then we'll see Her Majesty."

"Okay."

They made their way down the hall. The light from outside shining through the stained-glass windows gave the castle a calm radiance.

"So, what made you change your mind?" she asked.

"Well," he began hesitantly, "I guess I wasn't being honest with myself."

"Oh?" She looked at him questioningly.

"It's just been rough for me lately is all. Coming here not knowing how things are, it's frustrating."

"Yeah, you did mention that. Where are you from exactly? You never told us."

Isaac glanced at Raine then looked away. "I did some thinking. After we talk to Lucia, I'm going to tell you all where I'm from. I guess I need to try and be more honest with you guys if we're gonna be on the same team."

"What's with this change of heart?" Raine was pleasantly surprised.

"Look, what I said earlier, it's not like I don't want to help," he explained. "But a part of me doesn't want to always be the one that has to do something before others act. It's like I keep getting pulled into these events regardless of my decision. Back where I come from, I was part of something similar, and it kinda took its toll on me."

"We aren't gonna let you do everything, ya know," Raine reassured him. "Besides, I can't let you do the talking, you'll mess that up."

"That's a guarantee, I won't deny it." He chuckled. "You can be my spokeswoman."

"Haha, I was gonna do that regardless. You leave the relations to me, and you can assist me in battles, deal?"

"Assist?" Isaac playfully nudged her. "I think you have that backwards."

"Oh, I do, do I?" She laughed. "No offense, but you've got a long way to go before you reach my level."

"I'll get there."

"Oh, here we are." Raine paused in front of a door that was titled "Special Operations." They entered, and the room was filled with all sorts of what Isaac would describe as computers and digital boards of the world map.

"What the ...?" He looked around in shock. "This is way different than the rest of the castle!"

It was a fairly large room, and several people were working on various things.

Looking up from a computer, Vin jumped up and approached them. "Isaac!? What're you doin' here?"

"Nice to see you too."

"He's agreed to join us after all," Raine explained.

"Is that true?" Vin looked eager.

"Yeah, if that's okay with you." Isaac shrugged.

"Well, of course it is!" He smiled. "Glad to have you aboard! Does Her Majesty know?"

"Not yet," Raine replied. "We'll see her after we're done here. Did you secure a route?"

"Oh yeah!" Vin beckoned them to his computer. "I just found one a moment ago."

"Your destination is locked in, Vin." Bart came over to them. "Please let the queen know you can leave any time." He glanced over at Isaac. "What are you doing here?"

"I, uhh ..." Isaac started nervously as Bart stared him down.

"He's decided to join us," Raine stepped in for him.

"You ain't tryin' to pull anything, are you?" Bart narrowed his eyes.

"N-no! I swear. I just needed some time to think about it," Isaac explained.

Bart looked at him questioningly. "Fine. Since Her Majesty has taken a liking to you, I'll allow it, but know this: The operation we are conducting is top secret, you cannot reveal anything about it except to those of us involved. Got it?"

"Y-yes, sir."

"Good. I don't care if you're this so-called guardian. To me, you're worth is only as good as you give," Bart told him.

"I understand."

"Good. Glad we're on the same page. Carry this out success-fully, and I may take a liking to you."

After a slightly awkward pause, Vin spoke up. "Anyhow, we were able to secure a confidential transport out of the city and into Rial."

"Rial?" Isaac asked.

"It's a neighboring town." Raine pointed at the map on the screen. "There's a seer there who may be able to give us insight as to what's going on. It's also on the way to getting the artifact back."

"Since the council pretty much has the city locked down, they're preventing anyone from coming in or going out," Vin added. "So, we were able to secure a means of getting out via private train."

"Who's all going?" Isaac asked.

"Well, it was gonna be Vin and myself," Raine said. "We were going to look into another possible candidate, but since you're here, then it will be the three of us."

"Just us three? Will that be enough?"

Vin chuckled. "We can't have a large group moving about; it will be too suspicious. Besides, we've got the master mage and the master rogue on the team, along with the guardian himself."

"I just have one request," Isaac said. "I don't want to be called guardian. I'm not a fan of that title. I'm just me, ya know?"

Bart laughed. "I can agree to that. You aren't exactly cut out to hold that title as far as I'm concerned."

"I think that's supposed to be an insult, but I'm actually okay with it." Isaac gave a short chuckle.

"Well, enough talk," Bart ordered. "Go inform the queen that our route is secure, and we are waiting on her orders. Dismissed."

The three got up and left the room.

"Your Majesty, the south town has been filled with workers, and the east gate has begun repairs."

"Wonderful," Lucia replied. "Good work, everyone. Let us keep this up for now, and we shall focus on the north side tomorrow."

As the group dispersed, Raine, Vin, and Isaac approached. Upon seeing Isaac, Lucia gave a warm smile. "Took you long enough." She stood up and made her way to him. "I'm glad to see you changed your mind."

"Uhh," Isaac stammered, "you knew I'd come back?"

"Of course," she said confidently. "You're not as bad as people think you are. I believe wholeheartedly in you."

As usual, Lucia seemed overjoyed by Isaac's presence.

"Now, did you gather the requested intel?" She looked Vin.

"Yes, Your Majesty," he replied. "Bart says we can leave at any time."

"Excellent." Lucia nodded at them. "Please prepare accordingly. You should all go tomorrow night after the meeting with the council." She glanced at Isaac. "I humbly thank you for reconsidering this. I have no doubt you will be a beacon of hope in these dark times."

"I'll, uhh, try my best."

She smiled at him, then looked to Raine. "And do not worry about me. I've already found a temporary guard to watch over me while you are gone. Please feel free to utilize any of the facilities within the castle to prepare, but be sure not to reveal your intentions."

"We won't," Raine assured her.

"There's something I want to tell you all," Isaac said suddenly. Everyone looked at him curiously. "It's about where I'm from. I never mentioned it, but I want to tell you now."

"Oh yeah." Vin held his chin in thought. "I am curious about that."

"We're listening." Raine seemed eager.

Lucia didn't say anything; she only looked at him knowingly.

"I don't really know how to start, so I'll just say it," Isaac explained. "I'm not from this world."

Vin and Raine looked at him in shock. "What do you mean?"

"Well, I'm from a planet called Earth," he continued. "My world is very different than this one. That's why I'm not familiar with this place's customs."

"That ... actually makes a lot of sense," Raine said thoughtfully. "You couldn't really use aura when you first got here, and you don't know even the basics of anything."

"You guys believe me?" Isaac was surprised.

"Well, it kinda makes sense," Vin replied. "I kept badgering you for not knowing anything, thinking you were just stupid."

"Uhh ..."

"I guess I owe you an apology for all that."

Isaac shook his head. "No, it's okay. Perhaps I should have told you guys sooner. I just didn't trust anyone at the time. But we've already gone through quite a bit; I feel like I should be more honest with you guys from now on."

Lucia put her hand on his shoulder. "I'm so glad you told us, Isaac. I want you to know that you can trust us. We're here for you."

Isaac glanced down. "Uhh ... thanks, guys. Sorry if I was kinda rude before."

Raine chuckled. "Wow, I don't think I've ever seen you act so shy before." She smiled at him. "We're a team now, so let's look out for each other, okay?"

"Yeah." Isaac smiled back. "Thanks."

"You'll have to tell us about this world of yours during our travels," Vin said eagerly. "Kinda exciting to know there's a different world out there with intelligent life."

"I suppose you could say that," Isaac replied doubtfully. "But yeah, I'll tell you about it."

"That settles it, then," Raine said. "Let's go prepare. I'll help you figure out what to take, Isaac. Just let us know if you have any questions."

"I will, thanks."

Later that night, Isaac found himself wandering the castle halls. He didn't know what would happen on this secret mission, but he felt nervous nonetheless. He'd never done anything so crazy in his life. Earth had nothing like what he'd experienced so far here, and he realized that it was because he'd been granted these powers. A part of him enjoyed being able to use magic and have enhanced strength, but another part of him knew it would only bring him more problems.

As he walked down the long hallways, deep in thought, he passed a man talking to a maid.

"Don't worry, honey," the man told her. "Everything will be alright."

Isaac glanced over, and the maid locked eyes with him. For a moment, it seemed like her eyes were pleading with him.

The man noticed the maid looking away from him and followed her gaze.

"Can we help you with something, friend?" The man smiled at him.

Isaac shook his head apologetically. "Sorry, I was just passing by." He turned away from them and moved along as the man turned back to the woman.

The maids seem to get a lot of attention, he thought. No wonder Raine is always defending them.

As he continued along, he eventually heard a familiar voice.

"Oh, Isaac!" It was Lucia. "Fancy seeing you here!"

"Hm? Oh, hello, Your Majesty."

"No need to be so formal." She smiled warmly at him. "Please, just call me Lucia."

"Right, Lucia." He smiled back at her. "What are you up to?"

"Sometimes I like to go for walks around the castle," she explained cheerfully. "Would you like to join me?"

"Uh, sure." He nodded politely.

"How wonderful! Your company will surely make this more enjoyable."

"Y-yeah."

They walked together down the main hall and even up some stairs to a balcony overlooking the grand hall. Each time they passed a maid or one of the nobles, they would each bow to her politely.

"How have you enjoyed your stay here, so far?" she asked him. "Coming to a new world must be quite difficult."

"It's been ... interesting," he replied. "I think the biggest surprise is that everyone speaks my language."

"That is fortunate." She nodded. "Although it's kind of odd that you speak the same language that we do, don't you think?"

"I've actually thought about that a lot." He chuckled. "I don't really know how to explain it."

"It also must be tough being away from home." She gave him a sad look.

"Not really." He averted his gaze. "Can't say I miss it, to be honest."

"Well, I do hope this world will have more to offer you." She placed her hand gently on his arm. "I'm sure glad you're here, at least."

He looked at her, and her brown eyes twinkled back at him. He didn't understand why she was so comfortable around him, but oddly enough, he felt the same toward her, like they were connected somehow.

"May we sit for a moment?" She motioned to a bench that was overlooking the grand hall. "This is a nice, quiet place for us to be alone."

"Oh, uh, sure." He walked over with her, and they both sat down.

"Are you well prepared for your journey?" she asked him in earnest.

"Yeah, we got our bags ready and supplies in order. I guess we leave tomorrow night."

"That's good. I do hope you stay safe out there."

"I'm sure we'll be okay," he comforted her. "Not sure how much help I'll be, but hopefully we can come back quickly."

Lucia placed her hand gently on his shoulder. "I am sorry to have put this on you." She spoke softly. "I just feel you're the only one I can really turn to, and I know this journey may be hard on you, but please, do come back to me."

Isaac looked at her curiously. "Raine and Vin will be there with me. You can turn to them too, you know."

She looked over the balcony to the bottom of the grand hall, seemingly lost in thought. "When I was little, I'd always be afraid to go to sleep. When nighttime came and I'd lie in bed, the nightmares would happen. Even though they were just dreams, I would still wake up in fright. But there was always this man who comforted me. My mother told me I had nothing to worry about, that it was all in my head, but that didn't shake away the fear. I haven't seen that man in a long time, but I still remember the comfort he gave me."

Isaac watched her look back at him, and she stared into his eyes with a gentle expression. The next words she spoke would stay with him forever.

"You also make me feel safe."

He sat there, slack-jawed, not knowing how to respond.

She turned away timidly.

"My apologies!" She tried to hide her face as her cheeks turned red. "I just wish you well on this journey and want to send you off with my blessing."

"Um ... th-thank you ..." He turned away from her as well. "I'll be sure to bring your amulet back quickly."

"My amulet?" She paused questioningly.

"You know ... the artifact?" He frowned slightly.

"Oh!" She quickly smiled. "Right! I will look forward to having that back!"

"Right ..." He couldn't help but crack a smile at her as she fidgeted nervously.

"A-anyway." She composed herself. "It is rather late." Standing, she smiled brightly at him. "I really should be getting to bed."

He stood as well and nodded. "It was good talking with you."

"And I you." Her face softened as she bid him farewell. "Goodnight, Isaac."

"Huh?" He was about to respond, but she quickly turned and walked down the hall.

"Odd," he muttered to himself. "What was all that about?"

The black-haired woman smiled at Isaac. "Why did you change your mind?"

"I guess I just couldn't turn my back on someone in need," he replied.

"Is that truly it?" She laughed. "Or was there another reason?"

He remained silent.

"It was her wasn't it?"

Again, silence.

"It was!" The woman played with her black hair. "You saw something in her, that's why you wanted to help, isn't it?"

"I'm not sure what you mean."

"It's the same reason you killed that man in the tournament." She smiled as if she'd discovered a secret. "You knew he was working with the evil cult."

"I killed him because he pissed me off."

"Is that so?" She chuckled. "Or did your mind come up with an excuse so you would do it?"

Isaac looked down at the interrogation table, thinking.

"That's also why you didn't kill that girl, Tara."

"She was innocent."

The woman laughed. "But she caused you more trouble than the previous one. You could have killed her, yet instead you took a non-lethal approach, jabbing her with the hilt of your weapon instead of the blade."

"That's ... uhh ..."

"I wonder why that is." The black-haired woman sighed. "But I'm certain you will figure it out eventually. What happened next?"

"We met with some kind of seer," he explained. "She showed us these murals. I didn't really understand what they were, but apparently, they held some kind of prophecy."

"You mean the goddess' murals," the woman spoke knowingly.

"You know about them?"

"Of course." She smiled mischievously. "I created them, after all."

"What?" Isaac stared at her in surprise. "What do you mean? Just who ARE you?"

The woman giggled. "All in due time, my dear. There is still so much to learn, and I'm sure you'll find the answer eventually."

"No fair!" He frowned at her.

"Hehe!" She looked at him fondly. "You remind me of a dear friend of mine. I used to tease her just the same as this. I miss that sweet fox."

Isaac gave her a frustrated look.

"Now, now, don't be like that. Please continue. I prom-ise the pieces will come together soon enough."

"If you say so." He sighed dejectedly.

"Through fully understanding on your own, you can rise above the darkness," she told him. "But first, you have to come to terms with why you are here and that is not something I can tell you. Do you understand?"

"So, I'm on my own ..."

"No, Isaac." She reached out and took his hand. "I would never leave you. I can only guide you. But the answers you're looking for must be your own. This is your choice to make, not mine. I will help you, but in the end, what you do will be entirely your decision."

CHAPTER 10

PROPHECIES AND VISIONS

Isaac, Vin, and Raine stood at the lone train station near the edge of Adamas. It was nighttime, and the lights were all off to help conceal them.

"Looks like we're ready," Raine said.

Vin adjusted his backpack. "Yeah, I guess this is it."

Isaac remained silent.

They were waiting for Lucia and Bart to arrive as the people conducting the train were making preparations. After a few minutes, they approached the station.

"Forgive our tardiness," Lucia apologized. "We had to make sure we weren't spotted." She beamed at Isaac. "I do hope your journey goes well. Are you all ready?"

"Yeah," Vin said. "I made sure we brought the essentials, and Raine helped Isaac collect what he needed."

Lucia smiled. "Good. Please send a message if anything goes wrong. You have my number." She nodded toward Raine.

"Of course, milady." Raine bowed.

The sound of the train's engine began to roar. "We're ready when you are," the conductor called to them.

"Looks like this is it," Vin said.

"Keep your wits about you, Astor," Bart told him. "You're our best infiltrator. I don't want you winding up missing—or worse."

"Haha, I'll be fine, boss."

"Let's go." Raine nudged Isaac.

"Wait!" Lucia stepped forward. "I, uhh ..."

"What's wrong?" Isaac asked.

"It's just ... please be careful." She fidgeted as she lightly played with her long, black hair. "I do hope to see you come back safely."

"We'll be okay," he comforted her. "Will *you* be okay?"

She looked up at him with a smile. "Do not worry, just come back to me."

"I promise we'll make it back just fine."

"I really hope so." Lucia hesitantly made a motion as if to hug Isaac but meekly held back.

"Are you sure you're okay?" Isaac looked concerned.

She seemed slightly lost in thought. "Yes, don't let me hold you up. This mission is important." She waved them off. "I wish you success."

"Don't worry, Your Majesty, I'll keep him out of trouble," Raine said as she pulled Isaac's arm. "Let's go."

The three entered the train.

Lucia watched with worry in her eyes as the train departed. "It's up to you now, Isaac ..." she whispered to herself.

On the train, the three sat close to each other. They were the only ones aboard, aside from the conductors.

"So, Isaac ..." Raine eyeballed him suspiciously. "You gonna explain what the hell that was back there?"

"Huh?" He looked at her in confusion. "What are you talking about?"

"Don't play dumb." Her voice was calm, but her eyes told a different story. "Don't think I didn't catch that exchange between you and Her Majesty just a moment ago."

"Huh?" Now he was really confused. "What exchange? She was just saying goodbye."

"Hold up!" Vin grinned at them. "Is there something going on between you and the queen now?"

"What?" Isaac gave them a wry look. "How did you come to that conclusion?"

"I saw how she was acting toward you." Raine narrowed her eyes. "I don't ever see her act that way toward people except her family members."

"There's nothing going on!" he pleaded. "Why do you care, anyway?"

"I'm her personal guard, Isaac," she explained with a devilish grin. "It's my duty to make sure she's well taken care of and protect her from potential threats."

"I'm not a threat!"

"Sounds like someone's jealous!" Vin mused.

"As if!" She shot him a piercing stare. "The queen is like a little sister to me. I am very protective of her, especially when it comes to men."

"There's nothing between us, I swear!" Isaac explained desperately. "I'm not even from this world, and I barely even know her! How could I already be having a 'thing' with her?"

"Uh huh." She continued to stare at him suspiciously. "If you say so, but I'll be keeping a close eye on you."

"Oh ... kay ..." He sat there like a child after being lectured, and he didn't even know what he'd done.

The train continued along until they eventually passed the border out of Adamas. The night grew late as the lone train rolled along its rails. The grasslands and small houses lined the countryside.

"I think we're good," Vin told them as he watched from his window as the border to Adamas grew more and more distant.

"I guess this is goodbye for a while." Raine stared out her window thoughtfully. "Who knows how long we'll be gone?"

"I'm guessing you guys don't really leave the city often?" Isaac asked.

"I actually leave quite often for work," Vin told him. "But it's usually for only a week, maybe two."

"I'm always at Her Majesty's side, so I rarely leave," Raine explained. "And besides, this is a unique mission, and we don't have much information to go on, so this could take a while."

"Adventure awaits, eh?" Isaac leaned back in his chair.

They sat in silence for a while before Raine turned to him.

"Isaac ..." She looked at him curiously. "What's your world like?"

He scratched his head. "Well, it's similar to this one. Everyone knows English, so that's a plus."

"What's English?" she inquired.

"The ... language?"

"Oh, you mean Jadîm?" she corrected him. "The language we are speaking now?"

"Uhh, suuuure."

"That is quite fascinating now that I think about it." She nodded thoughtfully. "We're able to communicate with the same language. What are the odds of that?"

"I think it's convenient," Vin pointed out. "It sure saves you from having to learn an alien language."

"I don't even know how it's possible." Isaac shrugged. "There's still so much I don't know."

"Are there any other similarities?" She leaned toward him with interest.

"Well, the world is kind of the same. Trees, towns, the people. But there's no aura or magic whatsoever."

"How does a world function without aural energy?" Vin frowned. "We'd be screwed if we didn't have this power."

Isaac spent the next little while explaining Earth and the differences between the worlds that he'd noticed. They both listened earnestly, especially Raine who seemed rather excited to hear all about this other world.

"This is actually really fascinating," Raine said excitedly. "I mean, we always knew there had to be other life out there, but now here we are with you."

"Aren't you two worried or something?" Isaac said. "I mean, you guys just seem totally okay with it."

"Well ..." Raine started, "we've seen weird things happen before, so something like this isn't that strange."

"Yeah, but those demons during the invasion," Vin said thoughtfully. "Those were quite a surprise."

"That doesn't happen very often?" Isaac asked.

"Not really. It does every now and then, maybe once a year, but it's like one or two demons. Not a horde."

"This attack is just more reason to believe your appearance is a sign," Raine said to Isaac.

"For what?" he asked.

"Darkness," she explained. "There are forces in this world that seek to destroy it."

"The same darkness you sensed in me?" Isaac asked.

She frowned. "I'm not sure, but there's no mistaking you're the guardian."

"So, what exactly is a guardian?"

"To put it simply," she began, "they are heroes of legend that appeared in times of need. Their power was above all others, and they were able to smite the darkness that threatened our world."

Isaac thought for a moment. "Wait, if they could destroy darkness, then why does it continue to come back?"

"Because there will always be evil people out there who desire power, and they will seek any lengths to obtain it."

"So, the demons we saw were a portion of that dark power?"

"That's right." She nodded. "They were summoned from the abyss by evil cultists that serve a master. We thought they were after Her Majesty, but really, they were after the artifact."

"What's so important about this artifact?"

"It's said to house the power of the first queen of Adamas," Raine explained. "She was the first of Queen Lucia's bloodline, and apparently a powerful seer."

Isaac scratched his head as he listened, trying to understand.

"That's why our first stop is to the Architectural Lab in Rial. That's where a modern-day seer is. She may be able to give us insight as to the motives of our enemy and also about you."

"About me?" He frowned.

"Yes." She nodded. "We still need to learn why someone from another world would appear, especially when these horrible attacks are going on."

Something about me? Whatever, Isaac thought, *I just want to know how I got here.*

A few hours later, the train pulled into the Rial station. The three got off and headed into town.

"The lab is near the outskirts, just a short walk from the town here," Raine said.

"I'm just glad we were able to make it outside of Adamas' walls." Vin sighed.

The sun was starting to come up, peeking over the countryside as birds chirped and a warm breeze blew across the grass.

"I'm glad I took that nap on the train," Isaac said. "It's already morning."

"For sure." Vin yawned.

They found themselves in a small town with modest houses lining a paved road. After a brief walk, the three found themselves at the entrance to a mountain. Knocking on the door, a man covered in dust appeared.

"To whom do I make acquaintances with?" he asked, but upon seeing Raine, he beamed at her. "Madam Raine! What brings you here?"

"Well," she explained, "we need to see Orna. It's urgent."

"Of course, come in, come in!" The man motioned them inside. They walked down a long, winding corridor with glowing crystal reflecting off the brown walls. They eventually came out into an open chamber. Looking around, Isaac saw all sorts of pictures and crystals stuck into the walls as well as charts. It looked like a lot of history was here, which didn't interest him in the slightest.

"Orna is currently in her lab, this way." The man guided them. Eventually they entered a room filled with all sorts of books and testing equipment.

"Hello, Orna. It's good to see you again," Raine said politely to an older woman who was engrossed in a large tome.

Looking up from the book, the woman smiled deeply. "Raine! My word, it's been a while!" She hurried over to them. "How have you been?"

Raine smiled. "I've been good. Kept up on my studies just like I promised."

"That's good to hear, dear. Who are your companions?"

Raine motioned to Isaac and Vin. "This is Vin Astor."

Orna nodded to him. "One of Bart's operatives, I believe?"

"How did you know?" Vin looked at her in surprise. "Whoa, did you read my future or something?"

"The Queen Lucia told me about you." Orna laughed. "And I'm guessing this must be Isaac." She smiled at him.

"Oh, Her Majesty contacted you?" Raine looked at her curiously.

"Indeed, she did." Orna smiled at them. "It would seem you all have undertaken an interesting quest."

"We're trying to reclaim the queen's artifact that was stolen a few days ago," Raine explained. "We were hoping you could help us."

"Why, of course!" Orna told them cheerfully. "The queen has already asked me to assist you, although I am quite curious about him." She pointed to Isaac.

"What do you mean?" Raine asked.

"Well, I'm told he's not from around here, and I wonder why the queen would ask him to go on such an important mission."

"Well, he's from another world," she whispered into Orna's ear.

"What!?" Orna exclaimed. "For real?" She came closer to Isaac and looked him up and down. "How interesting."

"Is something wrong?" Isaac asked.

"Oh no, heavens, it's quite the opposite," Orna said excitedly. "If this information about you is true, it would mean you have no destiny here on Terra."

"What does that mean?" Raine frowned curiously.

"It would mean this boy's fate is blank. Anything could happen for him!"

"Is that good or bad?"

Orna thought about this question. "Hmm ... well, that would be up to him." She paused as her eyes lit up. "No way ..." She shifted excitedly. "Are you, perhaps, a guardian?"

Raine chuckled. "Always the clever one, Orna. Yes, he is."

Orna did a little hop-skip. "How exciting! Please, I must show you the murals!" She grabbed Isaac's hand and pulled him out of the room.

"Whaaa—" He had no time to react as he was dragged out into the corridor and up a flight of stairs.

The four of them were now in a grand hall where many people were studying giant, stone murals.

"This is the hall of The First," Orna explained. "Here, The First herself predicted several events throughout our history."

Oh boy, more history, Isaac thought. They were now standing in front of seven giant, stone slabs.

"Here we can see what transpired since the downfall," Orna went on. "Let's look at the first mural." She led them over to the first stone slab that had a picture of a city brimming with light. Over the city was a woman with long, black hair, her hands outstretched like a mother protecting a child. The slab was lit up with magic as prisms of light danced around it.

"This was during the time of prosperity, where the world was basked in light," she explained. "It was said the woman in the picture was a goddess, and she spread her light to every corner of the world. With her blessing, the people lived a wonderous life of joy and safety."

"It's written that during this time, the sky was vibrant with beautiful colors," Raine added. "Like the whole world was bathed in radiance."

"If only we could have seen what that was like," Orna mused. "But anyway, on to the next one!" She pointed at the second mural. This one depicted a city burning; the title above it was "Betrayal." It gave off a brilliant glow as the fire seemed to dance around the buildings.

"This was when the great treachery conspired," Orna explained. "The First was able to foresee these events, however, she was unable to prevent them."

"If it weren't for the traitor, we would be in a completely different reality today. One void of darkness," Raine added, looking at Isaac as she spoke.

"During this time, a being stole the goddess's power, and with it, brought in the age of darkness," Orna continued. "It was this betrayal that pushed the world to the brink of destruction."

"But you're all still here." Isaac frowned. "Perhaps this was all false?"

"Not a chance!" Orna shook her head. "The First was able to predict every event. She was always right."

"Which then brings us to the next mural." Raine pointed at the third stone slab.

The slab had a picture of people being enslaved. A sinister man stood over them, shrouded in darkness. The slab glowed with dark energies.

Orna spoke again. "This one was when the betrayer took over the world. He enslaved the people, and even The First was imprisoned. It was as if the end of days were upon us. That is, until ..." She pointed at the fourth slab.

The slab had a picture of five women, however, these ones looked odd. They had animal ears and tails, and they were all on their knees crying over the body of another woman whose eyes were glazed over. This slab, unlike the others, was not lit up.

"This one is where it gets really interesting." Orna put her hand on the slab reverently. "The woman dead in this mural was The First herself. She had predicted her own death."

"What's with those other women kneeling around her?" Isaac asked curiously. "They look weird."

"Those are the kitsuné," Raine told him. "They're fox spirits that reside in a forest near Esmeraldas."

"Yes, the kitsuné were benevolent spirits once," Orna added. "But something happened, and now they remain isolated in their forest where they will kill any and all who enter."

"That place scares the hell out of me." Vin shuddered. "Take my advice, dude, stay far away from that place."

"Um, okay." Isaac shrugged. "I don't even know where it is. But why isn't this mural lit up like the others?"

"That's what's most peculiar!" Orna exclaimed. "This mural never came to pass. The other three came true as predicted, but this one never happened. The First didn't die at this time, and it's unclear exactly how that could be, considering The First could predict the future in its entirety."

"Maybe her predictions actually weren't always accurate," he suggested.

"Oh, but they were!" she interjected. "That's what makes this mural so special! You see, after this, The First began documenting new historical texts about some mysterious warrior that appeared out of nowhere. She was very vague in her words, but someone had changed her fate. The only info I could dig up about our mystery person was that he held the image of the kitsuné, however, he was said to be a being of pure darkness."

"There's really no information about this person," Raine chimed in. "It's as if it was all redacted."

"Exactly." Orna nodded. "It almost seems like The First didn't want anyone to know the details of this person. We don't even know his name, just that he's referred to as Canis Lupus."

She went over to a small table next to the mural and picked up a book. She flipped to a certain page and held it up to them.

"This is the only picture we have of this person."

They looked at the image. It was a crude drawing, but it depicted a silhouette of some kind of beast. He had animal ears and a tail and was shrouded in darkness. But curiously, in his hand he held a giant sword of light.

"It was said that he drove the betrayer out of this world," Orna explained as they stared at the picture. "But see there, in his hand? That's a blade of light! It was believed that he was the first guardian to appear."

"So, what does this have to do with me?" Isaac asked.

"Ever since this mysterious Canis Lupus appeared, guardians have appeared throughout centuries. Each one possessing a weapon of pure light, just like him." She beamed at him. "May I see it?"

Isaac shrugged and then held out his hand. In a flash, he conjured his longsword.

"Incredible!" She looked at the weapon in awe. "I've never seen one in person before!" She looked at the blade with excitement.

"The last recorded guardian was over a century ago," Raine told him.

"Do you know how I got this power?" He looked at them intently.

"No idea!" Orna replied cheerfully. "However, it's been theorized that the goddess of light blesses those with a fragment of her power, which is why guardians are so strong in every aspect."

A goddess blessed me? Isaac thought. *No way!* Even if that were true, it wouldn't make any sense to give him this power.

"What about the other murals?" Vin pointed to the remaining three.

CHAPTER 10: PROPHECIES AND VISIONS

"Oh, yes, of course!" Orna walked over to the fifth mural. "This one is rather grim."

The picture on it was of several dark figures standing together. It gave off an eerie glow, the title, "Reapers." "This was many years after the passing of The First, but her prediction was accurate as the rate of reapers appeared."

"Reapers?" Isaac frowned.

"Dark beings," Raine clarified. "Creatures that can look just like regular people, but they are incredibly powerful."

"Yes," Orna said. "The reapers are so powerful, they can raze a village to the ground singlehandedly. Thankfully, we haven't seen a reaper in ages."

"I may have seen one," Raine said suddenly.

"What?" Orna looked shocked.

"Adamas was attacked, and someone entered the throne room wielding a weapon of darkness."

"Yes, I had heard you were attacked. What happened, dear?"

"I was able to kill him, but he said, 'we'll meet again.' It was strange; it was like the person I saw wasn't exactly the person I was talking to, if that makes sense."

Orna held her chin in thought. "Perhaps this reaper is able to control others directly."

They stood silent for a moment before she continued. "This doesn't bode well. Let us go on, at least." She moved to the next mural. The picture on this one was of demons ravaging the land. The title was "Hell." "This one predicted that demons would appear and harm the planet. You can see by its glow that this also transpired, but what's most curious is the last mural." She pointed to the seventh stone slab, which had no glow or activity on it. The picture was of two figures of darkness facing each other; one had a sword pointed at the other. The title was, "Choice."

"This one isn't lit up," Vin said.

"Yes," Orna replied. "This one is mysterious since it has yet to transpire."

"Since both figures are shrouded in darkness, that must mean they are both reapers," Raine stated. "But why would they be fighting each other?"

"That's the mystery," Orna explained. "Reapers have a unified goal, meaning there would be no reason to cause conflict amongst themselves. However, these creatures seem to have a disagreement. But what's really interesting is the title. *Choice.* What does it mean?"

"Do we have to choose something?" Isaac asked.

Orna looked at him thoughtfully. "We aren't sure. Since the event in this mural has yet to happen, we don't have a solid answer."

"Maybe it's a choice between the two figures?" Raine suggested. "What if we have to find both of these demons and choose between one of them?"

Orna shook her head. "Even if that were the case, either one of these reapers could doom the world."

"So, let's pick the lesser of the two evils," Vin suggested.

"Perhaps The First was trying to tell us something?" Orna scratched her head. "That's where we're stuck."

Choice. Isaac didn't really care about history. It was his least favorite subject. Two dark beings fighting that hadn't happened yet. Whatever.

"Well, it's no current matter," Orna continued. "I'm just glad you could see the murals and understand a little of our world's history." She smiled at Isaac.

"I still don't get it," he replied. "This doesn't tell us anything. If these events already happened, then how are they significant?"

"Well, after studying the ancient texts, we found that The First possessed keen accuracy on the future. However," she motioned toward the final mural, "there is nothing beyond this. Two Reapers in conflict. What happens after?"

"It's believed that the world ends ..." Raine said grimly.

"What?" Isaac frowned at her.

"Some of the events on these murals were hundreds of years apart," Orna continued. "It's possible this final mural is still ages beyond us. We have no way of knowing."

Well, whatever this is, Raine and Orna seem despaired, Isaac thought. "Uhh, maybe it's not as bad as you think. If this so called First made these, there has to be a reason, right?"

"Well, one thing I do know," Orna started, "is that now that you are here, I feel the hope of our world returning."

"Excuse me?"

"My powers as a seer are not near as effective as The First's, but I feel it deep down. Hope follows you, my boy."

Hope? Yeah right, he thought.

"Orna, do you sense something about him?" Raine asked.

"I can't explain it, but when I look upon him, I feel at ease, which is rare for me."

Raine looked at Isaac. *He's nowhere near as powerful as the previous guardians. Can he truly be this important?* she thought.

"What?" Isaac asked her with a tone of doubt.

"I was just thinking. Don't mind me."

"You keep mentioning 'The First,'" Isaac said. "She's the first queen of Adamas?"

"That's right," Raine replied. "The same one I told you about on the train."

"Is that all we know about her?"

"Well, apart from the murals and a few texts, we don't know much about her, now that you ask." Orna frowned in thought. "The biggest mystery is that we don't even know her name. She's only referred to as 'The First,' as if her legacy was written away."

"I'm not big on history, but doesn't that seem odd?" Isaac asked.

"Of course! We have been trying to find her name, or even her bloodline, but there are no texts. The only thing we know is that Lucia Elnur has the traits of said bloodline."

"The queen?"

"Yes, it has been passed down from kin to kin, the legacy of The First, at least that is what we have discovered."

Lucia was a descendant of The First? Isaac didn't know what was really going on, but it must have been important to everyone else.

"Anyway!" Orna said suddenly. "Let's go back to my study. You had questions?"

Back at Orna's study, the four sat at a table riddled with charts and graphs.

"Orna," Raine began, "we're seeking an artifact that was stolen from Adamas recently. We were wondering if you might have any insight as to where it would be taken."

"Would this artifact have anything to do with The First?" Orna asked knowingly.

"Yes, it's the amulet of The First."

"I see. That would explain my feelings as of late," she said thoughtfully. "I am unsure where it will be taken, but what I can tell you is that it is of utmost importance to the fate of our world."

Raine's eyes went wide. "So it's true, then. If that artifact is used, then our world will be destroyed?"

"What? Heavens, no!" Orna exclaimed. "I simply said it was important to fate, not that it would lead to destruction."

"Then what do you mean?"

"It's as if the amulet has been tied to destiny; it's simply a factor and piece of what is to come. There is more brewing than even I can truly decipher." Orna sighed. "All I can feel is that you must make your way to Esmeraldas. There was an attack there not too long ago. I believe what you seek lies there."

"Are you sure? We don't exactly have time to waste on side trips."

"Oh, did you have a place in mind?"

"Well ..." Raine said. "We were thinking of going to the town of Frede next."

Orna shook her head. "There's nothing there for you. I can't explain it, but if you go there, you will find nothing."

"You are certain?"

"Positive! Besides ..." Orna looked at Isaac. "I may not be able to read your destiny, but something tells me you need to go there."

"What? Why me?" Isaac asked.

"I cannot say for sure since you are shrouded in so much mystery, but it may have to do with you being this world's guardian."

"About that ..." Isaac said. "How are you all so sure I am what you think I am?"

"It's your aura," Raine said. "I have the ability to read any-one's aura flow, and you possess every type."

"What's that mean?"

"For instance," she pointed at Vin, "Vin utilizes speed; therefore, his type is yellow."

"Yeppers!" Vin said confidently. "That's why my weapon is yellow." His dagger appeared in his hand, shining its brilliant gold color.

"Your pal, Drake, wields a red axe," Raine continued.

"So, his aura is red?" Isaac asked.

"That's right. And his aura represents his large amount of physical power."

"And yours?"

Raine chuckled as she elegantly swished her blue hair. "Blue, which represents magic."

"And you're saying I possess all three?"

"That's right. Naturally I wouldn't be able to move near as fast as Vin or in many cases even react as quickly, however, he will never be able to use proper magic as I can. And neither of us can have the physical strength someone with a red aura has."

"I see," Isaac replied. "But there must be someone out there who has more than just one, right? I mean, take that Xander guy—he killed that dragon in one blow!"

"Xander is ... different," Raine started. "He has a red aura, but it's so powerful, he has developed some extreme forms of adaptability against the other auras. For instance, he's resistant to magic, and he can even keep up with a yellow aura long enough to overpower them."

"So basically, he's just really good at using his power."

"To sum it up, yes. You, on the other hand, can learn and master any form of power you wish. You just gotta practice." She winked at him.

To possess any power I want? Isaac thought about this. He didn't really want power, yet everyone seemed to think he needed it. "Cool, I guess."

"Damn, I just don't get you sometimes, man." Vin laughed. "Most people would kill to be a guardian, yet you don't seem to really care."

Isaac shrugged. "Don't know what to tell you."

"Anyway ..." Raine said. "We really should get going. I guess it's off to Esmeraldas."

Orna, who had been silently listening, suddenly spoke up. "Be careful," she told them. "I sense there will be terrible danger ahead. Stick close to each other and watch your backs."

"Don't worry, we'll be careful."

"I sense the darkness is a lot closer than we think," Orna added grimly. "A storm is coming, and the balance hangs in the air."

The three fell silent as they left the architectural lab. They made their way along the road toward the town.

"Is this so called 'seer' really a big deal?" Isaac asked suddenly.

Raine shot him an angry look. "Yes, she is. Orna may not be able to predict the exact future, but her premonitions have been precise."

"I'm just saying, she didn't seem to really know anything, except that we need to go to Esmeraldas."

"Do not take her words lightly. She has her vision and her reasons."

Isaac shrugged. "Fine, what's our next stop, then?"

"There." Vin pointed. "That's a flight pad, isn't it?"

"Yep," Raine agreed. "The queen pulled some strings, and we got ourselves a flight over to Dahli."

"We can't just go straight to Esmeraldas?" Isaac asked.

"Unfortunately, no," Raine replied. "We need to walk most of the way. Dahli just happens to be the closest we can get by aircraft. Let's go."

The three made their way to the flight pad.

On the flight over, the three talked about their destination: Esmeraldas. To Isaac's surprise, the main city was atop a massive ancient tree that the mages there tended to and kept strong. Below, around the trunk, were smaller towns where the less wealthy lived. The attack that happened over a month ago was by a cult group that worshiped the demons, and they caused a violent tornado to destroy a portion of the tree's branches, which caused part of the upper city to collapse. There may be a clue as to the motives of this cult group and if they were the ones that planned the raid on

Adamas. Raine said that was probably why Orna guided them in that direction.

"What is this town we are going to?" Isaac asked.

"Dahli. It's a small, quiet village," Raine answered.

"I've been there a few times," Vin added. "Nice folk, but they tend to keep to themselves and don't really like tourists."

As the sylphid approached the town, Isaac could see that it was indeed a fairly small place. The only thing that really stood out from it all was a rather tall tower in the center of the village.

"Prepare for landing," the pilot called as they approached a landing pad.

Stepping out, Raine thanked him, and the three made their way into town.

As they walked through, people gave them weird glances, but as soon as Isaac made eye contact, they would quickly look away.

"You weren't kidding when you said they don't like outsiders," he mused.

"Yeah." Vin chuckled. "They've always been like that. Almost like they're hiding something."

Glancing around, Raine looked at the staring people. "Actually, they really do."

"Maybe they're cautious because of the recent attacks," Vin suggested.

"Possibly ..."

They headed to a nearby shop. "We can get any supplies we need from here before we head out," Raine told them. The three looked at the assortment of goods available, ranging from food to tools. The whole time, the shop keeper stared them down.

"Why do I get the feeling we're being watched too closely?" Vin muttered quietly.

I'm not sure, Raine replied telepathically.

Isaac was waiting outside for the other two as he looked around. People were definitely acting sketchy. Making his way around the small town, he curiously wandered. The small buildings were closely intertwined, and if it weren't for his aural ability of heightened senses, he probably would get lost. He walked out into a large, open area with a fountain in the center.

As Isaac glanced around, an odd sensation came over him. He could hear whispering, but it didn't seem to be coming from the villagers. Locating where the whispers were coming from, he glanced up at the large tower in the center of it all; there seemed to be something familiar about it. He moved closer to the tower and stood at its entrance. Even though the tower was rather large; the door to the entrance was only slightly bigger than a standard door. A sound came from behind the door.

"How dare you ...?" it trailed off.

"What the—" Isaac pressed his ear to the door. That voice had sounded somewhat like himself.

Silence

He hesitated briefly but opened the door and stepped in. On the other side was a dimly lit staircase that spiraled up toward the top of the tower. As he took his first step, the door behind him slammed shut. Looking back, the door was gone.

"The hell?" Isaac said out loud. He felt a chill run down his spine. *This is just like at the tournament*, he thought. He tried to conjure his sword, but nothing happened.

"Shit ..."

Slightly shaking, he slowly made his way up the stairs. *I need to reach out to Raine, maybe she can snap me out of ... whatever this is.*

"You're weak!" the voice echoed around him. "You don't know what suffering is like!" It was Isaac's voice, but it was distorted.

He made it to the top, and now he was peering out at the town, however, the sky was unnaturally dark, and black tendrils reached down, encircling the town. There was no life, and blood dripped from the destroyed buildings, soaking the ground.

This is how it starts.

"I bet they told you that you're worth something," the voice echoed from the sky. "Everybody loves you. What would you know of loneliness?" There was the sudden sound of a crash, as if a building was being crushed.

"Please stop!" Raine's voice echoed out.

The pain.

The fear.

The loneliness.

"Raine!?" Isaac shouted into the dark world. His call was followed by the sound of Raine crying out in pain. "Raine! Where are you? Please answer me!" He stepped out a little farther and looked around the bloodstained town below him, but he couldn't see anyone, just a dark mist and the destroyed village.

"You're hurting me!" Raine's voice echoed around him. "Why ... this isn't you!"

It starts with anger, then leads to hate.

"Raine!" Isaac shouted again. "Who is it? Who's hurting you?" He started to panic. Without his powers, he wouldn't be able to really help her, but hearing her cry out like that ...

The feeling of helplessness driving you insane.

"Wait, lady! You need to stay away from him!" Vin's voice rang out. "It's not safe here!"

Vin ... Isaac looked at the sky, and the tendrils began to lash out. "What is this ...?"

Until eventually you become the very monster you despise.

"Don't do this, Isaac," Raine cried. "Please ... we're friends ..."

What ... Isaac stood there, dumbfounded. *What did she say ...?*

"Shut up!" the distorted voice of Isaac echoed. "I don't care about you! I don't care about this world!"

Isaac slowly started to back away. "Th-this ... what is ..." Tears rolled down his cheeks as everything felt horrifyingly familiar.

"You're not a monster ..." Raine's voice grew distant.

Isaac started to hyperventilate. *This can't be true.*

"It is true," a sinister voice whispered behind him.

He turned around, and standing before him was ... himself. His eyes were solid black, and his skin was the color of obsidian. A dark miasma pulsed from his very being. Isaac froze as he stared at the dark version of himself.

"This world doesn't want you," Dark Isaac said. "They'll get rid of you the moment you fulfill their desires."

"Wh-what?" Isaac said, shaking.

Dark Isaac leered at him. "Teach them a lesson. MAKE THEM SUFFER!" Suddenly he reached out and grabbed Isaac's throat.

"Uhh, can I help you?"

The voice came from right next to Isaac, and he jolted back to reality. "What?" He frantically glanced around and realized he was standing back at the entrance to the tower.

"Are you lost?" A stern-looking man was standing next to him.

Quickly gathering his composure, Isaac replied, "No ... uhh ... I'm fine. What is this tower?"

The man looked suspiciously at him. "This is the Zerzura tower. You have business here?"

Isaac shook his head. "No, I was just curious, never been here before."

"Oh, well, in that case ..." The man seemed to relax a little. "Allow me to explain." He gestured at the tower. "This tower has existed in our village since before we ever came here. It was prophesized that it would guide the fallen to their fate, whatever that means." He chuckled. "What's your name? Are you a tourist or something?"

"I'm Isaac. I guess you could call me a tourist. I don't know much about this place."

"Well, I hope you keep out of trouble while you're here. Lots of shady things going on lately; we're a bit on edge."

"Don't worry, I'm not here for any of that. I'll be careful."

After the man left, Isaac saw Raine and Vin approach.

"There you are," Raine said. "You just ran off all of a sudden."

"Sorry ..." Isaac replied, still a bit hazy from his experience. "I'm glad you're okay."

"What? We're the ones who should be worried." Raine chuckled.

"Right ..." He let out a deep breath. "Hey, isn't that ...?" Isaac pointed at an individual.

Raine followed his gaze, and upon seeing the figure, she walked over to greet him. "Hey there, Xander."

As she approached, Xander smiled. "Raine! What brings you here?"

"Work," she replied. "I see you were able to get out of the castle before the lockdown."

"Yeah, but this is surprising to see you all the way out here." He looked over at Vin and Isaac. "Oh, hey there, Vin and guardian dude."

Guardian dude? This Xander guy sure was full of himself.

"Hey, Xander, have you heard anything since the attack on the capitol?" Raine asked.

"Not really. It's been surprisingly quiet. I was able to sneak away right after the incident in order to watch over this place."

"What's so special here?" Vin scratched his head, glancing around.

"Well, for one, this is my hometown," Xander explained. "But also, there are no fighters here to protect this place, so I'm here to make sure it's safe."

"I see."

"Hey, are you guys heading out? Why don't you stop at my place for a bit? I may know something that might give you a clue."

"Sure," Raine replied. "Any info will definitely help."

The four made their way between a series of small buildings. Even though Dahli was a smaller town, the buildings were so close to each other it was almost like walking through a maze. Eventually they arrived at a modest house.

"Come on in." Xander opened the door and allowed them inside.

Isaac peered around the rather humble abode. There were some couches, a few paintings, but nothing too fancy. After they were all in, Xander closed the door, and a noise came from another room.

"Be mindful of Jax; he tends to not like strangers," Xander said as a dog entered the room. Isaac could tell it was a German shepherd breed, and the dog eyed the three of them cautiously.

"He shouldn't bother you guys as long as you don't provoke him. He tends to get really defensive." As he said this, Jax's eyes fell upon Isaac, and he began to move toward him.

"Jax, be nice!" Xander told him, but the dog continued.

As Jax approached, Isaac knelt down, a big smile on his face. He held his hand out. "Hey there, buddy!"

"Be careful. He bites ..." But to Xander's surprise, Jax started licking Isaac's hand and allowed him to pet him. "That's odd. Jax usually doesn't take a liking to people so quickly."

Raine watched Isaac curiously. "Neither does he." She was mildly shocked to see Isaac smiling so much.

"Aww, he's just a good boy!" Isaac said, scratching Jax's head.

"Anyway, have a seat." Xander motioned to the couches. "Tell me about your mission."

As they talked, Xander explained how he had heard of suspicious characters moving about recently, and all of them seemed to be making their way toward Rubens.

"So, Rubens *is* involved?" Raine pondered.

"We aren't sure yet," Xander replied. "But it seems likely."

"Damn cultists," Vin growled. "We've been keeping tabs on them for a while now, but they just pop up anywhere, it seems."

"So, are you guys chasing them?"

Raine nodded. "Yes, they stole something that we intend to get back."

"Well, with you on the job, I'm sure you'll retrieve it." Xander winked at her.

She chuckled. "Thanks."

Isaac remained silent as he listened to them. He honestly didn't really care about all that was going on. He didn't even fully know why he was on this quest to begin with. But deep down, something pulled at him to follow, albeit unwillingly.

"So, what about you?" Isaac glanced over as Xander asked his question. "Must be tough carrying the mantle of guardian."

He shrugged. "Not really."

"No? I can't imagine having all that stress." Xander chuckled. "But good luck to you."

Whatever, Isaac thought to himself.

"Don't worry, I've been training him well." Raine smirked.

It's as if they're treating me like some kid, Isaac thought irritably.

"Oh, well then, no worries." Xander laughed. "By the way, I should let you know that there have been rumors going on about Vaerun, since it's on the way to Esmeraldas."

"Oh? What about?"

"Apparently there have been some shady things going on over there. Mysterious figures, strange crates going in, but nothing coming out. I've heard from some of the people who've passed through there that the citizens were acting strangely—like they were keeping some kind of secret. Might be worth looking into for a lead."

You guys are also shady, Isaac thought.

"Thanks, we'll check it out. Hopefully it will set us on the right course," Raine said. "You've still got my number, right?"

As they talked, Isaac thought about his vision. What was it? He could feel a sense of dread. He just sat there in thought, silently listening to the others.

After a few more jokes and remarks from the three, it was time to say goodbye.

"Thanks for stopping by. Say hello to the queen for me next time you're back at the castle, and stay safe out there. Things are getting more dangerous as we speak," Xander told them.

"Don't worry," Raine replied. "We'll be fine."

They waved goodbye and headed off.

"Whew. This is gonna be a long hike," Vin said, giving Isaac a slight nudge. "I hope you don't get tired, 'cause I'm not carrying you, haha."

"Back at ya," Isaac said blankly. He still felt like a third wheel.

"We should be okay getting to Vaerun, but we will need to keep our wits about us out there if what Xander said was true." Raine added.

Isaac took a drink from his flask. *This is gonna be a long trip ...*

The woman leaned back. "So, you learned more about Terra from the murals."

"I wasn't really paying attention," Isaac replied.

She smiled and looked at him curiously. "Aww, that hurts my feelings."

"I just don't understand anything that's going on."

"It's quite alright." She grinned. "Having you here is all that matters now."

Isaac stared at her cautiously. "What's that supposed to mean?"

"You still haven't figured it out? Why you're here?"

"Why I'm here? Isn't it to 'save the world' or something?"

She shook her head. "Perhaps. Or maybe it's to realize your truest desires."

"Huh?"

"There must be something you want, more than anything." She looked at him playfully. "If not power, or fame, then what?"

Isaac remained silent.

"Do you even know?"

"What are you getting at?"

She sighed, licking her lips. "If you could have any one thing, would it be her?"

Isaac just stared.

"Hehe, in this reality, you could have her, you know." She smiled mischievously.

"That's not it!" he replied angrily.

"Oh? But my dear, you called out to her." She gestured to herself. "That's why I'm here."

Isaac shook his head. "But I didn't ..." he trailed off. "Did I?"

The woman tapped her fingers. "You can't hide from yourself forever."

"I'm not!"

"This journey is far from over. In the end, only you can face yourself."

Isaac gritted his teeth. "Whatever, I am who I am! I'm tired of others thinking I have to be something else!"

"They aren't the ones who think that," the woman replied. "Be careful of yourself, Isaac. The most dangerous foe we could ever face is the one that lies within."

CHAPTER 11

CONFRONTATION

"Milady? Your Majesty."

The words snapped Lucia back to reality. "Huh?"

"You spaced out there for a moment." Bart stood next to her in the throne room. "Something on your mind?"

"Oh!" She collected herself. "Forgive me, it's nothing." There were a few visitors in the throne room discussing political matters with her. "Let's continue." They chatted for a while before it was time to leave.

"Your Majesty," Bart said. "Is something troubling you?"

"Bart, how many times do I need to ask you? Call me Lucia." She chuckled.

"Sorry, milady, I'll, uhh, try to remember."

"I'm fine. You needn't worry."

Bart frowned. "Well, just take it easy, okay?"

"I will." Lucia smiled at him before leaving. It had only been about a few days since Isaac's group had left, and yet she couldn't help but worry about them. "Maybe I'll message Raine and see how they're doing," she said to herself as she pulled out her phone.

How's your progress? she texted.

Shortly after she got a reply: *We've got a lead out near Vaerun, so we are headed there now.*

She hesitated briefly to send the next message. *How's Isaac?* She held her breath.

A few moments later, Raine responded. *He's okay. We've been doing some training along the way, and he's picked up on these techniques rather well.*

Lucia smiled. *I'm glad,* she replied.

Adamas Castle was recently quiet since the aftermath of the attack had calmed down. Through various efforts, the people were able to get the resources needed to rebuild the damages, and, with the reluctance of the council, Lucia gave aid to the townspeople in need.

"Good day, Your Majesty," the maids said to her with a bow as she passed.

"Good day," Lucia replied. "Thank you for all you do." She looked around at how they kept the place clean. "You have all done a wonderful job. Please, take the rest of the day off." She smiled.

"Milady ..." they began.

"Please," Lucia pressed. "I insist."

The maids bowed. "Oh, thank you, Your Majesty!"

Lucia smiled as they hurried excitedly away. The town had been rattled because of the appearance of demons, and she wanted the people to spend time with their families as much as they could to help ease the shock.

As the days went, she had found herself thinking about the three she'd sent out to reclaim the artifact, but her thoughts always trailed to Isaac. He was hesitant to join their cause, and rightfully so. Lucia had felt terrible for trying to force such a task on him, but she was glad when he finally accepted. She worried about him.

"Good day, Your Majesty."

Lucia encountered Anwir as she made her way down the hall. "Oh, hello, Head Councilman, what brings you here?"

"Just collecting a few files needed for a briefing." He held a bundle of papers in his hand. "Taking the day off?"

"Yes." She nodded. "Thankfully, the rebuilding of our city is going rather well."

"Agreed. We should be back to a hundred percent here shortly," he stated. "By the way, I haven't seen Ms. Beria around lately, is she okay?"

Lucia nodded. "Raine is fine. Because of the attack, she requested a leave of absence. I am unsure of where she went, but she said she needed to take care of personal matters in the city."

"I see," Anwir said, looking thoughtful. "I haven't seen that guardian fellow either."

"I am unsure of where Isaac Wolfe has gone. He participated in the tournament, then after receiving the prize money, he simply left." She tilted her head. "I asked if he would join us, but he simply refused. Kind of odd."

"He did seem like a quiet one. If he really is the guardian, I would have expected him to be more willing to help us."

Lucia just shrugged. "I don't know ..."

"It's not like he seemed all that useful to begin with. Probably best it turned out this way. Well, I've really got to get going. It was good seeing you, milady." He continued down the hall, leaving Lucia by herself.

How dare you? she thought to herself, clenching her fists. *Don't you mock him!*

Lucia made her way to her bedchamber. She had been working nonstop to assist the people of the city, and she was glad to finally relax for a bit. She entered her bathroom and turned on warm water for a bath. As she waited for the water to fill, she poured in some soap and watched as the water produced a layer of foaming bubbles.

She let out a soft sigh as she sank into the relaxing, warm bath and lay her head back against the edge. Her thoughts wandered to the past few days, having to see the painful expressions on those affected by the attack. She shook her head. It was best not to think of that now. She just wanted to relax.

After her bath, Lucia sat at her vanity desk in a robe and slowly brushed her hair. She quietly hummed to herself as she stared back at her reflection. After a while, there was a knock on her door.

She opened it to see that Bart stood outside.

"I was just checking on you, Your Majesty." He smiled. "Are you doing okay?"

"Yes," she replied. "Thank you for checking on me."

CHAPTER 11: CONFRONTATION

"I've got my men all over town now and in the castle. Maybe you should take tomorrow off and rest up."

"Hmm, I might just do that. It's been a while since I got to sleep in." She sighed.

"Just let me know if you need anything. I'm right down the hall."

"I will, thanks."

"Goodnight, milady." Bart turned and left.

Lucia closed the door and got ready for bed. As she pulled her blanket over her, she glanced outside at the setting sun. Her mind wandered to the idea of what Isaac and the others were doing. Where were they at this moment? What were they doing? As she thought about this, she started to feel drowsy, and she soon fell asleep.

"You're really getting the hang of this," Raine said to Isaac as they spent time training in magic. Already, he had learned to make force fields as well as form and throw fireballs under her tutelage.

"You aren't very accurate though," she pointed out.

Being able to form the flame into a sphere was one thing, but to hurl it with accuracy was another.

"Just say when, and I'll toss another stone into the air," Vin said while holding a couple of large rocks.

Isaac's hand had several burns all over, but he continued to make fireballs regardless.

"Throw." As the rock was hurled upward, he readied a fireball. As the rock fell downward, he threw the flame at it, missing the stone by about a meter. "I never was good at baseball ..."

"What's that?" Vin asked.

"It's a sport they play on Earth. Throwing a ball is part of it."

"Let's take a break." Raine walked over to Isaac and took his hand in hers. Using magic, she was able to cool and soothe his burns. "We still have a bit of walking to do before we reach Vaerun. We can play a game on the way to help you practice your forcefield."

The three of them had been hiking since they left Dahli because there was no transportation available between towns.

Thankfully there was a small village where they were able to rest and restock some of their supplies on the way. They brought camping gear to sleep in during the nights, and Isaac was slowly adjusting to the outdoor life.

"How far away do you think we are?"

"Just a few hours," Vin replied. "We've actually made great timing. I'm impressed, Raine."

"Excuse me?" She shot him a harsh look. "You really think I would fall behind?"

"Well, speed users are known for their incredible stamina. I just didn't know how long you could go since you're a mage." He grinned.

"Don't underestimate me, Vin. I've gone on many long hikes before. This is nothing."

"I'm only teasing." He chuckled.

"The thing I'm curious about is how you stay so clean," Isaac said to Raine. "I've been sweating like crazy over here and am in need of a shower most dubiously."

Vin frowned. "Dubiously? Is that even a word?"

Raine laughed. "Misused, but yes, it's a word, haha." She flaunted her shiny, blue hair. "Unlike Vin's glorious stamina, I use my magic to keep myself from sweating."

"You can do that?" Vin looked surprised.

"There's a lot of things I can do." She smirked.

"You'll have to teach me someday," Isaac said. "Sounds really handy."

"Perhaps I will." She winked. "IF you ever learn how to control ice magic."

"That's all it takes?"

"Yep. Ice is probably the most advanced and versatile form of magic you could learn."

"But dangerous to the caster with no experience," he mused.

She nodded approvingly. "At least you've been paying attention."

After their break, the three packed up and continued toward Vaerun. On the way, Raine and Isaac played a game where she threw weak fireballs and Isaac would form force fields to deflect them. Unlike the fireballs, he had better control over creating barriers and eventually was able to easily deflect any of the fire she threw.

"Keep in mind, these are just weak fireballs I'm throwing, so neither of us gets hurt. In a battle, the enemy will use much stronger magic than this. You will need to learn how to create even denser barriers in order to stop enemy attacks," she explained.

A few hours, later they were at the edge of Vaerun, hiding behind a large boulder. The town was surrounded by a large wall, preventing them from seeing inside.

"Hold up," Vin said to them quietly. "Let me scout the area first before we head in."

"If you want to do that, go that way." Raine pointed to the left. "There are a lot of people opposite that direction."

"What can you see?"

One of Raine's many abilities was that of x-ray vision. Using her magic, she could see through nearly any object. "There's only one entrance, which is packed with people. As Xander said, they're moving crates into the town."

"Are they mostly near that entrance then?"

"Yeah, but it doesn't seem like they're doing anything shady. We could probably just walk in. The gates aren't guarded."

"Can't be too careful," Vin said. "I'm gonna scope the place out just to be sure. You two wait here; I work faster alone." He swiftly moved out, leaving the two of them in hiding.

"Is it normal for a small town like this to have a wall around it?" Isaac asked Raine.

"Not really. Walls are either to keep something out or keep something in," she replied. "But seeing inside the town, nothing seems out of the ordinary."

It was starting to get dark when Vin returned.

"Damn, dude, I thought they got you," Isaac said sarcastically.

"Hah hah," Vin replied dramatically. "Well, the place doesn't seem too suspicious, but that's where it gets suspicious."

"What?"

"It's kind of ... too quiet, ya know?"

Raine gave him a thoughtful look. "You think they are purposefully making it look normal as a cover up?"

"I can't say for sure, but it does seem rather off. That's not to say everyone in there is sketchy, but a lot of them seem to be."

"What's the plan, then?" Isaac asked.

"Let's just pretend we're travelers and we need lodging for the night," Vin suggested. "And Raine can keep her magic ears open for any gossip." He grinned.

"You'd be surprised what these 'magic ears' have caught you saying to people back at the castle." Raine gave him a cocky look.

"Ehehe, let's just go, okay" Vin gave a nervous chuckle as he stood.

They approached the gates where a few men were finishing up with the delivery of crates.

"Let me handle this," Raine whispered. She walked up to one of them. "Hi, are there any inns here we can stay at?" she asked politely.

The man looked at her wide-eyed. "Why yes, ma'am, there are." Some of the other men turned their attention toward her too, their mouths slightly agape. "That inn over there has availability." He pointed at a building farther inside the town that had three stories. "These guys with you?" He motioned to Isaac and Vin.

"Why yes, they are. Will that be a problem?"

"Oh no. I was just curious," the man said with slight hesitation in his voice. "Please, come right in." He gestured for them to enter.

"Thank you, that is very kind." Raine bowed slightly.

After they made it a little way down the main road into town, Vin gave a thoughtful hum. "That guy definitely seemed out of place."

"Yeah, I wonder what they're up to," Raine replied.

"We should search for clues."

"Let's not do anything that stands out, though," Isaac added.

"Exactly, so do not conjure your weapon," Raine told him.

"Right ..." A blade of light would definitely stand out.

The people in town seemed rather normal, for the most part. Isaac looked around and noticed the place didn't seem too off at first glance, but every now and then, someone would look at him only to quickly look away.

"Let's check in at the inn first, then have a look around," Raine suggested.

The woman at the front desk gave them a joyful smile. "Oh hello! Will you be staying here?"

"Yes, how much is it?"

As Raine talked with the woman, Vin scanned the room, looking over the building's detail.

"Thank you very much!" the woman said as she handed Raine the key.

When they got to their room, Raine spoke up. "Did you notice that?"

"What?" Isaac replied.

"She didn't even ask how many nights we were staying. She just handed us the key. Also, her facial features and body language were way off. She's hiding something."

Another ability Raine possessed was the intuitive nature of reading people. She could tell a person's intentions by simply watching their behavior. A useful skill for the right hand of the queen.

"Did you also notice the quality of this building?" Vin added. "It looks way more expensive than anything outside."

"I think our sketch-o-meter just went up," Isaac said.

"There's still a little light out. I doubt anyone would try anything this early. They would wait for us to go to sleep," said Vin.

"Good. That means I have time to shower!"

Later, the three decided to split up and explore the town for intel. Isaac, of course, headed to the local bar for a drink.

"What'll ya have?" the bartender asked.

"Whiskey with ice."

"That'll be five aurums."

Isaac handed over the money, and the bartender brought him his drink. He took a sip and scanned the place. There were only a few people there, and they didn't seem too out of the ordinary.

"So, what brings you here, stranger?" the bartender asked.

Isaac took another sip. "Just passing through."

"Oh? Where're ya headed?"

He gave the bartender a blank stare. "That's none of your business."

"Whoa, easy fella, I don't mean no harm." The bartender nervously held up his hands.

"Kinda rude to be prying, don'tcha think?" He took a large sip from his glass.

"My apologies." The bartender turned around and began to nervously wash glasses.

As Isaac finished his drink, the bartender set a new glass in front of him.

"Here, sir. Accept this with my apologies." He bowed to him. "It's on the house."

Isaac stared at the glass, then back at the bartender. "No thanks. I'm not a charity." He drank the last from his current cup, set it down, then headed toward the door. The bartender just stood there, baffled.

From the moment he had entered the bar, Isaac had been keeping an eye on everyone in it, especially the bartender; and what the bartender didn't know was that he'd seen him put some kind of substance in that "free" drink.

As he stepped outside, Isaac noticed an old man subtly trying to get his attention. He casually walked over to him. "What?" These people were definitely hiding something.

"You shouldn't be here." The old man seemed nervous.

"What are you talking about?"

"You and your friends need to leave this place." The old man glanced around.

"Why, what's going on?"

"I can't tell you more than that. They have eyes everywhere."

Isaac frowned. "Who? If you can tell me more, maybe we can help."

The old man lowered his voice. "Look, what you see above is just a cover up. The real problems are below." He glanced around some more. "They take people to the red house, and they aren't seen again. Please, leave before they get you too."

CHAPTER 11: CONFRONTATION

Without turning his head, Isaac used his magic to see behind himself, and he noticed someone had stopped to eavesdrop on their conversation. The old man seemed to notice too.

"Oh my god!" Isaac said angrily, making sure the passerby could hear. "Fine! Take the damn money!" He quickly drew some aurums from his pocket and thrusted them into the old man's hands. "Just please leave me alone! Shit!"

The old man seemed confused at first but quickly realized what Isaac was doing. "Oh, thank you, sir. I'm terribly sorry to have bothered you." He bowed dramatically.

Turning sharply, Isaac walked off with an angry look on his face. "Damn beggars! The sooner we leave this place, the better!" he shouted. People nearby looked at him curiously. As he pretended to stomp off, the eavesdropper turned and followed him. Isaac dropped his speed to allow the individual to catch up.

"Is something the matter?" The man approached him.

Isaac stopped and angrily stared at him. "Oh, dear god, not another one!"

"Excuse me?"

"I'm getting sick of you people begging for money. Look, I gave the last of what I can spare to the previous guy." Isaac waved his hand toward the man. "So, screw off, will ya? I'm busy!" He turned and continued on. The man quickly followed next to him.

"Easy there, guy, I'm not here to ask you for money." He gave an obviously fake smile.

"Then what the hell do you want?"

"I haven't seen you around here, are you new?"

Isaac stopped. "You're really nosey for a beggar. Just leave me alone, will ya?" He glared at the man.

"Beggar? Oh, heavens no, I'm not—" But before he could finish, Isaac walked away.

"Stop following me, or we're gonna have problems." He quickly made distance between himself and the shady character. He walked down the main road heading toward the inn. Upon entering, Isaac gave the hostess a brief smile and a nod.

"Turning in for the night?" she asked.

"Yeah," he replied. "People out there are being weird, and I'm tired."

She smiled disingenuously at him. "Well, it's safe here, have a good rest."

He headed up the stairs to their room. The others hadn't returned yet, but that wasn't Isaac's agenda. Without hesitation, he walked over to the window, opened it, and jumped out, landing silently on the ground below. Using telekinesis, he quietly closed the window.

While crouched, he swiftly made his way to a discreet spot away from prying eyes. Sitting down, he waited, and as predicted, eventually Raine appeared before him.

"Was waiting for you." He smiled at her.

"I noticed." She crouched next to him. "What was that all about?"

"I got a lead."

She looked at him, surprised. "You did?"

"Yeah, we're looking for a red house. Apparently, people are taken there and never come back. Also, the bartender attempted to spike my drink."

"Of course." She shook her head. "You *would* go to the bar."

"Where's Vin?"

She motioned behind her. "I gave him the signal, and he's circling around to us so he doesn't get spotted."

Isaac glanced around. "We should be safe here. Let's wait for him, then decide what to do."

A few minutes later, Vin joined them. "What's the info?"

"Looking for a red house."

"I may have seen one earlier near the south part of town." Vin pointed in the direction of the bar.

"Let's investigate," Raine said. "But stay close. My chameleon spell doesn't go very far. And if we move too fast, someone might notice the shift in the air around us." Being able to distort their very surroundings was a feat very few could pull off. Thankfully Raine was an adept mage and could handle the illusion well.

They made their way between the buildings and the outer wall that surrounded the town, stopping every now and then to allow people to walk by without alerting them of their presence. As they approached the location Vin had pointed out, they saw a discreet red building at the south part of town. It was set aside from the main hub. The building looked old and run down, but there was something about it. It had to be the place the old man had mentioned.

"What's the plan?" Isaac asked.

"One moment," Raine replied as she scanned the area. "There are a couple of people near the building. Probably guards."

"Should we wait until later?" Vin asked.

"Well, when we left the inn, I noticed some people were heading in that direction. Most likely to get Isaac."

"That's creepy," Isaac said.

"If they were going there, then they should know by now that he's missing," she explained. "I think waiting would only rouse more suspicion, and they may place more guards in this area."

Vin grinned. "So let's quietly bust on in, then."

"It seems we have no choice. You two take out the guards, I'll cover you from the shadows," Raine instructed. She waved her hand, and the air around her distorted until she was nearly invisible.

"Just you an' me," Vin said, holding out his fist.

Isaac glanced at him and extended his own fist in a fist bump. "Let's clean house."

The two split up and circled around the building, keeping an eye on each other's position.

"Two guards around that corner to your left, Vin," Raine whispered over the group's radio earpieces they all had on.

Vin swiftly and silently moved to the wall and peeked around the corner. Sure enough, there were two men casually sitting in chairs around a dirty table playing some kind of card game. Isaac quickly moved in on the other side and nodded to Vin, who pulled out a glove from his pouch. It gave off a slight crackle of electricity.

They both quickly moved in, and Isaac was briefly noticed, but it was too late. He grabbed his victim by the neck and sent a magical jolt of lightning through the man, and he crumbled to the ground. Vin did the same with his electric glove. The two dragged the bodies out of sight into the taller brush.

"You gotta be quieter than that," Vin whispered as they regrouped.

Isaac rolled his eyes but stayed silent. They inched around the building toward the front door when Raine spoke up over the radio.

"Hold up," she warned. "There's someone else, but he may have spotted you."

Vin glanced at Isaac in confusion.

"He seems to be heading for the front door as well, but from the opposite direction. Strange, I didn't see him until now. Be cautious."

The two carefully approached the corner of the building, rounding toward the front, then paused.

"He's near the opposite corner, but he stopped. I think he knows you're there."

Vin held up three fingers to Isaac and motioned to go. Isaac readied himself, and after three seconds, Vin darted out and conjured his bow. Isaac rounded behind him and held his hands up with lightning crackling in his palms. On the opposite side stood a lone figure, a blue katana in one hand, and several shuriken in the other.

"Drop it!" Vin commanded.

"You first," the man retorted.

The three stared at each other defiantly.

"I would do as he says." Raine appeared behind the man, her hands engulfed in electricity.

"You guys aren't from around here," the man said.

"No shit," replied Vin.

The man dropped his stance, and his blade dissipated. "Neither am I."

Vin lowered his weapon. "So, who are you?"

"You tell me first," the man ordered as he looked at Vin, then Isaac, his eyes narrowing. "Wait a moment, I know you."

Isaac frowned. "Funny, I was just thinking the same thing."

"Who is he then?" Raine asked cautiously.

"Can't put my finger on it, but you definitely seem familiar," Isaac said.

"From the tournament," the man explained. "That's right, you were in the finals. You're that so-called guardian." He looked at Vin. "Now that I think about it, you were his teammate."

Vin looked at the man thoughtfully. "Can't say I remember you, though."

"Wait a minute ..." Isaac began. "The first round. You were the one who competed in a maze."

"That's right," the man replied. "The name's Kaito Nishimura."

"Isaac Wolfe."

"I'm Vin, and that's Raine," Vin acknowledged. "What are you doing here?"

Kaito shook his head. "I could ask you the same. My reasons are my own, but I assume you're here about the strange things going on?"

"That's right," Raine said. "We are investigating the possible cause of the attack on Adamas, which I'm sure you are aware of."

"Of course. I helped to subdue the demons during the attack."

"Well, then, I guess that makes us allies." Vin grinned at him. "We should work together to figure out what's going on here."

Kaito stayed silent, only staring at them.

"Unless you'd rather go it alone."

"I work best alone." He looked back at Raine. "But if you want to help me, then I won't object; that is, as long as you stay out of my way."

"Do you know what's going on here?" Isaac asked.

"Haven't you heard? People have been going missing when they enter this town. My investigation has led me to this location." Kaito pointed at the door to the red house. "I assume you all came to the same conclusion."

"Yeah." Vin shrugged. "But we don't know what's in there."

"Give me a moment." Raine began to scan the building. "Interesting. This building is a decoy. The real place we are looking for is underground. There's a service elevator that can lead us down from inside, but it's hidden."

"Not hidden for you." Vin winked. "Let's head inside and go from there."

The four of them stepped inside and looked around. The rooms were dark, and even though Raine and Isaac could create light with their magic, they refrained from doing so to not attract attention from the outside.

"This sucks," Vin grumbled. "You guys are lucky to be able to have night vision with your magic. Too bad me an' Kaito are stuck following you two."

"Speak for yourself," Kaito responded as he confidently navigated the room.

"What? Oh, right, you have a blue weapon ..." Vin said dejectedly.

"Just follow the sound of my lovely voice," Raine said mischievously.

As he did, Vin tripped on something and ended up falling on his face. "Ow! Damn you!"

She giggled.

"Stop it, you guys," Isaac said. "We're gonna get caught."

"Oh shush," Raine retorted. "There's no one around to hear us, just the two guys you both knocked out."

Kaito ignored them and instead checked out the room. "Where's this secret elevator you mentioned?"

"It's over here." Raine entered a side room and made her way to a wall between two shelves. "It looks like the electrical cables run to here." She put her hand on an ornament sitting on one of the shelves. She pulled, and the wall opened, revealing a secret, lit up room.

"How cliché," Isaac muttered as the four entered.

Raine pressed one of the buttons inside the room, and the doors closed. "Down we go."

The elevator descended as the four stood together.

"So why did you join the tournament?" Isaac asked Kaito.

"I was hunting someone, a man named Magnus," he explained. "He was at Adamas during the attack, and afterward, I tracked him here."

"So, this place is connected to the attack," Raine said.

"I don't know about that, but what I seek should be here," Kaito said as the elevator came to a stop.

"Be ready for anything," Vin said.

The doors opened, and the four stepped out into a hallway more advanced than anything on the surface.

"Figured as much," Isaac said as he glanced around. The facility they now stood in looked like some kind of research lab. "Which way do we go?"

"I can only see so far down here," Raine said. "The place is filled with aural power."

"Let's just pick a direction and go. But stay on guard," Vin said, and they agreed on a path.

The hallway had some twists and turns to it, and there were several rooms which Raine verified to be mostly empty.

"I hope we don't get lost," Vin said. "This place is like a maze."

"I think we are heading in the right direction," Raine said. "Well, probably the right one. The aural density is getting stronger the farther in we go."

As they moved, Kaito checked every room they passed, never missing a single one.

"There's nothing in those rooms, you know," Raine told him.

"You can never be too sure," he replied.

Eventually they found themselves in an open, bay-like area that had large boxes and containers scattered about.

"Whoa!" Vin looked around. "This place is huge!"

"Watch out!" Raine grabbed Vin and pulled him back against the wall. "There's cameras all over the place." The four ducked behind some containers out of sight.

"This place is crawling with people." Kaito motioned to people in lab coats wandering the bay. "We need to be extra careful not to get spotted."

"Let's split up," Vin suggested.

"Hmm, the less we move as a group, the least likely we are to be seen," Raine suggested.

"Exactly. So how should we do this?"

"I'll go it alone from here," Kaito said. "I work easier from the shadows."

"Hold on, we don't know what's in this place yet. We should pair up so our backs are covered," Raine told him.

Kaito eyed them briefly before speaking. "Fine, but don't slow me down."

"If we can find the security room, we should be able to shut down the cameras and disable any alarms," Vin said. "Since I'm pretty decent at hacking, I'll look for that."

"And I'll be looking further into this place to see what these people are up to," Kaito said.

"I'll go with Vin then," Raine told them. "Isaac can go with you."

"Keep your comms on," Vin said. "If anything happens, let us know."

"Right," Isaac agreed.

"Let's go." Kaito started moving in the opposite direction of them.

"He doesn't waste time. Good luck, Isaac." Raine told him.

The four split up, and Isaac found himself chasing after Kaito. They made their way around the edge of the bay, hiding behind any crate or piece of equipment they could, making sure to avoid any cameras and people. They paused every so often to wait for a passerby.

Kaito came to a stop and pointed at the sign above a doorway. "That looks promising." The sign read "Weapons Research & Development." "But there are too many people near the door. We would be spotted."

Isaac glanced around at the equipment nearby. "Maybe we can cause a distraction."

"Let's pull the pins out of that crane." Kaito pointed at a vehicle with a cable line attached to it. On the cable was attached some kind of box. "We only need to undo one side to make it look like an accident."

"Let me try," Isaac said as he focused on one of the four pins holding the crate to the cable. Using his magic, he held his hand out and attempted to pull the pin with telekinesis, but the pin was stuck tight. Using all of his might, he jerked at the pin sharply, and just like that, it shot right out, causing the crate to dangle lopsidedly in the air.

"Good, that seems to have caught their attention." Kaito watched as the people nearby looked up in shock as they saw the crate swaying dangerously in the air. They ran to the crane, some shouting orders.

"What the hell!?"

"Quick, lower the cargo."

"Where do we put it?"

During the confusion, the two slipped through the door completely unnoticed.

"That was easier than anticipated," Isaac commented.

"Of course. They wouldn't expect anyone to discover their secret down here, so the thought of an intruder wouldn't be on their minds," Kaito mentioned. "As far as they're concerned, the people above are clueless."

Inside this new area was a bunch of testing equipment and machines. There were two other doors, one labeled "Assembly" and the other "Schematics."

"Let's check this way." Kaito made his way toward the assembly door. "I want to see what they are making down here."

They entered the door and were greeted by a few people.

"Who are you!?" they started but were cut off as Isaac and Kaito quickly dispatched them. Hiding their bodies, they surveyed the room.

"What the hell?" Kaito went over to one of the monitors. "This doesn't look like normal machine testing." He skimmed through some of the charts, and it was obvious these people were building something, but the design was peculiar. "They're using a prototype power source to build some kind of weapon."

"What kind of weapon?" Isaac asked.

"It doesn't say, but I have a bad feeling about this prototype power source. It doesn't look right." He moved away from the monitor. "Let's continue."

They made their way through the rooms, careful to take out anyone that might sound an alarm. The rooms held various machines and computers that seemed to be used for testing mechanical parts and weapon systems. A holographic projection showed what looked to be an arm with a cannon attached to it.

Isaac glanced at one of the monitors next to the projection. "It says this device utilizes the aura from the prototype to discharge energy at a rapid acceleration. However, due to the nature of the spent aura, a renewable resource must be used."

"A self-sustaining powercell? That's simply not possible," Kaito said. "Energy cells have to be recharged periodically when spent."

"Maybe that's what they're researching down here." Isaac shrugged.

The two continued farther into the underground lab, not knowing the horror that awaited.

Raine and Vin made their way through the bay rather easily due to Raine's chameleon magic. They were able to locate the security room and had to double back a short way to reach it.

"I hope those two are okay," Vin said. "We barely know anything about that Kaito guy."

"Maybe it was a bad idea to send Isaac alone with him," Raine added.

"Doubtful. If I know Isaac, he's the most suspicious of all of us."

They soon found themselves standing outside their target location.

"This room will be packed; you ready?" Vin conjured his bow.

"Ready." Raine held up her hands.

The two swiftly barged into the room. There were several guards sitting at various desks and monitors.

"What the—" The nearest guard started to rise but was struck down with an arrow. Others were a little slow to realize what was going on, and each one was hit with a bolt of lightning. Vin bounded up and used his electric glove to force another to the ground.

"Whew, was that all of 'em?" Raine glanced around.

"That was too easy," Vin said in satisfaction.

"Hurry up and disable the security. I'll keep watch."

Vin hopped onto a chair and began going through one of the computers. "This might be easier than I thought; they're logged in with admin credentials." He chuckled to himself as he clicked away at the keyboard. "Aww, someone sent this poor guy an email about their puppy."

"Quit fooling around."

"I know, I know!" A few moments later, he located the security software. "Bingo!" A few clicks here and there and ... "Done! Security is showing offline."

Raine poked her head outside and looked at the cameras. All the lights on them had turned from green to red. "Good job. Hey, Isaac, security is.down," she said over the radio.

"Nice, that should make things easier," Isaac replied over her earpiece.

"We still need to be cautious; don't go overboard."

"Right."

Raine looked over at Vin. "Let's go, we're done here."

The area that Isaac and Kaito had entered took a drastic change of scenery. There were large machines with parts moving along like an assembly line.

"Is that an arm?" Isaac watched as a giant, metal arm floated across the conveyor.

"These must be where they put the weapon together, but the parts we see look to be older models," Kaito said.

The following parts seen looked to be a torso, then a head.

"Are they building some kind of monster?" Isaac speculated.

"Who knows?" Kaito pressed on.

They exited the assembly area and found themselves in front of a door titled "Specimens."

"This has to be it." Kaito pushed the door open and entered.

Inside, a grim feeling settled over them. They looked out over a large area.

"What. The. F—" Isaac started. Down below them were several cages, and inside them were people.

"This must be where the missing people are brought," Kaito said nervously. "Let's get down there."

"Hold up." Isaac grabbed Kaito's arm. "There's someone down there."

Below them was a sinister-looking man that stood out from the rest. He had long, dark hair and his skin had a gray tint to it.

"Oh my god. That's him," Kaito said with fury in his eyes. "That's Magnus."

The man was with a few people wearing lab coats, and they were going from cage to cage.

"I want a full inventory on them. We need to make sure the right ones are available for the tests," he told them. "No more screw ups. We're already short on samples as it is!" He turned and left the area, leaving the few people behind.

"Now's our chance," Kaito said. He quickly got up and moved around the balcony they were on and hurried down the stairs to the cage floor. Without hesitation, he descended upon the researchers, and in seconds had subdued them all.

"Damn, dude, you okay?" Isaac came up shortly after.

Kaito was frantically checking the cells. Inside were people who stared out at them. They were clearly terrified.

"Kaito!" a girl's voice rang out. He quickly ran to the cell and peered at the person inside.

"Yuki!" He held her hand through the cage bars. She was a younger girl, looked to be around fourteen. "I finally found you!"

"We need to get out of here!" the girl cried. "They're doing horrible things to us."

"Don't worry, Yuki, I'm not leaving without you." Kaito inspected the bars. "This metal is too strong to tear apart without causing these people injury. We need to find the controls to open them." He looked at Isaac. "They should be nearby, let's search for them."

They looked around the confinement room and spied two doors opposite each other. "That one must be where Magnus went," Kaito said, pointing at one of the doors. "Let's check the other one first. As much as I would love to gut that bastard, my sister's safety is more important." He took off toward the opposite door, and Isaac followed behind him.

Raine and Vin found their way inside one of the laboratories. They were searching through any info they could find that would give them a clue as to where the artifact was.

CHAPTER 11: CONFRONTATION

"Check that computer terminal," she told him as she rummaged through a few papers on a desk. "I'll check these documents."

Vin began going through the system's files and reports. "Holy shit ..." he said. "They're testing on people down here. It looks like they're trying to harvest aura from people into some kind of energy source." He looked through the data and saw a few videos of test subjects screaming out in pain as some kind of device was used to forcefully rip the aural energies from them. "This is beyond messed up! None of the victims survived." He opened another video which showed of machine being powered up. "They're using the energy to power some kind of weapon. The core used houses all the aura from the victims."

"This is far worse than we anticipated," Raine said. "Let's find whatever info we can and get the hell out of here."

Vin pulled out a data drive from his bag and plugged it into the computer. "I'm going to collect all the data and send it back to HQ." As he skimmed through the info, he paused on a transmission. "Hey, I've got something!" He beckoned Raine over. "It looks like the artifact was originally going to be brought here, but they ordered it to be sent elsewhere."

"Is there any clue to where it would be going?"

"Checking ..." Vin skimmed through a few more messages until he found the location. "Apparently it's being sent to some secret facility near Esmeraldas."

"No shit ..." Raine said curiously. "Looks like Orna's prediction was accurate." She put her hand on her earpiece. "Isaac, are you there?"

"What's up?" came the reply.

"We got what we came for, where are you two at?"

"We found Kaito's sister as well as several others. We're trying to find a way to free them."

"That could get messy," Raine said. "There's too many people here; the chance of everyone escaping is slim."

"Any suggestions?"

She thought for a moment, then Vin spoke up. "What if we caused a distraction to get everyone away from that area?"

"I don't think that will work," she protested. "We would need everyone to leave, but they would keep people behind as guards."

"So we just need to clear a path for the prisoners to escape, right?" Isaac asked.

"Right, but that's easier said than done."

"We still need to find the controls that open the cells. Let me know if you come up with an idea," he added.

"No promises." Raine glanced at Vin. "This is already beyond our scope of the mission."

Isaac and Kaito searched the area, making sure to take out any people they saw. Kaito grabbed one of them and got him to disclose the location of the control room.

"We're almost there," he said as they made their way to the given location. Upon entering the room, they were faced with about five people in lab coats. "Hi there," Kaito said as he and Isaac rushed them. "Keep one of them awake," he told Isaac.

After they knocked out four of the five, Kaito held his blue katana blade to the last one's throat. "You're the lucky guy that is going to tell us how to open those cages."

The guy looked like he would try to resist so Kaito pushed his head into the nearby wall. "You aren't doing yourself any favors by struggling." He pushed his weapon's blade into the man's cheek till a stream of blood ran down his face. "You're running out of time, buddy."

"Okay, okay!" the man squealed. After a moment, Kaito and Isaac knew how to operate the controls.

"Thank you," Kaito said blankly as he hit the man in the back of the head. The man crumbled to the ground.

"Any idea how we can get the rest of them out?" Isaac asked.

"If I had more time, I could come up with a plan, but I'm more concerned about my sister."

Isaac glanced at the equipment in the room. It was a control room, but he noticed there were other devices that worked different machines rather than just opening the cell doors. "Hmm." He walked over to a panel that had a bunch of dials and switches on it labeled "Core Generator."

"I wonder what this does," he said mischievously as he started to twist the dials and flip switches that were all geared toward higher power cycles.

"What are you doing?" Kaito narrowed his eyes.

"I'm not really sure," Isaac replied. He kept flipping switches until the monitor flashed red and displayed the message, "Overheating."

"Stop, do you have any idea what that will do!?"

"I kinda do ..." he continued. "Hopefully it causes people to evacuate the facility."

Kaito gave him a shocked look, then realized his intentions. "So, this is your distraction?"

"Yep, if anything, they'll get a team down here quickly to change the settings back. During the panic, we can quickly escape with the prisoners."

"That's pretty reckless." Kaito frowned. "But it just might work."

"Get ready to run," Isaac said. "Go back to the cell room. I'll open the cages once I've finished here."

"You're crazy, you know that?" Kaito replied as he made for the door. "Don't mess this up."

Isaac chuckled. "Don't worry, I'll meet up with you afterward."

"Raine, come in," Isaac spoke to her over her radio.

The whole facility began to blare a resounding alarm, and evacuation lights activated.

"What the hell did you do!?" she growled at him. "The emergency alarm is going off!"

"I, uhh, kinda caused a reactor meltdown ..." he replied. "We need to get everyone out of here. This distraction may allow that to happen."

"You should have said something beforehand," she said in irritation. "You definitely caused a panic, that's for sure!"

"We don't really have time to think. I'll meet you guys up top."

"You better!"

The emergency alarm was blaring, warning of an imminent meltdown. Isaac quickly hit the switch to open the cages and saw on a monitor that Kaito was taking his sister's hand and leading her out of the containment area. "Gotta go," Isaac said to himself as he turned and ran out of the control room.

"Hey! YOU, there!" Three guards stood in Isaac's way.

"Sup fellas!" He charged them, dodging a sword swipe, and brought his own blade to clash against another attack. He blasted one of them into the wall and swiftly drove his sword through the back of the first attacker. He grabbed the wrist of the second guy as he attempted to attack, and with a twist of his arm, Isaac caused the man to drop his weapon.

"This was a bad idea for you," he said as he surged electricity through his hand and into his opponent.

The third guy recovered and attempted to attack Isaac from behind, but he quickly turned and pushed his electrified opponent into the third, and with a swift bound, Isaac charged up a fireball and pushed it into the men at point blank range, causing them to explode.

"Shit!" Isaac shook his hand as the flames scorched it.

He continued toward the containment area.

"C'mon, everyone, hurry!" Kaito shouted to the prisoners. "We're getting out of here, and there's no time to waste!" He pointed to the exit. "Keep going that way, and you'll eventually find an elevator you can take to the surface!"

The group of prisoners continued running through the hallways. Thanks to the confusion, it was easy, since everyone was focused on evacuating.

"C'mon, Yuki, stick with me." Kaito took his sister's hand and led her in a different direction.

"Where are we going?" she asked.

"I promised that other guy we would meet up," Kaito explained. "There are two others in here that helped me out, so I want to make sure they are also able to escape." They moved down a hallway toward the main bay area. "We'll meet with them over here."

Magnus stood in the command room of the underground facility.

226

CHAPTER 11: CONFRONTATION

"What the hell is going on!?" he shouted.

The other people with him moved about frantically.

"Someone turned the power up on the core generator. It's overheating at an accelerated rate," one person said. "At this rate, the whole facility will be destroyed from the meltdown."

Magnus's eyes flared. "How did someone enter this place without us knowing!? You people were supposed to keep this place a secret!"

"Sir, we got the security cameras back up. It seems someone disabled them, and we found the security team half dead."

"You all got complacent," Magnus growled. "Show me the camera footage!"

On the monitors, he could see Kaito moving down the hallway with his sister. "Hmm, he looks familiar. He must be that boy from Sapphirus. I'll deal with him; you all activate the weapon. This facility is already lost. We cannot lose the core!"

"Yes, sir!" The researchers fumbled with their computer terminals. "Booting up the Behemoth. Running diagnostics. Check."

Magnus stormed out of the room. His goal was to pursue Kaito.

Kaito and Yuki entered the main bay.

"They should be here soon." He looked around.

The area was mostly deserted with everyone having evacuated in a panic.

"Look over there," Yuki said, pointing to a large ramp near the back of the bay. It appeared that the ceiling had opened up, and revealed an alternate route to the surface. Several people were headed that way.

"That must be an emergency exit or a loading dock," Kaito said. "Let's check it out."

They made their way in that direction when someone suddenly jumped in front of them.

"So, you're the rat that caused this chaos." Magnus stood before the two. "Do you have any idea how much research will be lost due to your meddling?"

Kaito moved to shield Yuki. "You kidnapped my sister, you piece of shit! I don't care what you were doing down here, it all comes to an end now!" He conjured his blue katana and took a defensive stance.

A red broadsword appeared in Magnus's hand. "Foolish boy, not only will I kill you, but I will kill your sister as well." He lunged at Kaito, who quickly deflected his attack and pushed Yuki away.

"Run, Yuki!" he shouted at her. Yuki turned and fled as Magnus grabbed a nearby container and hurled it in her direction. Kaito waved his hand, and a blast of wind pushed the heavy container aside, barely missing her as it crashed into the ground. "Asshole! Your fight is with me!" he shouted as he swung his katana, causing an energy blast to fly at Magnus.

Hitting the blast aside, Magnus moved toward Kaito with fury. He swung his blade in an attempt to overpower the magic user. Kaito skillfully dodged the attacks and bounded off a large container, hurling magical shuriken at his opponent. Magnus dodged most of the small blades, but one slashed his arm. He angrily jumped at Kaito as he landed but was not aware that a sigil had been placed by the skillful ninja. The blast threw Magnus away, but he quickly recovered. "Your little tricks don't phase me," he growled as he jumped back to his feet and launched himself at his prey.

"Go!" Kaito shouted to Yuki. "Get to the exit!"

Magnus continued his assault. "Oh, you aren't leaving this place." He pummeled Kaito with several sharp sword swipes.

Kaito did his best to deflect the attacks, but Magnus was far stronger than him, and he soon felt himself being overpowered. Changing his tactics, he quickly ducked and rolled out of the way. Aiming his arm, he shot a grappling cable at Magnus's legs, tangling him. As Magnus went to cut the cable, Kaito followed up with a charged lightning blast.

Magnus ripped the cable from his legs as the lightning hit him in the chest. He growled in anger as the electricity encased him.

Kaito recovered and quickly moved toward Yuki. As he got close, a large container dropped between them, and Yuki cried out as she jumped out of the way.

Kaito turned as Magnus threw his weight into him, knocking him into a nearby crate. He stumbled and fell over the medium-sized crate and looked up in pain as his opponent approached Yuki.

"Ugh, you bastard!" Kaito struggled to stand. How the hell was Magnus able to recover so quickly from his attacks?

"You're very skilled, I'll give you that, but now you get to watch your sister die, just like your mother," Magnus said wickedly. He moved the container he had thrown, revealing the scared girl.

"You leave her alone!" Kaito got to his feet, but it was too late. Magnus raised his blade for the killing blow. "NOOO!"

The red broadsword arched through the air toward her head but was suddenly stopped by a magical force field. Magnus was thrown aside from a blast of wind as Isaac charged into the area. He used his telekinesis and hurled a container at Magnus, who regained his balance just enough to catch the object. Isaac leaped up and kicked the container into him, forcing Magnus to slam against the crane in the large bay. The crane toppled over from the impact and crumbled to the ground, dragging several scaffoldings with it, burying Magnus.

Isaac jumped back and made a force field around himself and the girl. "You okay?" He called over to Kaito.

Kaito quickly composed himself and made his way over to them. "Y-you ..." he stammered in relief. "You saved my sister."

"Sorry I took so long; I didn't know where you guys ran off to," Isaac said. "I let the others know where we are, they should be here soon."

The blaring alarm sounded around them, and a voice echoed over the intercom. "Warning! Core unstable. Evacuate immediately. Detonation imminent!"

"We need to leave. Now!" Kaito said, pointing toward the large ramp. "We can get out through there!"

"Raine, there's an exit through the main bay area. Hurry up!" Isaac said over his earpiece.

"We're almost there," Raine replied. "Just get out."

The three of them moved toward the exit when movement came from the crane.

"Oh, you have got to be joking ..." Isaac said in disbelief as Magnus emerged from the rubble.

"You're going to pay for that," he said as he stepped toward them.

Isaac and Kaito's weapons appeared in their hands.

"What's this?" Magnus said, staring at Isaac. "A guardian? How interesting." He saw the glowing blade of light. "I can add your death to my list."

"Pretty full of himself, isn't he?" Isaac frowned.

"Yuki, stay back!" Kaito said to her as Magnus approached, broadsword in hand.

Isaac stopped Magnus's attack with a force field as Kaito shot a torrent of flame at him. The evil being stepped back, away from the flames, and hurled his sword at Kaito. Using his katana, Kaito parried the incoming weapon, but Magnus jumped at him with his fists. Kaito's parry left him vulnerable, but Isaac grabbed Magnus's arm and tried to bring his sword around to stab him. Magnus quickly threw Isaac aside.

Isaac fell to the ground and quickly rolled to his feet. Kaito took advantage of the brief opening and swung his katana at Magnus, cutting the tough opponent. On the second swipe, though, Magnus's sword re-appeared in his hand, and he blocked the attack.

Kaito jumped away from the red blade and threw a few smoke pellets at Magnus's feet, engulfing him in a thick smoke. Isaac used his telekinesis to hurl a container at the smoky area, slamming Magnus across the bay.

"There!" Isaac shouted. "Run!"

Kaito took the opportunity to grab Yuki, and the three of them hurried to the ramp.

"You won't escape!" Magnus yelled with fury as he violently shoved the container aside and chased after them.

Isaac hurled more crates and containers at Magnus as they made a sprint for the exit, but the evil juggernaut dodged and leaped over them with ease.

"Isaac, keep going!" Raine's voice shouted through the earpiece. "We've got you covered!"

CHAPTER 11: CONFRONTATION

In an instant, Raine and Vin appeared ahead of them. Vin leaped on top of a large container and fired several arrows at Magnus from his bow. The arrows found their mark, one in his shoulder and two in his legs.

Magnus staggered from the pain, fury in his eyes. "You damned rats!"

Raine followed up with a giant, magical fist that slammed Magnus to the back of the bay, but she wasn't finished. She formed a massive fireball above her head and hurled it at the ceiling. It exploded with a thunderous boom, and the cement and metal shattered, raining destruction down on Magnus.

As he was pummeled by debris, Magnus's eyes turned demonic, and his face distorted into a hideous monster. He sneered at them in anger as the ceiling came down, burying him for good.

Isaac and the rest wasted no time in ascending the ramp as they burst out into the morning light. They sprinted across the area, passing the red house along the way as the ground began to shake violently. As they ran into the main part of town, the entire area behind them, where the red house was, erupted for a brief moment and then collapsed into a massive sinkhole.

"Holy shit!" Vin said aloud as the dust cleared.

Raine glared at Isaac. "THAT was a very stupid thing to do!"

He gave her a sideways look. "Oops ..."

Around them, people seemed shaken by the event, and a few men approached.

"What the hell happened here!?" they shouted.

Isaac turned and gave them an angry look. "We took down your hidden lair and killed your boss."

"What!?"

Raine quickly stepped in. "This was unintentional." She shot Isaac a look. "However, you were kidnapping innocent people and locking them up. What do you have to say for yourselves?"

"Th-that ... we were simply ordered to bring people here and ..." one guy began.

"And what?" Raine snapped.

"We don't question them. You don't understand who these people are, what they're capable of!"

"Unacceptable!" She pointed at them. "They were treating people like guinea pigs in there. Experimenting on them!"

"We didn't know."

"Where are the people that escaped?" She watched as they pointed out the group standing a good distance away from them. "I'm gonna make this very clear. You are to stop this nonsense. These people are free to leave. If you do not comply, I will bring the entirety of the royal guard of Adamas down upon this town!"

The men swallowed hard. "A-Adamas? Please, no."

While Raine berated the people of the town, Kaito turned to Isaac. "We'll be leaving," he told him. "I've got what I came for, so there's no reason for me to stay." He held out his hand. "Thank you for saving my sister."

Isaac shook his hand. "Sure."

"Thanks so much," the girl said. "I never got to introduce myself, did I?" She smiled at him. "I'm Yukiko Nishimura. If it weren't for you, I wouldn't have made it out of there."

Isaac nodded. "Don't worry about it. I'm just glad you're okay."

"Do you guys need a lift somewhere?" Kaito asked him.

"What do you mean?"

"I have a ship just a ways from here," he explained. "Since you helped me out, it's only fair I offer you a ride."

"That would actually be quite helpful," Vin said. "If you're sure, then why not?"

"Then it's settled. I'm parked just beyond the south part of the town wall. I'll get things prepped; you meet me there when you're ready to leave. Please don't take too long." Kaito and Yukiko turned and proceeded toward the town entrance.

Isaac and Vin waited for Raine to finish scolding the townspeople, and she also checked on the freed prisoners. After a few minutes, she approached the two.

"Now that that's over with," she stared hard at Isaac, "we need to talk about what you did."

"Can it wait?" Isaac asked bluntly. "Kaito said he'll give us a ride, and I don't want to keep him waiting."

"A ride? On what?" she asked.

"Said he had a ship outside of town."

"A ship way out here?" She frowned.

"That's what he said."

"Fine, but you're getting an earful later." She narrowed her eyes at him.

"What do we do about this place?" Vin motioned to the town.

"I let the people here know that if they try to do anything more to the escapees, there would be consequences," she explained. "The only real good that came from Isaac's recklessness is that they are terrified of us now."

After a few more minutes, they were ready to leave, and as they headed out, a rumbling could be heard coming from the wreckage of the facility.

"What the—" Vin said as the rubble in the sinkhole started shifting.

They cautiously approached the edge, and a few other townspeople also peered curiously into the pit.

The rumbling increased, and soon something burst out of the sinkhole.

"Get back!" Raine shouted, and they all turned and fled. "Something is coming out of there!"

Isaac watched as a giant, metal arm shot out of the sinkhole, followed by another. The arms placed their hands on the edge of the pit, and the thing pulled itself out.

"What the shit is that thing!?" Vin shouted.

Standing before them was a twenty-foot-tall, mechanized robot. It had an assortment of weapons attached to it, and at the center of the main body was a glowing sphere encased in the chassis.

"That must be the weapon they were creating down there!" Raine said. "Look there at its chest. That must be the prototype energy core they were using people's aura for!"

The eyes of the steel beast turned from yellow to red, and it seemed to be staring at them.

"*Targets acquired,*" a mechanical voice echoed.

"Looks like we're in for a fight!" Raine told them. "We also can't allow that thing to run free. All the poor souls that lost their lives for that core need to be avenged."

"Let's bust this thing up, then!" Isaac said as he conjured his sword.

The townsfolk fled as the robot took an aggressive stance, leaving the three of them alone with the beast.

"Looks like we're on our own," Vin said unenthusiastically.

"Don't lose focus!" Raine told them. "It's going to take all of us to bring this thing down!"

The Behemoth aimed its arm cannon at Isaac, and a hail of energy blasts were fired at him.

"Shit!" He sprinted to his left as he created a force field in front of himself.

Vin fired a few arrows, but they harmlessly bounced off the steel giant. "That's not good."

Isaac ducked behind a giant boulder. The hail of energy crackled against the massive stone. "I could use some help here!" he shouted.

Raine waved her hands through the air, and a giant sphere of electricity appeared above the Behemoth. Another wave, and it came crashing down on it.

The robot only sputtered slightly as the lightning engulfed it, but it resumed its attack after a brief moment.

"Oh great, the thing is magic resistant," Raine grumbled. She quickly put up a force field as the thing turned its guns on her, the energy bullets ricocheting in random directions.

Vin scaled up the nearby town wall to get a better view. "We need a strategy."

Isaac stepped out from behind the boulder and charged up a lightning blast which he fired at the Behemoth. It hit its chest but didn't seem to have an effect.

The Behemoth approached Isaac. While still firing at Raine, it used its other arm to fire at him. Isaac put up a shield and hid behind the boulder again.

"I'm open to suggestions!"

Vin glanced around. There were several trees and boulders littering the ground from the wreckage of the facility. He also spied a few metal posts sticking out of the ground from the foundation. "See if you can lure it near those trees and metal posts," Vin told them. "I have an idea."

Raine moved behind a building for cover. The Behemoth's energy blasts were shredding the house apart. "Oh, I hope no one is in here," she murmured to herself.

It ceased fire, and a suspicious pod opened on its shoulder. "Raine, you might want to move!" Vin shouted at her.

Raine dashed from her hiding spot as a barrage of missiles hammered the building, crumbling it to the ground.

Isaac took the opportunity to sprint from his hiding spot to a place near the location Vin had suggested. He kept his force field up as it absorbed several energy blasts.

"Keep it distracted, Isaac!" Raine told him.

Isaac fired several lightning blasts at it in quick succession, eventually gaining the Behemoth's full ire. It moved in his direction at a quick pace, firing both cannons at him. He quickly ducked behind another boulder as the energy shots began to rip it apart.

"What now, genius?" Isaac shouted at Vin.

"We might be able to trap it in that debris if we can get it to stand in the center," Vin replied as he pulled several small pellets the size of marbles from his pouch. He made several arrows appear, and he notched a pellet to each one. Sizing up the area, Vin fired the arrows around the designated trap he had in mind. The arrows stuck into the ground and then vanished, leaving the pellets embedded into the dirt.

The Behemoth walked up to where Isaac was and brought its arm down upon the boulder he was hiding behind, shattering it. Isaac had quickly dodged out of the way and repositioned himself closer to the trap.

Raine charged up and blasted a large fireball at the giant; it exploded against its arm, forcing the Behemoth to stagger.

Isaac took the opportunity and approached the steel beast. He jumped onto its leg and climbed up to one of its arms. While the Behemoth was recovering, Isaac jammed his longsword into a crevice where the energy cannon was. He kicked at the blade in an attempt to break off the weapon. "C'mon, damn you!" he grunted. After a few kicks, he could feel the cannon slightly loosen.

The Behemoth had recovered and reached around to grab at Isaac.

"Shit!" He jumped off and backed away from it as it moved toward him. "This thing has really tough armor."

"It's after you—try to get it to stand in that spot I mentioned," Vin said.

Isaac dodged from side to side as a rain of energy was fired at him. He kept his force field up, but if it took too many hits, he wouldn't be able to maintain it.

"It's almost there," Vin said. "Just a bit more."

"Allow me!" Raine appeared behind the Behemoth and formed two giant, magical, blue fists that floated in the air. She moved her own fists in a punching manner, and the blue fists began slamming into the back of the steel giant. One, two! The fists hammered it, forcing it towardsthe trap. The Behemoth stopped its attack on Isaac, and its torso turned to face Raine. It held its cannon toward her and began to fire.

Isaac focused his attention on Raine and put a force field around her. "Keep hitting it!" he shouted. "It's almost there!"

Raine smirked in thanks and continued her assault. Soon the Behemoth had been pushed into the trap.

"It's in!" Vin shouted, holding a device in his hand. "Now, get back!" He hit the switch as Isaac and Raine moved away from the trap. In an instant, there was an explosion as all the pellets detonated. This caused the ground underneath the beast to shift, and its legs sank into the dirt.

"There, it's stuck!" Vin exclaimed.

The Behemoth was indeed trapped within the ground, and it struggled to break free, but with the loose dirt constantly shifting beneath it, it was unable to.

"Isaac, help me drop this boulder on it!" Raine called out to him. She was pointing to a rather massive rock that looked like it weighed several tons.

Isaac swiftly dashed over, and they both combined their telekinetic powers to begin lifting the massive boulder.

On top of the wall, Vin fired continuous arrows at the Behemoth to draw its attention away from the other two. Being incredibly fast, Vin was able to outrun and dodge the spray of shots aimed at him.

"Steady!" Raine told Isaac. "We almost got it!" The two of them strained as they moved the boulder above the Behemoth's head. "Let's hope this can do some serious damage!" The boulder was several meters above the steel beast. "Okay, let it go!"

Isaac and Raine both stopped their powers, and the boulder crashed down upon the Behemoth in a shower of sparks.

"Did we do it?" Isaac watched as the dust cleared.

The Behemoth's head had been completely obliterated, and the shoulders and collar area were badly damaged, but the steel giant was still moving.

"Oh my god ..." Isaac said in irritation.

"Let's hit it again," Raine said, and they began to lift the boulder once more.

Without warning, the Behemoth stirred, and its torso began to smoke.

"What's it doing?" The question was answered as the Behemoth detached from its legs, and the torso began to float into the air, propelled by rocket thrusters.

"Are you KIDDING ME!?" Isaac shouted.

"Wow. Of course, it flies ..." Raine said as they dropped the boulder. "Now what?"

"Run!" Isaac said as the Behemoth flew after them, its cannons spraying energy shots their way.

The two dashed from cover to cover as the flying machine chased after them.

"This just got way worse!" Raine shouted as she surrounded herself in a force field. "We need a new plan!"

The hiding spots were becoming scarce as they moved around the town.

Vin used his advantage of being unnoticed by the Behemoth to follow behind it. "C'mon, just a bit more," he whispered to himself as he prepared to strike. In the relentless pursuit of Isaac and Raine, the Behemoth didn't notice Vin quickly run up a nearby building. With gusto, Vin leaped toward it, throwing a grappling hook that entangled itself around the beast's arm.

As a speed user, Vin was able to easily climb onto the back of the giant, and as it tried to grab him, he was just out of reach. "My time to shine!" He grinned as a dagger appeared in his hand. Using it, he was able to bend back a part of the damaged metal and dropped several pellets in between the joints of the Behemoth's shoulder. After finishing the job, he jumped off, doing an acrobatic roll as he landed. "Try this," he said as he detonated the pellets in a fiery explosion.

The Behemoth's shoulder plating broke off, and the joint holding the arm to the torso was mangled.

"There!" Vin shouted at Raine. "Try to rip it off!"

Raine nodded, and using her magic, she threw a long rope of lightning at the flying beast. It wrapped itself around the damaged arm, and, using the lightning as a lasso, a blue hand appeared and gripped it. Pulling with all her might, Raine was able to rip the arm from the Behemoth.

"Hell yeah!" Isaac shouted. "Now let's see about the other one!"

The steel beast shook as its arm fell to the ground. The bottom of the torso opened and several lasers shot out at a steady stream, ripping up the area underneath it.

"Really!?" Vin grumbled. "Just how many tricks does this thing have??"

The Behemoth flew around Isaac and Raine, its lasers threatening to cut them to pieces.

"This thing is trying to get above us. Run!" Raine said.

"It's also avoiding any place that might allow me to jump onto it," Vin added.

"It's adapting!"

"I'm really glad this thing is just a prototype, otherwise a more complete version would be devastating," Isaac commented with irritation.

The three of them didn't stop moving as the giant continued its pursuit. After a moment, there was the loud sound of an engine roaring in the sky.

"What now!?" Vin said in disbelief.

CHAPTER 11: CONFRONTATION

Up in the sky was an aircraft that looked like a high-tech jet. It hovered above them.

"Wait, isn't that—?" Isaac started.

"Looks like you could use some help," Kaito's voice echoed from the ship. A cannon appeared from the underside of the aircraft and began raining blasts down on the Behemoth.

"All right!" Isaac said with a fist pump. "I didn't know he had a *combat* ship."

"He's having a hard time hitting the robot, though," Raine replied. "We need to stop it so he can get a clear shot."

"Right, I'll distract it, you grab it." Isaac darted out from his hiding spot and threw several bolts of lightning at the Behemoth. Between Kaito's assault and Isaac's lightning, the beast didn't notice Raine throw a lightning rope around it. The blue hand appeared once more, and she began to pull.

"Grrr, c'mon!" Raine said as she used all of her might to hold the robot.

"Yes! Hold it right there," Kaito called from the ship.

"It's chest!" Vin yelled up at him. "Hit its chest!" He waved his hands and pointed at his own chest, gesturing toward the Behemoth.

Kaito must have noticed because he maneuvered the ship around for a clear shot. The cannon on the underside began to glow brightly as it charged up a lethal shot.

"Hold it steady, Raine!" Isaac called out to her.

"The hell do you think I'm doing!?" she snapped back at him as the lightning tightened around the Behemoth.

After a few moments, Kaito's ship fired a massive blast that found its mark where the core of the Behemoth was. There was a thunderous crackle as it exploded into several fragments.

The Behemoth hovered for only a moment before it came crashing to the ground.

Raine dissipated the lightning and collected herself, breathing heavily.

"Did we do it?" Vin asked as he cautiously approached the wreckage.

Isaac walked up to the Behemoth and peered at the core. There was a faint light, but overall, it was damaged beyond repair. "Let's make sure it's toast," he said as he used his telekinesis to pull the core from the torso and smash it multiple times on one of the many boulders until there was barely anything resembling a sphere.

"Well, that was fun!" Vin said somewhat cheerfully.

Raine gave him a disgusted look. "You shut the hell up!"

CHAPTER 12

LOOMING SHADOW

Zagaan.

A being shrouded in darkness.

One of the many reapers on Terra. Possessing the ability to control his minions from a distance, this sinister figure worked from the shadows. Having orchestrated the attacks on the separate nations as well as Adamas, he continued his goals with ease.

With several leaders under his grasp, he used his influence and fear to achieve his will. He sat in an undisclosed location as his followers carried out his tasks.

"Report," Zagaan said to a nearby cultist.

The cultist fumbled nervously. "We have tabs on the activity inside Esmeraldas. Several informants are inside the city, and Ligeia is luring people away from the hidden base inside the kitsuné's domain."

"Are the kitsuné still under suppression?"

"Yes, milord."

"Good, those vile creatures are a nuisance," Zagaan growled. "How far along are we on that project?"

"We are making great progress," the cultist replied. "Once we receive the queen's artifact, we can begin summoning Omega."

"Excellent. Once the bringer of death has arrived, our ultimate goal will easily be achieved," Zagaan said with malice. "The others may doubt me, but they shall see."

Other cultists in the facility began to shift nervously, and one of them shakily approached the reaper. "Uhh ... s-sir?"

"What is it?" Zagaan snapped at him.

"Eep!" The cultist was startled. "It's ... uhh ... i-it's Vaerun ..."

"What about Vaerun? Has Magnus reported in?"

"Well, no ... uhh ..."

Zagaan glared at him "Speak clearly! I hate it when you people stammer!"

"Y-yes, milord!"

"Then tell me what it is!"

"The, uhh, beta site in Vaerun. It's been destroyed ..." The cultist paused in fear.

Zagaan stared blankly at him for a moment before speaking. "What?"

"Uhh ... we've lost all communications with the facility directly, but ... uhh ... one of our informants at the site says it ... e-exploded," he fumbled.

"Is this some kind of joke!?" Zagaan hissed. "Because if it is, there will be hell to pay!"

The cultist took a step back. "N-no, sir! It isn't! The informant says that the guardian exited the facility right as it was destroyed. He must have done it!" His words came out quick and panicky.

"The ..." Zagaan narrowed his eyes. "Don't tell me you believe that crap!" he growled. "You're telling me that someone entered the facility and blew it up from the inside?"

"Th-that, is correct ..."

"Unbelievable ..." Zagaan's face was full of anger. "What about the prototype? Did the core make it out?"

"Well, yes, but ..."

"So, it's secure then? That core is important! You'd best tell me that they have it."

"The, uhh ..." The cultist was shaking furiously. "The guardian ... destroyed the prototype and ..." He swallowed hard. "The core."

Zagaan's eyes flared. "Destroyed!?" He stood up. "Have you any idea how long it took to create that!?"

"I'm s-sorry, s-sir." The cultist bowed. "I'm just relaying what I was told. It was the guardian who—"

"Stop calling him that!" Zagaan sneered. "He is NOT a guardian. There's no such thing! That boy is nothing but a low life!" He towered over the quivering cultist. "And to think that you people would let him walk into our facilities and destroy them!?" He kicked the cultist savagely across the room. "I want Magnus to report directly to me! He has a lot of explaining to do!" He shook with anger as he stormed out of the room. "Pfft, guardian …" he muttered angrily to himself. "What a joke!"

After the battle with the Behemoth, Isaac and the others confronted the townspeople of Vaerun and made certain that the prisoners who had been held captive inside the now destroyed facility would be freed. Raine had been very persuasive, especially after they had seen her incredible power used against the steel beast. After they were thanked—with a few praising Isaac particularly due to his status as guardian, which he irritably waved off—the three of them boarded Kaito's aircraft.

"So where are you guys headed?" Kaito asked as he piloted the ship.

"To Esmeraldas," Raine replied. "We greatly appreciate your assistance, but how, might I ask, did you get a license to fly in this area? Usually aircraft aren't authorized."

"I didn't," he replied. "My ship can't be detected, so I can go anywhere I want."

"You have technology that can avoid aural sensors?" She narrowed her eyes.

"That's right. It's a new technology developed by Sapphirus researchers," he explained. "We've been working on it for years now, and we've finally got the first model created and installed on this ship."

"Incredible," Raine said. "That must have been why even I couldn't see you."

Isaac sat with Vin as the other two chatted.

"Damn dude, I can't believe you blew that place up," Vin said.

"I mean, technically I didn't really know what was gonna happen," Isaac replied with a shrug.

"That was pretty reckless."

"Yeah, yeah, Raine already gave me an earful."

"But between you an' me," Vin leaned in, whispering, "that was totally awesome!"

They secretly high-fived each other.

In the back of the ship, Yukiko was sleeping quietly. After all that she had been through, she was exhausted.

"How close can you get us to Esmeraldas?" Raine asked.

"Probably to the outpost near the north of the main root of the great tree," Kaito replied. "I would get you closer, but even my cloaking can't avoid the detection of the kitsuné."

"Yeah, that could be a problem." She frowned. "I guess that means we'll have to take the long way around."

"What are kitsuné?" Isaac had moved next to them.

"Vile creatures," she explained. "Their lust for blood is only matched by their extremely violent behavior."

"You never heard of a kitsuné before?" Kaito asked with a frown.

"I'm, uhh, not from around here," Isaac replied.

"Nobody goes into their domain," Raine added. "It's extremely dangerous."

"Well, nobody in their right mind," Kaito scoffed. "Some people get stupid and make bets to see who can go in the farthest and come out alive. Almost all who go in never return."

Isaac frowned. "Seems kinda like superstition to me."

"Trust me, Isaac," Raine told him sincerely. "Do not ever go in there. This isn't superstition."

"Well, I don't even know where it's at, so no worries, I guess." He shrugged.

They flew on for nearly an hour over an endless sea of trees. The forested area below them seemed to go on forever. Eventually, in the distance, a massive tree that seemed to touch the very sky could be seen.

"What's that?" Isaac looked at the tree in amazement.

"That's Esmeraldas," Raine explained.

Even though they were several miles away, the tree could easily be seen from where they were.

"Whoa, that thing is huge!" Isaac's eyes were wide as he stared at the large tree in the distance.

"It's the biggest tree in our world."

"Hold up," Kaito interrupted. "First you don't know about kitsuné, and now you don't know about Esmeraldas? Where exactly did you come from?"

"Oh, ya know, from another world," Isaac said calmly.

Raine gave him a sideways glance.

"Really ...?" Kaito said with a tone indicating he almost believed him.

"Totally."

Kaito just sat there for a moment before giving a short, "Hmm."

"You know," Raine said, "you really shouldn't just tell that to random people."

"Wait ..." Kaito frowned. "That was the truth?"

"Maybe," Isaac said sarcastically.

"Oh, haha, you two are joking."

Isaac and Raine remained seriously silent.

"You, uhh, are joking ... right ...?"

"So, this tree," Isaac changed the subject. "Just how big is it?"

"The trunk goes on for several dozen miles in diameter," Raine explained. "The main city sits on top within the branches."

Kaito glanced back at them in confusion.

"An entire city on top of a tree?" Isaac was surprised.

"Yep. Not as big as Adamas, but still huge."

Kaito shook his head. "You guys are strange."

As they drew nearer to the large tree, eventually it felt as if the branches and massive leaves hanging from them would devour the ship. They flew above the edge of the tree roots that shown from the ground.

"Those roots have to be at least a quarter mile thick!" Isaac commented.

"They stretch even farther lengthwise under the ground. Some even go as far as the edge of Adamas," Raine told him.

"That's insane!"

"Over there," she added. "That's the kitsuné's domain." She pointed at a part of the endless forest that stood out from the rest. The leaves on the trees seemed to sparkle, and colored lights shone from within.

"Wow, it's beautiful." Isaac never thought he would say such a thing, but the image of that section of forest was captivating.

"Yeah, that's what most people would say before they walk in, only to never come back," Raine said, narrowing her eyes.

"Is it really that dangerous?"

"Yes."

Isaac stared at the section of forest illuminated by brilliant lights. It seemed peaceful to him. A place to just live carefree.

What am I thinking? he thought to himself as they flew around it, avoiding the area.

After a while more, Kaito began the descent. "We've reached the northern outpost."

"Damn, I was just enjoying the relaxation," Vin said with a yawn.

"No time to be lazy," Raine told him. "We still have a mission to complete."

The ship hovered near the edge of a tiny settlement and landed in an open clearing.

"Before you go," Kaito said as the three of them got ready to head out. "Here." He gave Isaac a piece of paper. "That's my contact info. You saved my sister; if you ever need help with something, give me a call."

"What, you're not coming with us?" Vin joked.

"Honestly, I would, but I need to get my sister home so she can recover," he explained. "My mission was to find her and bring her home, so I will finish that first."

"Thanks for the ride." Isaac smiled.

"A guardian, huh?" Kaito looked at him. "I don't know if I believe in any of that, but if it weren't for you, I may never have seen my sister again. Thanks." He held out his hand.

"I guess we'll never know," Isaac said, shaking Kaito's hand. "I don't really believe in this guardian stuff myself."

Kaito chuckled. "Well, may our paths cross again someday."

"I hope I get to see you again." Yukiko had appeared beside Kaito. "Thanks for everything."

Isaac gave her a nod. "I'm sure we will."

The three of them waved goodbye and headed toward the outpost as Kaito and Yukiko took off.

"Daaang, you're becoming quite popular," Vin said playfully.

"Am not," Isaac grumbled back.

"Aw, you're just embarrassed," Raine added with a chuckle.

"Not really."

"Hey look!" Vin said suddenly. "A snack shack!" He quickened his pace toward a particular building. "I'm starving!"

"He gets distracted so easily." Isaac chuckled.

"If only his distractions would keep him away from the castle maids ..." Raine retorted.

The outpost, though small, still had a bustle of life about it.

"This doesn't seem like a regular outpost," Isaac mentioned.

"What do you mean? They're all like this," Raine replied.

Well not in my world, Isaac thought.

The two of them found a resting spot and sat down.

"Once Vin gets back, we'll decide our next course of action," she said. "By the way." She looked at Isaac. "Do you really not believe that you're a guardian?"

Isaac stared back at her. "Not particularly."

"But you've already been able to accomplish so much. Plus, you're the only one with a blade of pure white light."

He shrugged. "Doesn't mean anything to me. Besides, you're still more powerful than I am."

"Yeah, that's true," she replied smugly. "But you know, even if you don't believe in it, you can still bring hope to everyone."

He gave her a quizzical look. "Hope for what? It's not like I'm some great hero like Xander. He can be the one to bring everyone hope."

"There are a lot of people that do look up to him; some even believe he's actually the guardian," she mused. "But I can see people's auras, and he's only got one. You have a unique aura that I've never seen before."

"Maybe it's because I'm from another world. It doesn't necessarily mean I'm your chosen hero or anything."

"Hmm, you may have a point." She held her chin in thought. "But the queen believes in you."

"I don't see why ..."

"You don't get it," she told him. "In all my years of serving her, she has never put her trust in someone so strongly. She genuinely believes in you more than anyone else that I've seen. Even myself."

"That makes no sense." He shook his head. "I don't even know her; how could you tell me that she believes so strongly in me when I've barely even had a conversation with her?"

"I don't get it myself." She sighed. "But it was completely her idea for you to join us in this mission. She even talked to the council about requesting you to stay there with her. They rejected it, of course. But you should have seen her face when they denied you."

Isaac listened in confusion. "What do you mean?"

"She didn't say anything, but I could tell that she was furious. I rarely see her get angry like that." Raine looked at Isaac solemnly. "But she has a strong faith in you."

He shook his head in bewilderment. "It's probably because you guys think I'm a guardian."

"Actually, she never mentioned that. Not once. She only mentioned your name and that she wanted you close."

Isaac looked at Raine and frowned. "That REALLY makes no sense."

"I agree, but Her Majesty has always been a great judge of character. If she believes in you, then so do I." She smiled at him.

They stared at each other for a moment in silence.

"I, uhh, don't know what to say," Isaac muttered. "Maybe you shouldn't ..."

"Why's that?"

He looked away. "Because I'll probably let you down."

Raine also glanced away. "Well, I'm not sure exactly what it is you're supposed to do, but I hope that maybe, when the world is in trouble, you'll join and help us."

Isaac didn't reply; he just sat there in thought.

"Yo! I brought snacks!" Vin's voice broke the silence, and he came marching up, holding an armful of food.

"You could have just put that all in your bag, you know," Raine said, standing up as if their conversation had never happened.

"But then I couldn't eat them!" Vin said as he stuffed a small sandwich in his mouth. "Mmmf, dis ish gud!"

"Don't speak with your mouth full!" Raine said sternly. "How improper."

Isaac just watched as the two of them argued. *I'm sorry, Raine,* he thought. *I don't think I'm the person you want me to be. I can't save your world. I can't even save myself ...*

Back in the interrogation room, the black-haired woman smiled at Isaac. "Seems like you're quite the reckless one."

Isaac stared at the table. "I was just ... angry. How could they do those things to all those people?"

"Careful now," the woman said. "You may actually start to care, haha." She cocked her head. "Besides, I like reckless. You're more interesting than I thought."

"What's that supposed to mean?" He frowned at her.

"You need to stop lying to yourself." She licked her lips. "I want to see the true you."

"What are you talking about? I'm right here."

The woman gave him a knowing look. "This version of you is here, but I'm looking for the true you."

"That makes no sense."

"Only because you complicate it." She laughed.

Isaac just stared blankly at her.

"Did you ever figure out why she believes in you so much?"

"No." He shook his head.

"Well, I'm right here, you could just ask, hehehe." Her laugh was devious.

"You aren't her."

The woman's eyes grew wide. "Oh my, but you said so yourself, YOU are here, so how come I can't be 'her'?"

"Uhh ..." Isaac didn't know how to respond.

The woman laughed loudly. "You are so cute when you get stumped. HAHAHA!"

"Shut up!" he growled.

"Aw, that's not nice of you. You wouldn't tell *her* to shut up."

"What do you want from me?" he demanded.

"Me?" She held her hand to her chest dramatically. "I didn't bring you here." Her eyes narrowed as she stared at him. "You did."

"What?"

"Do you remember what happened before you came here?"

Isaac thought about it and remembered how he had lost control of the darkness and attacked Raine. "I was ..."

"You did something terrible, didn't you?" The woman wore a serious expression.

He only nodded.

"Why would you drag yourself to a place like this?"

Isaac was confused. "But I didn't—"

"Was it to protect them?" She grinned. "From ... you, perhaps?"

"I don't know ..."

"Fear, Isaac." She leaned toward him. "It will seek to control you. Don't let it."

He remained silent.

"You're the only one who can get out of this," she told him. "I can only guide you, but you will have to be the one who opens the door."

"And if I can't?"

The woman wore a sad expression. "Then you will be lost to oblivion."

CHAPTER 13

ILLUSIONS

The sea rocked the ship softly as it floated helplessly on the water. It was midnight, the power was out, and there seemed to be no life on board except for Isaac. He wandered the hallways of the dead ship hopelessly, knowing there was no way off.

"Anybody there?" he asked cautiously. The only response was a groan from the ship as it rocked side to side.

"Of course." His only source of light was a small flashlight he carried with him. It barely lit up the pitch-black hallways. He had been wandering around trying to find anyone else, or maybe a way to turn the ship back on.

Out on the deck, there was no moonlight and no way to see out into the vast ocean. In fact, he couldn't tell if the ship was even on water. The empty void that stretched out before him may have well been another dimension.

Inside was a twisting hallway with not a soul around. He made his way carefully through the ship, trying to locate the engine room.

"I don't know where the hell I'm going," he muttered to himself as he continued to search. Eventually he found his way down a staircase and into a large room.

"This has to be it." He glanced, searching for a way to start the engine back up. Making his way through the darkness, he found a control panel of sorts. He tried pressing a few buttons, but there was no response.

"Come on, dammit!" He had no success. Was he doomed to be trapped here forever?

In the distance, there was a noise. He froze. Even though it was mostly incomprehensible, there was a distinct whispering that was getting closer.

He wanted to call out to it but decided not to. He couldn't tell if it was friendly or not. The whispering grew louder as whatever was causing it drew closer.

He turned off his flashlight and quietly backed against the wall, holding his breath. The whispering moved passed where he had been previously standing.

It paused.

He did his best to keep his breathing as quiet as possible as he listened. It was so dark that there was no way anyone could see without some form of light. He stood there motionless, hoping that whatever this thing was would leave.

The whispering continued, and eventually, it slowly moved away from him. As it was leaving, Isaac could make out some of the things it was saying.

"The angels are coming ... beware ... they took my baby ..."

He waited until the whispering was far off in the distance before he turned his flashlight back on.

"What the hell?" he said quietly. What was that thing? With the darkness, he obviously didn't see what it was, but he felt that if it saw him, he'd be in danger.

He made his way out of the engine room, cautious to avoid whatever that thing was. *Angels are coming? Beware? What was it whispering about?* He decided to get back on deck and see if there might be another ship out there or something.

Walking through the outer hatch, he stepped out onto the deck. The world was still dark, and he couldn't see anything beyond his flashlight. He walked around the deck, peering into the darkness.

"Not a goddamn thing," he said dejectedly. As he was about to re-enter the ship to try looking for power again, he saw something in the distance.

"What's that?" He saw a weird light on the horizon, but what was odd about it was that it didn't illuminate anything; it just sort of floated in the nothingness but was slowly coming closer.

Isaac just stared at it curiously. Was it another ship? Was he finally getting help? His answer came in the form of a piercing howl that echoed from the direction of the light. Suddenly, the ship began to shake as if the howling had hit it like a shockwave.

"The angels are here," he heard the voice echo from inside the ship. The howling increased as he quickly stepped back inside. *There's nowhere for me to run to. I'm trapped here.*

He swiftly moved into the main hallway and glanced around. Shining his light down the corridor, he saw a figure. It slowly walked toward him. As it got closer, he saw that it was some kind of sickly, thin creature of average human height, but the odd thing about it was its mouth was moving at a rapid pace as it whispered non-stop. It continued to walk toward him.

"So that's what you are ..." he muttered as he backed away from the creature. There was a flicker from the flashlight, and in the brief moment it went out, the creature had seemingly teleported closer to him through the darkness.

Isaac stumbled back, keeping the light trained on it. Quickening his pace, he stepped through a nearby hatch and quickly swung the door shut, sealing it tight. The creature slammed against the door, its claws scrapping the other side. After realizing it couldn't get through, it turned and continued down the hallway.

Isaac could hear the whispering shoot down the corridor at an alarming rate.

It knew where he was.

It seems this thing moves faster in the darkness, he told himself. He quickly moved to a different section of the ship in an attempt to lose the creature.

Outside, the howling was getting closer, and he started to hear it even through the thick walls of the ship. He turned a corner and stepped into a nearby room, shutting off his flashlight. He pressed himself against the wall, the whispering darting down the corridor he'd come from.

It paused.

Did it know where he was? As he stood motionless, trying to calm his breathing, he could hear his own heartbeat. The whispering slowly grew closer. How sensitive was this creature's hearing? But it didn't matter at this point. He held his breath as the whispering entered the room.

Raine had woken up in the middle of the night. For the last few days, they had been hiking around the great tree of Esmeraldas, making sure to avoid the kitsuné's domain as they headed for the entrance at the western side of the trunk that would take them to the main city. They had come to a nearby village where they took lodging for the night. The three of them shared a room together and were sleeping in their own separate beds, but she had woken up suddenly before the light of dawn arrived.

She rubbed her eyes and looked around. Vin was snoring in his bed, and she shook her head in disgust. *How annoying*, she thought. But she immediately felt an evil set of eyes upon her. Glancing around, she discovered the source.

There, sitting upright in his bed, was Isaac. His eyes were solid black, and he wore a sinister grin as he stared at her.

Raine froze as she looked back at him. "Isaac ...?" she whispered as they stared at each other. There was no response. He simply continued to stare at her. She briefly glanced in Vin's direction, but he was still asleep. Looking back at Isaac, she cautiously got out of her bed and approached him.

"A–are you ... okay?" she stammered as she stood next to his bed. Isaac just looked at her with his demonic, black eyes and wicked grin.

Raine, using her abilities, peered at his aura. It was tainted with darkness and completely different than normal. "You aren't Isaac ..." she whispered to him defensively.

The demon gave a low, raspy chuckle. "Soon."

"What?" she asked nervously.

"Not much time left now." His voice was not Isaac's but a warped, raspy, demonic voice. "Soon he will be gone." He cocked his head slightly as he leered at her, flashing an evil, toothy grin.

"Who are you?"

The demon licked his lips. "I'm your friend. Don't you recognize me?" He laughed.

"Leave him alone," Raine told him. "Get out of him!"

Isaac cocked his head from side to side, mocking her. "The convergence is almost complete. There's no stopping it," he said with a smile. "You just keep pushing him along. You're doing a wonderful job." After saying this, he sat motionless, staring at her, grinning.

"Who are you?" Raine asked again, her voice shaking slightly.

The demon didn't budge, nor speak.

"Who are you?!" She raised her voice.

Vin started to stir in his bed.

Isaac's eyes began to glaze over, and the blackness started to disappear. In a jolt, he appeared startled and fell out of his bed.

"What's all that noise?" Vin said groggily.

Raine looked down at Isaac on the floor. "Isaac, are you okay?"

He glanced around, somewhat in a panic. "The angels!"

"What?" She noticed his eyes had changed back to normal. "What angels?"

He realized where he was and looked up at her. "Uhh ... n-nothing ... I was just having a nightmare ... yeah."

She scanned his aural reading, and he was back to normal. "You scared me." She gave a nervous chuckle. "Are you okay?"

He stood up, grumbling. "Yeah ... I think so." He looked at her and gave a fake laugh as he smiled weakly. "Guess it was just a dream."

"Yeah ..." she replied. "Just ... just a dream, haha."

"That must have been a hell of a dream," Vin said as he stretched his arms. "You startled the crap out of me."

"Haha, sorry," Isaac replied.

"What were you dreaming about?" Vin asked.

"It was ... it's nothing," was the reply. "Whew! It's kind of early!" he said, trying to sound positive. "I'm, uhh, gonna go for a little walk and get some water. You should go back to sleep while you still can." He headed for the door.

"Isaac ..." Raine said. He turned and looked at her. "Please ... just be careful."

"Haha, don't worry. It was just a dream. Really."

"Right." She watched him leave and then lay back down on her bed.

"That was weird, huh?" Vin chuckled as he rolled over, closing his eyes. "Kinda funny though," he added. "Isaac, freaking out over a nightmare, haha."

Raine lay there in silence, staring at the ceiling. That dark feeling just now. It was the same one she felt back at the castle that one morning before the tournament.

The convergence is almost complete.

She didn't go back to sleep.

After the sun had risen, the three of them packed up and continued their journey.

Raine couldn't help but continually look at Isaac. She kept checking his aura for any signs of change, but he was completely back to normal, and it seemed he had no memory of what happened.

"This forest is way more colorful than anything I've ever seen on Earth," Isaac said as he glanced around. "Kinda makes me glad I left. Other than all the fighting and conflict on this planet, it still seems like a better place to live."

"Are there many conflicts on your planet?" Vin asked him.

"Not like here where we are able to settle them ourselves. On Earth, we have a police force to keep the public safe, kind of like the town guards," he explained. "If anyone acts out, they get arrested immediately, so most people are usually non-violent. But every now and then, a bad apple turns up and the police go after them."

"It's not like there's conflict everywhere here," Vin said. "It's just a part of the job we've taken on. Since we're dealing with these cultists that summon demons and experiment on people, we're bound to run into conflict."

"I guess that's true."

"Do you guys also have aural technology on Earth?"

Isaac shook his head. "No. Actually, there's no aura whatsoever on Earth."

"Not even a little?" Vin looked puzzled.

"Nope. It's a rather boring place."

"Then, how do *you* have aura?" Vin asked.

CHAPTER 13: ILLUSIONS

Isaac thought for a moment. "I'm not really sure. Just one day I had a weird dream and then next thing I know, I'm waking up here on this planet with these abilities."

This statement only confused Vin more. "That's really weird," he said. "Wait! Maybe that's how guardians get their powers, ya know? Like you were chosen or something."

"Maybe?" was the reply.

Dreams, Raine thought to herself as she pictured what happened earlier in the morning. *How long has Isaac been having these dreams?* she wondered.

"Yo, Raine!" Vin nudged her playfully. "You've been awfully quiet this morning. Usually you're yapping away." He grinned at her.

"Sorry, I'm just lost in thought at the moment," she replied.

"Huh, she didn't snap at you." Isaac grinned jokingly. "Everything okay over there?"

Raine stopped walking, and the other two stopped and stared at her. "Hey, Isaac." She looked at him.

"Uh oh, she's gonna get you, dude," Vin said with a smirk.

"I, uhh, need to talk with you in private, okay? Come this way." She headed toward a clearing.

"Um, okay?" Isaac followed her.

"If you don't come back, can I eat your snacks?" Vin shouted as they left.

Raine stood facing Isaac in the clearing away from Vin.

He closed his eyes dramatically. "Okay, do it. Just make it quick, I beg of you," he said sarcastically.

She looked at him seriously. "Isaac, do you know anything about illusion magic?"

He opened his eyes and saw how serious she was. "Can't say I have. What's that?"

"Okay, training time," she replied. "I want you to pay very close attention to what I'm about to tell you."

He looked at her, his normal serious expression returned. "Alright."

"Illusion magic," she started, "is when you get trapped in a reality that isn't true. It may seem very real but can be very dangerous if the victim does not get out of it in time."

She glanced around the clearing, and Isaac followed her gaze. "It could even be possible that we're in an illusion right now."

Isaac looked around as she explained. He stared at the grass, the trees, even the sky.

"But there's a big difference between illusion and reality. For instance, there's no wind in an illusion," she told him. "Right now, we can feel the breeze and the wind on our faces, therefore we know we are, in fact, not in one."

"Why isn't there any wind?" he asked.

"Because an illusion is a spell on your mind. Whatever location you are at is fake, and since there's no wind in your head, there wouldn't be any in your thoughts," she explained. "The illusion creates a subconscious reality formed from your own thoughts or memories. You may feel certain emotions or pain, even physical, if those memories or ideas were the same at the time of the memory. Basically, the spell causes you to create your own illusion unwillingly."

"Are there any other indicators that I'm stuck in one?"

"Yes," she continued. "In an illusion, the people around you may not act like they do in reality. It could be a friend or a family member. If you notice that someone you know is behaving out of character, it's a good indication that you may be trapped in an illusion."

"Well, damn, I guess anytime Vin compliments me, it means I'm probably trapped," Isaac joked.

"This is serious, Isaac." Raine stared at him. He went silent and continued listening. "It's probably going to get more dangerous from here on out, and I needed to tell you about this now. I should have explained it before, but it didn't cross my mind until ... recently."

"I'm listening."

"Illusion magic is extremely dangerous. If you ever find yourself trapped, you need to do whatever it takes to get out of it. If you stay in one too long, your mind will become twisted, and your personality will change for the worse. Permanently," she told him. "No one who has been stuck in an illusion for an extended period of time has ever come back the same. Some become braindead, while others become monsters and begin to hurt the ones around them. Even their friends."

"How do you get out of one?" he asked.

"It depends," she replied.

"On what?"

"The individual. There's not a sure way to get out. The illusion is created from the individual's mind, so it's really up to that person to figure it out."

"You seem to know a lot about this. Have you ever been stuck in one?" he asked.

"Yes." Raine looked grim. "I was stuck in one for around thirty hours."

"What happened?"

"I don't want to go into detail, but what I can tell you is that it took a lot for me to get out of it." She looked down, remembering the pain it had caused her.

"What did you do?"

She looked back up at Isaac. "I confronted and overcame my fears."

"Did, uh, did you have any ... weird things happen while you were trapped?" he asked carefully.

"Yes," she revealed. "There were these ... things that attempted to hurt me."

Isaac's eyes went wide. "Things?"

Raine placed her hands on Isaac's shoulders. "Isaac, if you ever get stuck in an illusion, and something comes after you, you run. Got it?"

"O-okay ..."

"Because those things are manifestations of your fears, and if they get you ..." Her voice was slightly panicky. "If they get you, there won't be a 'you' left."

"What's that mean?" Isaac was a little shaken.

"It means you'll become that thing in reality," she told him. "In an illusion, you cannot use your aura to protect yourself because it is being used to manifest and distort your mind. All you can do is search for a way out, you understand?"

Isaac nodded. "Y-yeah. I understand."

Raine took a step back and let go of Isaac. "Good. Sorry, it brings back memories of my own illusion when I talk about it, so I kind of got a little weird just now."

"When you said you were trapped for thirty hours, didn't someone come looking for you?" he inquired.

"That's the tricky part," she told him fearfully. "From my perspective, I was in it for that long, but in reality, I was only trapped for around five minutes."

Isaac wore a shocked expression. "That's ..."

"That's why you need to understand how dangerous it is," she added. "If you get stuck for too long, there's no coming back. There's no one to save you."

"How long is too long?"

"Unknown," she said. "We keep records of people who get trapped and come back the same as they were before, and the longest time we've ever recorded was fifty-seven hours. Those who went insane have never mentioned their time. It's like they became something entirely different."

"How often do these illusions happen to people?" he questioned.

"Thankfully, not very often," she answered. "It's incredibly difficult to force someone into a fake reality. Even I cannot use illusion magic. It's mostly brought on by the individual."

"Is there a pattern to the ones affected?"

"Yes." She gave him a somewhat sad expression. "It mostly happens with people who have mental illnesses, and their mind turns their aura against them. Usually with those who are suicidal. It can also be caused by an individual with a weak resistance to pain. Even to a guardian."

"Weak to pain?" Isaac asked curiously.

"Yes, those who meet hardship that they cannot overcome. Those types of people will quickly fall into depression and a feeling of helplessness. That can cause them to get trapped in their own mind."

He simply nodded in thought.

The two of them stood there in silence for a moment.

"Well, training's over," Raine said, trying to sound cheerful. "Just remember all of this, and be careful."

"I, uhh ..." Isaac nodded in thought. "I will."

CHAPTER 13: ILLUSIONS

She nodded. "Let's continue on, then, shall we?"

Isaac followed behind her, thinking about what she had told him.

Please overcome this, Isaac, Raine thought to herself. *I fear there's nothing I'll be able to do if it gets worse.*

"Dammit!" Vin said as they regrouped with him. "I was really hoping to get your snacks."

"Get your own, you pig!" Isaac jabbed at him.

"Do I look fat to you?" he retorted.

"Yep," was the quick reply.

"Lies!"

As the two continued joking with each other, Raine remained silent. She thought about the demon and the things it said.

You just keep pushing him along.

You're doing a wonderful job.

How was I 'pushing him along'? she wondered. *Is it possible that I'm somehow causing this?*

She glanced at Isaac.

There's gotta be something I can do. I must save him from this. That place. That horrible, horrible reality. No one should have to suffer from it. I don't know how, but I'll find a way. I will save you, Isaac.

She shuddered from the memories of her own nightmare and held her hands together as if in prayer.

I WILL save you ...

CHAPTER 14

THE HOWLING CRESCENDO

Back at the architectural lab, Orna was at her desk going over several books and graphs. Her research into the first queen of Adamas' history and predictions were almost an obsession for her. The final mural depicting two dark beings in conflict baffled her. Who were they? Why were they fighting? What would happen to the world after this event came to pass? The strangest thought that always went through her head was when she was confronted by that sinister being. She knew that it was going to happen and what to tell him. And what she told him, she knew, would lead to the events in the final mural.

A while back, Orna was approached by a man who clearly had ill intentions. His face was hidden behind an emotionless mask.

"I demand your insight," the man told her.

"And to whom do I owe the pleasure?" Orna replied with caution.

"I am Zagaan, and I require information," Zagaan said. "I'm searching for something, and I was informed that you are a seer."

"I am only a partial seer," she explained. "The premonitions that I get are simply informational. What you do with my knowledge is up to you."

"Partial?" he growled. "You mean you cannot see into the future?"

"My abilities are nothing like The First. I can only learn realizations, as if reading pieces of the future from a book but not knowing the full outcome."

Zagaan frowned. "Then just tell me everything you know. Have you ever heard the name Omega?"

"Omega?" Orna thought for a moment. "It ... seems familiar."

"Tell me everything," he demanded.

She searched her thoughts, focusing on the name. "I don't ..." Her eyes went wide. "Wait ... Omega."

"Yes? Well?" Zagaan leered at her. "Tell me!"

Orna stared cautiously at Zagaan. "Tell me first: What is your interest in this being?"

"That is not your concern," he growled. "You will tell me what you know, or I will take your life."

She pondered her answer for a moment before speaking. "If you seek Omega, go to the kitsuné's domain." Her voice was solemn.

"The forest of spirits?" Zagaan asked questioningly.

"Yes," she told him firmly. "That's all I know. If you go there, you may find something."

He frowned at her. "Is this all your power can do? Give precarious insight?"

"I told you, I cannot peer into the future," she replied. "When I think of the name Omega, the forest of spirits enters my thoughts. I have no doubt that your Omega and the kitsuné are somehow linked."

"Those vile creatures?" he pondered. "I'll admit, that makes some sense considering how dangerous they are." He glowered at her. "Is that everything you can tell me?"

"No, there's one other thing," she answered, her face growing serious.

"Tell me."

"This is a word of warning," Orna began. "Beware."

"Excuse me?" Zagaan's voice grew dangerous.

"Beware of Omega." Her tone was sincere. "For should he take up the blade and fight, it will be the doom of you and your kind."

Zagaan laughed. "You are greatly mistaken, woman."

She looked at him in silence.

"Omega is the Bringer of Death. A being born from darkness. An enemy of humanity."

"I can only tell you what I know," she explained. "And I assure you, Omega is not your friend."

He scoffed at her. "We shall see." With that, he turned and left.

Ever since that encounter, Orna devoted herself to finding as much information on this Omega as possible. But every text she read that hinted at his coming all ended abruptly. Even The First knew very little. It was truly as if he were the end of it all. Why did she feel that this being of darkness was the key? She searched everywhere for information.

After her meeting with Raine and the guardian, she felt some strong connection to their journey and Omega's awakening. "There must be a link between the guardian and the Bringer of Death," she muttered as she poured over her books. She skimmed over one of The First's riddles. A poem of the past that mentioned the future.

The End is coming, a choice must be made.
Two souls are bound by destiny.
One is darkness, one is light.

"One is darkness, one is light," she read aloud. "If the guardian is light, then is Omega the darkness?" How were they linked? Just who was Omega? Orna flipped through the pages and came to one of The First's final verses.

Upon the fangs of vengeance, evil burns.
Heed this warning, betrayer, before encroaching.
Beware, for he is the storm that is approaching!

"Beware ..." Orna thought back to the final mural that had yet to pass.

Choice.

The one that showed the two dark beings in conflict.

"Evil burns at the fangs of vengeance ... if this is referring to Omega, then wouldn't that make him an enemy of darkness?"

No matter how hard she tried, she couldn't come up with an answer. There simply wasn't enough information to go on, as if fate itself were erased. But somehow, deep down, she believed that one of those dark beings depicted in the mural was this Omega, and if so, who was the other?

"Hey, I just talked to the queen," Raine told Isaac and Vin. "The council is getting a little suspicious of the situation. Apparently, my absence is concerning."

"How's Her Majesty?" Vin asked.

"She's a little worried about us, but she's keeping the mission a secret, at least. She's good at that stuff."

The three of them had recently passed the kitsuné's domain and were within a day's walk to the entrance of Esmeraldas. Upon passing the domain, Isaac saw a glimpse of the radiant sparkle that emanated from the area. Raine had once again warned him not to go in even if it looked welcoming.

"The kitsuné are vicious creatures," she told him. "They will kill you without hesitation."

"And then they'll feed on your flesh!" Vin added with a shudder.

Isaac just stared at them suspiciously. "You sure you guys aren't just exaggerating?"

"Trust us," she reassured him. "That place is dangerous."

He glanced one last time at the colorful trees of the kitsuné's domain. Around a few of the trees, he could see several butterflies hovering around. It was strange, but they seemed to be watching him.

They continued quickly away from the domain.

"We should hurry. If Orna's prediction is true, hopefully we can locate the exact place the artifact is being kept from someone in the city above," Raine explained.

"Where's this entrance at?" Isaac asked.

"Just a few miles up ahead," Vin said. "Should be there in a few hours."

A few days hiking in the forest started to drag on a bit for Isaac. It was just an endless sea of trees, but at least the hike was quiet enough.

"I can't wait to get out of this forest," he muttered.

"We'll be there before you know it," Raine told him.

They continued, and after about an hour, they came upon a large settlement.

"Let's take a break," Vin said.

"Good idea. This is the last town before we get to the main city," Raine replied.

The three entered the town and made their way to what Isaac would describe as a coffee shop. They sat at a table, and a waiter approached. "What can I get you all?" he asked.

"Hmm, I'll take the emerald cream," Raine told him.

"A heavy espresso," Vin added.

"Huh," Isaac muttered. "They have those here?"

"Hurry up and order, Isaac," Raine said.

"Right, I'll, uhh, take a strawberry liqueur."

Vin shook his head slowly. "Of course ..."

After the waiter left, Isaac looked to his companions.

"It's really strange," he pondered. "A lot of the things here on Terra are the same things on Earth."

"You mean there's coffee on Earth?" Raine asked.

"Yeah, and there's other things, like how we all speak English."

"Well, it's called Jadīm on this planet," she reminded him.

"I mean, some things are different by name, but it's basically the same thing," he told her. "It's just ... weird."

"Well, I'd say it's pretty convenient," Vin stated. "This way you aren't struggling to learn how to communicate or wonder about the little things."

"Yeah, I guess that's true," Isaac agreed.

The three of them chatted for a while before the waiter came back to their table.

"Here's the bill," he said to them. "Also, be careful out there. We've had a lot of people go missing in the forest."

Vin rolled his eyes. "Don't tell me the trend of wandering into the kitsuné's domain is becoming a thing again ..."

"Unfortunately, no. We haven't had many reports of the kitsuné in a while," the waiter explained. "The reports are from the forest near here. A lot of people are staying within the town here because of the alarming rate of people that go missing."

"Haven't they sent some kind of investigation team?" Raine asked.

"They did ... but they have yet to return. Stay safe out there." He left the table after Raine paid him.

"What is it with missing people wherever we go?" Isaac wondered out loud.

"Something tells me this is different than Vaerun," Vin said.

"Either way, we need to be cautious," Raine told them. "Let's just get into the main city and go from there. This issue is not our concern."

The three of them finished up and left the coffee shop. They decided to refresh their supplies from the local vendors before heading out.

"Hey, I want to check out this shop really quick," Raine said, pointing to a nearby building. "It will only take a moment."

"Alright," Isaac said. "I'll wait out here for you."

Vin was off in another shop gathering tools to create explosives and whatnot.

Isaac sat down on a nearby bench and watched the people around him as he waited for his companions. He spied a dog wandering the area and gave a whistle to call it over. The dog noticed and quickly ran over to him.

"Hey, buddy!" Isaac said as he pet the dog. "What's a good boy like you doing around here?" He smiled as the dog wagged his tail happily. He noticed that the dog was quite thin. Probably a stray. "Aww, you must be hungry. Here you go." He brought out some beef jerky from his bag and gave it to the dog, who ate it quickly. "Wish I could give you more." He smiled sweetly as the dog looked up at him gratefully. "Take care of yourself, buddy." He watched as the dog walked away, curiously sniffing around.

Isaac glanced toward the building Raine was in. She was still browsing around, and he felt himself getting a little impatient.

A short time went by when he heard a yelp from a nearby building across the road.

"Git outta 'ere, you dumb mutt!" A middle-aged man angrily kicked the stray dog away from his place of business. The dog went flying a few feet and lay there, cowering.

Isaac stood up, his eyes wide with fury. "HEY!" Without hesitation, he sprinted across the road and viscously grabbed the man by his throat, slamming him into the wall of the nearby building.

"*You. Piece. Of shit!*" Isaac growled at the man. "Why did you hurt that dog!?"

The man gurgled as he choked him against the wall. Passersby watched on in shock as the white blade appeared in his hand.

"Isaac, wait!" Raine came running up to him. "Stop! Please!" She noticed a very faint linger of darkness from his aura. "Let him go. Please ..." She stood next to him.

Isaac's eyes seemed to burn a hole through the man as he stared him down with hatred.

"Please, stop this," Raine pleaded again.

He briefly glanced at her, then back at the man. His sword vanished, and he grabbed the man with both hands, throwing him violently to the side. The man hit the ground and gagged as he lay there.

"You lucky bitch," Isaac sneered at him. "Don't you ever do something like that again, because next time, I won't stop!" He turned and walked over to the dog. Kneeling down, he pet the dog's head. "You okay, buddy?" His voice was calm and soothing. The dog looked up at him with a whine. "Don't worry, no one else is gonna hurt you." He glanced over at the man who was still recovering on the ground. "*Are* they?" His voice became dangerous. The onlookers watched Isaac in silence.

"Let's go." Raine tugged on Isaac's sleeve. "Please, let's just go."

A moment later, the dog got back on its feet and ran off. Isaac stood, and together with Raine, they left the area while a few people moved in to check on the injured man.

A ways away, out of sight from other people, Raine turned to Isaac. "So, you want to tell me what that was about?"

He shook his head angrily. "What a piece of trash," he growled. "Hurting a dog like that. I should have killed him!"

"Just calm down." She put her hand on his shoulder. "Deep breaths. This isn't like you."

He looked at her. Her deep blue eyes peering into his was calming. "I'm sorry," he told her. "I just couldn't stand back and do nothing." Even though his voice was calmer, he still shook slightly with anger. "The nerve of someone hurting a defenseless animal like that," he said, looking at the ground. "He's just a ... a freak!"

Raine continued trying to calm him down. She rubbed his back as she used her magic to sooth him. It was shocking for her to see him explode like that. Even from within the store, she saw how quickly he had attacked that man. A behavior he had never exhibited before since he had always been fairly calm and collected—and even when he lost his temper, it wasn't anything like this.

"I'm okay," he told her. "Really."

"We'll meet up with Vin and head toward the entrance to the city," she told him. "Let's just try and forget this ordeal, okay?" She didn't want him to focus on that kind of anger. The faint hint of darkness that seeped out of his aura had Raine worried, and she didn't want it to get worse. She figured that once they completed their mission and returned to Adamas, she would research a way to suppress that evil.

The two made their way to the gates of the settlement where Vin was waiting for them.

"What took you two so long?" he asked with a smirk. "You guys run off and make out somewhere?"

"Why yes, actually," Raine answered. "We were so over-joyed with your absence, that we took this chance alone to taste each other's lips for a while."

Vin frowned. "Wait ... really?"

"Yep, let's go." She marched off down the path toward the ancient tree.

Isaac, even hearing what she had just said about the two of them, stayed silent and followed behind.

"You were just kidding, right?" Vin asked her with a playful tone.

"Nope." She didn't look at him; she just kept walking.

"Uh huh," he replied.

"Why, you jealous?" She grinned.

"Pshh, nah." He waved her off.

"I mean, if you wanna make out as well ..." she joked, "you could always ask him. He's right there." She pointed to Isaac with her thumb, a smirk on her face.

Vin rolled his eyes. "You know, a part of me was hopeful for a second, but I pretty much knew you were gonna do that." He glanced back at Isaac. "You just gonna take that from her?"

Isaac shrugged. "Not really paying attention, to be fair."

"Whatever, man." Vin chuckled.

"I'm just thinking about how delicious Raine's lips tasted," Isaac added seriously. He was trying to shake off the anger he felt earlier.

Vin coughed. "Hold up ..."

Raine closed her eyes and slightly curled her lip. *Hey, you aren't supposed to say something like that,* she told Isaac telepathically.

You started it, he replied.

The three continued down the visible path for a bit. The forest was still just as thick as when they'd entered, and there was no seeing beyond a short distance. Raine was a great navigator, however, since she could see through every tree, so there was no way they could get lost.

"Hey," Raine said randomly, "let's take a break for a moment." She pointed to the left. "I can see a little stream this way. Looks like a nice place to take in the sights."

"Sounds good to me," Vin said. "My back has been slowly getting more and more exhausted carrying my pack."

"You big baby." She laughed.

"I don't have magic or strength aura like you two," he responded. "My endurance comes from cardio, not carrying heavy shit."

"Pfft." Raine shook her head, and the three made their way through the thick trees off the beaten path until they came upon a beautiful stream with a fairly open area to sit in. The trees here were thinned out, and the sun shone over the stream as the light glistened off the water. Grass lined the banks and provided a nice place to relax.

"Oh wow," Vin said with wide eyes. "You weren't kidding. This place looks great!"

Isaac glanced around. "Yeah, it's nice."

"Would be a great place to bring a lucky lady," Vin added with a wink.

"I wouldn't consider her lucky." Raine chuckled.

"Rude!"

The three took off their packs and found spots to relax. Isaac sat the farthest from the other two and was staring at a photo he had in silence. Raine had a travel cooking set and was heating three cups of tea. Vin had a small, collapsible fishing rod and was attempting to catch a fish, albeit with no success.

"Ya know, I just can't see it," Vin called over to Raine as he cast his line into the water.

"What are you talking about?" she responded, adding tea bags to the cups.

"You and Isaac," he answered. "I just don't see you two dating or whatnot."

"Wow, you're still on about that?" She shook her head in disbelief.

"Just sayin'."

"Well, I just don't see *you* with any of the castle maids," she jabbed.

"Hah! *You're* still on about *that?*" he scoffed.

"They're probably really enjoying this time that you're away." She poured hot water into the cups, stirring slightly.

"Nah, they miss me. I'm sure of it." He grinned.

Raine rolled her eyes. "Whatever, here." She stood, levitating two of the cups while holding her own. She waved her free hand, and one of the cups floated next to Vin.

"Why thank you, my lady." Vin gave a dramatic bow.

She shook her head with a grin and made her way to Isaac. He was sitting on a rock staring blankly at the stream, a photo of a dog cupped loosely in his hands.

"Your dog?" She sat next to him and motioned to the picture.

Isaac was slightly startled by her sudden question, and he glanced over at her. "Didn't hear you come up," he said, turning the photo facedown. "What's up?"

Raine offered the second floating cup. "Here. It's tea."

"Oh, no thanks. I don't really like tea," he said politely.

"Aww, but you haven't even tried mine." She hovered the cup within a foot of his face. "Come on. Just a sip? It'll warm you up."

Isaac took the cup. "It's the middle of summer. I'm already warm." He tipped the cup to his mouth and took a sip.

"Well, how is it?" she asked eagerly.

"It's okay," he replied. "Tea always has a bland taste."

"Darn." She gave a wry smile. "Well, at least you tried it."

"Sorry."

"Don't worry about it. Is that your dog in the picture?"

Isaac paused for a moment. "He was."

"Was?"

"Yeah," he said faintly. "He's gone."

"Oh ... I'm sorry to hear that."

"It is what it is." He flipped the picture back over and looked at it. "He just got too old. Everyone dies eventually."

Raine looked at the picture. It had only a large, black dog sitting in a house, smiling back at her. "What was his name?"

Isaac looked back at the stream, somewhat embarrassed. "Dozer."

"He seems really big for a dog."

"He was," he stated. "Weighed over two hundred pounds. But don't let the size fool you, he was a gentle creature, and my best friend ..."

She glanced at him. "Is that why you got mad earlier?"

"Yeah." He nodded. "I've always loved dogs. There's a reason they're considered man's best friend."

"I see."

He stared at her. "Look, it may seem silly to favor a dog over a human, but Dozer was always there for me when I needed him most; no one else was."

"No one else?" Raine asked, bewildered.

Isaac looked away. "Forget it." He tucked the picture back into his pocket. "I don't know why I even brought it up."

"I'm sorry. I didn't mean to pry."

"I'm fine, Raine." He looked back at her. "I'm fine ..."

"What? Oh, I didn't mean that ..." she tried to comfort him.

"You've been acting really weird around me since a few days ago," he explained. "I dunno what's going on, but I'm okay. You don't need to worry about me so much." He frowned.

Raine was about to reply but paused. There was a bit of awkwardness in the air, and she eventually responded. "Isaac, I'm sorry. I guess maybe I have been getting a little worried." She fidgeted with her teacup. "I guess I have a bad habit of that. Always worrying too much. It's the same when I watch over Her Majesty."

"You don't have to watch over me, you know," Isaac responded in his usual calm tone.

"I know, I know!" she stammered. "I'll try not to be so nosey from now on. Anyway, we should probably get ready to head out." She stood up. "I'll get everything packed up, so don't worry about it." She quickly walked away.

What am I thinking? she thought to herself. *He was starting to open up, and I quickly killed the mood somehow.*

You just keep pushing him along. You're doing a wonderful job.

Am I making this worse? She felt her gut clench. *I don't know what to do.*

She finished packing up the equipment as Vin packed up his fishing rod, and soon they were ready to continue their hike.

"Can't wait to get up to the city!" Vin stretched. "Soft beds, good food, and of course, probably a lot of cute girls." He stared at the sky as if daydreaming.

"Unbelievable," Raine muttered. "You're such a simpleton."

"I enjoy the simple things in life, that's all." He winked.

"That's not what I meant." She shook her head slowly.

Isaac glanced at the trees around them. It seemed as if they went on forever. "About how long do we have till we get there?" he asked.

"Probably another hour and a half," Raine answered.

"That's not too bad, I guess."

They walked for another thirty minutes, and the forest still didn't open up. The trees were so thick Isaac couldn't even see up the massive tree's trunk. "You sure you know where we're going?" he asked with a frown.

"I'll have to teach you how to see through objects one day." Raine chuckled. "Trust me, we're on the right path."

"Hey." Vin stopped suddenly. "I just realized where we are." He glanced around him, his eyes stopped to their right. "Yeah! There's a shortcut this way!" He pointed and started heading in that direction.

"What are you talking about?" Raine asked him sternly. She approached him as if to lecture him. "That's not the ..." She paused. "Oh wait, you're right. I remember now. Wow, it's been a while."

"You know what I'm talking about, right?" Vin asked her excitedly.

She chuckled. "Yeah, I didn't understand at first, but now I remember." She started to head off with Vin. "Come on, Isaac. It's this way."

Isaac glanced around. Everything seemed the same to him. "Um, okay ..." He just decided to trust them since this forest was alien to him.

"This way will make things much easier," Vin said ecstatically.

"Well, it wasn't that tough to begin with ..." Isaac mentioned.

"Well, I don't have strength aura like you do," Vin sneered.

"Yeah, Isaac. You should be more sensitive," Raine added.

Isaac stopped walking for a moment. What the hell? That last comment was very unlike her.

Raine and Vin both stopped and stared at him.

"You coming? It's not much farther," Raine said.

"Are you two okay?" Isaac asked cautiously.

"Of course we are. Are you okay?" Vin frowned.

"We were just teasing you, Isaac," Raine said to him extra sweetly. "Don't take it so personally." Her voice was uncharacteristically alluring.

Maybe I'm still just wound up from my encounter earlier, Isaac thought. "Right, sorry."

"It's no big deal," Raine said with smile.

They continued walking for what seemed like forever. Raine and Vin would occasionally start humming, only to randomly stop at times. Isaac remained silent as they moved through the ever-thickening trees.

"I really can't wait till we get there," Vin said happily.

"Me either!" Raine added with a skip.

The two of them seemed more joyful than before they'd chosen this "shortcut."

"Any idea how close we are?" Isaac asked carefully. He had checked the time, and based on what Raine had told him earlier, they should have been to their destination about ten minutes ago.

"We aren't too far now," Raine said, glancing back at him, a big smile on her face. "Why aren't you excited? This is gonna be so much fun!"

He was about to argue but realized the look in Raine's eyes was different somehow, and her behavior was off. "I am excited," he told her, forcing a smile. "I just can't wait, you know."

"I totally get you, dude!" Vin said, clapping his hands. "It's just right up here! Oh, I can't wait to see her!"

"Yeah, yeah!" Raine agreed. "To be in her radiance is gonna be awesome!"

Now Isaac was confused. "Um, who are you talking about?" After he asked this, Raine and Vin stopped. "Uh ..."

They turned to him, their expressions serious.

"I'm sorry, what?" Vin asked almost threateningly.

"What's your problem?" Raine hissed at him.

Wait a minute. Isaac remembered something Raine had told him a few days ago. About illusions.

People you know, such as family or friends, will act out of character.

He thought for a moment. Was this an illusion? What else ...? Oh yeah!

There's no wind.

Isaac held his hand up and, to his surprise, he could feel the wind blowing. *So, it's not an illusion?* he thought.

"We asked you a question!" Vin snapped at him.

Swallowing hard, Isaac answered, "I'm sorry, my mistake. Of course, I remember her, I was just curious if you meant someone else." He forced another smile and did a little hop skip as he approached them, trying to mimic their behavior. "Let's get going!" He chuckled.

Raine and Vin immediately grew smiles on their faces. "That's the spirit!" they both said in unison. They turned and continued with Isaac cautiously behind them.

"So uhh, when do we get to the city?" he asked with a joyful tone.

"What city?" Raine replied with big eyes and a wide grin.

"You know, Esmeraldas?" He gave a nervous chuckle.

"Oh heavens, why would we go there?" Vin said with shock.

"I don't know, I just thought ... that was where we were going ...?"

Raine did a little spin in mid-step and began walking backward while staring at Isaac. "She's not in the city." She tilted her head slightly, the grin still on her face. "She's down below here with the others."

"The ... others?" he inquired, continuing to force a big smile.

"They're all waiting," she continued. "They can't begin the ceremony without us."

Ceremony?

"Hey, uhh, you guys ..." Isaac just remembered something. "Do you remember when that waiter told us about people going missing? Something strange is going on ..."

"You shouldn't lie, Isaac," Vin growled. "I remember no such thing. Right, Raine?"

"Yup!" She was still walking backward, but her face turned to a sneer. "You don't seem too excited to be in her presence, Isaac ..."

"I'm following, aren't I?" he told her. "If I wasn't so excited, I wouldn't be coming along, don't ya think? Hehe ..." He clapped his hands like Vin did earlier.

Raine turned around and was now walking normally. "I sure hope so. She wouldn't like anyone who isn't ..."

Isaac felt a chill at that last remark. *Who the hell is "she"?* he thought. *I'll just have to play along and find out. This isn't good.* He didn't know what to do in this situation. Since he clearly wasn't in an illusion, then what was wrong with his companions?

They continued walking for another half hour, making their way around the thick trees, avoiding heavy foliage and whatnot. Eventually in the distance there was an evident break in the trees. The area around them had become very dark, and Isaac suspected it was nighttime. He heard an ominous sound coming from the direction of the opening. Eerie music could be heard. The closer they got, the quicker Raine and Vin's pace was.

"We're almost there!" Raine squealed with excitement.

"I wanna see her first!" Vin said, and he started to run.

"No way, I get to see her first!" Raine chased after him. "Come on, Isaac, she's just through here!"

Isaac's first thought was to stop them, and he gave chase, but upon seeing what was through the opening, he stopped and quickly ducked out of sight, hiding behind a nearby tree.

What he saw sent a chill down his spine.

Vin, followed by Raine, entered a large clearing where several people were knelt down in front of a large, grotesque creature. The creature towered over them, had ragged wings, scaly skin, and a twisted face with bloodshot eyes. The creature was clearly female due to the lack of clothes and its feminine physique. She played a harp, somewhat elegantly, and she peered out over the dozens of people surrounding her in worship. Isaac had seen this type of creature before from ancient lore on Earth. The creature was a siren.

"Come forth, dears." The siren beckoned to Raine and Vin. "Come into my flock." She continued playing her harp with that eerie music.

Raine and Vin both clapped their hands together. "Ah! She noticed us!" They beamed. "Let's go show her our appreciation." They laughed moved toward the creature.

"Wait a second ..." Raine paused. "Where's Isaac? He should bask in her glory, too." She glanced around.

Isaac held his breath from his hiding spot. *What do I do? I can't fight that.*

Yes, you can ... the voice within told him.

"What are you doing?"

He jumped at the sound. Raine was standing next to him, her eyes wide and dangerous. With her powers, it would be impossible to hide.

"I was, uhh ..." Isaac stammered. "Playing hide and seek?" He gave a sheepish grin. *This is bad. This is really bad.*

"You're being an asshole!" she snapped at him. "Show some *goddamn* respect!" She grabbed him and pulled him out into the open. Her strength was stronger than normal, and

Isaac couldn't pull away. He fell into the opening, in sight of the siren.

"What have we here?" the siren sang out. "A third? The more the merrier!" She cackled.

"Get off me, Raine!" Isaac struggled against her grip and was forced to shove her away. She stumbled back a few feet and glared at him.

"Oh? What's this?" The siren stared at him, confused. "Are you not grateful to be a part of my flock?"

Isaac stood defensively as he glanced between the siren and Raine.

"You're out of line, Isaac!" Raine hissed at him.

"And you're acting really weird!" Isaac chimed back.

"You're the one who's acting weird, dude!" Vin glared.

The siren narrowed her eyes as she leered at Isaac. "Who are you?" She whistled a haunting tone. "Bring him here!"

Isaac slowly backed away as Raine and Vin approached him. "Snap out if it, you guys!"

"You're being a bitch!" Vin told him with malice.

Raine waved her hand, and several magical blue ropes circled around Isaac. He quickly put up a shield around himself as the ropes tightened.

"Stop it, Raine!" He struggled to hold the ropes back, but she was far stronger than him.

"You're such a loser, Isaac." Raine looked tauntingly at him. "Why even struggle? You know you can't win."

What are you doing!?

Isaac's shield shattered, and the ropes wrapped themselves around him, binding him tight. He fell to the ground on his back as Raine and Vin grabbed him.

"You've been so disrespectful," Raine said to him as the two dragged him toward the siren. "You should be ashamed of yourself."

He tried to struggle, but it was futile.

Why do you hold back? Unleash me!

His anger started to spike. Around him, the other people just looked at him with disgust. Even his own companions had turned on him.

He was alone.

"You could have joined us," Vin spat at him. "But you had to go and act all weird."

"This is your fault you know," Raine added.

Isaac's chest tightened as he heard their words. This was just like before.

The two threw Isaac at the feet of the siren. The other dozens of people surrounded him.

"How fascinating." The siren stared down at him with her hideous, bloodred eyes. "How come you're not under my spell?"

"Maybe 'cause your music sucks!" Isaac snapped at her.

Vin kicked him in the stomach. "How dare you say such things, Isaac!" he shouted as Isaac groaned from the pain. "And to think I called you a friend!"

I warned you this would happen. They don't care about you.

Isaac conjured his blade in an attempt to cut the magical ropes from him, but Vin put his foot on it, pinning it to the ground.

"You ...?" The siren perked up upon seeing his white blade but never stopped playing her harp. "So, you're the one Zagaan told me about." She cocked her head. "Even still, there's no reason you can be immune to my magic."

There was nothing he could do. Pinned to the ground by the very people he trusted, he could only listen to the siren's words.

"I suppose I should introduce myself, reaper." The siren's voice was like a song. "I am Ligeia, Zagaan's eidolon, and you are now my prisoner." She laughed. "I will keep you and your companions until you turn." She smiled wickedly. "There is no escape for one as pathetic as you. Isn't that right?" She looked at Raine and Vin.

They both chuckled.

"You always were a weakling," Raine told him. "I don't know why I wasted my time training you."

"I only pretended to be your friend, you know," Vin added. "Only because I took pity on you."

Isaac's eyes began to water. Was it all a lie, just like he thought?

They only wanted you for your power, but they realized how weak you were, so they'll just toss you away.

This whole time, was it all for nothing? *Why did I even come on this journey? It's not like anything will change.*

You know what you have to do. Unleash me! Destroy them!

The siren, his companions, these dozens of people now peering at him. Tormenting him.

But.

They were just being mind-controlled, right?

Right?

A storm began to well up inside Isaac's mind. His vision blurred as tears poured from his eyes and anger took over.

This was just like before ...

"Push him again!" A group of kids laughed as one of them pushed a young Isaac, who stumbled backward, tripping over the foot of another. He fell to the ground hard.

"Haha, look, he's already crying!" another boy said with a snort.

Isaac's face was covered in tears. He cowered before the group of bullies.

"What a crybaby," a girl said out loud. "He's such a loser."

A boy leaned down close to him. "How long are you gonna cry for, huh?" He pushed Isaac's head into the ground. "You're such a wimp."

"L-leave me a-alone ..."

"What was that?" the boy growled.

"I said ..." Isaac grabbed a rock lying next to him. "Leave me ... ALONE!" He pulled his head away and swung the rock at the boy, hitting him in the head with it. The boy fell backward, a trickle of blood running down his face.

"UGH!" The boy held his head in pain. "You bitch!"

Isaac quickly stood, anger and tears in his eyes. He moved toward the injured boy with the rock raised above his head.

"What is going on!?" an older voice rang out. The group of kids scattered, revealing one of the schoolteachers. She saw Isaac standing over the boy with a rock in his hand.

"*Oh my god!*" She ran over to him. Isaac quickly dropped the rock and backed away.

"It's not what you think ..." he tried to say.

"I've had about just enough of you." The teacher grabbed his arm viciously and dragged him back to the school. "I am calling your mother."

"No! Please don't!" Isaac sobbed.

As he was dragged off, the bullies chuckled. "What a loser. We'll get him good next time!"

Inside the school, the teacher called Isaac's mom, and shortly after, she showed up.

"Your son is a problem child," the teacher told her. "All he does is pick fights with the other students."

"I don't pick fights." Isaac pleaded. "*They* attack *me!*"

"Don't you lie!" the teacher snapped. "I saw you beating another kid with a rock."

"That's not ..." he tried to explain.

"Are you *kidding* me!?" His mom leered at him. "We are sooooo gonna have a talk at home!"

"I hope you straighten out your son, Ms. Cunningham. He does nothing but cause problems for everyone!" The teacher folded her arms in disgust as she glared at Isaac.

"Oh, don't you worry," Isaac's mom replied. "There's gonna be hell to pay when we get home!" She grabbed Isaac's arm and pulled him out of the classroom.

"Mom, it wasn't my fault. You gotta believe me!" Isaac pleaded yet again.

"I've had it with your *shit*, Brennon!" she whispered in his ear as they stood in the empty hallway. "I had to leave work early because of you! You are nine years old; you should know better!"

Isaac began shaking in fear. "I-I swear, I'm telling the truth."

His mom smacked him across the face. "You're gonna learn to stop talking back to me, you little shit!" She dragged him helplessly out of the school. "You are SO disrespectful!"

Isaac wouldn't stop crying that night. No one would believe him. No one.

He was alone.

Anger. Hatred. Fear. Pain.

The darkness that lay dormant within Isaac began to stir.

Unleash me! I am your true power!

Isaac closed his eyes as the siren watched him with glee.

"There is no escape," Ligeia repeated. "Once your trans-formation is complete, this world will be ours." She laughed.

He mumbled something under his breath.

"What was that?" Ligeia taunted him. "I couldn't hear you under the sound of your suffering." She cackled even louder.

"I ... hate ... you ..."

Ligeia frowned, sensing a change in his behavior.

A deep, raspy breath came from Isaac. "I HATE YOU ALL!" He opened his eyes and looked up at the siren. His eyes were solid black, and a slight mist of darkness poured out from them. "ALL OF YOU!"

In an instant, a massive blast of darkness pulsed from Isaac's body, disintegrating the magical ropes that bound him and engulfing everyone around, including Vin and Raine. They all fell to their knees, groaning.

"What??" Ligeia said with surprise.

Isaac rose and stood angrily before the siren. "Never again ..." His voice was deep and dangerous. "*Never!*"

The seal binding your heart has been undone. This is your true self!

Ligeia changed the music on her harp. "Stop him, my flock!"

Raine attempted to cast a spell at Isaac, but he shot an orb of darkness at her. As it hit, her aura dissipated, and she fell back to her knees.

"What ... is this?" she stammered. "Milady, my body feels heavy," she pleaded toward Ligeia.

The siren hovered a few feet off the ground and floated slightly away from Isaac. "This is a surprise." She wore a serious expression. "But no matter." She played a sharp note from her harp, and a blast of wind brushed the darkness from the area. "You cannot use the power of darkness to your advantage here."

Isaac curled his lip in hatred as he watched the people around him recovering. "No more holding back, then," he growled. His sword appeared in his hand, but instead of the brilliant, white blade of light, it was dim with darkness pulsing from it.

Raine and Vin got to their feet. Vin's daggers appeared in his hands, and Raine's crackled with lightning.

Isaac turned and glared at them. "I'm gonna snap you out of this, one way or another!" His black eyes leered at them. "I'm not playin' ..." He raised his blade.

Someone rushed Isaac from the side, and he swiftly dodged over their weapon, kicking them away. Another came in from his back but was met with a jolt of lightning as he surrounded his body with an electric barrier.

Raine raised her hand and began summoning a massive fireball. Vin rushed toward Isaac with his daggers and unleashed a flurry of swift attacks, but they were matched equally with Isaac's blade as he blocked each one. After a few more swipes, Isaac got the upper hand over Vin, and he knocked the daggers away. Grabbing his companion, he flipped him over his shoulder and slammed him on the ground, knocking the wind from him.

Several people charged him with their weapons drawn.

"Fight all you like, you'll never win." Ligeia laughed. "Unless you are willing to kill them all."

Through Isaac's fury, anger, and hatred, he still felt deep down that he didn't want to hurt his friends, no matter how much he hated them. He performed several spinning attacks as his darkness rained down on them, pushing them back and subduing them.

Don't hold back! Stab. Maim. KILL!

Isaac growled as he tried to keep those destructive thoughts from consuming him. He glanced at Ligeia with fury.

The harp.

She never stopped playing it. That must be the key to her mind control.

Raine had finished charging her giant fireball. She hurled it at Isaac, who put up a shield as he dodged out of the way. The flame flew past him, but then arched around and came for him again.

Isaac sprinted toward the siren, pushing several individuals aside with blasts of wind amplified lightning. The fireball drew near as he bound upon the giant creature.

283

"It's futile," Ligeia said calmly as she floated higher into the air, away from Isaac.

"Hmph." He turned around when he was under the siren and reached out at Raine's fireball, snatching it out of the air with his darkness enhanced telekinesis. Waving his hand, he guided the flame straight at the siren at a startling speed.

The blast hit a shield that surrounded the creature, causing Ligeia to reel.

"How dare you attack me?" the siren wailed.

Raine began summoning more magic.

You just keep casting, Isaac thought. *Because you're gonna help me destroy that harp.*

Several balls of flame as well as lightning came flying at Isaac from different individuals. He held his dark infused blade at the ready as he dodged from side to side, batting away a few of the magical spheres.

Vin fired a steady stream of arrows at him, causing him to duck behind a tree. Someone wielding an axe came slamming into the tree, cutting it down in one swipe. Isaac quickly did a flip through the air, avoiding the axe.

Dammit, these guys are everywhere, he thought. But he already had a plan. He shot a blast of darkness at the axman, sapping his aura.

Each time Isaac would weaken someone with his dark power, the siren would clear it with a tune from her harp, but that didn't bother him; he was trying to get Raine to charge an even bigger orb of magic by making her believe she was safe behind the onslaught of people.

Stop resisting me!

Isaac grunted, briefly dazed. His sanity was slipping the longer he used the power of darkness.

No, he thought. *I can't lose control! I promised!*

He steadied himself as Vin opened fire another volley of arrows.

Thanks, dude. Isaac waved his hand and stopped the arrows midflight in a stasis field. He sent out a blast of darkness, infusing them, and he pointed them upward into the sky. He moved away, leaving the multitude of arrows frozen in time.

"This struggle is pointless," Ligeia sang out. "Just submit to the darkness."

"Not a chance, hag!" Isaac snapped as he dodged several attackers.

Raine had finished charging another massive sphere. Not of fire, but pure aural energy.

"How dare you insult her?" Raine said with malice. She floated briefly off the ground and fired the sphere at Isaac.

Okay, I only get one shot at this! Isaac moved to position himself closer to Ligeia and waved his hand, releasing Vin's arrows from stasis. The arrows shot straight up into the sky above the siren.

Raine's energy sphere flew dangerously fast toward Isaac, and he knew he couldn't dodge it, but he wasn't trying to. He shot a blast of darkness into the air in front of Ligeia, detonating it in a large cloud of blackness. She swiftly played a few notes to clear it as Isaac snatched Raine's magic and, with all his might, hurled it at the creature.

As the dark cloud cleared, Ligeia reeled back as the energy sphere slammed into her magic shield, taking her by surprise; for a moment, the shield broke.

"Ugh!" Ligeia growled. She went to put up another shield, but soon a rain of arrows came flying down at her, infused with darkness.

"Gotcha!" Isaac charged up a huge blast of wind from under himself as the arrows struck the siren with deadly accuracy. He launched himself at Ligeia. She held her arms up to protect her head as the arrows pierced her, causing the harp to fall. Isaac came flying toward the creature and slammed into her with a blast of darkness, knocking her out of the sky. He kicked off her and toward the tumbling harp. With his telekinesis, he yanked the instrument toward himself and, arching his body with sword in hand, he shattered the harp into pieces.

Ligeia hit the ground as Isaac landed a good distance away from her.

Immediately everyone around him began to mutter amongst themselves.

"What? Where am I?"

"What's going on?"

Everyone looked around in confusion.

Raine and Vin were doing the same thing.

"What have we been doing?" Vin seemed dazed.

"I'm not sure ..." Raine replied as she looked around.

"*Hey!*" Isaac shouted at them. "You awake now!?"

"Isaac?" She looked at him with shock. "Oh my god ... your eyes ..."

"*Shut it!*" he snapped at her. "We have a bigger problem!" He pointed at Ligeia, who was now getting back on her feet. "Everyone, listen to me!" he barked at the few dozen people. "If you want to live, then fight!"

The siren's body began to pulse with a dark energy. "How *dare* you?" she hissed at Isaac. "That was a *big* mistake!" She floated into the air once more, and blood ran from her eyes as aural energies pulsed from her body. "DIE!" She held her hands toward the sky, and the very air around everyone began to shift.

"What is this?" someone cried out in fear.

"FOCUS!" Isaac shouted at everyone while conjuring his tainted blade. "There's no time for hesitation!" He waved his hand in a circle in front of himself, and several fireballs appeared. "You hesitate, you die!" He fired the magic orbs at the siren at a rapid speed. The shield surrounding Ligeia absorbed the flames.

Vin's bow appeared in his hand, and Raine readied herself. "I don't know how we're gonna fight this thing," he said. "This is way different than our other battles."

"We'll just need to figure something out, and quickly." She stared at Isaac. His aura was tainted with darkness and was different than what it was before.

"I'll make you suffer!" Ligeia growled at Isaac. She waved her hands around, and the sky crackled with lightning.

"Not good," Vin said as he fired a few arrows at the siren. "We need to get past that shield."

Isaac bounded up toward the creature with blade in hand. "Don't just stand there, you morons!" he yelled at everyone. "*Fight!*" He hurled an orb of darkness at Ligeia as a cascade of lightning showered the area. The orb slammed against her shield, but it didn't break.

Several people were struck by the lightning bolts, and they fell to the ground motionless. Red, blue, and yellow weapons appeared in everyone's hands, and they prepared to attack.

"Focus on taking down that shield of hers. Once it's down, give it everything you've got!" a large man wielding a red bastard sword yelled out. "Form up! Reds in the front, blues in the back! Yellows lend support where you can. Blues, use range attacks and shield our front line!" Everyone was finally coming to their senses and began moving to their designated locations. Vin and Raine decided to join the strategy as well. Isaac, on the other hand, was directly assaulting Ligeia with bloodlust.

The siren floated around the large clearing, trying to keep her distance from him as he hurled multiple spells at her. "You'll pay for this!" she howled, waving her hands again. This time the ground began to glow bright red in certain areas.

"Move! Don't stand in the light!" Raine shouted, and everyone who was standing in the red quickly moved out of it. The light erupted and fiery pillars shot out from them, lighting up the dark forest.

"Burn! All of you!" Ligeia growled with malice. She began casting another spell.

Isaac bounded off several trees in an attempt to reach her, and he threw himself toward the flying creature with a swing of his dark sword. He slammed against her shield in an explosion of darkness. The shield flickered briefly.

"Strike now!" the large man shouted, and everyone took up arms and attacked.

Isaac continued striking Ligeia until she was forced to land. "Die, bitch!"

The siren snarled, and a blue mist began to pulse from her body as several magic spells flew at her, damaging her shield.

"Watch out! Incoming!" Raine shouted. "Shield yourselves!" She jumped out in front of everyone and put up a large energy shield, defending a portion of the group.

Isaac backed away from Ligeia and put up his own shield of darkness.

The creature screamed, and the area was engulfed in a blast of blue power, burning away all the grass and leaves off the trees in the clearing.

Those who weren't protected by a magic shield were thrown away, and only a few barely survived.

Raine grunted under the immense power of the siren, and her shield started to crack. "Everyone hold on!" she called as she used her other hand to rip a nearby tree down in an attempt to crush the siren.

Ligeia swiftly moved out of the way of the falling trunk, cancelling her spell in the process. "You worms are annoying me!" she hissed.

Isaac charged a dark infused fireball and left it floating in the air. Drawing his blade, he charged the siren. "You should have thought about that before coming here," he told her in a dangerously raspy voice.

Vin charged up an arrow from his bow, training it on the siren's head.

A volley of spells flew toward Ligeia as Isaac continued his onslaught of attacks. Eventually, Raine had charged up a massive sphere of aura, and she hurled it at the siren. The orb exploded on the creature's shield, and it went down.

"Now! Give it everything you've got!" the large man shouted, and everyone charged at Ligeia with weapons in hand.

Vin fired his arrow and found its mark in one of the siren's eyes. He gave a fist pump in victory as the arrow struck deep and she howled in pain.

Isaac took the opportunity to unleash his fireball of darkness that he had created previously. It slammed into Ligeia's back in an explosion of fire and darkness.

The creature began thrashing about as several red weapons tore into her from the attackers. She slammed several of them across the forest. "How dare you disrespect me this way?" she screamed. "I am a demi-god! You are all beneath me!"

Isaac leaped up onto her back and drove his blade through her neck with devastating force. "Now you're a dead demi-god," he whispered maliciously in her ear. Twisting the blade, he violently ripped it out, nearly cleaving her head off.

Ligeia slumped to the ground with a gurgle, and her body began to dissipate.

Everyone watched as the siren's body vanished in a cloud of aural mist.

"Is it over?" someone asked.

"Yeah, I think it is!"

Several people collapsed to their knees. The time they spent under Ligeia's control was finally catching up to them.

Raine ran over to Isaac, who stood there, glaring at her with those demonic, black eyes.

"Isaac?" she called to him carefully. "Are you still ... you?"

He stood there, his darkened blade still in his hand.

She cautiously walked up to him and put her hands on his face. "It's me. It's Raine. Please come back to me." She stared into his eyes, trying to find a hint of the person she knew. "I'm so sorry. I didn't mean to hurt you." Even though her memory of being controlled was hazy, she knew she had done something to him to cause this outburst of darkness.

"Raine ..." Isaac said softly. "Are we ... friends?" The darkness in his eyes began to fade.

"Of course we are!" she told him. "I'm here for you!"

"Really?" He closed his eyes and shook his head. The dark blade disappeared.

"Please believe me. We're friends." She felt her chest tighten as she held back tears.

He opened his eyes, and the darkness was gone, revealing his usual blue eyes. "I want to be alone." He moved her hands away, and he left the area.

Vin tried to say something, but Isaac just brushed past him. Raine looked at his aura, and even though the darkness had mostly faded, she saw that it was still slightly tainted.

"What the hell just happened?" Vin asked, approaching her. "One moment we were headed to Esmeraldas, and next we're here with that creature, and Isaac was ..."

"I don't know. Some kind of mind control," she replied. "We're lucky to have survived."

"If Isaac hadn't done whatever it was using that dark power, we probably wouldn't have made it," he noted.

"Vin, that power is not good. Even if it saved us this time," Raine said. "If he continues to use it, it'll consume him, and Isaac will be no more."

"What do we do?"

She shook her head and looked at the other people recovering in the clearing. "I don't know," she muttered grimly.

The black-haired woman tapped the table. "So, your friends turned on you, did they?"

"They were being mind-controlled," Isaac explained. "They couldn't help it."

"Oh really?" She smiled. "Because their words seemed to cut deep, even awakening the evil that lays within your soul."

"What is this evil?" he asked with a frown.

"The manifestation of a lifetime of suffering that you have kept pent up all this time," she replied. "You can't hold all that anger and hatred back forever, you know."

He didn't respond, just sat there in silence.

"You know where it all comes from, don't you?" The woman rested her chin on her hand.

"Maybe ..." Isaac stared at her knowingly.

"To be betrayed by everyone around you, even if they were being controlled. That didn't bode well for you," she said with a sad expression. "This was the beginning of your downfall."

"If I didn't do anything, we probably would have been killed by that creature," he told her. "I didn't have a choice."

"You made the choice to go on this journey, did you not?" she asked. "That was your choice that led you to this point. Everything you do will lead to a consequence, for better or worse. You need to understand that anything you do will lead you somewhere, and the destination will be of your own making."

He stared blankly at her. "You make it seem like this outcome was my fate or something."

She smiled warmly. "That's exactly what I'm saying. Fate is a very fickle thing. It only takes a single choice to alter the destiny of the world."

"What are you saying?"

"I'm saying," she said with a secretive smile, "that your fate has brought you to me for a reason. One that I foresaw a long time ago."

"I don't follow." Isaac folded his arms.

"You don't have to. All will be revealed in due time." The woman spoke with gentleness. "The fate of this world is headed toward oblivion. A choice must be made to alter that course."

"What choice?"

"Yours."

PART III

SINISTER SHADOWS

The visions end, but I am not afraid.
As I peer into crimson-gold eyes, a new pact has been made,
the wings of redemption take flight, a new beginning by design,
the loyal wolf brings about a dark divine.
I see it, this vengeful beast whose gentleness brings a connection,
the kind kitsuné have given him their eternal affection.
Whatever the future holds, we gratefully sigh a relieving breath.
The path of uncertainty is worth more than a path of death.
I know not why you have come, nor why you protect us,
but as I touch your face and look into your eyes, all I can say is
Thank you, and ...
... I love you.

—Aurelia

CHAPTER 15

THE EMERALD CITY

The weather was calm in Adamas, and Lucia was spending her time in the castle courtyard enjoying the sunshine. She sat at a bench reading a book about the ancient queens, namely The First. She pondered over the small amount of history they had in writing, and the tales of old were always vague. Every queen of her bloodline all knew of their ancestor's legacy, just as her mother had taught her. The First was considered a goddess by all rights and brought happiness to the world. That is, until the calamity struck, and the betrayer stole away her power, leaving the world doomed.

The tales always mentioned the coming of would-be heroes who wielded weapons of pure light, like Isaac's longsword. There was nothing written about the purpose of these people, except that one day, someone would come and reclaim what was stolen. That was when the legend of the guardian came about, spoken from the speculation of the past. The legendary warrior, who challenged the betrayer long ago. It was thought that these people were descendants or reincarnations of that brave warrior, and that they carried the light of hope with them as the new heroes of light.

But what became of those people? Why did the darkness linger still? Several historians had pondered this mystery, for if these heroes were supposed to rid the world of evil, then why did they vanish?

But Lucia knew the truth. Instead of focusing on the past, she instead focused on the present, on the current world's "hero of light." Her belief in Isaac was unbreakable, and she knew she had to aid him in any way possible. But she didn't fully know how.

Sending him on this journey, she had hoped for him to see their world and understand their plight. But that wasn't enough. Why did the others disappear? Would he disappear too? She shook her head at the thought. *I must find a way*, she thought to herself.

"Good day, Your Majesty."

Lucia, who had been lost in thought, was startled by the sudden greeting. She looked up and saw a peculiar individual walking into the courtyard.

"I didn't think to find you out here." The man gave a bright smile.

She slowly closed her book and took a deep breath. "How can I help you, Vetis?"

Vetis, the councilman with the suspicious cat, stood a short distance away from the queen. "You seem somewhat irritated today, might there be something I can help you with?" He smiled widely.

"I would prefer to be alone," she told him firmly.

"Come now, certainly you could use some company?" He sat down on a bench across from her.

She stood up, looking away from him. "I certainly don't want company at the moment, but thanks for your inconsideration." She began to leave the courtyard.

Vetis quickly pursued her. "Milady, I did not mean to offend. It's just not very often you and I get to speak."

"I've got nothing to talk about." She headed into the castle and down the hall.

"If there's something bothering you, maybe I can help?" he insisted with that same big smile.

"There's nothing you can help with." She turned a corner and came upon the command room.

Vetis noticed where she was headed. "Well, if you do need my assistance, you only need ask." He gave a bow and was about to turn and leave.

"There is one thing," she told him. "Please, this way." She entered the room.

He followed, and inside, several people were busy at work. Lucia made her way to a certain individual presiding over the others.

"Good day, Bart," she said warmly.

"Ah, Your Majesty, what brings you here on your day off?" He looked at her with concern, especially when he noticed Vetis behind her.

"I was wondering if you would kindly explain to the councilman here why I do not appreciate him bothering me. That is all." She gave Bart a slight curtsy and left the command room, seeing Bart give a stern look to a baffled Vetis.

She quickly made her way across the castle to Isaac's room, which had been left empty since his departure. She entered and locked the door.

Even though she gave off a strong attitude and confident demeanor, deep down, she was scared. The way Vetis would stare at her, and how his cat would watch her sleep at night. She didn't feel safe around him.

After the battle with Ligeia, the survivors regrouped. Several people had died during the fight, and many more were wounded. The large man with the bastard sword that had taken charge had turned out to be the commander of Esmeraldas. Kirk was his name. He contacted the city above, and a rescue team with supplies came to assist.

As for Isaac, Raine, and Vin, they had proceeded on ahead since they were barely injured. Isaac hadn't said a word to them as they rode a giant lift all the way to the top of the massive tree. Upon entering the city, they were greeted by a marvelous display.

The city had a beautiful green glow to it, and the structures were very ornate as if the whole city belonged to kings and queens. There were several walkways made of thick glass where they could see the forest down below, and the place was busy with activity.

"The great emerald city," Raine commented. "Let's be sure to check in. We don't want to cause any trouble." She motioned to a checkpoint where visitors were being scanned.

The three approached, and Raine produced a writ of transit signed by Lucia herself.

"We come on behalf of the queen," she told the man at the counter.

"Ahh, Her Royal Majesty's seal," the man said. "Please, step through the scanner, keep your manners, and welcome to Esmeraldas."

After the three of them had entered fully into the city, Raine turned to them. "Let's find lodging and rest for today." She took a half glance at Isaac. "I think we could use a break after what just happened."

"Right ..." Vin agreed solemnly. "I've only been here a few times so I'm not sure where the inns would be."

"I've been here many times," she explained. "I know a good inn just inside the main gate here." She pointed to a grand entrance with a shimmering, green gate about thirty feet in height. It was large enough that dozens of people could move through it even if they were shoulder to shoulder. The town stretched out before them with several shops, almost like a massive outdoor mall.

The three of them passed through the gate, and Raine led them a good distance in before they came to a fancy-looking hotel. The sign read: "The Final Rest."

"The *Final* Rest?" Vin questioned. "What kind of name is that?"

"Since the forest is considered the 'forest of spirits,' there is an old tale about how when someone dies, their soul goes there to rest," Raine explained. "Therefore, this inn is just a play on words."

"Well, if you *do* enter the forest of spirits, you *will* meet your final rest." Vin shuddered.

"Let's just get a room," she said as they entered.

Inside, the place was filled with glowing crystals that illuminated the building, giving it a magical feeling.

"Welcome. How many will be staying?" the woman at the counter asked them.

"Just three," Raine answered. "I was wondering, is Lily here?"

"She is, may I ask who is requesting her?"

"Raine Beria."

"Sure, one moment." The woman stepped into a separate room behind the counter.

"You sure do know a lot of people," Vin mused.

"I've done a lot of traveling and diplomacy in Her Majesty's stead," She explained. "Also, be polite." She gave him a serious look.

He gave her a confused look.

A few moments later, a young woman approached them. She had lovely blonde hair and blue eyes. Her skin was fair, and she smelled of jasmine.

Vin's jaw dropped, and Raine sharply elbowed him. "Hello, Lily, it's so good to see you again," she said with a smile.

"Raine! Oh my goodness, it's been so long!" Lily came over, and the two hugged. "What brings you here, and are these guys with you?"

"Yes, they are my companions, and we are here on business," Raine explained. "This is Isaac, and this ..." She paused, staring Vin down. He wore a sheepish grin. "Is no one you should concern yourself with."

"Hey!" he said, only to turn his attention to Lily. "I'm Vin, it's good to make your acquaintance." He gently took her hand in his and slightly bowed with a smile, his gaze never leaving hers.

"It's good to meet you two," she replied politely. "Wow, Raine, you never cease to have men chasing you wherever you go." She winked.

"What? That's not ..." Raine started. "Never mind. We're sorry to bother you. We were wondering if you had a vacant room available for us to use for a little while."

"Just one room?" Lily gave a coy look at Raine. "The three of you, together?" She chuckled.

"It's not what you think." She gave a humorless look. "We just need a place to stay."

Lily laughed. "I'm just teasing!" She beamed at them. "It just so happens I have a few rooms available. What is the reason for your stay?"

"We're on an errand for the queen. It's quite urgent."

She thought at this answer. "The queen has done so much for me in the past ..."

"Well, you needed help, and we needed your help, so it all worked out," Raine assured her. "We don't need much, just whatever you can spare, if that's alright."

"Nonsense." Lily smiled. "I probably wouldn't have been able to maintain this inn if it weren't for her and you. In return, I'll help any way I can."

"Thanks, Lily. It really means a lot."

"You can stay in the luxury suite."

"The luxury suite!?" Raine was baffled. "You have one of those?"

"Haha, yes we do!" Lily winked. "The boys can stay in one of our standard rooms on the ground floor."

"Wait ..." Vin frowned. "You mean, we don't get to stay in the suite?"

Raine was just as shocked. "What do you mean, Lily?"

She laughed. "Well, I wouldn't have a couple of men staying with a lady like you, Raine, now would I? She can take the suite for herself, it's only fair." She smiled sweetly at Vin. "Right?"

"But, uhh ..." Vin was about to protest, but Isaac interrupted him.

"Thanks, we'll take it," Isaac told her. His face was calm as he looked at her.

"Well, well, a gentleman." Lily chuckled. "I'll bring you your keys. Don't worry about the money."

Vin just stood there stammering.

"We're getting the room for free," Isaac told him. "You should just be thankful, you know."

Raine looked at him with concern. His personality had changed slightly since their last encounter, and a part of her couldn't blame him.

"I know that, it's just ..." Vin started.

"Don't look a gift horse in the mouth," Isaac lectured him.

Vin seemed like he wanted to argue for a moment, but upon noticing Isaac's serious expression, he simply said, "You're right."

Lily returned with three keys and handed them out. "Your guys' room is down that hall, number thirty-two. Raine, come with me; yours is at the very top with the best view of town." She giggled as she headed for the elevator.

"I'll see you two later," Raine told them as she followed Lily, only to glance back for a moment at Isaac, who didn't acknowledge her.

He headed down the hall in silence as Vin followed behind. Upon entering their room, Isaac noticed how clean and spacious it was. For a supposedly low-priced hotel room, it was actually quite nice. There were two beds with fluffy emerald sheets, the carpet was soft, and there was even a display similar to a TV on a desk. The whole room was illuminated by colorful crystals.

"See, this isn't so bad," Isaac told Vin as they entered. "It's actually quite nice."

"It's not too bad," Vin replied. "But I am curious about that luxury suite."

"Just ask Raine if you can check it out later."

"Maybe." Vin shrugged.

They took off their packs and settled in. Vin flopped on one of the beds, and Isaac sat on the other.

"That shit was pretty crazy," Vin said. "I don't even recall what happened."

Isaac didn't reply.

"But damn, dude." Vin glanced at him. "I've never seen power like that."

"She said she was a demi-god. Maybe that's why."

"Not her." He pointed. "You. You used darkness and killed her. How did you do that?"

Isaac slightly glanced at Vin. "I'm not really sure."

"But you never did anything like that before." Vin sat up. "I was really surprised."

"It doesn't matter." Isaac stood up.

"I would definitely say it does. No one just uses the power of darkness without a cost."

Isaac looked at Vin and shrugged. "Maybe it's part of my 'guardian' powers." He shook his head. "I'm gonna go check out the town. Later." He moved toward the door.

"Alright ..." Vin replied. "Just, uhh, be careful, man."

Up in the luxury suite, Lily was giving Raine the grand tour.

"Wow, this suite is huge!" Raine exclaimed. "You really didn't have to do this."

"Of course I did!" Lily told her. "I owe you one."

"I feel bad for leaving the other two out ..."

"Don't worry about them. This way we can catch up," Lily said joyfully. "Come on, I'll show you around."

The suite was split up into separate rooms and covered the entirety of the top floor of the building. It took a special key to get in from the elevator. Unlike the rest of the building, the inside of the suite had an elegant, gold glow to it. The living room had a golden table topped with an assortment of liquors and wines. A fireplace was built against the wall, and the area was encircled by a luxurious couch.

"Wow!" Raine stared. "Isaac would love this." She stared at the drinks and the calm atmosphere.

"The loud one?" Lily asked. "He doesn't seem like a fun drunk to be around." She chuckled.

"No, the quiet one," she replied.

"Oh ..." Lily said. "Well, at least he wouldn't talk your ear off."

"Oh my god, is that a hot spring?" The path in the suite led to a giant balcony overlooking a good majority of the city. A giant hot tub with a fountain was in the center of the marbled deck. Steam rose from the water.

"It's been so long since I've had a good hot soak," she said with glee.

"Haha, I knew you'd like this part." Lily giggled. "It's always a woman's dream to relax in a hot spring after traveling. Albeit this is only an artificial hot spring, but we tried to make it as authentic as possible."

"It's perfect!" Raine smiled.

"Let me show you the rest of the place."

Lily guided Raine to the large walk-in showers that had complimentary high-quality soap and whatnot at her disposal. There was even a large tub for bathing. In the bedroom was a giant, king-sized bed with fluffy blankets on an ornate bed frame with a canopy.

"You've really outdone yourself with this suite," Raine said. "There was nothing like this here before."

"After you left, business started booming, and soon we had customers from all over," Lily explained. "Eventually we earned enough to remodel, and then we decided to add this suite to try and bring in royalty when they visited."

"Have you got anyone like that to come?" Raine asked.

"Just one. But he gave us high praise for it, which really boosted our reputation."

Eventually the two settled on the circular couch in the main area.

"So, what have you been doing this whole time?" Lily asked her, pouring a glass of wine for the both of them.

"I've mostly been protecting the queen lately," Raine answered. "But right now I'm searching for something."

"Like what?" she replied, handing Raine a glass filled with red wine.

"Have you seen or heard anything suspicious?" she replied, accepting the wine. "There was a group that attacked Adamas recently."

"Like the way Esmeraldas was attacked a few months back?" Lily asked.

"Yeah, we're trying to find a group of the same cultists that stole something from us. Have you heard anything?"

Lily shook her head. "I see a lot of strange people come and go, but I don't know if any of them are those crazy cult members." She sipped her wine.

"I guess they wouldn't just tell people, huh?" Raine chuckled.

"Those guys with you, though," Lily began. "Are they from Adamas as well?"

Raine nodded. "One of them is. That's the loud one." She shook her head, amused. "He's not really that bad of a guy. But don't tell him I said that."

"My lips are sealed." Lily grinned. "What about the other one? I didn't really get to meet him."

"Umm." Raine looked down at her wine glass with a some-what sad expression. "He's, uhh, quiet but kind ..."

Lily frowned upon seeing Raine's change of behavior. "Is he your boyfriend or something?"

"What? No, no!" She shook her head.

"Oh, you just seemed really deep in thought after I asked about him."

"It's not like that," Raine explained. "Isaac, he ... well, let's just say I may have done something really bad to him recently." She averted her eyes.

"Like what?" Lily asked sympathetically.

Raine held a thoughtful expression. "It's hard to explain, but I know that I hurt him, and I feel really bad about it." She thought back to the feeling she had after they'd killed the siren. Even though Isaac had become enraged, the look in his eyes after wasn't of anger, but of pain, and she knew it was something she had done while she had blacked out from the mind control.

"Maybe you can do something to apologize?" Lily suggested.

"I've tried thinking of something, but I just don't know how," Raine confessed. "I don't want to make things worse."

Lily gave her a smirk. "Have you tried seducing him?"

Raine choked a little on her wine. "E-excuse me!?"

"Ya know, maybe give him some attention until he lowers his guard, and then tell him how you feel." She narrowed her eyes mischievously. "Men love a woman's attention, and a beauty like you would easily put him under your spell." She grinned.

"Uhh." Raine fidgeted. "It's not that simple. You see, he ... uhh ... he's kind of ... different ..."

"Wow, you seem really nervous." Lily laughed. "He must mean a lot to you." She sipped her wine with a playful look.

"You've got it all wrong," Raine replied frantically. "Isaac's just a friend, that's all."

"I'm just teasing you." Lily giggled. "But if you want to grab his attention, you just need to flirt a little. Men love that stuff."

"Why am I taking advice from you?" Raine joked. "I'm not just some pretty face, ya know."

The two of them continued their chat into the evening.

Isaac was at a bar, seated outside. He stared at people passing by, glancing at all the activity around him. He was sipping a glass of whiskey when a waiter approached him. This guy was middle-aged.

"Can I bring you another drink, sir?" the waiter asked him.

He looked up at the man and glared. "You can bring me another waiter," he said forcefully. The waiter stared at him slack-jawed.

"I beg your pardon?"

Isaac continued to glare. "Did I stutter?"

The waiter looked at him for a moment before turning away and leaving. A moment later, another waiter approached, this time a young woman.

"Good day, sir." She spoke softly to him.

He looked at her and gave a gentle expression. "Good day to you too." He smiled.

"May I bring you another drink?" She smiled brightly at him.

"Yes, please. Whiskey with ice," Isaac replied. "I appreciate it." He smiled again as she nodded and left. He watched her go, using magic so he didn't have to look directly at her. She seemed shy and timid but quite kind. Using his enhanced sense of hearing, he listened to her conversation with the previous waiter.

"So, what did he say to you?" the first waiter said with a rotten tone.

"He was quite nice," she replied. "Kinda cute too." She began making Isaac's drink.

"The dude was a total asshole!" the first waiter said angrily. "Unbelievable!"

The woman finished pouring whiskey into a glass with ice cubes. She didn't look at the other waiter as she made her way back to Isaac. He looked up as she approached and gave her a gentle smile.

"That was quick," he told her sweetly.

"Here you go, sir." She placed the glass on the table in front of him. "Is there anything else I can get for you?"

"Perhaps you could tell me your name?" Isaac looked kindly into her eyes.

The waitress blushed slightly. "Oh, it's Tessa."

"Thank you, Tessa. I'm Isaac," he responded. "Might I also ask who that other waiter is?"

She paused and looked back at the entrance to the bar, then back at Isaac. "You must be talking about Quinn," she said, her smile slightly fading.

"I gotcha." He winked at her. "I won't keep you any longer. Thank you for the drink." He nodded politely. She smiled warmly again and left.

Quinn, Isaac thought. *I'll remember that.* He continued drinking with his new glass of whiskey as he stared out into the city around him. The sparkling emerald glow was very different than anything on Earth, and it was fascinating to him. As he watched people coming and going around him, his magic gaze would often focus on Tessa as she worked. She was kind and polite to the customers, a real sweetheart. He would also watch Quinn and how he looked at her.

He drank the last of his whiskey, feeling a slight buzz. It was late in the evening, and the sun was starting to go down. Since their battle with Ligeia, he and his companions had been up all night and day, but even still, Isaac was restless. The encounter had awakened a newfound power in him, and with it, a certain clairvoyance. A sixth sense that he could not ignore.

He stood and made his way into town. It was going to be a long night.

There was a knock at the door, and Vin answered. Raine stood outside of the room looking back at him. She seemed somewhat buzzed.

"Hey there, Miss Royalty." He gave her a smirk.

"Hello, peasant. Is Isaac around?" she responded with a grin.

"Why no, Your Majesty, he isn't," he said sarcastically. "But maybe I can help you with whatever it is you need." He winked at her.

Raine's expression changed to a frown. "I think I'll pass. Anyway ..." She glanced past him into the room. "I really want to talk to Isaac; you aren't hiding him back there, are you?"

"He's really not here," Vin told her sincerely. "I'm not sure where he is. Said he wanted to check out the town."

"Man!" she said dramatically. "What if he's lost?" She giggled.

"You've been drinking." He looked at her with a half grin.

"Maybe ..." she replied with a secretive smile.

"Well, I'm tired and was getting ready for bed. If you want to join Isaac for a drink, then you go find him." He chuckled.

Raine turned to leave. "Well, if he comes back, let him know I wanted to see him, would you?"

"I'm not gonna play a role in your guys' complicated love story." Vin closed the door.

"We aren't ..." She was cut off as the door clicked shut. "You're just jealous!" she called out to him.

Nighttime had fallen on Esmeraldas, and the calm air was met with the soft glow of emerald as the city slowed down. The streets that were once busy had gone quiet.

The bar closed, and the employees were leaving. Tessa packed up her uniform and was about to head home.

"Heading out?" Quinn asked her.

She paused, not looking at him. "Yes," she replied softly.

"How about I walk you home?" He grinned at her.

"I'm fine," she replied, avoiding his gaze.

"Come on, don't be like that." He moved close to her and rubbed her shoulder. "It's dangerous out there. You don't want to get hurt, do you?"

She stiffened at his touch but didn't say anything.

"How many times do we have to go through this?" he said.

Tessa pulled away from him. "I'll be fine. I'm going home now." She headed out the door, and Quinn quickly followed.

"What's the matter?" Quinn asked as he stalked her. "You don't appreciate my company?"

She quickened her pace. "It's not that ... I just want to be alone, alright?"

The area was empty except for the two of them; not another soul was in sight.

"Hey, I'm talking to you." He reached out and grabbed Tessa's arm. "Do you realize how much trouble you're causing me?"

She stopped and stared at him, fear in her eyes.

"I've been going out of my way to make sure you're safe. You should at least show your gratitude." He grinned wickedly.

"Th-thank you," she muttered.

"Thanks isn't gonna cut it." He leaned in and smelled her hair. "How's about you show me your gratitude back at my place?" He smirked.

"Please stop," Tessa muttered quietly.

"Maybe I should just let them take you, then you would know how much you really needed me." Quinn's voice was stern.

"I–I ..."

"She told you to stop," a voice came from nearby.

Looking around, Quinn spotted the source. A man dressed in black with a large mask over his face. "And who the hell are you?" He glared at the mystery man.

The man approached him. "You aren't very good at following directions," he growled.

"You might want to back off, buddy. You don't know who you're messing with," Quinn threatened, but that didn't stop the masked man, who grabbed him and threw him into a nearby wall. He crumbled to the ground in pain.

Tessa stood frozen as the masked man glanced over at her.

"It's okay," he told her. "I won't hurt you." He gently placed his hand on her shoulder. "You should go home. He won't bother you anymore."

She slowly nodded. "Thank you." She gave a weak smile and then turned and walked away.

Quinn groaned as he tried to stand. "You're making a mistake."

"You're the only mistake here," the man replied as he walked up and shoved Quinn against the wall. "You think stalking a young girl like that is acceptable?"

"Screw you!" was the reply.

The man twisted his wrist roughly. "This is about to get real ugly for you," he told him. "Why were you stalking her?"

Quinn whined in pain. "You think I'll tell you?"

"Yes, I do," the man answered calmly. "Or I'm going to break every bone in your body and leave you dying on the street." He twisted harder until Quinn's wrist snapped.

He howled in pain, and the man grinned at him.

"This is fun, isn't it?" the man said dangerously. "Let's try this again. Why were you stalking her?"

Quinn was breathing heavy from the pain. "I-I was asked to."

"By who?"

"I don't know," he gasped.

"Wrong answer." The man savagely kicked his leg, breaking his knee.

Quinn fell to the ground with a scream.

"Screaming won't help you, only answers will." The man crouched down next to him. "Who?"

"It's the ... syndicate." He struggled to get the words out. "They run the place."

"Who are they? I want specifics."

"I just work for them. They're looking for candidates for some kind of special experiment or something." His voice was weak as he held his knee with his good hand.

"Where do I find them?" The man leaned in threateningly.

"The church. The priest there works for them." Tears poured from Quinn's eyes. "Ask him, I'm just a grunt."

"Interesting." The man stood up. "You're gonna stay away from that sweet girl, Quinn," he threatened. "Because if I catch you even looking at her, I'll come back, and I'll break you 'till there's nothing left to break." He kicked him hard in his ribs. Quinn howled in pain as he went sliding into the wall. He struggled to steady himself on the ground, and when he was finally able to focus, he noticed that the man was gone.

The man in the mask stood on the roof of a quiet part of the city, out of sight from any prying eyes. He took the mask off, revealing his face.

It was Isaac.

Since the encounter with the siren, he had noticed a change in his visual powers. He could see through walls, just like Raine, and he could see people's aura, but not like the aura that she described; it was like Isaac could tell which people were good and which were bad.

When he was at the bar, he noticed Quinn's aura was incredibly dark, revealing him to be a bad person. Tessa's was light, which indicated she was good, and based on her kind personality, this had proven to be true.

He spent a good part of the evening observing Quinn and noticed his behavior toward Tessa, and he knew something was going on, so he followed them after they left the bar. Isaac's hunch had proven true. But the information on a so-called syndicate was surprising. If there were others involved in things like what Quinn was going to do, then he felt a strong desire to destroy them.

He hopped off the roof he was standing on and landed on the ground. Heading for The Final Rest, he now knew this city had secrets, and he was going to uncover them. The anger that welled up inside him needed to be vented, and what better way than to let it out on horrible people?

PRELUDE
OF VENGEANCE

Morning came, and Raine had slept well during the night. She prepared for the day as she showered and put on clean clothes. It had felt like an eternity since she'd gotten to relax so comfortably. Soaking in the hot spring did wonders for her the night prior, and she looked forward to doing it again. She entered the elevator from the suite and descended to the ground floor.

"Good morning, Raine," the woman at the counter greeted her with a smile.

"Good morning. Have you seen my friends?"

"Why yes, one of them left about thirty minutes ago," the woman replied.

"Which one?"

"The one with brown hair."

Raine nodded. "Thanks. Do you know where he went?"

"He didn't say." The woman shrugged.

"Gotcha." She smiled and left the inn. She wasn't going to bother waking Vin up.

The city had come alive, and the green glow was radiant. Raine found her way to a coffee shop and purchased a mocha. She then walked down the main city path, sipping her coffee, when she noticed a commotion.

City guards were at a bar questioning people, and among those people was Isaac. She hurried over to him, and the guard he was with looked over at her.

"Sorry, ma'am, there was a crime here last night, and we are questioning individuals about it." The guard held up his hand as if to warn her to back off.

"Don't worry, she's with me," Isaac told him calmly.

"What's going on?" Raine asked with a frown.

"A man was hospitalized last night," the guard told her. "He works at this bar."

"What does this have to do with Isaac?" she asked.

"I was on my way here for a drink, and they stopped me." Isaac shrugged. He turned back to the guard. "Like I said, I was here yesterday, but left before the sun even set. I don't know what happened," he told him.

"You didn't see anything suspicious?" the guard pressed.

"The man in question was pretty rude," he told him. "Can't say I really appreciated the guy. Maybe he pissed someone off, I dunno." He shrugged. "Look, I just wanted a morning drink. I didn't expect to get held up by the city guards for simply minding my own business." He stared blankly at the guard.

"We're just trying to find the culprit, sir," the guard told him. "Any information will help."

"Look, sir," Raine spoke up. "We just got here yesterday. We're from Adamas. Isaac here wouldn't have any information on the matter, of that I assure you."

"He's not under arrest," the guard explained. "We're just doing our job. If you find any information on a masked assailant, please notify us immediately."

"I'm sorry, a masked assailant?" she asked with a puzzled expression.

"Yes," the guard replied. "Apparently the individual that attacked the employee was wearing a mask. There was no identification."

"We'll be careful," Isaac said. "If we find out anything, we'll let you know." He turned to leave.

"We appreciate it." The guard turned away to question someone else.

"That's odd," Raine said as she and Isaac walked away from the bar. "I wonder what really happened."

Isaac didn't answer as he was closely listening to a certain person being questioned.

"I didn't see his face." The waitress known as Tessa told a guard. "He just appeared out of nowhere. I don't know who he is."

He grinned slightly as the two of them headed into the major part of the city.

"Were you really getting a drink so early in the morning?" Raine asked him with a frown. "The crystal isn't even yellow yet."

"Yeah, why not?" he replied nonchalantly.

"You may have a drinking problem." She chuckled.

"It seems you might as well," he said mischievously.

"What?" Her eyes went wide.

"Vin said you were looking for me, and that you were pretty drunk." He smirked.

Raine pursed her lips. "I was not drunk!" she said sternly. "I had a few drinks, yes, but I was not drunk."

Isaac shrugged. "That's just what he told me."

"That guy ..." She was about to continue, when he suddenly stopped. "What's wrong?"

He was staring at a peculiar building. "Is this ... a church?" he asked, looking at a building that stood out from the rest. It had elegant architecture that resembled Catholic churches from Earth.

"Yeah, it's the only one in Esmeraldas," Raine answered. "It's actually hailed as a historic monument of the city. Are you religious?"

Isaac stared at the building in thought. "I'm not, it just reminded me of Earth. The designed is very similar," he told her. "Kinda weird."

"You want to look inside?" she offered.

"Nah." He shook his head. "I don't care for that crap." He continued walking.

Raine followed after him. "Hey, uhh ..." she began. "I was just wondering. About the other day ..."

He stayed silent, not looking at her.

"I'm not sure exactly what happened, but I wanted to apologize again," she told him.

"About what?" Isaac responded somewhat sarcastically.

She paused, realizing that whatever happened still bothered him. "How can I make things right?" she asked him sincerely.

He didn't respond.

"Look, I—"

"What's our plan, by the way?" he interrupted her.

"What?"

"Our plan." He looked at her with a frown. "You know, for why we're here. The plan. The artifact we're looking for?" His expression was blank as usual.

"Oh ..." she stammered. "Right. We need to go to the palace here and speak with the king. We should be allowed entry with our letter from Her Majesty."

"So, you mean you can go and talk to him." His words weren't a question, but a statement.

"Huh?" she looked at him, confused.

"You can talk to him. You don't need me," Isaac said without looking at her.

"Don't you want to see the palace?" she asked, almost pleading.

"Nope," he responded. "I'll go sightseeing elsewhere." He turned as he walked away from her.

"Okay ..." She watched him leave and sighed. She wanted to reach out to him, to fix what it was that she'd done. But she didn't know how. It was like he was growing more and more distant in just the last two days. She was worried about him. The darkness had tainted his aura, and she felt that it may have taken over his mind.

Raine continued on toward the palace of Esmeraldas. After she spoke with the king, she would go to the royal library and search for knowledge on a possibility of suppressing that darkness.

Isaac made sure he was out of sight from Raine before he turned back and headed toward the church. He wanted to investigate which priest had a connection to this mysterious syndicate. He couldn't explain it, but the idea of there being some organization causing pain to innocent people drove him crazy. He wanted to know more, and if possible, to end their charade. He also knew that Raine would tell him to stay out of it, so he was going to make sure she didn't know what he was doing.

He walked into the church and looked around. The inside was very formal, with stained glass windows showing pictures of beautiful women with angel wings. The interior was painted white, similar to Earthly churches. Rows of pews lined the building. He glanced at some of the people inside. Most were wearing regular clothes; probably worshippers, but one individual stood out from the rest. He wore an elegant attire that clearly fit that of a priest. He approached him.

"A new face," the priest spoke joyfully. "How can I serve you?"

Isaac scanned his aura. It was bright. "Are you the only priest here?" he asked with a polite smile.

"Oh, I'm not a priest," the man replied. "I'm just an acolyte. Priest Edwin is currently in a confession. Are you seeking confession yourself?" He smiled kindly.

"Yes, actually, I am," Isaac replied. "Do you know about how long the wait will be?"

"It shouldn't be much longer," the acolyte said. "If you would like to have a seat and maybe read the scriptures, you are welcome to."

"Sure." Isaac sat at a pew and took a nearby book in his hands. He pretended to read while he scanned the area.

There were several adjacent rooms connected to the main cathedral. Peering into those rooms, he located a source of darkness. Two people were seated next to each other, and he believed that the one with a dark aura was the priest Edwin. He also checked for cameras. There were none. This was good, since he was about to raise some red flags.

He sat in silence, listening to everything around him as he waited for the current confession to end. A few minutes later, the acolyte approached him.

"The priest is available to take your confession now." He smiled.

Isaac had already been standing since he saw the individual leave the confession booth. "Thanks. Where do I go?" he asked with innocence.

The acolyte pointed at the room with the dark being. "Just through there. May God be with you."

May God be with your priest, Isaac thought as he entered the confession room.

"Good day, son," the priest said to him as he sat in the dark room of the confession stand.

"You must be Priest Edwin," Isaac said to him. There was a wall between them, probably to maintain the secrecy of the confessions.

"That I am, child," Edwin answered. "How may I serve you?"

Even though he could easily see through the wall between them, Isaac had to make sure this Edwin couldn't see him. "I have a confession to make," he said as he held up his middle finger at the priest.

"I am here to listen. God is forgiving," Edwin replied, not reacting to Isaac's hand.

He made a funny face toward the priest as he answered, "I've done something horrible." He stuck his tongue out at him.

"Take your time. I am here for you." No reaction.

Isaac leaned back, satisfied that he couldn't be seen. "It was a while ago. I did a bad thing."

"You can tell me, no one will know."

"You see, I was doing a job for The Syndicate." He paused as he noticed Edwin hold his breath at the statement. "And I was with others, when a person in black showed up." He made his tone sound sincerely apologetic.

The priest swallowed. "Did you happen to see who that man was?"

"No, he wore a mask," Isaac explained with a smirk. "As soon as he showed up, I quickly hid. He didn't notice me."

"What happened to the others?" Edwin asked slowly.

"They were killed," he answered, holding back a chuckle.

"And have you reported this incident?" The priest sounded almost stern.

"Uhh ..." Isaac pretended to be scared. "That's what I'm confessing. I haven't reported this to anyone."

There was a pause. He watched Edwin's face change to that of someone eager.

"There was an attack last night," the priest said. "One of ours was hospitalized by the same masked man." His tone was different now. "If you have any information on him, they will need to know."

Bingo. Isaac made his voice shaky as he answered, "That's the thing, I don't know who to go to." *Come on, spill the beans, asshole.* He listened for the reply.

"This is a very serious matter," Edwin said darkly. "You will need to inform the secretary about this."

"I don't know who that is." He tried to sound innocent.

"How long have you been in the organization?"

"Not very long." What did that matter?

"The cemetery," Edwin said. "Be there at midnight. I will arrange a meeting."

A cemetery? Seriously? "I'm not in trouble, am I?" he asked with a grin.

"We will discuss that tonight." The priest's face was serious.

"O-okay, I'll be there," Isaac replied and quietly left the confession booth.

"Good, now let me see who you are before you leave so we know who will arrive," Edwin said.

There was no reply.

"You don't have to be afraid." He stepped out of the booth and opened the door to the other side. It was empty. He looked around in confusion.

Isaac chuckled as he stood outside of the church. He had exited out the window before the priest even noticed. "What a sucker." This whole thing was becoming quite interesting. Who would he be meeting in the cemetery? He would have to wait till midnight to find out.

Raine had spoken to the king's attendant and informed them of their situation in hunting down the artifact. Since the king of Esmeraldas and the queen of Adamas were close allies, the king agreed to assist and sent messengers to try and discern the location of the stolen amulet. Afterward, she made her way to the library within the palace in hopes that she could find information on suppressing dark magic.

"Excuse me." She approached one of the librarians. "I was wondering if you had any books on dark magic."

The librarian gave her a puzzled look. "From my knowledge, there's not much information on darkness. What would you need to know about it?"

"I'm looking for a way to suppress it," Raine explained.

"Well, I can give you a list of books that may help, but I wouldn't hold my breath." The librarian tapped away at her computer.

"Anything might help," Raine said as the librarian eventually handed her a document with a list of books and their locations in the library.

"Dark magic isn't to be taken lightly," the librarian added.

"I know, that's why I need all the information I can get." Raine nodded politely and began to search for the books on the list.

After acquiring them, she sat at a desk going over the pages. She spent at least an hour trying to find anything about darkness, but all that came up was how bad it was.

"I know it's bad, so how do I stop it?" she muttered to herself irritably. Another hour later, with no luck, she quit searching. Placing the books back, she felt somewhat disheartened. How was there no solid information on dark aura?

"I'll just see if I can talk to Isaac for a bit." She pulled out her phone. "I hope he agrees. I really want to make amends." She sent him a text and was anxious when he replied. She sighed in relief upon seeing him agree to meet her. She texted back a location for them to talk.

A while later, the two of them met at a bar near the palace.

"Thanks for coming," Raine said with a smile as they sat down.

"How can I refuse free drinks?" he responded with his usual calm demeanor.

"I just realized that it's not very often that I treat you to a fun time."

"Did you find out anything at the palace?" he asked her.

"At the palace?" Her eyes went wide. "Uhh ..."

"About the amulet?"

She snapped out of her daze. "Oh, right. Of course. The king has people looking into it. Hopefully they return with good news," she said with relief after thinking Isaac was mentioning dark magic.

"So, we just wait then," he said. "Guess we should order drinks."

After the two had obtained their own beverages, they continued their chat.

"So, how was your day?" Raine asked him. "Do anything fun?"

"Not really." Isaac sipped his drink. "Mostly just wandered around exploring."

"It's a beautiful city, isn't it?"

"I guess ..." He continued to sip his drink.

She watched him for a moment; his expression was always blank as if he really didn't care about anything.

"I have an idea," she told him. "How about you join me tonight in the suite?" She smirked at him. *Come on, be flirty,* she thought.

"Why?" He frowned.

"It's really nice up there, and there's a hot spring!" She tried moving her hair to look more appealing to him. "We could both go for a soak together." She put her finger to her cheek with a big grin.

"Not really in the mood to swim," Isaac replied.

Raine was somewhat taken aback. He was still mad at her. She decided to try a different approach. "There's lots of alcohol up there. Good quality stuff, and free at that!" She winked.

Isaac placed his hand on his chin in thought.

"Come on." She nudged him. "Let's get drunk together. Whadya say?" She grinned happily at him.

"No thanks," he replied while taking a long drink from his whiskey. "No offense, but I just don't feel like it."

"He said WHAT!?"

Back at the inn, Lily was dumbfounded. She and Raine were up in the suite. The sun had set.

"I told you, he's ... different." Raine was sulky. "I just don't know how to get through to him. It really bugs me that there's this awkwardness between us now."

"How could a guy refuse to sit in a hot spring with a gorgeous woman like yourself?" Lily shook her head in disbelief. "He's not gay, is he?"

"I don't think so," Raine replied, taking a sip of wine. "I just want things to go back to normal. He won't even let me train him anymore."

"This really is a predicament," Lily told her. "Alright, it seems you'll need my assistance." She beamed at Raine. "I'm gonna help you land this fish!" She clapped her hands together confidently.

"It's not like that!" Raine said to her with a chuckle. "I just want us to be good friends again."

"Don't worry, I'll help ya. By the time I'm done, he'll be totally under your spell!" Lily smirked.

"You aren't even listening ..." Raine shook her head in amusement.

It was close to midnight, and the priest had left the church, making his way across town. He didn't notice the silent shadow that followed him. He walked for several minutes until he came upon a cemetery.

Isaac watched from the top of a nearby building as a few people stepped out of the shadows and approached Edwin.

"Is everything secure?" one man spoke to the priest.

"We should be on schedule. The shipment leaves in two days," Edwin replied.

"Good, I'll inform the councilman. With this, we should be able to move forward with the next step," the man said. "With all luck, the king won't know what's going on till it's too late."

Under Isaac's mask, his eyes frowned. *This is some sneaky stuff going on*, he thought to himself. *Would be a shame if someone sabotaged it.*

"What about that other matter?" another man asked the group.

"You mean the incident last night with Quinn?" the first man asked.

"Yes, and the man in the black mask."

"Don't worry. One guy isn't going to be a problem," the man said. "Someone wanted to be a hero last night, and if he pokes his head up again, we'll cut it off."

CHAPTER 16: PRELUDE OF VENGEANCE

"Someone came into the confession booth today and mentioned the masked man," Edwin said. "He told me that the man in black showed up the other day and killed the group he was with."

"I haven't heard of anything like that." The man frowned. "Who was the individual that reported this?"

"I don't know; he left before I could see him." The priest shrugged. "He was supposed to show up tonight."

"That's curious," one of the others said.

"It doesn't matter," the man told them. "Back to the topic of Quinn. What about that girl, the waitress he was trying to get?"

Isaac perked up.

"We've sent someone else to get her. She should be at the storage site now," one of the men answered.

"Good, we'll deliver her to the duke as a means of securing our trade route through Rubens." The man grinned. "He's always loved young brunettes, and that girl is top of the line. I'm sure he will be pleased."

Isaac's lip curled in anger.

"Go check on her and make sure she's prepped for delivery in the morning. The sooner we secure that trade route, the sooner we can move the goods," the man told the one who'd mentioned Tessa.

"Right away." He walked off.

Isaac snapped a photo of the men with his phone. *I'll find you guys later*, he thought as he turned his attention to the man leaving the area. *I have to save that girl first.*

He silently followed the suspicious man by hopping from rooftop to rooftop. Eventually, he came upon an open area filled with people.

Isaac grumbled. *Why are there so many people out this late at night?* He silently dropped to the ground and removed his mask. He would just have to blend into the crowd while he stalked his prey. He casually stepped into the open after putting the mask into his pocket, pretending to be a regular civilian.

"Hey sweetie, you busy right now?" a woman in a skimpy dress called out to him.

"Not interested," he replied. So that's why so many people were around. It was a red-light district. He ignored the prostitutes and solicitors as he watched the suspicious man walk down a sketchy alleyway. He moved down a different alley while watching the man through the buildings.

When he was out of sight, he put his mask back over his eyes and quickly closed the gap between himself and the man.

It wasn't long after that the man came to a large warehouse. He glanced around a moment and then entered.

Isaac stood outside, hidden, as he scanned the building. After a moment, he located Tessa. She was locked in some kind of box with no windows. His eyes flared.

"You shitbags," he muttered angrily under his breath.

The building also had several other people, most likely the ones who were going to move her in the morning.

But that wasn't going to happen.

The storm inside Isaac's head raged as he prepared to enter the warehouse.

"You're all going to die tonight!"

There was a rapid knocking on the door.

Vin glanced over and rolled his eyes as he heard the voices from the other side.

"Isaac! Come out and play!" Lily's voice rang out.

"Don't keep us waiting, silly!" Raine was also there.

Shaking his head, he walked over and opened the door. He was greeted by two tipsy women.

"He's not here," Vin said with a playful look.

"Nonsense," Raine told him. "You can't hide from us, Isaac." She pushed her way into the room.

Lily giggled. "I feel like a kidnapper."

Vin dramatically held his arms out. "Please, just let yourself in ..." He sighed.

The two women glanced around the room.

"Wow, he really isn't here," Lily said with disappointment.

"Has he been back at all?" Raine asked Vin.

"Nope," was the reply. "He even came back really late last night."

"He's probably hanging out at the red-light district," Lily suggested with another giggle.

"That doesn't sound like something he would do," Vin said doubtfully.

"Think we should go check?" Raine grinned.

"Oh my god, if we were to find him there ..." Lily laughed.

"Aren't red-light districts kind of dangerous for women?" Vin asked.

Raine tilted her head in thought. "You're right, that's why you should accompany us, Mr. Bodyguard."

"Say what?"

Lily giggled again. "Aww, you don't want to? You'll get to hang out with two cute girls." She fluttered her eyes at him.

"Well, when you put it that way, why not?" He grinned mischievously.

The three headed out toward the red-light district.

"How's the girl?" the suspicious man asked someone near Tessa's crate.

"She was a little loud at first, but we quieted her down quick," he replied.

"You better not have hurt her," the man said. "We need her in perfect condition to present to the duke."

"Don't worry, boss, she's fine. She's just taking a nap right now." He smirked.

Farther into the warehouse, a shadow moved.

"Watch duty is so boring," one man said to another. "Why do we always get chosen to watch the cargo?"

"I dunno, man," the other guy said. "Maybe they just don't like us."

They continued to chat, oblivious to the one that was watching them. Isaac moved closer, keeping himself out of sight. Eventually he was within a few feet of them.

"That girl we have, though, she's damn gorgeous, isn't she?" one of them said.

"I kinda wish I could keep her for myself." The other laughed. But their chat was cut short as Isaac jumped out behind one of them and swiftly broke his neck.

"What the hell!?" A red mace appeared in the second man's hand. Isaac dodged the incoming attack and struck him in the belly, bringing his other fist up and smashing it in his face.

The man gasped, trying to catch his breath. Isaac grabbed him and slammed him onto a nearby wooden table, shattering it. He stomped the man's head in, crushing his skull.

Leaning down, he picked up one of the broken table legs. One side was splintered in a pointed shape. He made his way toward the rest of the men who were surrounding Tessa's crate.

Isaac knew not to use his aural blade, since that would give away his identity. Instead, he would have to improvise.

The men sat around, not knowing that two of them had been killed off. The warehouse was large and spacious, and since it was nighttime, only small overhead lamps dimly lit the area. Some of them joked about how creepy the building was at night. They didn't realize just how creepy tonight would become.

Isaac counted the number of enemies. There were seven. He readied the wooden spike in his hand.

It was about to become six.

Preparing himself, he knew that once he began, he would have to face them all.

There was a pause in the air as the men sat around. But that pause was broken as the wooden spike came flying through the air, impaling one of them from the back. Everyone stood and glanced at their companion. A trickle of blood ran from his mouth, and he slumped to the ground, dead.

"Shit!" one of them shouted.

Isaac rushed into the area from a different angle, catching one of them by surprise. He savagely kicked him, and the man went flying into a metal pole. He struck the pole hard with a loud thud, and Isaac followed up by slamming the man's head violently into it.

Five.

"It's the man in the mask!" another guy shouted, and aural weapons appeared in the remaining thugs' hands.

The suspicious man from the cemetery stared at Isaac wide-eyed. "Kill him! I don't care how you do it!"

They came at him.

Isaac ducked an attack from a sword and punched the man in the gut. He held his hands up and caught another attacker's aural club. He twisted the man around as someone attempted to get him from behind with a spear, but the attack was met by the man holding the club. The spear cut through the man's chest, and Isaac kicked him away.

Four.

The man with the sword recovered from Isaac's blow and charged at him. He grabbed Isaac and shoved him into a nearby wooden crate. He smashed through the crate in a shower of splinters.

"Grr," Isaac growled as he hit the ground.

Two other men ran up on him, their weapons at the ready. Now lying on his back, Isaac waved his hands, causing the splintered wood to float around with telekinesis. Another wave, and the splinters surrounded the men, stabbing into their skin. They growled in pain, putting their hands up to protect themselves. It gave Isaac enough time to get back on his feet.

The one who'd shoved him came charging up as he was recovering. He swung his red blade at him. Isaac ducked and then brought his arms up to block a kick from the assailant. Another sword swipe, but Isaac caught the man's wrist as it passed dangerously close to his face. He brought his other hand upward to the man's elbow, breaking his arm. The man howled in pain. Isaac then did a spin kick, forcing the man onto the ground.

The other two men recovered from the splinters and were coming at him once again. Looking around, Isaac spotted a long, metal rod; he pulled it to his hand with telekinesis and slammed it down on the man who was lying on the ground.

Three.

Twirling the rod like a staff, he faced the last two attacking thugs, the suspicious man only watched anxiously. He blocked their attacks with the rod and delivered counterattacks in kind. One of the men dropped his guard momentarily, and Isaac took advantage of it by slamming the butt of the rod into the man's shin, causing him to slightly double over in pain, which allowed him to bring the rod up into the man's chin, knocking him clean out.

The final attacker stood little chance one on one against Isaac, and soon he was on the ground, dead.

Two.

Isaac stared at the remaining individual through his mask as he walked to where the unconscious man was. He drove the rod downward through the man's skull.

One.

Throwing the rod aside, he approached the final victim.

"Have you any—" the man started.

"Idea who you are?" Isaac finished his sentence. "No, and I don't give a shit." He grabbed the man and threw him to the ground. He put his foot on the man's back and grabbed one of his arms.

"You're going to answer some questions, or you won't be walking out of here alive," Isaac growled at him. "This shipment that leaves in two days, where is the location?"

The man grunted as his arm was slowly being twisted. "I can't tell you. They'll ... they'll kill me!"

Isaac's eyes flared. "Bitch, I'll kill you!" He twisted the man's arms roughly, causing him to cry out in pain. "Are you serious right now?"

"Please." The man struggled through tears.

"You should have thought about that before abducting an innocent girl." He twisted the man's arm till it popped.

The man screamed.

"That's one arm," Isaac told him as he grabbed the other. "I'll make the pain stop, all you gotta do is answer my *god-damn* question!" he growled.

"If I tell you, you'll let me go?" the man cried.

"Yep."

"It's at the loading dock near the flight pads. Section B." The man was breathing heavy.

"You aren't lying to me, are you?" Isaac's voice was dangerous.

"No, no, I swear! Oh god ..."

"God can't save you." He glared down at the evil man.

"What? But you said ..."

Isaac grinned. "That I would let you go and end the pain? That's exactly what I'm going to do." He reached over and grabbed a cinder block lying near a corner of the warehouse with telekinesis. He slammed it down on the man's head, killing him instantly.

Zero.

He quickly walked over to the crate and forced it open, looking inside.

Tessa was lying there, her eyes closed and her breathing calm.

"Tessa ..." He reached out and felt her face. It was warm. She didn't seem to have any injuries on her. The air was fairly warm inside the crate, and Isaac waved his hand, cooling the air around her with magic. He gently shook her.

"Tessa, wake up." As he shook her, she started to stir. "There ya go. Come on."

She opened her eyes and looked up at him groggily. "Huh? Where ...?" Her eyes began to focus, and she recognized him. "It ... it's you ..."

Isaac helped her sit up. "You okay?" He spoke to her gently.

"I-I think so." She looked around. "Where are we?"

"Probably best if you don't look around." He gently tilted her head back so she was looking at him. "Can you stand?"

She nodded, and he helped her to her feet. "I was so scared. These men, they came after me and I just ..." She started to tear up.

"I know. It's okay now," he reassured her. "Let's get out of here." He guided her through the warehouse, making sure to avoid the bodies. They eventually made it outside.

"Is there somewhere you can go? Somewhere safe?" he asked her.

"My brother's," she said. "He works for the guards; it should be safe there, I think."

"I'll take you to a nearby guard. Would he be able to escort you home?" Isaac gently had his hand on her back as they walked. He didn't remove his mask.

327

"Yeah, I believe so ..." She was still shaking from the ordeal, and Isaac couldn't blame her.

"Then let's go find one."

Tessa looked over at him as they continued through the city, alone. "Why did you save me?"

Isaac thought for a moment. *Why did I save her?* He couldn't really explain it. Normally he wouldn't involve himself in such things, but after acquiring the sight of seeing good and evil, he just ...

"Because I wanted to. That's all." He spoke calmly.

"Thank you ..." Her eyes twinkled in the moonlight as she looked at him gratefully.

He didn't respond, and she didn't notice him blush slightly under his mask.

Eventually they found a guard on patrol, and Isaac scanned his aura. It was bright.

"There's one," he told her. "Go, let him know what happened. And ..." He paused for a moment. "Stay safe." He patted her shoulder softly as he said the last part.

Tessa looked at him as she slowly moved toward the guard. "I won't forget you." She smiled thankfully to him, and he returned the smile with a nod.

She approached the guard and began to tell him what had transpired. After mentioning the man in the black mask, she pointed to where Isaac had been, but he was gone.

"Do you see now?" The woman with black hair smiled gently at Isaac. "That there's kindness in your heart?" Her eyes sparkled.

Isaac averted his gaze. "I guess it doesn't really matter now, after everything that I did ..."

"That's not true," she told him sweetly. "Everyone has their bad days."

"By destroying a village and nearly killing the one trying to defend it ... from me?" He gritted his teeth.

"Why did you save that girl?" The woman's eyes peered at him with empathy.

He simply shook his head. "I don't know."

"Sure you do." She reached out and took Isaac's hand in hers. "You may put up a fake façade for the world to see, but deep down, you're really a sweetheart."

He stared back into her eyes, almost hypnotized by them. "Uh ..." His cheeks turned slightly pink as he didn't know how to respond.

She giggled, still holding his hand. "Aww, you're blushing!"

Isaac looked away nervously. "No, I'm not."

The woman took her hand off his and leaned back. "You're doing it again."

"Kinda hard to think how nice I am when I've killed so many people ..." He frowned.

"They would have done far worse to her," she told him. "I don't have to spell it out. You did what you had to, to protect her. They would have just gone after her again. You possess a rare sense. The ability to see the true nature of people. You've always had it, but now you're able to see it plain as day."

"What do you mean?" he asked.

"Do you remember back to the tournament? You told me you killed the man in your first battle, but then you let that girl, who was supposed to be an enemy, live?" She looked thoughtful. "Why do you think that is?"

He shrugged. "It was just a feeling I had."

"Exactly." She tapped her fingers. "Your ability allows you to see the truth."

Isaac stared back at the woman with curiosity. "I asked before, but you never told me. Why do you look like her?"

She smiled back at him almost lovingly.

"You aren't going to tell me, are you?" He looked at her blankly.

"Not quite just yet." She winked at him. "There's still so much to learn about you before you can learn about me." She clasped her hands in front of her, resting them on the table. "Please, continue. Did you take down this syndicate?"

Isaac tilted his head. "I guess it depends on what you mean by 'take down.'"

"Did something happen?"

"Yeah," he said grimly. "A lot of things. Even Raine, she was ..."

The woman nodded. "Tell me everything. I want to hear every detail."

CHAPTER 17

AN UNEXPECTED MEETING

At an unknown location, Zagaan sat, watching his followers obeying his orders, when one of the cultists approached.

"Lord Zagaan, I bear ill tidings." The cultist spoke carefully.

"What is it?" Zagaan hissed, his eyes leered at the quivering man.

"It's about Esmeraldas and Ligeia." He swallowed hard. "There have been reports coming in about survivors of a battle in the forest and the death of ... a demi-god."

Zagaan sat up straight, and he stared hard at the cultist. "What do you mean!?"

The cultist paused for a moment to compose himself. "It appears that a man with a blade of light destroyed the creature that had everyone under her mind control."

The reaper just sat there for a moment in silence. He searched his aura for a sign of his eidolon's life. "What is this ...? I cannot feel her presence." He stared back at the cultist. "What are these reports?"

"Apparently," the cultist answered, "there was a group of people who showed up to the city and reported a battle in the forest against a large demon with wings, and that the guardian had slain her."

Zagaan's eyes flared. "Impossible!" He held his hand out. "Ligeia! I summon you!"

Nothing.

"Ligeia!" he tried again.

No answer.

He sat there in silence, fuming. Never had an eidolon, a demi-god bound to a reaper, ever been killed.

Until now.

"She should have mind-controlled him," he snapped. "How did someone surpass the power she possessed!? *It's impossible!*" He slammed his fist on the table next to him, shattering it. Several cultists looked at him in fear.

"This boy is more troublesome than any of the others ever were." He breathed heavily in anger. "I'm going to have Magnus drag that bastard to me one way or another!"

At the red-light district, Raine, Lily, and Vin walked down the main road.

"Holy crap, this place is wild!" Vin said with a grin.

The entire area was busy with people in skimpy outfits, and the buildings had sexual pictures on the windows. There were shops that sold adult toys and videos as well as a multitude of strip bars and brothels. The usual emerald glow of the city was different here, instead replaced with pink.

"There's no way Isaac would be in a place like this," Raine said, looking around. "But it's kinda funny that a sophisticated city like Esmeraldas would have such an area." She chuckled, holding a cup of wine in her hand.

"Even if we don't find him, this could turn out kind of fun!" Lily said with a giggle.

They had all gotten drinks at a nearby club and were walking around the district sightseeing, as well as keeping an eye out in case Isaac was there.

"How you doing, baby?" a random man made a pass at Raine.

"In your dreams, dude!" She laughed back at him.

"Don't be like that, honey." The man grinned at her as he grabbed her arm. "I'm just being friendly."

"You might want to let go of her," Lily sneered at him. "She's a powerful mage, she'll kick your ass!"

Raine made a spark of electricity appear from her eyes as she stared at him. "I bite!" She bared her teeth.

The man quickly let go and backed away. "Whoa now, easy. I was only teasing ya, no need for that." He smiled nervously and turned away from them.

Raine and Lily giggled with each other.

"You two are crazy." Vin shook his head. "It's kind of adorable."

"You're only lucky because we know each other." Raine poked at him. "But don't you dare get any ideas."

"I know, I know." He held his hands up. "I learned my lesson a long time ago."

Lily perked up. "Oh, I have to hear this." She laughed. "Tell me, tell me!"

Raine looked at Vin mischievously. "Sorry, Lily," she said. "That's between us two."

"I don't want to remember," he said in fear. "It was terrible!"

"For you, maybe." Raine chuckled.

"Now I REALLY wanna know!" Lily pleaded.

"Maybe I'll tell you later." Raine winked.

The three continued to stumble down the district before they saw a familiar face.

"Oh ... my god." Raine stopped and stared at the individual. "I don't believe it."

Vin wore a slack-jawed expression.

"So, he IS like that." Lily smirked.

They approached their friend who was wandering down the main road of the red-light district.

"Wazzup, Isaac!?" Lily shouted at him. "Fancy seeing you here!"

Isaac paused as he saw them. "Wh-what are you guys doing here?" he stammered.

"We're asking the questions here!" Raine said in a tipsy voice. "We were wondering what you were doing out so late."

He stared at her with a frown. "I was, uhh ..." He frantically thought for an excuse.

"Well?"

"I, uhh ..." He gave a cheesy smile. "Was, uhh ... looking, for a hooker."

The girls looked at him in surprise. "Really ...?" Lily asked doubtfully.

"Yep."

"Mah man!" Vin held his hand up for a high-five.

Isaac merely looked at Vin with no interest and then back at the ladies. "Why are you guys here?"

"Actually, we were looking for you," Lily told him with a drunken smirk. "Raine was worried about you."

Raine looked wide-eyed at Lily. "What!? It's not like that!" She looked at Isaac. "I was just curious where you ran off to," she said, flustered. "I, uhh, was just wanting to say hi!" She gave a goofy, drunk smile.

"Hi," Isaac replied and turned to leave.

"Whoa, whoa!" Lily moved in front of him. "*Now* where are you going?"

He frowned at her, slightly irritated. "I told you, to get a hooker." He held a serious expression.

"Wait, you're serious!?" Raine was flabbergasted.

"Unbelievable!" Lily gave him a stern look. "Your lady friend here has been waiting all night to throw herself at you, and you've been looking for a cheap whore?"

"Hey!" Raine punched Lily's arm. "That's not what happened!"

"Cool story," Isaac dismissed her and stepped around Lily.

"Get a good one, dude!" Vin cheered him on.

This time it was Raine who stopped Isaac. She tugged on his shirt before he could take a step. "Come on, Isaac, don't you wanna hang out with us?"

"Nope." He pulled away from her and walked off.

She just stood there with a devastated expression. "B-but ..."

He was gone.

Lily was shocked. "He really is different ..." She glanced at Raine, who looked as if she would cry. "Hey, you okay?"

"I just don't get it." She shook her head sadly. "Where did we go wrong?" Her eyes reddened as her chest tightened and the alcohol kicked in.

"It's okay," Lily tried to comfort her. "Let's go back. We can chat and drink till you pass out." She took Raine's arm in hers. "Let's have a girl's night in."

"Can I join?" Vin asked.

"Girls only!" she hissed at him.

He shrugged sadly. "Man ... I don't deserve this."

The following morning, Isaac was in his room with Vin watching the news on the TV.

"Several men were murdered last night in a warehouse near Rouge Street," the reporter said.

"What the hell?" Vin muttered. "Weren't we near that area last night?"

"I don't really know the city that well," Isaac replied. "Maybe?"

Vin nodded. "Right, you're not from here." He lay back in bed. "That's crazy, though. Nine men were killed."

"Not our problem," Isaac replied. "Let's just find this artifact and leave."

"We're still waiting on an answer from the palace," Vin told him. "That's what Raine says, at least."

Isaac got out of bed and started getting dressed. "This waiting is a drag."

"I hear ya, man." Vin yawned. "Where are you headed?"

"Nowhere in particular," Isaac replied as he put on his shoes.

"Why don't we get some food together?" Vin suggested.

"I'll pass. I want to be alone," Isaac told him as he left the room.

Vin watched him leave. *Huh*, he thought, *maybe Raine is on to something. Isaac has been pretty distant lately.*

Tomorrow night was when the apparent shipment of whatever would take place. Isaac wanted to see the location before he made his move. He purchased a map from a nearby store and soon located the loading docks. *Site B*, he remembered as he walked around the area. Having the handy ability of being able to look in any direction with magic without actually turning his head would keep him from looking suspicious. He scanned the area and noticed a section that was marked as reserved. This was probably the spot they would put whatever goods they were transporting.

Guess I'll have to ruin their plans. Isaac grinned to himself. This was getting entertaining. The way he'd been feeling lately—this would be a good way to vent.

Raine woke near noon. She drank a glass of water as she nursed a slight hangover. It had been a while since she'd drank so much in a single night. She sat on the couch in the main area of the suite watching TV. The news was on about a mass murder in a warehouse.

"That's odd," she thought out loud. "Wasn't that near the red-light district?" She continued to watch, thinking how peaceful the city was when she'd last visited. Maybe things had changed since then, especially with the attacks by the cultists.

After a while, she got dressed and headed out. She stopped by Isaac's room and knocked on the door. Vin answered.

"He's not here," he said with a sigh.

"That's okay," she told him. "Maybe you would like to join me? I'm going to the palace to see if there's any news on the missing artifact."

"Sure, as long as we can grab food on the way. I'm starving. Let me get ready. One moment." He closed the door and got dressed.

Soon the two of them were outside heading to a diner.

"Is it just me, or does it seem like Isaac is avoiding us?" Vin asked her.

"He's avoiding us," Raine replied with a sad tone.

"I don't get it." He frowned. "What did we do?"

"I don't know," she replied. "Do you remember the other night in the forest when we fought that thing?"

"Yeah ..."

"Well, do you remember how we got there?" She looked at him.

Vin thought for a moment. "Not really. We were walking, then my memory gets fuzzy, and next thing, we're standing with a large group and Isaac was shouting at us to fight."

"It's the same for me, but do you remember his eyes?" Her voice was almost a whisper.

He nodded. "Yeah, they were freaky."

"It wasn't just that," she added. "I peered at his aura, and there was this swirl of darkness around him."

They arrived at the diner and stood there staring at each other.

"What does it mean?" he asked.

"I'm not sure, but he's acted strange ever since."

"What's his aura look like now?"

"It's mostly back to normal, but ..." She looked grim. "It's tainted. There's still a faint hint of darkness. It may even be having some kind of effect on his mind."

He looked puzzled. "What kind of effect?"

Raine looked solemn as she answered. "It could instill anger, fear, sadness, I'm not entirely sure. There isn't much information on the effects of darkness." She reached for the door into the diner. "Let's just eat; we can figure it out later."

They mostly ate in silence. Once they finished, they headed toward the palace.

"Damn that was good!" Vin said loudly while rubbing his belly.

"You're so dramatic." Raine shook her head.

He shrugged. "Whatever, that pulled pork was delicious."

"Funny how food can lighten the mood," she speculated.

"And it allows you to rhyme." He winked at her.

After a bit, they arrived at the palace.

"Hello, we're here about our request to the king?" Raine asked one of the receptionists.

"Raine Beria, correct?" the receptionist asked.

"Yes, that is correct."

"It's just down the hall. There's a waiting area at the end in room fifty-seven." The receptionist pointed down a hallway.

"Thank you." Raine bowed, and they turned and headed down the hall.

Unlike Adamas Castle, the Esmeraldas palace had a more modern look inside, with the walls lined with ornate green crystals and chandeliers hanging from the ceiling, with clean, not too modest carpeting of a turquoise color.

As they moved down the hallway, Raine noticed a familiar face, and she swiftly ducked out of sight into a nearby room. She quickly ushered Vin to do the same.

"What's up?" he asked in confusion.

"This is bad," she whispered. "I just saw one of the councilmen down the hall."

"What? They aren't supposed to be here," he replied. "They were all under lockdown at Adamus."

"That's what we thought." She used her magic to see through the walls and spied the individual. "But there's no doubt that's Ubel."

"What the hell would he be doing all the way out here?" He frowned.

"I don't know, but we can't let him see us," she told him. "He knows our faces, especially me. If he finds out we're here, the queen will have to answer for it."

They waited for the councilman to leave the area before proceeding down the hall.

"We need to also let the king know not to mention us to him." They entered the waiting room.

"If a councilman is here," Vin started, "then that means he broke the lockdown rules."

"He must have a good reason. I'm not sure why, but I don't feel like asking him." She smirked.

"Probably not a good idea," Vin agreed.

They waited for a moment before being allowed entrance. In the throne room sat the king. He was an older man with long hair and a grand beard. The people of the city knew him as King Roland, but Queen Lucia knew him as her uncle.

"Good day, Your Majesty!" Raine and Vin bowed politely to him.

"Welcome back." Roland smiled at them. "I'm afraid there's still no information on the queen's artifact. But we are almost quite sure it's not here in the city. There's been no activity of any cultists or their demons entering Esmeraldas."

"Is there anything we can do to help speed up the search?" Raine asked politely.

"Afraid not. We've got our best scouring the surveillance systems and tracking any movement down below in the forest," he explained. "All we can do is just be patient."

"Well, if we have to wait," Vin chimed in, "I was curious if you've heard of the masked vigilante that made the news today."

"Vin!" Raine shot him a nasty look.

"I have, actually," the king confirmed. "We've been look-ing into it. Normally these kinds of cases are left to the local guard, but since they have no information on this individual, we've decided to assist in unmasking the killer."

"Maybe we can help with that," Vin suggested.

"No!" Raine snapped at him. "This isn't why we're here!"

"Raine is right." Roland nodded. "You two need to stay hidden and keep a low profile. We'll work on finding out who this assassin is." He glanced at them curiously. "By the way, didn't you say there was a third member of your group?"

"Yeah," Raine answered. "He decided not to come today."

"I see. Well, I sure would have liked to meet this person Her Majesty has put her faith in." He shrugged.

"Sorry," Raine apologized. "We're kind of having a squab-ble at the moment. Nothing too big, just some things were said and now we aren't talking much."

"Well, hopefully he knows to keep a low profile," Roland advised. "If my niece Lucia trusts him, then I'm sure he won't get into any trouble."

Nighttime had come, and Isaac was wandering the town, keeping an eye out for anyone with an evil aura. His restless-ness was getting the better of him.

Since the battle with the siren, he could feel a darkness tugging at him, and he yearned for conflict.

I should pay that priest a visit, he thought. *Maybe beat more info out of him.* He grinned at the thought as he headed in the direction of the church.

It wasn't long before he saw a peculiar sight. Through the buildings, he spied two individuals. One had an evil aura and the other did not.

Don't tell me this is another kidnapping, he thought as he put on his mask and made his way closer. As he approached, he recognized the individual with the bright aura. She was with an unknown man. Isaac decided to eavesdrop on their conversation.

"Payment is coming up," the man told her. "How long are you going to keep us waiting?"

"I'm sorry," the woman replied. "I'm trying to bring in more money, truly I am, but things have been complicated since the attack on the city a few months ago."

"I don't want to hear your excuses!" the man snarled at her. "We have a deadline, and if you don't do your part, we all get busted."

"I know that!" she said, slightly panicked. "I'm doing the best I can. I'll make sure the money and the goods are delivered on time."

"You'd better. I'm not going down because of you!" He glared at her, then turned and walked away.

Normally, Isaac would have chased him down and beat the crap out of him, but right now he was more interested in the woman. He watched her walk in the opposite direction of the man, and he followed her. When they were in a secluded area, he approached her.

"Fancy seeing you out here, Lily." Isaac stood in front of her.

Lily gasped. "What? I, uhh ..." She stared hard at him in shock. "Oh my god ..." She trembled. "Y-you're ... the man in the mask."

"You know about me, huh?" He took a step toward her. "I guess you would since it appears you're working for The Syndicate."

Her eyes went wide. "You ... you saw that?"

"I also heard it." He smirked at her. She clearly didn't recognize him with the mask over his face, and they had barely talked so she didn't recognize his voice either. "So, what's a girl like you doing dicking around with The Syndicate?"

She swallowed. "It's not my fault, they forced me to."

"Really?"

"It's the truth!" She was clearly scared of him. "Oh, please don't kill me." Her voice was frantic.

"I assume you saw what happened at that warehouse?" he asked her.

She nodded. "Yes, they told me it was you. Saw you on cameras."

"Good." He smirked. "Then they know that I'm out here. But now I want to know what you know. Who are they? Where do they hide?"

"I don't know where they sleep, but I do know several members," she answered. "Some of them are even high in rank within the palace." Her hands were shaking.

"Calm down, Lily, I'm not going to hurt you," he told her. "Why do you help them?"

She took a deep breath to try and calm herself. "They have my father. If I don't do what they say, they'll kill him."

"I see." He walked closer until he was a few feet away. "How do you think Raine would feel if she knew that you were out here?"

"She would probably freak out." She paused. "Wait a minute. How do you know about her?"

Isaac reached up and pulled his mask down to his neck, revealing his face.

Lily gasped. "Isaac ..."

"So, it seems you know my secret, and I know yours," he told her with a smile. "If you want to keep it that way, I suggest you help me."

"How?" She glanced around her.

"There's no one out there. Trust me," he assured her. "And you can help by giving me information."

"Why are you doing this?" She frowned. "You aren't even from here, are you?"

"Do you not want to stop them? See your father again?" he asked her sternly.

"Of course I do!" she said somewhat angrily. "But they're too powerful. Everyone is scared of them."

"I'm not. If you help me, we can bring them down and save your father. Help me, Lily."

"So, you weren't looking for a hooker," she said. "You were coming back from that place."

"Correct." He grinned.

"Why did you go to that warehouse? Why did you kill all those men?"

"They kidnapped a young girl," he explained. "They were going to trade her to a duke in Rubens as a sex slave."

Lily looked at him in shock. "So, you did that to save her?"

"Yes."

She looked down in thought before looking back up at him. "I'll help you," she decided. "The things they do the people here, especially the women, is unforgivable."

"We need to keep this between ourselves," Isaac said firmly. "We cannot tell anyone, not even Raine or Vin." He put his hand on her shoulder. "Do you understand?"

She nodded.

"Because if anyone finds out about this, they won't just come after us."

"I know..." she said. "They'll go after the people you love. They'll do what they can to hurt you. I don't want this to continue."

"We won't let it. We'll stop them," he said confidently.

"I'll tell you everything I know, but this could get tricky. They say there's a powerful, high-ranking individual who runs the whole thing. Apparently whenever something is about to be uncovered, this person twists the leadership to make it all vanish."

"We'll take it one step at a time. Let's go back to the inn; we'll talk there. This is only the beginning for them, and if they've talked about me to each other, it means they're shaken."

She nodded, and the two walked to The Final Rest. With an insider on his side, Isaac felt confident that he could bring them down.

CHAPTER 18

SHAKING
THE HORNET'S NEST

The next morning, Isaac and Lily were walking through the city.

"I'll show you the locations that I know of," she told him. "I don't know everything, but these places should give you a head start."

After they had gotten back to the inn last night, Isaac had convinced Lily that he could take down The Syndicate, and she offered up all the information she knew. She also promised not to reveal his identity to anyone or even talk about the matter, and he promised the same for her.

"They have a shipment supposedly moving out tonight," Isaac said. "After that, I think I'll pay that priest a visit." He scowled.

Lily had told him about Edwin, that he used the church as a means to lure victims to The Syndicate. He used the confessions he held as a way to enslave people.

"Anyone who knows of him stays away from the church," she explained. "He's a terrible man."

"You won't have to worry about him for long," he assured her.

"You're going to kill him."

"Yes."

"Good." She held a firm expression.

Isaac glanced at her. "You aren't bothered by my methods?"

"No," she replied. "These assholes have been terrorizing us for too long." She clenched her fists. "They do as they please, and somehow the king doesn't know about it. I want them all dead!"

He grinned. "Then I guess we are in agreement."

"Yeah." She looked at him. "If you do this, then I guess I'll owe you big time, just like I owe Raine."

He shook his head. "I'm not doing this for a reward, you know."

She looked at him curiously. "Then why?"

"I dunno. Seems like a fun thing to do."

"Fun?" she gasped. "This is fun for you?"

"I didn't even know there was a syndicate," he told her. "I just saved a girl from a bad person, then I found out there was more shit going on." He shrugged. "Guess I just decided to go down the rabbit hole."

"Why don't you tell Raine? Maybe she can help."

Isaac stopped walking and stared at her. "No."

"Why?" She stopped as well.

"I don't want Raine knowing." He frowned at her. "This isn't her business, and besides, she wouldn't approve."

"What is it with you two?" she asked him. "She said you two were close, and now you're distant."

He narrowed his eyes. "Come here." He grabbed her and pulled her into a secluded alley. Once he saw that no one was looking, he conjured his blade of light and held it up to her. "You see this?" he asked her somewhat forcefully. "*This* is why I'm with her. You said the other day that 'boys just follow her around,' but in reality, the only reason she has me here is because of *this*."

Lily gasped in shock as she looked at his aural blade. "W-wait ..."

"*There!*" His sword vanished, and he pointed at her. "That expression right there!" He shook his head in anger. "Your reaction toward me just changed because you saw that. That's the only reason Raine wants me with her."

"But you're a ..."

"I am NOT a guardian!" Isaac hissed at her. "I'm just *me*, okay?"

Lily just stared at him in shock.

"I'm doing this as me, not as a guardian," he said. "If everyone only thinks of me as this sword, then I'm not using it!" He wore a solemn expression. "I'll do this my way. Raine can just sit this one out!" He turned and walked out of the alley. Lily followed.

"You know, you're more than just a sword," she told him. "If you possess that kind of power, you could change the world."

"Screw that," he replied. "I'm only doing this because we have to wait, and I don't care for waiting."

Lily stared at him in thought. He wasn't like anything she had ever learned of about the guardian, also known as the Sotér. He didn't carry a heroic attitude or sweet personality, but she still felt that he could save this city from the terrible people who ran it from the shadows.

"I trust you," she said. "You aren't what I was raised to believe, but that doesn't matter."

Isaac looked at her with a frown.

"I just hope you stop The Syndicate, and I will help you anyway I can." She smiled.

His expression softened. "We'll do it together." He held out his hand to her.

She took his hand in hers. "Let's do it!"

That night, Isaac had told Lily to stay at the inn. She wanted to come along, but he insisted that it would be too dangerous. Instead, she decided to hang out with Raine while he took care of business.

At the loading dock, he watched the busy activity. There were people moving several crates onto some kind of vehicle. From his perch high above, he spied a rather sinister-looking man. The dark aura surrounding him was darker than any he had previously seen.

"Make sure this shipment gets sent," the man spoke to another. "Lord Zagaan needs these supplies sent to the base within the kitsuné's domain."

Kitsuné's domain, Isaac thought. That's the place Raine had told him about. The place to avoid. *I've also heard that name before. Zagaan.*

"Yes, sir. It will be done," the henchman replied.

"I came all the way out here to see this through myself," the man told him. "Do not fail." He turned and left.

The dark aura surrounding that man was deep. Isaac could tell he was pure evil. He took a picture of the individual with the intention of hunting him down later.

"Alright, everyone, get that last crate loaded, and we are done here," the henchman said to his crew.

Oh, we are not done here. Isaac grinned as he put the mask over his face. He descended from his perch and landed a short ways away from the loading bay.

The people working were oblivious to the chaos about to happen. As they were loading up the final crate, a fireball came flying at it, blasting it into pieces. Isaac had been practicing his aim, and he used his wind power to propel the flame as he guided it with telekinesis. The people near the crate were thrown back from the explosion.

"What!?" Everyone looked around, confused, as a figure swiftly ran up on them.

Isaac delivered a flying kick to the nearest man, and he flew into wall.

"Sup, assholes!" He smirked at them. "Your shady dealings have ended, as of five minutes ago!"

"Shit, it's the man in the mask!" one of them shouted as weapons appeared in their hands.

"Wow, you're smart, huh?" Isaac said sarcastically as he waved his hand, causing a shower of lightning to rain down upon them. Several of them jumped out of the way, but a couple were struck, and they fell to the ground.

"Stop him!" one of them shouted. "We must protect the cargo!"

Isaac moved toward him. "You are so falsely hopeful." He chuckled as his aural shield deflected a few magic bolts.

"He's just a mage!" one of the ones wielding a blue staff shouted. "Get in close and kick his ass!"

Isaac cocked his head smugly as two men rushed him with their red aural blades. He dodged left and right as they tried to hit him. He caught the arm of one of them and kicked the other away. Twisting his body around, he threw the man across the loading bay into a metal light pole.

"What the hell?" Some of them were dumbfounded. "How did he overpower them!?"

"What aura is he using?"

Confusion set in as Isaac tore them apart one by one. They would try to hit him with magic, but he would deflect it with his barrier. They would try to overpower him with strength, but he would swiftly dodge their blows. They would try to outperform him with speed, but he met their attacks one for one.

Eventually the loading bay went quiet as he took down the last of them. He turned his attention to the only living individual. The one who had spoken with the evil man from earlier.

"Who the hell *are* you!?" the man asked in fear.

"I don't think you get the concept of the mask, dude," Isaac replied as he encircled the man in a funnel of flame. "But this is about to go really badly for you." He chuckled dangerously. "I want to know who that individual you were talking to was back there."

The man stared back defiantly. "You'll just have to kill me. I will not reveal that information."

"I'll find out regardless," Isaac told him. "But if you want to die so badly." He shrugged, and the flame began to contract closer to the man.

"You don't understand the powers that be," the man told him. "They'll get you and destroy you. You cannot stop them!"

"Too bad they don't know who I am." Isaac smirked as the flames grew dangerously close. "Last chance, dipshit. Answer my question or die!"

The man closed his eyes. "If I tell you who he is, they'll kill me either way."

"Well, that sucks." Isaac chuckled. He held his hand out and clenched it into a fist; the fire engulfed the man, burning him to a painful death as his screams cut through the air.

He turned toward the cargo that now lay in pieces all over the loading bay. There was mostly machine parts and electrical pieces. He wondered why they were so important, but that didn't matter now. He saw several people heading in his direction.

He decided it was best to sneak away and make his way to the priest.

Lily and Raine were bathing in the hot spring, sipping on wine. The night sky twinkled down on them.

"This really feels like a vacation," Raine said with a smile. "I can't thank you enough for letting me stay up here."

"We don't really get a lot of royalty, anyway," Lily told her. "So the suite usually goes untouched except for the monthly cleaning."

"Well, I certainly feel like a queen right now."

There was the ringing of a doorbell at the suite elevator.

Lily and Raine glanced over in confusion.

"Who could that be?" Raine asked. "I hope it's not Vin. He keeps trying to sneak a peek at me in my bathing suit."

"I'll go check," Lily offered, but Raine stood up quickly.

"Nah, I'll get it. It's probably him, so I'll just tell him to go away." She made her way to the elevator and pressed a button. "How can I help—" she began sarcastically, but then immediately paused. On the monitor, she could see who was in the lobby ringing the bell. It wasn't Vin; it was Isaac. "I-Isaac?"

"Umm, hi ..." Isaac replied with a big smile. "How's it going?"

Raine stood there dumbfounded. "Uhh, everything's going okay, haha." She suddenly felt nervous.

"So, uhh, can I come up?" he asked politely.

"Come up ...?" She blinked. "OH! Yes, one moment!" She fumbled with the controls on the wall. "Okay, the elevator should bring you right up."

"Thanks." He stepped through the door, and the elevator began to rise.

Raine's head was abuzz. This was the first time in over a week that Isaac had requested to be around her. She hoped that she didn't screw this up. She wanted to make amends with him.

The elevator doors opened, and Isaac stepped into the suite. "Sorry for the sudden call ..." He glanced her over. She was wearing a rather revealing bikini.

"Oh, it's no problem," She told him as she felt his gaze on her. She could feel her cheeks turning red as she realized what she was wearing.

He looked back at her eyes and simply gave a nod with a positive, "Hmm." He glanced around at the suite. "So, this is the fabled suite you keep trying to lure me to." His expression was blank as usual.

"I don't try to 'lure' you here," she stammered with embarrassment.

"Not bad." He walked towards the living area. His eyes lit up upon seeing the booze. "Damn! That's a lot of alcohol!" He grinned.

"I knew you'd like this part." She stood next to him.

Lily came walking in and froze upon seeing Isaac. "Uhh, hello Isaac ..."

He looked her up and down as well. She was also in a revealing bikini, and water was still dripping off of her. "Wow, you two look great!" he said with wide eyes. "What's the occasion?"

Lily's face immediately turned red.

"Well, we're just relaxing in the hot spring," Raine explained. "Remember, I told you there was one up here?"

"Oh yeah. Guess I forgot."

She smiled sweetly at him. "Why don't you join us?"

Isaac blinked. "What?"

"There should be some swim shorts up here," she told him. "Why don't you come swim with us?"

He blinked again. "You're inviting me to share a hot tub with you two?"

"Well ... yeah ..." She looked at Lily. "Isn't that right?"

Lily paused for a moment. Hers and Isaac's eyes locked. "Y-yeah. Come play with us, Isaac!" she said with a sheepish smile.

"I don't know ..."

"This is an offer exclusively for you!" Raine said flirtatiously. "It'll be just the three of us!" She wanted to try and make Isaac feel welcome, and hopefully he would open up to her.

"Uhh." Isaac looked baffled. "Why only for me?"

"Well," she explained, "you're not pervy like Vin."

"And how do you know I'm not?" he asked with a smirk.

"Well, it's simple. You told me you can see through walls now, so it's not like keeping you out of the room would help anyway." She grinned jokingly.

Lily's expression turned to shocked embarrassment. "Wait! You can see through WALLS!?"

"Yep." He gave a half smile.

"So, that means ..." Her face turned bright red. "You could ... you ... could ..." She froze in fear.

"He totally could." Raine looked at Isaac humorously. "So it doesn't really matter if you're here or not." She took a drink of her wine. "But I trust you." She winked at him.

"I see." He gave her a knowing look. "But you know, you could do that too."

She giggled. "I suppose I could." She gave him a nod of approval. "Needless to say, I'm especially grateful that Vin does not possess this ability."

"Thank God for that," Lily added, rolling her eyes. "He tends to hit on me a lot. It'd be really scary if he could check me out at will."

"Being able to see through walls is an incredibly rare gift," Raine told them. "It took me years of training just to develop it, and I didn't actually obtain it until ..." Her voice trailed off. "Anyway, Isaac! Go get changed!" She pointed at a room. "Don't keep us ladies waiting."

Eventually the three of them were all in the hot spring, relaxing.

"So what made you want to come up here, Isaac?" Raine asked.

"Well, I saw you two cuties in bikinis, so I figured I'd say hi." He grinned at her confidently.

"That's not something you would normally say." She narrowed her eyes.

"Well, you did invite me, after all." He took a drink from a glass of whiskey. "I'm just super glad I get to spend this time with the ladies." He gave Lily a wink.

"Well, then." Lily gave him a coy look. "Since you get to hang out with us ladies, we get to ask you some questions." She smiled mischievously.

"Oh?"

"Have you ever snuck a peek at Raine?" She grinned.

"Uhh ..." He frowned at her.

"Isaac isn't like Vin," Raine told her, drinking more wine.

"You have to answer!" Lily pointed at him sternly. "Honest answers only!"

"I'm not answering that," Isaac said blankly.

"No fair!" She pouted. "Fine, then how's about this one."

"There's more?" He looked at her, uninterested.

"If Raine were in danger and you were the only one to save her, would you do it?" Lily ran her finger around her wine glass as she anticipated Isaac's answer.

"What's with these questions?" he asked her, narrowing his eyes.

"I'm a little curious myself," Raine added. "Would you save me, Isaac?"

"Is this what you two do up here?" He looked at them both. "Ask each other weird questions?"

They giggled, sinking lower into the water. "Sometimes," Lily answered. "We usually talk about boys, though."

Isaac eyed Raine. She was a lot more girly when she was with Lily. Her bossy side seemed to melt away. "I see ..."

"Come on, tell us," Lily urged him. "Would you?"

"Nope," he replied casually. "She can handle herself; she wouldn't need me."

Raine gasped dramatically. "You mean you wouldn't come to my rescue?"

"Why should I? You can just burn up whoever is trying to get you, right?" He smirked.

"That's not the point!" Lily eyeballed him playfully. "Don't you want to be her knight in shining armor?"

"Not really." He sipped his whiskey while staring back at her.

"You would leave me to perish?" Raine added dramatically.

"Don't really care." He shrugged. "As for the first question, the answer is yes." He looked up at the night sky as he waited for a response.

"Wait ..." Raine paused. "You have?"

"Yep."

"When?"

He grinned mischievously. "Not telling."

"So, you're not gay?" Lily asked him with a hopeful tone.

He frowned at her in puzzlement. "Never said I was ..."

"Well, I kind of figured you might have been with how often you refuse Raine's passes at you." She giggled.

"Hey!" Raine glared at her. "I don't make passes at him!"

"It's so obvious that you do!" Lily poked at her.

"I would never!" Raine started then paused when she noticed a change in Isaac's expression. He seemed amused until she said that, then his expression became sad. "Not that you aren't attractive or anything," she tried to recover. "In fact, I'm sure there's lots of women that find you attractive." Her attempt at saving face didn't work.

"I see." Isaac took a large drink from his whiskey, emptying the cup.

"Look, that's not how I really feel. I think you're—" she started.

"Don't worry, I already know how you really feel about me," he interrupted, looking down at his empty cup.

There was an awkward pause between them as they silently sat in the hot spring.

Raine realized that she had hurt him. Again. She stood up and got out of the hot spring. "I'll, uhh, get us more drinks," she offered with a weak smile.

Isaac held his cup up over his head, and she gently took it. She made her way back into the suite, leaving him and Lily alone.

"Look, Raine didn't mean—" Lily began, but Isaac used his telekinesis and pulled his phone to his hand. He pulled up the photos he had taken and showed them to her.

"Do you know who this is?" he whispered as he moved to sit right next to her. "He was there tonight giving orders, but he left before I could confront him."

She looked at the photo and shook her head. "He seems familiar, but I'm not really sure who that is."

"Any of these?" He flipped to the photo from the night Tessa was kidnapped.

"Oh my god, that's the prime minister!" She gasped, pointing at one of the men. "And he's with Priest Edwin ..."

"The priest is dead," Isaac told her.

She looked at him in shock.

"I'm back—" Raine returned and stared at them both now sitting side by side. "Whatcha guys up to?"

That was fast! Isaac thought as he tried to figure out an excuse. He quickly closed out of the photos and opened the camera. "We were about to take a selfie together!" He smiled and held the phone up as he leaned into Lily. She forced a cheesy smile, and he took the picture. "Yep, that's a keeper!" he said. "Well, I guess that's it for me." He stood up and stepped out of the hot spring. "I'll see you guys later."

"But I just brought you more whiskey," Raine said, trying to be friendly. "Don't you want to stay a bit longer?" She held out the cup to him, almost like an offering.

"Nah," he replied calmly. "I'm gonna go to bed." He walked past her into the suite. He gathered his clothes and headed for the elevator.

"Isaac, wait." Raine frantically came up to him as he waited for the elevator. "I'm sorry about earlier. I didn't mean to hurt you." She wore a sad expression.

"Whatever do you mean?" he replied softly. "You don't need to apologize. I'm not worth your time, after all." He stepped into elevator as the door opened. He pushed a button and descended.

Raine stood there in sorrow. *I just keep hurting him*, she thought. Her chest tightened as she started to feel the effects of the wine she had been drinking. It was like what he told her that night when he seemed possessed. That she was just pushing him along, making it worse. She felt her eyes begin to tear up. Was there really no way to save him?

The following day, Isaac and Lily met up and headed into town.

"If the prime minister is a part of this, he may be the leader," he told her. "I think I'll investigate him next."

"Taking down the prime minister will not go well with the king," she told him. "You can't just kill him."

"Then I'll have to dig up some evidence on him," he said. "Solid proof that will nail him to the wall."

They walked around the main square as they chatted. Lily was giving Isaac information on the people he encountered in the graveyard that night—he prime minister of Esmeraldas being one of the key players, probably the leader. She mentioned how it made sense that any evidence brought up about a mysterious syndicate got shutdown immediately in the past. He was twisting the policies in their favor.

After a while, Isaac had all the info that he needed, and they decided to take a break at a coffee shop.

"You know, Raine is really worried about you," Lily told him. "She feels bad for whatever it was that she did."

"Whatever," he replied, staring out into the city.

"I don't know what happened between you two, but she just wants to make up, you know." She looked at him, trying to be comforting.

"It doesn't matter," he said, giving her a quick glance. "I'm not bothered by it."

"You clearly are. I know you said you didn't care last night, but I think you do."

He looked at her blankly. "Did I say that?" He took a sip from his coffee as he played dumb.

"I know you care about her," she insisted. "If you didn't, you wouldn't be so hurt over how she thinks about you."

He looked away without replying.

"Because if you didn't, her words would have had no effect." She felt that she was starting to understand him, even though they'd only known each other for a short time.

He was about to reply when a puzzled expression settled over his face. He motioned to a TV that was in the shop. On it, the news was playing.

"Another report of a mass murder last night came up at the dock B loading bay."

"That's ..." Lily stared in shock at the screen.

"These murders have even caught the attention of our prime minister who had this to say."

Isaac perked up. "That's him ..."

The prime minister appeared on the screen. "People of Esmeraldas, there is a criminal among us. There have been several attacks in the dead of night by a masked individual."

A picture taken from a camera at the loading bay showed Isaac with his mask on.

"I urge the people: If you see this individual, report him to the nearest guard immediately. This is not to be taken lightly. Do not approach this man, he is highly dangerous." The prime minister wore a serious expression. "And if this person is watching right now, I promise you, we will find you and bring you to justice."

Isaac glared at the screen. *Oh, we'll see about that,* he thought.

Lily looked over at him with fear. "They've made you a public enemy."

"Don't worry," he assured her. "Let's say worst case scenario, they catch me; I will not reveal that you're helping me." He smiled at her. "But they aren't going to catch me."

"So, what now?"

"Nothing's changed," he replied confidently. "But I think I'll pay a visit to the good prime minister tonight. Send him a message for all to see." He grinned wickedly. "I'm gonna stir this hornet's nest and expose them all."

She stared at him, wide-eyed. "This could get rough."

"I'm counting on it," he told her. "You just keep helping them like you normally would. Don't give them any reason to suspect you." He frowned at her. "I don't want you to get hurt because of this."

She smiled sweetly at him. "Be careful. You might actually start caring."

That night, chaos erupted.

Lily and Raine were back up in the suite relaxing when an emergency news broadcast appeared on the TV.

"We have breaking news," the reporter said. "An attack on the prime minister has happened!"

Raine stared hard at the TV. "What the hell!?"

Lily froze in fear.

On the screen, it showed a massive fire at the prime minister's home. But what was most peculiar was on the wall of the home. There, spelt in blue magic, were four words: *Death to The Syndicate.*

Oh my god, she thought. *He's really done it. This will definitely get their attention.*

"We don't know what to make of this," the reporter said as onlookers watched the flames in confusion. "It seems this is a message from the masked man mentioned in the prime minister's speech earlier."

"What's The Syndicate?" Raine muttered as she frowned at the TV.

"Well ..." Lily began. "They're apparently an underground group of criminals that have been controlling the city for years now. At least, that's what I've heard."

"I've never heard of that," Raine replied.

"It's only hearsay," Lily explained. "There was a reporter about a year back that tried to expose them, but his story was removed as being false and he was demoted."

"What is going on out there?" Raine looked puzzled. "A few murders, and now this?" She shook her head. "I hope Isaac and Vin are okay. Maybe we should stay indoors at night."

Lily gave her a sideways glance but remained silent.

"There has been no comment from the prime minister at this time, but we will keep you all informed until then," the reporter said as the camera panned over the vandalized building.

Outside, Isaac made his way to a certain building. It was one that Lily had pointed out, and he had scouted it, peering through the walls at the activity inside. There were several dark auras and a bunch of computer equipment. The building itself seemed rather plain, and any passerby would have no idea what was actually going on inside, but with his ability, he could see plain as day that The Syndicate controlled the place.

The fire that he had started and the message he had sent to the prime minister wasn't just for show. It was also a distraction.

Isaac checked to make sure that the small data drive he'd purchased was still in his pocket. If there was any evidence on the computers in the building, he wanted to get it. He forced open the back door and let himself in. All the dark auras were in the basement, and he quietly made his way down.

There were several people huddled around computers and TV screens. The news was on every channel, and they all looked at Isaac's handiwork.

"What the hell?" one man said. "Who would attack the prime minister?"

"We don't know, but somehow he knows that he's with us," a woman replied.

"Just who is the guy in the mask?"

Isaac stepped into the room. "Who indeed?" He smirked at them all. "Nice place, by the way."

"Holy shit!" One of them stood up in shock.

"Whatcha all working on?" he asked them in a friendly tone.

They all stared at him, dumbfounded.

"Nothing? Alright then." He blasted a nearby person with fire. "Then let's get started."

It was only minutes before the building fell silent as Isaac killed the last of them.

"Let's see what secrets you've been hiding." He sat at one of the computers and began going over the files. He did this with a few more and soon he had collected a substantial amount of evidence.

"Dang, this is some juicy stuff you guys were packin'!" he said out loud with a grin. He had even collected intel on locations and personnel involved in the operations. He spent about half an hour checking over documents and emails, gathering everything he could and putting it on the data drive. After a while, he had what he needed.

"I got a load of stuff, thanks guys!" he shouted to the dead bodies as he left the building triumphantly. "Now I gotta find a way to release this information so everyone can see."

Lily had mentioned an investigator that got demoted when he tried to expose The Syndicate. Isaac had tracked him down and prepared to confront him.

"Who the hell—?" The man saw him and froze.

"I'm not here to hurt you," Isaac told him. "I heard you tried to expose The Syndicate a while back."

The man slowly nodded. "I tried, but it didn't happen."

"I'm sure you saw the news," Isaac stated. "You know who I am and that I'm trying to do the same."

"It's not as simple as just killing a few thugs," the man explained.

"You're right, that's why I've collected evidence." Isaac held up the data drive.

"I've already tried to give evidence," the man told him. "There's someone in the palace that will just sweep that stuff under the rug."

"Then how do we get this information out there?"

"We don't," the man said. "I lost my wife to them; I don't want to lose my son as well." He turned away from Isaac.

"What if we can get rid of them for good?" Isaac said. "What if we put them down so no one else gets hurt?"

"The only way to do that is to get evidence on the one who's orchestrating it."

"And who's that?"

The man shook his head. "Nobody knows. We thought it was the prime minister, but he seems to just be the spokesperson for the real leader."

"So, someone more powerful than a prime minister would do this ..." Isaac cocked his head in thought.

"We've tried to even get information to the king, but it seems nothing we do can reach him." He clenched his fists. "There's nothing we can do until whoever is at the head is gone."

"Who is 'we'?" Isaac asked.

"Anyone," the man explained. "Anyone who tries to do something, they just get shut down."

"They haven't shut me down," he replied.

"Not yet." The man shook his head again. "You're just wasting your time."

"If I find out who the leader is, and remove him, would you consider publishing this evidence?" He held the data drive out.

The man stared at the drive in thought. "I don't know."

"People are suffering," Isaac told him. "If we don't stop them, who will?"

The man just stared at him.

"People like your wife will get hurt or killed. We can't let them continue with this."

"I know," the man said dejectedly. "But what can we do?"

"If I can take down the leader, then maybe we can get this evidence published and exposed," Isaac replied. "We can make sure the king is aware of what is going on."

"I'll help you, but only if you can guarantee the leader is gone," the man told him. "I fear if I attempt to expose them again, it won't end well for me or my son."

"I understand," Isaac said. "I'll make sure you'll be safe at that point. You have my word."

"Well, until then, I'll just be waiting." The man shrugged. "What do I call you?"

Isaac thought for a moment before replying. "Just call me Mors. And you?"

"Name's Talim, though you've probably already heard of me," he said. "I don't know how you plan to do it, but if you can remove the head of this snake, come find me."

And with that, their conversation ended.

Isaac now had a set goal. Find the leader and wipe them out. Only after that would he be able to get Talim to publish the evidence and expose the whole criminal organization.

The next day, Raine was about ready to head to the palace when Isaac appeared.

"Hey!" He approached her. "You headed to the palace?"

She looked at him with surprise. "Uhh, yeah I was ... why?"

"I figured maybe I'll join you." He gave her a slight smile.

"You ... you will?"

"Yeah, I guess with all this waiting we've been doing, I'm kind of bored," he explained.

"Well, sure, if you want to come along, then great!" She forced a smile. "Are you ready to go, then?"

"Yep."

"Okay, let's go." They headed toward the castle.

Isaac stayed silent as he looked around the city. Raine wanted to apologize again but decided to pretend like nothing had happened.

"It's a pretty cool city," she said. "I always enjoyed coming here when taking up tasks for the queen."

"It's also kind of chaotic with all that's been going on with the news," he added.

"It's rather odd," she said thoughtfully. "All the times I've visited, nothing like this has ever happened." She looked over, and their eyes met. "With that person going around and killing people, it's probably best if we stay indoors at night."

He shrugged. "I'll be fine. I just like to hang out at the bars and watch people. It's a very populated area, so nothing bad should happen. I think."

"Maybe I'll, uhh, join you some time." She smiled at him.

"No thanks," he told her. "I like to be alone during that time."

"Oh." She looked away, feeling sad. It appeared he really was avoiding her and Vin.

They walked in silence the rest of the way until they came to the palace.

"Looks big," Isaac said nonchalantly.

"It's even bigger on the inside," Raine told him. "Come on, let's go." She motioned to him as she headed up the long steps toward the main doors.

Inside was a reception desk, and Isaac watched as Raine pulled a letter from her bag and presented it to the woman there. The woman nodded and let the two of them enter.

"The nice thing about having a letter from the queen is that we're basically ghosts here," she explained. "Our presence doesn't get recorded, so we can do our business without the risk of being caught."

"How come we get that kind of privilege?" he asked.

"The queen and the king have a strong unity. They've helped each other many times, and their trust is great," she answered. "The king understands that discretion is required when we come, so he makes sure that our identities remain secret."

Well, that's convenient, Isaac thought.

They ended up waiting for a representative to inform them of the status of the artifact, and as they waited, he scanned the building, looking for any signs of evil people. He was looking for someone who could possibly be of higher rank than the prime minister, and he bet they would be here somewhere in the palace.

"I'm sorry, my lady." The representative had arrived. "We're still looking into the matter, but with all the happenings going on in the city, the king has allowed the visiting council member to investigate the situation as a top priority."

"You mean the murders?" Raine asked her.

"Yes, it has caused quite a commotion, especially since the prime minister has been involved," the woman replied.

After she had left, Raine sat there in thought.

"What the hell?" She shook her head. "If the councilman is getting involved, this might be really serious." She looked at Isaac. "We need to be extra careful. This might interfere with our mission."

"Well, I hope it doesn't interfere with my drinking," he replied with a playful shrug.

"Let's go. We'll just need to wait for this mess to blow over." She stood up, and they both left the room.

Oh, it won't blow over, Isaac thought to himself.

As they were walking down the hall, he paused. "Who's that?" He pointed at a man with the same dark aura he'd seen that night at the loading bay. He was accompanied by another evil man with a similar dark aura.

"Oh, shit!" Raine said as she quickly ducked into a nearby room, out of sight. *What are you doing? Come on!* she told Isaac telepathically.

Why? he replied with his own telepathy, still standing there.

That's Councilman Ubel. If he spots us, our cover is blown! she told him.

So that's who the person was that night. Isaac stared at him as Ubel drew closer. He started walking in his direction.

The hell are you doing!? Raine hissed at him.

He doesn't know who I am, he reasoned with her. *I'm going to go talk to him.*

You're gonna what!?

Isaac approached Ubel and gave him a bright smile. "Mr. Councilman, what brings you here?" He gave him a fake puzzled look.

Ubel looked at him and returned the smile. "Just some small business. Who might you be?"

Are you out of your mind!? Raine yelled at him.

"My apologies." Isaac slightly bowed. "I'm Kristoff. I didn't expect to see someone like you here. I hope I'm not bothering you."

"Well met, Kristoff. I am a little bit in a hurry, but it's always nice to meet the good people of this city." He beamed at Isaac.

What a freak, he thought. *This guy is good at keeping up a fake façade.* "Well, be careful out there," he told the councilman. "A lot of us are scared of the guy that's been mentioned on TV. We've been staying inside at night."

"That's a good idea," Ubel told him with an approving nod. "But don't worry, we're looking into it, and we'll apprehend him soon." He gave a confident smile.

Bullshit. "I sure hope so. I have a family to look after," Isaac said with a look of innocence. "I believe in you, sir." He chuckled in his head at his lame joke.

Ubel smiled brightly at him. "Don't worry, you're safe with me here. Now I really must be going." He motioned to the man with him. This other person was just as evil as Ubel; his face looked somewhat ... off.

Isaac bowed properly as Ubel and the other man left. *Someone higher than a prime minister*, he thought. *Ubel has to be the leader.*

"What were you thinking!?" Raine came out of hiding and snapped at him.

"Don't worry, he doesn't suspect anything," he dismissed her.

"Please, do not do something like that again!" She waved her finger at him. "We need to stay discreet on this mission."

"Alright, alright," he told her. "I promise I'll lay low."

She shook her head. "Why did you do that, anyway?"

Isaac shrugged. "I dunno, guess I was just curious."

"Curious!?" She looked sternly at him. "Let's just go, we've already lingered here too long."

"Sorry," he replied, but could help the satisfaction swelling within him. He was able to get a lot from Ubel. His voice, his posture, even the scent of darkness on him. Now he would be able to track him down.

Later in the evening, Isaac met with Lily.

"It's the councilman, Ubel," he told her. "He has to be the one pulling the strings."

"The council!?" She looked at him in shock. "You must be mistaken!"

"I'm not."

She shook her head. "It can't be a councilman, they're the ones who help unify the five nations!"

"Why can't it be?" He frowned at her. "Anyone in a position of power has the potential to abuse that power."

She sat there in thought. "It just can't be ..." She glanced at him wide-eyed. "Wait, what do you plan to do?"

"Kill him, of course," Isaac replied blankly.

Lily took a sharp breath. "You can't do that!" she stammered. "He's part of the council! To kill him would be one of—if not the—worst treasonous acts you could do!"

He shrugged. "They don't know who I am."

"It doesn't matter!"

"Hey, do you want The Syndicate to keep hurting people?" He stared at her seriously. "Because if we just look the other way, nothing will change."

She didn't reply.

"If we don't stop him, your father—and anyone else's loved ones—doesn't come home." He folded his arms, his gaze still on her. "I don't care if this guy is a councilman, he's evil and I'm taking him down."

Lily looked away. "I don't want them to keep making people suffer, but this is a whole other level of bad."

"I promise, I won't compromise you," Isaac assured her. "I'll do what's needed to protect you. This is my fight, after all."

She shook her head. "No, it isn't just your fight." She let out a deep breath. "A lot of people in this city know what's going on, but everyone is too scared to do anything about it, and now, knowing a councilman is leading it all, it makes sense why they get away with everything." She looked at him with pleading eyes. "I've talked with a lot of people who want nothing more than to see The Syndicate brought to justice, and they're all silently cheering you on." She relaxed slightly and looked into his eyes. "*I'm* cheering you on."

Isaac was speechless at Lily's next words. He looked at her in surprise as she took his hand in hers.

"Please. Save us."

CHAPTER 19

FALLING APART

Ubel sat alone with the prime minister.

"He raided our data center," the minister growled. "After vandalizing my house, he attacked it. It was all a distraction." He threw a desk ornament across the room. It shattered against the wall.

"Calm yourself," Ubel told him. "If he leaks any of the information, I will make sure to have it discredited and swept away. However, this is getting troublesome." He narrowed his eyes in thought. "Lord Zagaan needed that shipment by now, and the report I had to give him about the attack has irritated him. We need to deal with this masked individual immediately."

"I can hold another press conference and have the city guards do a search," the minister suggested.

"No." Ubel shook his head. "I will hold the conference and have the city locked down. We will make an enemy of this man. As one of the council, my influence will have the citizen's attention, and they will reveal the identity of him to us."

"Isn't that a little suspicious, though?" the minister asked with a frown.

"With all the reports going out as murders and the people learning that the priest Edwin was killed, they will not question the need for action," he explained. "Besides, no one will go against the words of a member of the council." He grinned wickedly. "We'll have that masked intruder discovered and killed. Set up accountability with the guards. I want to know who has come into this city. Check every resident for irregularities. We will discover who this person is, one way or another."

Raine had called Isaac and Vin into the suite. She explained that it was urgent. Lily was also present as she secretly knew what was going on, along with Isaac. They were all watching the TV.

"We have an emergency report from Councilman Ubel himself," the reporter explained.

"This has gone from really bad to way worse!" Raine said in disbelief as she stared at the screen.

On the TV, Ubel appeared in front of the podium.

"I am calling a state of emergency," he declared. "We have just learned that the kind priest Edwin, has been murdered."

Isaac and Lily quickly exchanged glances.

"Murdered by the man in the mask," Ubel continued. "This individual has also made a threat against our prime minister. Our city is no longer safe; therefore, I am calling to have the city put under lockdown until this criminal is apprehended."

"Lockdown!?" Vin frowned. "This is NOT good."

"Looks like we're at the part of being hindered." Isaac looked at Raine, who glanced between him and the TV.

"I am calling for an active search of the city," Ubel told them. "I want every registered citizen to be checked and anyone who has entered this city within the past month to be investigated."

Vin shot a look at Raine. "THAT'S not good!"

She held her hand up. "Calm down," she told him. "We weren't registered upon entering, so we shouldn't be questioned."

Isaac looked at her. "How sure are you?"

"I mean, I've never been questioned before when I visited ..."

"We should still remain cautious," Isaac said.

She nodded.

"I apologize to the good citizens of this city, but this has escalated to a crisis," Ubel continued. "The masked man cannot be allowed to roam our streets and kill whoever he wants. I am calling upon the citizens to be vigilant and report any sightings of this individual. We will find this killer, and we will bring him to justice. I urge you all to stay indoors at night unless it's an emergency."

"This is messed up," Vin muttered.

"Shit!" Raine snapped out loud. "There goes checking in at the palace. They'll have halted their search for the artifact to focus on this issue."

Isaac watched her stomp out of the living area of the suite. He took a glance at Lily. She was staring at him with worry.

We need to bring them down, he told her telepathically. *If you can, try to find one of their buildings of high importance. We need to show them that we cannot be intimidated by them.*

She nodded but remained silent.

This was about to get messy.

Throughout the day, the city was full of activity. The guards were basically going door to door, investigating everyone. Isaac, Raine, and Vin stayed indoors, keeping out of sight. Lily had been questioned but revealed nothing about the masked man.

"Things are starting to calm down a little," Raine said, "but we still need to stay out of sight. If our cover is blown, we're screwed."

"At least you have plenty of booze up here," Vin said with a grin. "We can just kick back and have a little party."

"Oh no, you don't!" she scolded him. "You can go party down in your room."

"B-but ..." he stammered.

"I don't want your prying eyes on me all night." She frowned at him. "Especially with Lily here."

"Huh?" Lily quickly glanced at them. "Oh, uhh, yeah. Go to your own room. Jeez."

"That's so mean!" He looked at them sadly.

"I know your game," Raine told him. "We've worked in the same castle for years now. You aren't fooling me."

He gave her a dejected look. "Fine, fine. I'll just go hang out at the red-light district, then."

"Even though there's a search going on?" She gave him a stern look.

"In case you've forgotten, I'm one of the best infiltrators in the royal guard. Avoiding detection and blending in is my specialty."

"Whatever. Just don't get caught." She shook her head.

The evening was coming slowly, but there was still some light outside.

"I have to head out," Lily told Raine. "I'll try to be back later."

"Be careful," Raine cautioned. "Things are a mess right now."

Lily nodded and made her way out of the inn. She walked to a nearby alleyway, and Isaac was there waiting for her.

"Did you get any information?" he asked.

"I did some digging and asked around," she replied. "Apparently there's a certain building the prime minister goes to often. It's on the north end of the market district."

"What's so special about that?" He frowned.

"Like I told you, a lot of people have noticed what's going on, and some of them even keep tabs on The Syndicate," she explained. "That building seems to be where the prime minister holds his meetings in secret." She took out a folded piece of paper from her pocket. "I marked the building on this map." She unfolded the paper. On it was a building that was circled with a marker. "The word is there's going to be a meeting tonight in order to discuss how to get rid of you."

Isaac smirked.

"If you can record the meeting that would be pretty damning evidence to bring down the prime minister," she said. "After that, it would be like a domino effect."

"I'll just have to make sure the councilman is killed before the evidence is released, that way he can't block it," Isaac replied.

"Exactly," Lily agreed. "And I do believe that investigative reporter, Talim, would be willing to publish the evidence if the councilman is out of the picture."

"I'll talk to him tonight. If all goes well, we can end this soon."

"A lot of people are counting on you." She looked him in the eyes. "For the first time in a long time, you've given us something to hope for."

Something to hope for, huh? he thought to himself.

"Don't worry. We'll stop them," he told her confidently. "I need to go. I'll scope out that building and get the evidence."

"Alright." Lily nodded. "I have to meet up with a member of The Syndicate tonight. I'll try to brush them off as fast as I can, then return to the inn."

"Be careful." Isaac placed his hand on her shoulder. "This is about to get chaotic."

The sun set, and the city grew dark. There were guards everywhere on the streets, but that didn't bother Isaac. With his ability to see through walls, he was able to easily avoid them. He made his way to the building Lily had marked and then waited. He kept the mask over his face, even though no one was around. With all the sensory input from his powers, having the mask over his face helped him focus.

It was only about an hour before he noticed a few people approaching the building. One of them was the prime minister. Lily's intel seemed accurate. They glanced around briefly and then entered the building. Isaac watched them walk through the hallways and enter a large room. He also searched for a quiet way in.

It wasn't long before he was inside the building and standing outside of the door to the room the meeting was being held. He reached into a small bag he had with him and pulled out a wire with a camera on it. The wire was connected to a recording device, and he slid the wire under the door to spy on the meeting and record it.

"Let's get right to the topic," the prime minister told the others. "Have we turned up any clues on the identity of the masked man?"

"None," another man said. "We did a thorough search of the city. Everyone who entered the city in the last month was clean."

"How is that even possible?" a third man commented. "We made sure to get everyone on the list. There's no way someone was able to avoid being questioned."

"Unless this individual isn't on the list," the second man replied. "We'll keep doing searches every day until we find him."

"We need to do it quickly," the prime minister told them. "Lord Zagaan is furious about this whole situation. If we don't get a secure trade route to Rubens and deliver that shipment to the itsune's domain, he may very well send a few demons to the city, and we cannot have that."

"Lord Zagaan is pretty scary when he's upset," the third man said. "I would like to avoid dealing with him if possible."

The others nodded. "Then let's find the masked man quickly and get rid of him," the prime minister said. "And be sure to keep this information from the king."

Isaac grinned from behind the door. This evidence should be enough to at least incriminate the prime minister, and with the other evidence he had collected, the whole operation could be taken down.

He continued recording for another half hour, and once the people inside began to wrap up, he silently put the camera and recorder back in his bag and left.

These assholes were sure in for a surprise.

Lily was waiting at the location to meet up with The Syndicate. It wasn't long before a couple of men approached her.

"Were you spotted?" one of them asked.

She shook her head. "Of course not."

"Good." He walked up to her and grabbed her arm. "Because you're coming with us." He grinned at her.

"What?" She tried to pull away, but the other men circled around her, blocking her escape.

"Seems like you've been a bad girl," the man sneered at her. "Digging your nose into places you shouldn't." He began to pull her into the shadows. "You should have just kept to yourself and did as you were told. Now the boss wants a word with you."

She tried to scream, but one of the men put his hand over her mouth as they dragged her away.

Isaac made it back to the inn safely and without being detected. He was heading to his room to wait for Lily when he saw Raine coming from the same direction.

"Oh, Isaac!" She looked at him in surprise. "I was just looking for you."

"Is that so?"

"I was hoping maybe you would join me up in the suite." She smiled at him. It was evident that she was a little tipsy.

"What for?" He frowned. "Lily isn't even here. She said she had things to do."

"I know that," she said. "I was just hoping maybe it could be the two of us tonight."

"Look, if you're still bothered by the other night, don't worry about it." He shook his head. "It doesn't bother me."

"It's not!" she pleaded. "I just, uhh, wanted to spend time with you. That's all."

He looked at her with the intention of turning her down, but upon seeing her expression, he decided to go along with it. "Jeez, don't look so sad ..." He tried to put on a happy face. "Fine. Let's go."

"Really?" She said joyfully.

"Don't wait for me to change my mind." He motioned for her to lead the way.

"Okay!" She walked to the elevator, and he followed. "This is gonna be fun!"

He couldn't help but give her a slight smile. "You sure are enthusiastic."

"It's not often you and I get drunk together." She giggled. "Since the city is under lockdown, there really isn't much more we can do, so I say let's at least enjoy tonight while we have the chance."

They arrived at the suite, and Raine ran over to the lounge area. "I'll pour you a drink."

"You sure have been drinking a lot since we got here," he told her. "You act more girly when you're tipsy."

"What do you mean 'more girly'?" she asked him sternly.

"You're usually so bossy, but right now you're actually kinda cute," he said with a smirk.

"Don't get used to it." She eyed him. "Once we're done here, I'm going back to my bossy ways." She laughed as she handed him a drink.

They both sat on the circular couch, close to each other.

"So, how do you like Terra?" Raine asked Isaac as she took a drink from her glass.

He shrugged. "It's better than Earth."

"You seem to not like your planet." She looked at him with curiosity.

"I don't." He sipped from his glass.

"How did you even get here?" she asked.

He gave her a sideways glance. "I actually don't know."

"So even that's a mystery." She took another drink.

"It doesn't matter," he dismissed her question. "I'm here, and that's that."

"It's still pretty interesting," she said. "Someone from another world ..."

He didn't reply. He just turned his glass in his hand as he glanced at the elevator. Where was Lily?

Raine noticed him looking at the elevator. "You want to leave already?" She held a sad expression.

"That's not it," he replied.

"You've been avoiding me ever since we got to this city," she told him. "Isaac, whatever it was that I did, I'm—"

"It's nothing." Isaac looked at her with a solemn expression. "Don't sweat it." He took a sip from his glass.

"I'm worried about you," she said after taking a long drink. "I feel like you've grown distant these past several days."

"What do you care?" He frowned at her. "It's not like I'm here to be your friend or anything." He shook his head slowly as he stared at her.

"That's not true!" she said, her words starting to slur. "I'm your friend!"

"Are you, though?" He gave her a doubtful look. "The only reason I'm even here is because you saw my aura."

Raine started to stammer. "Why do you have to be so mean?" Her face was red with drunkenness. "I've been trying my hardest to make amends with you."

"Make amends for what?" He gave her a blank stare. "What would you have to make amends for? I told you not to worry about it."

She took another long drink and began to pour more into her glass. "I don't know what I did that night, but it really bothered you, and I'm sorry."

Isaac shrugged. "It's whatever."

"Please, Isaac ..." She gave a slight hiccup. "I didn't mean whatever happened."

"I get it, Raine." He sounded irritated. "You don't need to apologize. I know how you really feel. Once we get back, I'm gone. You won't have to deal with me again."

"What?" She looked at him with drunken puzzlement. "You aren't going to stay with us?"

"Oh please." He sipped his whiskey. "It's not like you even want me here. You made that very clear from the start."

"What are you talking about?" she questioned. "Of course I want you here."

"Do you?" He narrowed his eyes at her. "Do you actually want me here, or just my power?"

"I-I don't understand ..."

"You remember when we first met?" he explained. "You didn't want us to enter the castle. That is, until you saw me."

She was struggling to focus as she nervously took another drink from her glass.

"You looked at Vin and told him no. You looked at Drake and told him no." He started tapping his foot as he stared hard at her. "Then you looked at me and were about to say no, but you didn't. Do you know why?" He waited for her to respond.

Raine averted her eyes from his. "Please stop ..."

"You told me yes because you saw my aura," he said. "That's the only reason I'm here. You and Vin only care about me being some legendary guardian. You don't care about me." He shook his head as he felt a subtle surge of anger welling up. "Hell, Vin started calling me his friend only after he saw my aural blade."

"You're wrong!" she blurted out with a slur. "I was sad when you said you didn't want to join us."

"Yeah right." He looked away from her in disgust.

"Why did you choose to come with us?" She leaned toward him, her body swaying as drunkenness began to kick in. "If you hate us so much, why are you here?"

"I don't know," he replied. "I guess I thought maybe things would change, but I was wrong." He watched her as she struggled to reply.

"You ... don't know ..." she slurred. "The queen ... she likes you ..."

"Raine, you're drunk." He stared at her seriously.

"And you're a douche!" She tried to stand up but clumsily fell back onto the couch.

There was an awkward feeling in the air.

"I see." Isaac looked away from her as he stood up.

"I–I didn't mean that ..." she stammered. "I'm ... I'm sorry ..."

"Whatever." He made a motion to leave.

"Please!" She shifted down the circular couch toward him. "Don't leave!"

"Why, so you can just insult me more?" He shook his head. "I don't have to take this." He placed his glass on the table.

"I don't want you to go." Raine's eyes started to tear up. "I'm hurting ..."

"You're too drunk." He sighed. "You'll feel better if you sleep it off." He started to walk away.

"Isaac!" She tried to stand again but fell back onto the couch. Rolling to her side, she lay there. "I'm ... sorry," she mumbled. "I just ... want to ... save ..." Her words trailed off.

Isaac let out a deep breath. His first thought was to just leave, but he turned back and looked at her. She had clearly passed out from the alcohol.

Why do you put up such a defensive persona?

Walking over to her, he knelt on the ground.

"You are such a lightweight," he grumbled as he gently shook her shoulder. She mumbled something but didn't wake up. He waved his hand and turned off the lights in the suite with telekinesis.

You should tell her how you really feel.

He gently put his hands around her legs and her back, then picked her up off the couch. He carried her across the suite into her bedroom.

CHAPTER 19: FALLING APART

"You are not going to have a pleasant morning," he said, even though she was oblivious. He gently placed her on the bed and pulled the blanket over her. Leaving the bedroom for a brief moment, he returned with a glass of water and a couple of painkillers. He placed them on the nightstand next to the bed.

Before leaving, he paused and stared at her. Even though she was passed out drunk, she still looked beautiful to him. He held a solemn expression as he watched her sleep.

"I'm sorry, Raine." He looked at her with sadness. "I lied to you." Even though he knew she wouldn't respond, he spoke to her. "I do care ..." He put his hand on her forehead and used his magic to cool her off. "This should help your hangover in the morning." Even though his magic wasn't as strong as hers, he could still help ease the headache she would have.

He took one final glance at her and then left the room. It was dark inside the suite, but with his abilities, he could easily see, and he's looking through the walls of the building down at the lower floors looking for Lily. She was nowhere to be seen.

That's odd, he thought. She should have been here by now.

He remembered how she mentioned having to meet with The Syndicate. With the lockdown and the searches, she may have run into trouble. Going over to the balcony where the hot spring was, he looked out over the city. Using his magic, he descended the building.

I'll just have to find her, he thought, putting on his mask as he made his way down the street.

CHAPTER 20

I DO CARE ...

Lily sat in a secluded room with several men from The Syndicate. One of them backhanded her in the face.

"Who is the man in the mask?" Councilman Ubel was speaking to her from a remote location. His face was on a monitor.

"I don't know!" she said with a shaky voice. "He never showed me his face."

"Do not lie to me!" Ubel growled at her. "I know you've been helping him."

"I swear, I don't know who he is!" She flinched as one of the men raised his hand at her.

"Enough," Ubel told the man. "She's clearly not going to tell us."

Lily stared at the monitor with tears in her eyes.

"Well, since you've been spending so much time helping him," the councilman said to her, "you're now going to help us capture him."

"What ...?"

"Surely he'll come looking for you," Ubel said. "And when he does, we'll spring our trap."

"You don't know what he's capable of." Lily looked at him defiantly. "You won't be able to trap him!"

One of the men in the room grabbed her by the hair and pulled her head back.

"Your faith in him is ill placed," Ubel told her. "Once we've dealt with him, we'll make sure to deal with you in kind."

CHAPTER 20: I DO CARE ...

The man brandished a knife at her throat.

"You will regret ever helping him." Ubel gave a sinister grin.

Outside, Isaac was searching the city. The location Lily had told him she was going to was empty except for one individual. He approached this person.

"So, you came just like he said you would." The man grinned at Isaac. "The man in the mask."

"Where's the girl?" Isaac asked with a dangerously low tone.

"Don't worry, I'm gonna tell you," the man replied. "She's close. In the building toward the back of this very district."

Isaac took a few steps forward. "That all?" he asked.

The man took a step away. "Hold up, now." His voice was shaky. "You have to go alone. If you don't, she dies."

"Good talk." He pulled a softball-sized rock to his hand with telekinesis. He raised it, ready to bash the man's skull in.

"W-wait!" The man stumbled backward. "If you kill me, she dies." He pointed to a nearby building. There on the corner was a camera pointed at them.

Isaac glanced at it, then back at the man. "What about maiming?" he asked. "Any rules on if I'm allowed to break you in half?"

"Uhh ..." The man looked at him in fear.

Isaac smiled at him, then using wind to propel the rock, he hurled it at the man's leg. It struck hard, and the man cried out in pain as he fell to the ground, his knee broken.

"I'll be back for you," he told the man as he walked toward the mentioned building. It didn't take him long to find it. Scanning the area with his x-ray vision, he saw the building in question. The place was filled with people, and he knew this was all a trap.

It's so obvious, he thought. Telling me where she is, having the whole place packed with killers. But that didn't matter to him. He had to get Lily out of there.

After scanning the whole building, Isaac decided to take a more reckless approach, and he ended up breaking through the front door. There were a few people in the main lobby, but he had no issue taking them out. The hallways twisted and turned, but surprisingly, he had very little resistance getting through them.

He knew they were trying to box him in, but he pushed on anyway. Lily was his only priority. The building was fairly large, and he had to make his way through several rooms. Eventually he found his way to the room she was in.

He took a deep breath and smashed the door open. The men in the room conjured their aural blades, and the one standing next to Lily tried to stab her with a knife, but a force field deflected the blade. The men rushed him, and he ducked under their attacks and threw his fists into them, dropping them to the ground. Another attacker was met with a cascade of lightning from his hands. Soon the room went quiet, and Isaac went over to Lily.

"You okay?" he asked as he noticed the injuries on her face.

"You shouldn't have come!" she cried with tears in her eyes. "It's a trap!"

"I know," he told her. "But I'm not leaving you with them. I can handle a trap, but you can't."

"You didn't have to come for me," she whimpered. "You could have just taken them down."

"I won't leave you like this!" He put his hand on her shoulder. "Come on, let's get out of here."

"Before you go ..." a voice called out to him. "I do believe we haven't met, yet." It came from a monitor in the room. Ubel's face was on the screen.

"Ubel ..." Isaac growled at the monitor. "You have some nerve taking her."

"I'll admit, I'm quite surprised you were able to protect her so easily," Ubel replied. "You see, I was going to have her killed regardless, but I needed you here first."

"That's too bad." Isaac smirked. "But you might want to worry about yourself."

"Indeed," Ubel said calmly. "I am quite aware that you have certain evidence of our group. But I wouldn't get too hasty just yet. You see, I always come up with a contingency in case someone decides to do something stupid."

Isaac chuckled. "You really think this little trap of yours is gonna stop me?"

"Not at all," he answered. "You see, while this is definitely a trap, it is not a trap for you."

"What?" Isaac frowned.

Ubel chuckled. "While we were doing our investigation on the people of this city, trying to find you, I noticed a certain individual when investigating your friend there." He motioned toward Lily.

Isaac glanced at her, then back at him.

"Our investigation failed to give light to your identity, but I recognized the woman that was with her, and so I wondered: What would the queen of Adamas' right hand be doing way out here?" He smiled maliciously. "Raine Beria. She wasn't registered on entry to the city, and she had two others with her."

Isaac's mouth twisted in a snarl as he listened to Ubel.

"Adamas is supposed to be under lockdown since the demons attacked, but she's here. Why is that? Then I realized the other two that she was with, one of them, the blond, was always hanging around the inn, but the other, the one with brown hair," he pointed at Isaac from the monitor, "was always missing."

"Get to the point," Isaac growled.

"My point is that I believe you're one of Raine's companions, and since you're staying at the inn Lily owns, that's why she's been helping you."

"Oh boy, you found me out," Isaac sneered at him. "You still won't stop me."

"I would rethink your position," Ubel told him. "See, while you're busy fighting your way out of here, I've sent a group of rather skilled people to collect your blue-haired friend."

A deep anger began to well up inside Isaac.

"Raine's a powerful mage; your people won't be able to touch her!" Lily snapped at Ubel.

"Oh, I am quite aware how powerful Ms. Beria is," he replied. "That's why I sent this particular group. They'll easily be able to overpower her." He grinned at them. "So, here's the deal. If you wish to see your friend again, you will return all the evidence you've collected and give yourself up. You'll be caught regardless; you might as well make this easier for everyone."

Isaac gritted his teeth in fury.

"I would hate to think of what would happen to her were you not to comply." Ubel wore a sinister expression. "She's quite the find. She would make for a good pet."

Isaac waved his hand, and a blast of wind smashed the monitor to pieces. He quickly pulled out his phone. "They were waiting for me to get here first," he said frantically. "So they haven't gotten to her yet."

"Are you trying to warn her?" Lily looked at him with panic.

He looked at her grimly. "She's passed out in her bed," he explained. "I'm calling Vin. He's closer to her."

"What ...?" Lily looked at him in horror.

The phone in Isaac's hand rang, but there was no response. "Come on, answer!" His voice was a mix of fury and panic. He tried to call Vin again.

"Why isn't he answering?" Lily was wide-eyed.

Over in the red-light district, Vin was chatting with two women.

"So, then I snuck into the thieves' lair and stole back the crystal chalice." He grinned at them.

"Wow, that's so cool!" The women giggled.

His phone was on silent as he drank and shared stories with them. He didn't notice the missed calls.

"Answer your damn phone, you bastard!" Isaac yelled. "Raine's in trouble!" The call failed to go through. "SHIT!" He looked down the hallway. Several people were headed in their direction.

"Oh my god." Lily put her hands to her mouth in shock. "Raine ..."

"You stay right behind me!" he told her frantically. "I have to get to her, so we're busting out of here!" He tucked his phone back into his pocket. "We cannot waste time. Do not fall behind!" He turned down the hallway; his fists began to pulse with darkness as anger gripped him.

"Okay ..." Lily gulped as she prepared to move.

Isaac shot out into the hallway with fury. The men that now crowded it took up defensive stances as chaos erupted.

Slamming into the nearest person, Isaac hurled several fireballs that blazed down upon the group. He shoved another into the wall and fired a blast of wind that forced a hole between them.

"Hurry!" he called to Lily. They quickly ran past as the people fought off flames and recovered from being thrown aside.

After they got a good distance away from the thugs, Isaac shot a blast of fire at the ceiling, causing it to collapse in the hallway, sealing the entry from pursuers. Moving into the next room, two men jumped out at him. He blocked their attacks, countering one of them with a fist of lightning, sending him flying into the wall. The second guy tried to stab him, but Isaac grabbed his arm and viscously turned the weapon toward him, stabbing the man in the chest.

Throwing the man aside, he moved to the next room.

"Keep up!" he told Lily. "I'm only going to cut down the ones we need to!"

She nodded and quickened her pace as they rushed from room to room.

Isaac was a whirlwind. In his panic and fury to reach Raine, he could feel the darkness pulling at him. His eyes started to blacken under his mask.

Several people rushed him as they entered the lobby.

We're almost out, he thought. He dodged several attacks from both weapons and magic. He struck his assailants with a violent anger, breaking bones and burning them with fire and lightning. He grabbed one of the men and, using him as a shield, he charged toward the exit, dragging him in front as blasts of magic tore at the pathetic thug.

Lily was hot on Isaac's tail as they burst through the doorway to the outside.

Throwing the dead corpse aside, he turned around and fired several flaming orbs into the lobby. They exploded, filling the room with fire. Using a bit of dark power, he focused on the structural supports of the doorway. He gave a loud growl as he used magic to rip them out, collapsing the doorway and the rest of the thugs' exit.

Lily stood there in shock as she looked at Isaac. He wasted no time. Turning, he took off down the street at an alarming speed. "W-wait!" She called after him.

Raine can't wait! He replied telepathically. *Hurry back to the inn, I have to save her!*

Even though she was shaken, she gave chase after him.

In his office where he monitored Isaac and Lily's escape, Ubel narrowed his eyes in thought. He had observed Isaac's onslaught from several cameras inside the building, watching him battle his way out.

"So, that's why my men had such trouble with you." He scratched his chin. Glancing over, he looked at his assistant. The man with the strangely shaped face. "Prepare for battle. He will be joining us sometime tonight, but do not kill him; we only need to capture him and bring him to Lord Zagaan."

The assistant simply nodded.

Ubel smiled. "Of all the people, you were the one that showed up. How fascinating." He continued to play over the footage of Isaac's battle.

At The Final Rest, seven men entered the lobby. It was nearly midnight, and the building was dark and quiet. They made their way behind the front desk, and one of them located a spare key to the elevator.

"Boss says she's up in the suite. You guys ready?" one of them asked the others. They all nodded and entered the elevator.

In the suite, the men stepped out of the elevator and glanced around. The room was dark, and only light from the moon gave any illumination. They spread out, motioning to each other. Upon entering the bedroom, three of the men approached Raine who was still passed out in her bed.

"She's in here," one of them called to the others.

Another reached down and pulled the blanket off her. "Wow!" His eyes went wide as he looked at her. "She's a babe!"

"She also reeks," one man said as he glanced down at her. "She must have drank a lot tonight."

"Guess this is gonna be easier than we were told." The first guy smirked. "See, she's totally passed out." He shook her shoulder, causing her to slightly mumble, but she didn't wake up.

"Damn, she is fine!" the third guy said as he ran his hand down her leg.

"Let's just grab her and go." One of them reached down and lifted her up from under her shoulders. "Grab her legs."

The two men lifted her off the bed and began heading toward the door.

In the main part of suite, the other four were checking the place out.

"This place is pretty fancy," one of them commented, taking a drink from a bottle of scotch.

"Hey morons, call the elevator; we've got the girl," a guy called out to them from Raine's bedroom.

"Yeah, yeah ..." one of them grumbled as he went over to the control panel.

The air in the suite drew thick as the men carried Raine out of the bedroom. The seven of them were fairly scattered around the place: three carrying Raine, three in the living area next to the hot spring, and the last next to the elevator. None of them noticed the masked figure enter from the hot spring balcony.

Isaac quickly ran up to the closest man and dealt him a devastating blow, using the power of wind to send him flying with the force of a sledgehammer. The man struck the wall next to the elevator and crumpled to the ground.

"What the ...?" The two men in the living area and the one next to the elevator glanced over at him. "What's *he* doing here!?" Their aural weapons appeared in their hands.

Isaac wasted no time. He moved in toward the next guy, hurling a bottle of wine from the living area table at him.

The man blocked the bottle with his blade in a shower of glass and wine. Isaac kicked the blade out of his hand and moved in, throwing several punches. The man blocked and dodged most of them as the second man came in from behind wielding an axe. He swung at Isaac, who skillfully ducked out of the way, and then grabbed the first guy, twisting him around and shoving him into the man with the axe.

The two men stumbled briefly but quickly recovered just in time to dodge a torrent of flame.

The men carrying Raine looked at each other in confusion. "What the hell!?" The one holding her shoulders looked at the others. "See what that is? We've got to get her out." He motioned to the one holding her legs, and they began to move toward the elevator. "Get that door open!" he called to the one at the control panel.

In the living area, Isaac dodged an axe swing and swiftly kicked the feet out from under the man. He followed up with a lightning attack, slamming himself into him in a blast of electricity, causing the man to stumble out of the living area and fall into the hot spring.

The man with the sword lunged at him. He dodged left and right as the man swiftly attacked, the blade coming dangerously close to Isaac. Spotting an opening, he caught the attacker's arm and twisted around. He pulled, throwing the man into a nearby wall. The man tried to get up, but Isaac leaned down and slammed his fist into his face. He fell to the ground, gasping for breath. The battle out of that building and the sprint across town had Isaac breathing heavily. He laid there for a moment, trying to catch his breath, but he didn't have long before another guy ran up on him.

Giving an irritated grunt, Isaac reached up and blocked the kick the man took at him. He quickly got up and blocked the next few swings from his new attacker. The man that was thrown into the hot spring had gotten himself out and was making his way back toward the battle.

Isaac spied the two men carrying Raine and swiftly hurled a bolt of lightning at the one holding her legs, being careful not to hit his friend. The man dropped her legs as he was struck. He howled in pain as he dropped to the ground.

Isaac's attacker conjured a yellow staff and was spinning it around, attempting to overpower him with speed. Unfortunately for the thug, he could match his speed, and he caught the staff with his hands and wrenched it from the man's grasp, slamming the butt of it into the now recovered axman who approached him from behind. He spun the staff and swung it at its owner's head, but before the weapon connected, it vanished in Isaac's hands.

"Shit, it's him!" The man holding Raine's shoulders looked at Isaac. "We need to deal with him first; we'll get the girl after." He placed her on the ground and turned toward the man at the elevator. "Don't just stand there!"

The axman had recovered and quickly jumped in behind Isaac, who was dealing with the man with the staff. He wrapped his arms around him, pinning his arms to his side in a bear hug.

The man with the staff attempted to take easy shots at Isaac, who was being held in place by the bigger guy, but his attacks were met with an aural shield. Isaac brought his feet up and slammed them into the man, causing him and the axman to stumble backward. He brought the back of his head into the axman's face. As they stumbled, he used the momentum to jump backward with the big man still holding onto him. They crashed into the living room table that had all the booze on it. The axman growled in pain as his back shattered onto the many bottles causing the broken glass to cut into him. Isaac reached back and grabbed a bottle, smashing it into the axman's head. He crawled off the motionless figure, gasping for breath as two more rushed him.

He rolled out of the way toward the fireplace as they descended upon him. Reaching over, he grabbed one of the fire irons and held it up to block their weapon attacks. He kicked at one of them, causing him to stumble backward, and he swung the fire iron at the other. Before the first one could recover, Isaac reached out and, using telekinesis, grabbed a large amount of the hot spring water from the balcony and covered the man's head with it. The man thrashed around, trying to get the water off.

While that one was struggling with the water, Isaac focused on the other one. He swung the fire iron at his attacker, but it was met with the man's red blade. The one with the yellow staff had recovered and was now closing in.

With a few staff swipes, Isaac parried the weapon. Using wind to blast the one with the red sword away, he took the opportunity to force the staff from the wielder using the fire iron, and with a clear opening, he thrust the poker upward into the man's jaw, killing him instantly.

As the man with the sword recovered, Isaac quickly shot a bolt of electricity at the one with the water on his head. The lightning hit the water and sent a jolt of power through the man, causing him to collapse to the ground.

The man with the sword rushed him, and he attempted to pull the fire iron from the head of the previous man, but it was stuck. He turned and ducked a few attacks, but the man grabbed him and forcefully threw Isaac across the suite.

He fell to the ground near the elevator, and as he started to rise, the thug who'd been guarding the control panel charged and tackled him through a nearby door. The door shattered as the two fell through into the suite's bathroom. Isaac grunted as they hit the ground; the man was now trying to strangle him. He used his feet and pushed against the brute to keep him from gaining leverage.

Looking back, he spied the toilet. He reached out and pulled the ceramic lid off the tank with telekinesis and hurled it into the big man's head. It shattered, stunning the attacker. Isaac grabbed one of the broken shards of the lid and stabbed the sharp end into the man's neck as he pushed his body off him.

Getting to his feet, Isaac leaned against the wall just outside of the bathroom as he tried to catch his breath, but he didn't have that long of a break as the man with the red sword and the other that was previously carrying Raine's legs came at him.

He ducked an attack and struck the man in the ribs, bringing his other fist across the man's face, dazing him. The second attacker swung at him with red gauntlets on his hands. Isaac blocked most of them, but one punch grazed the side of his head, causing him to stumble backward. The man moved in for another attack, but Isaac caught his arm, pinning it on top of his shoulder. Twisting his body slightly, he brought his other fist down on the man's elbow, breaking it.

The man shouted in pain as Isaac grabbed him by the throat and slammed him to the ground, crushing his neck.

The man with the red sword lunged at him, and he quickly kicked the man's leg out while dodging his attack. He pushed the man into the nearby wall and fired a pointblank blast of wind, smashing his head through the wall.

Gasping, Isaac moved away and put his back against the wall, sliding down until he was sitting on the floor. He gave sharp breaths as his heart hammered away in his chest. He took a quick glance around, making sure there were no more attackers. After a moment, his breathing began to calm.

"Ra ..." he gasped, his voice shaky. "Raine ..." He glanced over at her still form lying right outside her bedroom. "Raine." He struggled as he crawled over to her. Pulling the mask down around his neck, he looked at her and reached out and felt her face. She was still passed out, but otherwise, she was okay.

Isaac breathed a sigh of relief as he focused on calming himself. "I've got you ..." he whispered as he placed his hand gently on her shoulder.

Down in the lobby, Lily had finally made it back. She headed toward the front desk and paused as she saw the elevator descending. The doors opened, and Isaac stepped out carrying Raine.

"Oh my god!" Lily gasped.

"It's okay," he told her, stepping out of the elevator. "She's just asleep." He moved toward the hallway leading to his room. "Come on, let's get her to my room."

They entered the room, and Lily locked the door. Isaac took Raine over to his bed and gently laid her on it. "Where the hell is Vin?" he muttered.

"What happened up there?" Lily asked him with concern. "You look terrible."

He sat beside Raine on the edge of his bed. "You're gonna need to send a cleanup crew for your suite," he replied. "Also, someone to dispose of the bodies."

Lily looked at him with wide eyes. "Great ..." She looked over at Raine. "Well, I guess it's better than what could have happened to her." She gave him a gentle look. "You not only saved me tonight, but you also saved her."

Isaac didn't look at her. "You two wouldn't have been in danger if I hadn't started all of this." He rubbed his face with both hands as he let out a sigh. "I didn't expect things to get this bad."

"It's okay." She sat on Vin's bed opposite him and Raine. "You just wanted to do the right thing."

"No. That's not it." He glanced in her direction, but he didn't make eye contact. "Ever since we got out of the forest, something within me changed. I feel faster, stronger, and on top of that, my vision has improved. I can see people for who they really are. I can see the ones who are good, and the ones who are bad."

"How is that even possible?"

"I can't explain it," he told her. "But when I see people, I know the true intentions in their hearts. But there's more," he added. "Along with these added abilities, I've felt this deep anger welling up inside me. You see, I've always hated bad people, but with this newfound power, it feels like I'm going insane. Each time I see someone who is evil, I get the strong desire to destroy them." He clenched his fist as he stared at it. "Those people who bring suffering to others. I want to wipe them all out!"

"That may be, but isn't that because you care about others?" She gave him a gentle look. "Because you want to protect those around you?"

He shook his head. "There's a monster inside of me," he explained. "Deep down, I enjoy hurting them, those terrible people." His expression had a hint of pain. "It's like, if I beat the hell out of them, then it makes up for the times others have hurt me and I wasn't able to defend myself."

"That's not entirely true," she told him. "Even though your face was covered, I could still see your reaction when Ubel mentioned kidnapping Raine. You were worried. Why else would you have fought across the city to get to her?"

He didn't reply.

She smiled knowingly at him. "You do care, don't you?"

He looked at her "Yeah."

"Then why do you keep pushing them away?" she asked. "She's been so worried about you, ya know."

He looked over at Raine, who was still asleep. He stared at her face for a few seconds before replying, "I guess, I'm just scared." He continued to look at her. "Seems like anytime I try to get close to someone, I just end up getting hurt."

"Did she say something to hurt you?"

"Yeah ... I know she was being mind-controlled and that she probably didn't mean what she said, but ..." He wore a sad expression. "Hearing those words come from her mouth, it hurt a lot." He let out a deep breath. "It just reminds me of all the times in the past when the people I thought were my friends ended up treating me like garbage. It's like no matter what I do, I'm just going to end up hurt. So I push people away. Better to feel nothing than to feel pain." He fidgeted with his hands. "I'm just so tired, ya know? I'm tired of everything. Hell, I even attempted ..." He paused as he realized what he was about to tell her. "It doesn't matter." He shrugged. "It didn't work anyway, so here I am!" He gave a weak chuckle.

"You should tell her how you feel." Lily looked at him with concern. "I'm sure she'll understand."

"Maybe."

"Raine really does care about you," she insisted. "And you clearly care about her. Tell her."

Isaac looked at Raine once more. He thought about the argument they had earlier. "It's tough," he said. "It's difficult for me to trust people after all the betrayals I've been through."

"You said you can see the good in people now," she told him. "What do you see in her?"

Raine had a gentle glow of light illuminating from her body. "She's kind-hearted."

"See, she wouldn't try to hurt you." Lily smiled at him. "You don't have to second guess people now."

Isaac didn't respond. He just silently watched Raine sleep.

A few moments went by, and there was the sound of a key entering the lock of the door.

Lily glanced at the door, startled, but Isaac gave a stern look.

Vin walked into the room and shut the door behind him. Upon seeing the three of them, he paused. "Uhh, hey guys, what's going on?"

"Where the hell were you?" Isaac snapped.

"I was, uhh ..." Vin look at him with confusion. "Is something wrong?"

"Yeah. Raine was attacked. I tried to call you!"

Vin froze as he looked at Raine. "Is she ..."

"She's fine," Isaac told him. "No thanks to you."

"Isaac, please," Lily said. "It's not his fault."

Isaac shook his head with a hint of anger. "I was counting on you ..."

"Shit, dude ..." Vin looked shocked. "What happened?"

"The Syndicate tried to kidnap her," Isaac explained. "They set a trap, and she was the victim."

"What do you mean?" Vin frowned.

Isaac stood up. "I need you to stay here and look after them. It's going to get ugly tonight. If anyone other than me walks through that door, you put an arrow in their head."

Vin stood there dumbfounded as he watched Isaac walk toward the door.

"What are you going to do?" Lily asked him.

Isaac placed the mask over his face once more and looked back at her. "I'm going to end this."

CHAPTER 21

JUDGMENT

It was past midnight, and the streets were still busy. Guards roamed around watching for signs of the man in the mask.

Isaac was careful to keep out of sight as he headed for Talim, the investigative reporter's house. It wasn't long before he reached his destination.

"I have the evidence you need," Isaac told him after Talim answered the door. "We need to stop them tonight."

"And how do you plan on doing that?" Talim asked him. "Even if I were to get this sent to every news outlet, you really think the king would believe it?"

"He will," Isaac assured him. "There's even a video of the prime minister plotting against the king in those files."

"That's not the issue," Talim told him. "The council-man will just discredit this information as false. It'll never go through."

"I am aware of that," Isaac explained. "That's why I'm going to take him down. He can't sweep this stuff under the rug if he's dead."

Talim looked at him in shock. "You're going to ... you can't!"

"Oh, I can. And I will!"

He shook his head. "The council is untouchable. Simply suggesting an assassination on even one of them carries a severe punishment."

"I won't compromise you, if that's your worry," Isaac reassured him. "This is on me. I will deliver the evidence on Ubel personally to the king after I have killed him."

Talim frowned. "And how will you accomplish that?"

Isaac grinned. "I have my ways." He held out the bag with the evidence he had collected. "Once Ubel is dead, you get all of this out, and we can bring them down."

Talim stared at him. "You do know what will happen if you fail." He took the bag.

"I won't." Isaac turned to leave.

"Why are you doing this?" Talim asked him. "Why help us?"

Isaac didn't look at him. "I guess you could say I'm sick of assholes treating people like garbage." He clenched his fists. "They'll hurt anyone for their own gain. I despise them and all of their kind. Those freaks who prey on the innocent, who take happiness from others. I'll take them all down!"

"I see ..." Talim replied. "You know, if you pull this off, you'll be saving a lot of people from their tyranny." He held a solemn look. "You've given a lot of people hope these last several days. If you do this, it will have consequences."

"Just get that evidence sent out," Isaac said. "After I deal with the councilman, it's in your hands."

Talim nodded. "How will I know when to release it?"

"Trust me, you'll know." Isaac began to walk away. "Just listen for the pandemonium."

Ubel and his assistant made their way to the church. With everything going on, he had made sure that the two of them were alone.

"He'll be here eventually," he told the assistant. "We need him alive. Lord Zagaan will be greatly pleased once we bring him in."

The assistant simply nodded.

"He thinks he can expose us," Ubel scoffed. "How naïve."

The assistant's face shifted slightly. The skin moved as if it weren't attached.

"Patience. You'll have your fun." He grinned. "I would like a word with him before he is destroyed."

At the inn, Lily had explained to Vin what was going on.

"So, that's what he's been doing this whole time," He said in shock.

She nodded. "Yeah. I don't really know how he's been able to do it, but somehow, he's been taking them down one by one."

"He's been acting so strange lately," Vin said thoughtfully. "I've never seen him like this."

"He told me that he can see the good and evil in people," Lily told him. "He also said that's he's really angry and needs to vent."

He looked at her with confusion. "He said that to you? Really?"

She nodded.

"That doesn't make sense." He cocked his head to the side. "He can be rude, irritable, sometimes even reckless, but I've never seen or heard of him doing something like this before."

"He said something changed after you guys left the forest," she explained. "Something about going insane."

Vin looked at her with a frown. "The forest ..." He glanced at Raine, who was still asleep. "Raine told me that his aura had changed. That there was a hint of darkness." He wore a grim expression. "She also said that there was a chance this darkness was affecting his mind."

Lily looked surprised. "What does that mean?"

He shook his head. "I don't know. But if Isaac's been out there fighting, and he's using this dark power ... he might change for the worse."

"But he was worried about her." Lily motioned to Raine. "Even if his aura is tainted, he still cares, even if he doesn't show it."

"We'll need to be careful. We don't know the extent of the darkness's influence."

They sat in silence for a moment before Lily turned on the TV.

"We should probably watch the news for now," she said. "I think ... I think it's about to get ugly out there."

Isaac scouted the city, looking through walls, scanning auras until he finally found the one he was looking for. Two evil auras were inside the church at the altar. He checked the area and noticed they were the only ones there. Ubel was waiting for him, that much was certain. Instead of sneaking in, he decided to enter through the front door.

"You took longer than anticipated," Ubel greeted as Isaac slowly walked down the aisle of the nave. Ubel was standing behind the pulpit, his assistant close to his side. "I was beginning to wonder if you'd even show up."

Isaac stopped halfway across the nave and glared at Ubel from under his mask. "Your attempt to kidnap Raine failed, asshole!" he snapped. "She's safe, unlike you."

"It was interesting to see how you handled my people so easily," Ubel told him. "Here I was thinking you were just some common vigilante." He leered at Isaac maliciously. "I didn't expect to be dealing with a guardian."

Isaac gave a cocky smile. "Too bad for you, huh." He held his arms out to his sides. "Guess the cat's out of the bag, and it looks like you're the only one left to kill."

Ubel narrowed his eyes at him. "You're quite different from the other guardians. The others had aspiring dreams of becoming heroes. They had a sense of morality and honor about them." He held his chin in thought. "It was because of those ideals that they were easily manipulated. But you ... you seem to be quite the opposite. You kill without mercy. Without any moral code. That's why I was surprised at the realization of what you were."

Isaac chuckled. "I don't care what you think of me." He pointed at him. "You're going to pay for the suffering you've caused others—with your blood."

"You really have no idea what's going on." Ubel shook his head. "Threatening one of the council is a serious crime."

"Like I give a shit!" Isaac spat at him.

"I wonder," Ubel continued. "If you're with Raine, then that means you must have come from Adamas. I saw you at the tournament, after all."

"So? That speculation isn't going to save your life."

Ubel shrugged. "I was just curious. What would you people be doing all the way out here?" He smiled secretively. "Unless perhaps you were looking for something?"

Isaac frowned. "What makes you think that?"

"What indeed." He laughed. "Let's not play games. It's no mere coincidence that the stolen artifact the queen holds so dear is being sought after by her own trusted people, and the guardian, no doubt."

"How do you know about that?" Isaac asked cautiously.

"Well for one, I am a member of the council." Ubel smiled. "But also, I was one of those that orchestrated the attack. You see, we need that artifact for an important experiment of ours."

"How convenient," Isaac said sarcastically. "The evil mastermind reveals his plan right before his demise." He laughed. "I already know the artifact is somewhere down in the forest. It'll only be a matter of time before I find it."

"I would think again on that," Ubel said dangerously. "I only tell you this because I want you to understand your failure."

"Really?" He motioned around the church. "I don't exactly see any guards here to protect you. Just your ugly ass assistant there." He pointed at the strange figure.

At this statement, Ubel smiled wickedly. "You truly are naïve." His eyes flared dangerously. "You really think I would be here without protection?"

"Bring it on, asshole!" Isaac shouted. "I took down your operations! I got the evidence to put you all in the ground! It's over!" He clenched his fist at Ubel. "We beat you! *I* beat you!"

"I'm afraid you are quite mistaken," Ubel growled as he motioned to his assistant. "You've fought demons before, right?"

The assistant moved until he was standing in front of Ubel, facing Isaac.

"You see, those were lesser demons," Ubel continued. "And I am aware that you faced the eidolon known as Ligeia down in the forest. However, you had help with her." He grinned. "But now you are alone, and there will be no escape for you."

The assistant waved his hand, and the door to the church sealed itself as a curtain of bluish black flame encircled the walls, trapping Isaac in with them.

"You see, there are different types of demons," Ubel went on. "And no one has ever survived an encounter with the elite demon known as a revenant."

Isaac watched as the assistant's face began to shift violently as his body twitched.

"Even the guardians of the past couldn't stand toe to toe with these arch demons." Ubel smirked. "You're journey ends here."

The skin on the assistant's face began to tear, peeling away to reveal a set of gray, glazed over, dead eyes as blood trickled down his body. His back arched as the flesh covering him ripped away, falling to the ground to expose his true form.

"What the fuck?" Isaac stared in disgust at the creature before him. It was large with grisly, bloody skin and those dead, unseeing eyes. It was muscular with forked hands and feet. Sharp horns protruded from its ridged head.

"You shouldn't have meddled in our affairs," Ubel told him. "But you shall be removed soon enough." He nodded toward the revenant.

A battle axe appeared in the revenant's hands, but this was unlike any aural blade Isaac had ever seen. It was bloodred but had no glow to it, and it seemed to be dripping blood. As each drop hit the floor, it would splash in a flash of sparks, then dissipate.

Isaac's sword of light appeared in his hand.

The revenant approached, its axe held at the ready. Isaac charged up an orb of electricity and hurled it at the demon. The monster swung its axe and deflected the orb, but Isaac held out his hand and clenched it into a fist, causing the orb to explode before it was too far away. The demon flinched as it took the full blast of sparks. It continued to move closer.

Isaac jumped to the side as the revenant brought its axe slamming down where he was standing, shattering the floor to pieces. Turning quickly, he hurled his blade, causing it to spin rapidly toward the demon, who deflected it with its axe, sending it flying away. The revenant charged him. He re-conjured his sword and used it to block the demon's axe. The demon pressed down on him, and he began to slide backward.

Isaac gritted against the strength and weight of the monster but could not push it away. The revenant reached out and grabbed him by the throat, lifting him into the air. He kicked at the demon, trying to break free. In a single movement, he was hurled across the church, crashing into several pews and lay there, groaning in pain.

Ubel simply watched on with a sinister smile.

The revenant approached Isaac, who was lying in the middle of the shattered wooden pews. It leapt into the air, preparing to stomp down on him.

Isaac saw the demon jump and forced a blast of wind from himself, pushing away all of the debris, clearing the area around him. He swiftly rolled out of the way as the demon's foot shattered the ground where he'd just been. Getting to his feet, he paced around the revenant as it slowly followed him, its axe at the ready.

"You can't hope to win this fight," Ubel taunted. "You should just give up."

Isaac paid him no attention as the revenant leered at him. He backed away as the demon quickened its pace.

Stop holding me back! The voice inside him urged.

He curled his lip in anger as he felt the darkness pulling at him.

The revenant swung at him, causing him to duck out of the way, but the demon was quick, and it used its other hand to strike him to the ground.

"It's really too bad," Ubel said smugly. "Her Majesty will be highly disappointed to hear that her champion fell so easily."

Get up!

Isaac tried to move, but the revenant put its foot on his back, pinning him to the ground.

"It won't matter for her, though," Ubel continued. "Once we've dealt with you, she'll be next." He chuckled as if telling a joke.

At these words, Isaac felt a strong emotion rising from the depths of his heart. He couldn't explain it, but the darkness pulled at him even more, as if urging him to fight.

"Lucia ..."

Her name barely escaped his lips as the revenant held its axe above its head, ready to strike him with the blunt part of the handle.

If you don't fight, she'll die!
Anger. Hatred. Fear. Pain.

There was a violent aura from deep down, trying to break free, and the hunter within began to lose control.

As the demon prepared to strike him with the final blow, Isaac felt the darkness taking over. The thought of Lucia back in Adamas filled his mind, and somehow, he knew she was in danger.

There was no turning back.

The air in the church thickened. The revenant brought its axe down toward Isaac's head, but it was stopped inches from its mark. A veil of darkness shielded him from the attack.

"Get ... off ..." Isaac growled dangerously.

"What ...?" Ubel frowned as he watched the atmosphere darken around Isaac and the revenant. "What is this?"

A black tendril appeared out of Isaac and grabbed at the revenant, hurling the demon off of him into a nearby wall. His sword re-appeared in his hand, but the glow of light was nearly gone as it pulsed with darkness. He rose, facing the demon as it got back to its feet.

Ubel looked at Isaac with wide eyes. "You're already turned? This isn't possible!" He took a step back. "How are you still in control!?"

Isaac glared at the revenant as darkness began to pour out of him like a thick mist. "You just stay there, old man." His voice was raspy and cold. "You're the one who's next!" His movement was swift as he slammed into the demon, forcing it back against the wall. The revenant swung at him, but the dark blade met the demon's axe with conviction.

The demon struggled, but Isaac wouldn't budge. It shoved with all its strength but wasn't able to push him away. It growled as aura began to build up in its axe.

"Stop him!" Ubel shouted.

Isaac waved his hand, and a cascade of darkness-infused lightning bolts rained down upon the revenant, scorching its skin. The demon jumped away as it hissed in pain. He didn't let up. Hurling his sword toward the demon, it dodged the spinning blade, but in the blink of an eye, Isaac had appeared where his sword was, behind the revenant, and violently attacked. The dark blade pierced the demon's skin, leaving a trail of blood as he ripped the blade from the demon's flesh.

The revenant howled as it brought its axe slamming to the ground. A blast of aura erupted from the impact, destroying the immediate area within a ten-foot radius.

Isaac gritted his teeth and held up his arm as a dark barrier surrounded him, fending off the powerful attack.

"This can't be ..." Ubel's previous smugness was shaken as he watched his revenant now struggling against the enraged darkness that Isaac now wielded.

The demon swung its axe in a fury, slashing left and right. Isaac's heightened power allowed him to anticipate every attack. He dodged frantically as each powerful swing came within inches of him, but none connected. He extended his arm in a punch as the darkness formed into a giant fist, hammering the brute away.

The revenant held its forked hand toward Isaac as a condensed sphere of energy flew at him. He brought his dark sword up and blocked the magic, causing it to break apart into several smaller orbs that flew away in random directions. He was about to retaliate when he noticed the orbs circling around and coming back at him. He held his hand up and surrounded himself in a dark barrier reflecting the magic as it struck his shield.

The demon dropped its shoulder and charged him. Isaac was thrown backward as the revenant broke through his barrier and slammed into him. He hit one of the pillars near the center of the nave, causing it to crumble apart as he hit the ground.

"It would seem you don't have as much control of the darkness as I thought," Ubel stated as he watched Isaac get to his knees. "Hurry and subdue him before he gets too far out of control!" he shouted to the revenant.

Isaac stared at the demon as he knelt by the broken pillar. He grinned sadistically as he wiped a trickle of blood from his face. The demon readied its axe and charged. Isaac swiftly vaulted over its head and into the air. As he fell to the ground, he conjured a lightning rope from his hand that wrapped itself around the demon's leg. Landing on the ground, he pulled the rope, tripping the revenant. He jumped onto the monster's back and drove his blade into the demon's thick skin. The revenant growled angrily and reached around, grabbing Isaac's arm and pulling him away. He re-conjured his blade in his other hand and swung it downward at the demon's arm. The revenant pulled its arm away as the dark sword cut a large gash, leaving a trail of blood.

Isaac looked up at the ceiling above the revenant and spied a chandelier. The large, ornate object of interest had a design that ended in a sharp point at the bottom. Using his dark magic, he targeted the chains holding the chandelier to the ceiling and ripped them out. As it fell, he guided it with telekinesis toward his target.

The revenant jumped out of the way as the chandelier crashed into the ground. It was about to counterattack but was stopped short. Isaac had bounded up to him and delivered a devastating kick to its chest, pushing the demon back toward the fallen chandelier. He followed up with a blast of fire, briefly stunning the demon enough to deliver the final blow, smashing the revenant's head onto the broken mess of metal, forcing several of the chandelier's bars to pierce its skull.

The demon gurgled for a moment and then lay still. Its body burst into flames and was soon nothing but a pile of dead ash.

Ubel stared at his slain revenant in shock. "Impossible ..."

Isaac grabbed his head and fell to his knees, growling in pain. The darkness was pulling at him as if trying to tear his body apart.

"It would seem you used too much." Ubel narrowed his eyes as he watched the darkness swirling around Isaac's body. "Only a reaper could singlehandedly best a revenant, after all."

Isaac's vision was becoming hazy. He could feel his negative emotions overcoming himself, and his mind was filled with bloodlust.

His memories.

His friends.

His life.

It was all becoming distant as the darkness continued to take hold. He didn't know why he had set out on this journey to begin with or why he continued to fight. His mind was now filled with an everlasting hatred for all things.

As Isaac felt the last bit of his sanity slip away, he paused. The part of him that he held deep within began to stir. His hands shook as he stared at the picture that lay on the ground before him.

It can't end this way.

His vision began to clear, and his thoughts came flooding back to him.

You promised.

"Buddy ..." he barely whispered as the dark mist began to dissipate from his body and his eyes turned back to normal.

He didn't know how it ended up on the floor. Perhaps he took it from his pocket without realizing, but there, on the floor, was his picture of Dozer.

"This can't be ..." Ubel looked at Isaac in confusion. "How are you pushing it back!?"

With the darkness being suppressed once more, Isaac took the picture and slowly rose to his feet. He felt drained after using that power, but he shrugged it off.

"I told you ..." He spoke carefully as he put the photo in his pocket. "It's over." He looked at Ubel as he struggled to keep his composure.

"This doesn't change anything!" Ubel growled. "You can't hold that darkness back forever. It'll only be a matter of time before you succumb."

Isaac approached the councilman. "Too bad for you; today is not that day." He conjured his blade. It had regained its glow of white but was slightly dimmer than before.

"Killing me won't stop them!" Ubel took a step back. "You think you can protect her? She's already doomed!"

Isaac made his way across the church and grabbed Ubel by his throat. He drove his sword into the evil man's leg. "How dare you mention her!" He twisted the blade, causing Ubel to cry out in pain.

"Y-you ..." Ubel gasped. "You don't ... even know why ... you protect her." He gave a hysterical chuckle.

Isaac's sword vanished, and he punched Ubel in the face. "Don't you bring her into this!" He struck him again and again.

Ubel gagged as blood ran from his mouth. "It's ... too late," he stammered. "We've been keeping an eye on her ... for years, now." He laughed. "You cannot save her."

Isaac kicked him savagely to the ground. "What does that mean!?" He glowered down at him. "Who else is involved!?"

Ubel laughed harder. "You really have no idea ..."

The sound of bones breaking could be heard as Isaac mercilessly kicked his body.

"Y-you don't ..." Ubel gasped as he lay there paralyzed with pain. "Don't even ... understand ... why you're angry." He barely gave out a laugh as Isaac drove his sword through his chest.

"We'll see about that." Isaac glared down at Ubel's corpse as he drew his blade from the evil man's heart.

He took a deep breath to calm himself. He knew there was more to be done tonight. He had to get this information to the king so that Talim could release the evidence and put The Syndicate behind bars.

He pulled out a recording device from his jacket and inspected it. There was slight damage, but thankfully the protective case he had covered it in had kept it intact. He had the entire recording of Ubel's confession.

Looking down at the dead body of the councilman, he knew how to get everyone's attention and bring light to the evil that plagued Esmeraldas.

King Roland was alone in his bed chamber inside the Esmeraldas palace preparing for the night. It was late, and he'd had to spend more time than anticipated on meetings and urgent matters. He sat on the edge of his bed and stared at the crystal on his dresser. It had a dark blue glow to it. It was past midnight.

He sighed and turned off the light on his nightstand. As he was about to lie down, he paused. There was a figure standing at his window.

"Who's there!?" he demanded.

CHAPTER 21: JUDGMENT

"Calm down," the figure spoke calmly. "I'm not here for trouble."

"Who are you?"

The figure stepped closer till Roland could see him in the moonlight.

"It's you ..." He frowned as he stared at the man in the mask.

"I'm sorry to have bothered you so late at night," Isaac told him. "But there's something you must see." He pulled out the recording device and held it up to the king. "I have evidence that Councilman Ubel was plotting against you and the Queen of Adamas."

"That's absurd!" Roland replied. "There's no way any member of the council would do such a thing."

"I'm afraid it's all true," Isaac replied. "I have his confession on video." He turned on the device, and a holographic image appeared. It showed the confrontation he'd had with Ubel and the revelation of treason against Roland and Lucia.

The king watched the video with a frown. He saw the revenant and the revelation of conspiracy.

Isaac stayed silent as he let the king view the whole video. After it was over, the two of them stood there for a moment before Roland responded.

"I don't know what to think." He shook his head. "This is a serious turn of events."

"He's been manipulating everyone in your city," Isaac explained. "He formed The Syndicate and has been keeping your people tied down with blackmail and threats for years now."

Roland didn't reply.

"He was able to keep his identity a secret because the leaders appointed under you were working for him—the prime minister being the main source."

"You have evidence of these claims?" the king asked him.

Isaac nodded. "Yes. A reporter will be releasing all of it to the press here shortly."

Roland stared at him. "What? You mean to release this to the public?"

"That's right," Isaac told him. "I apologize if this goes above your authority, but this matter involves not just the

403

castle, but the citizens who have been involved and silenced for years now."

"If what you're telling me is all true, then the attack that happened a few months ago would have been organized by ..."

"By your own trusted people."

The king went silent in thought.

"Here." Isaac pulled a data drive from his pocket. "I kept a copy of all the evidence for you." He handed the drive to Roland. "They need to be brought to justice."

"You know," the king looked at the drive in his hand, "Queen Lucia mentioned someone like you."

"What?" Isaac frowned.

"I met with Raine," he explained. "If she's here, then that must mean the one Her Majesty mentioned is with her." He looked at Isaac and nodded. "I've been paying close attention to the issues involving the man in the mask. I never would have guessed it involved a criminal organization here within my city." He gave a calm smile. "If what you say is all true, that would mean you have done our country a great service." He glanced over at his dresser, and Isaac followed his gaze. There was a picture of Roland and Lucia in an ornate frame. "We go way back," he explained. "I've known her since she was a child, and her judgment of people has always been spot on. She is my niece, after all." He glanced back at Isaac. "Which means you must be Isaac."

Isaac stiffened.

The king chuckled as he saw his suspicion confirmed. "She told me a lot about you. Said you would help us when we needed you."

Isaac reached up and took off his mask. "She talked about me?"

Roland nodded. "She spoke very highly of you. I've never heard her speak of anyone with such affection."

Isaac felt a sense of warmth in his heart at hearing this revelation. A part of him couldn't believe what he was being told. "She did?"

"Oh, yes." The king nodded. "Ever since she was young; it was always how Isaac would save her and whatnot." He chuckled fondly.

"What do you mean when she was young?" Isaac was confused.

"Oh, since she was a child." Roland smiled warmly. "Seemed I was the only one who believed her since she constantly mentioned you after all these years, and yet, here you are!"

Isaac stared at him in disbelief. "But how could she have known about me?"

"Weren't you two friends?" he asked. "She always said her best friend was always with her."

Isaac just stood there, baffled.

"If she trusts you, then so do I." The king looked back at the drive. "I'm not sure if I approve of your methods, but if my own people are involved in what you have claimed, then I will personally make sure to put an end to it."

"There have been a lot of people involved that are being used by them," Isaac said. "The girl who runs the inn called The Final Rest said her father is being held against his will, as are many others."

Roland nodded. "I will go over all of this information tonight. We shall bring those responsible to justice." He looked at Isaac with approval. "And thank you for looking out for my niece."

Isaac simply nodded.

Back at the inn, Raine had woken up and sat in the middle of the bed. The morning was approaching, and Isaac had not returned. Even though her head was spinning from being hungover, she had managed to listen to Lily as she explained what was going on.

"How did I not notice?" she said, holding a cup of water. "He didn't even mention anything about what he was doing."

The three of them sat with their own thoughts until the TV drew their attention.

"We have disturbing news," the female reporter said with a grave look. "Just late last night, there was an attack at the church."

Lily turned the volume up, and they all watched with interest.

The picture on the TV showed the inside of the church in ruins.

"There seems to have been some kind of fight that took place. The investigators are looking further into it." The reporter continued, "But the worst part is the most recent report."

Raine's eyes widened in horror as she listened.

"We cannot show you the footage due to the grisly nature of it, but Councilman Ubel is dead," the reporter said with a hint a fear. "His body was found outside of the prime minister's house."

"Oh my god ..." Lily whispered. "He actually killed him."

Raine and Vin remained silent.

"Passersby saw the body and reported it to the guards this morning. We believe the destruction in the church was where it happened."

The footage on the TV did not show the body, but there was a large group of people crowded near the prime minister's house trying to get a glimpse of the scene as guards had the area cordoned off.

"There is no evidence at this time, but we believe the killer is the man in the mask," the reporter explained. "Even though the investigation is underway, there was also a mass leak of evidence released from an investigative reporter by the name of Talim Larrs."

The TV now showed several videos of the evidence Isaac had collected, including the meeting with the prime minister.

"According to Talim, he had been quietly investigating the criminal organization known as The Syndicate and had collected the data he is now releasing. He claims to have no connection to the man in the mask."

"Holy shit," Vin said as he stared at the TV. "That's some damning evidence right there."

"I can't believe what I'm seeing," Raine muttered.

On the TV, it showed several guards escorting the prime minister in handcuffs as well as a few people who were part of the castle leadership.

"Oh my god!" Lily gasped as she saw the next part of the report.

"There have also been several people found during the morning investigation that are believed to be victims of The

Syndicate." The TV showed several people being taken care of by rescue teams. Among them was Lily's father.

"He did it," she said with tears in her eyes. "He actually did it."

"The investigation is ongoing, and there will be more to follow." The camera cut back to the woman reporter. "As for the man in the mask ..."

The three of them perked up at this statement.

"His identity is still unknown."

Outside in the city, Isaac sat on one of the buildings over-looking the commotion. He watched as guards were frantically running up and down the streets and people were watching on in shock.

The morning had come, and with it, the fall of evil.

He stared at his hand as they shook slightly. The power of darkness still lingered, and he could feel its tempting pull. How much would he have to rely on that power?

CHAPTER 22

STILL BOUND TOGETHER

As the morning went on, more and more individuals were arrested as the leaked evidence was released publicly by Talim. He was also taken in for questioning and even King Roland with his copy of the evidence given by Isaac was going over the data.

The royal guard was activated, and investigations were ongoing. It was simple to say that The Syndicate that had long held the city hostage in secret was being dismantled swiftly. A system that took years to be built up was ended seemingly overnight because Isaac had acted based on the unique ability he now possessed of seeing the good and evil in people. A power he didn't fully understand but couldn't ignore.

Raine, Vin, and Lily remained at the inn long after the sun had come up. Raine was still nursing a hangover as she drank water, and the other two were watching the news. It was shortly after the crystal had begun to glow green that Isaac returned.

He entered the room as the three looked at him in silence. He took a few steps and leaned back against a nearby wall, closing the door behind him.

"It's over," he said, looking at the ground. His face had mild cuts with a couple of small bruises. His clothes were somewhat in tatters, and his hair was messy.

"We saw," Vin said quietly as he glanced at Isaac. "You okay, dude? You look terrible."

Isaac nodded with a wry expression. "Ubel was a bit tougher to take down than expected," he replied with a scoff. "He, uhh, summoned a demon."

"A *demon* did that to you?" Lily asked with wide eyes.

"It was ... a *big* demon," he answered, holding up his fingers sarcastically as if measuring something.

"I'm glad you're okay." She smiled at him.

He gave her a brief smile before speaking. "You know," he glanced toward Raine and Vin but didn't meet their eyes, "down in the forest, when we fought that creature, some things happened."

Raine stared at her glass of water without replying.

"You guys said some pretty terrible things to me," Isaac continued. "I know you weren't in control and normally this kind of thing wouldn't have bothered me, but ..." He rubbed his face with both hands as if gathering his nerves. "We've been together for a while now and, uhh, well, I guess you could say I see you both as my friends, so when you said those things to me, it hurt. A lot." He made a quick glance at Lily. She smiled warmly at him. "I never told you guys how I got here. It wasn't my choice."

Vin frowned. "What do you mean?"

"I told you that I'm from another world," Isaac explained. "But I was actually brought here against my will."

Raine looked at him in surprise. "How?"

"I'm not sure," he answered. "After I committed—" He stopped himself, then shook his head. "I remember there was darkness, then I heard a voice."

Brave soul who does not fear death. Heed our call.

"I don't know who it was, or what they wanted," Isaac said. "But after that, I woke up in Terra and I had these powers." He looked at his hand and softly clenched it into a fist. "I don't really know why I'm here, or who brought me, but I didn't want this."

Raine looked away from him, and Vin stared at the ground.

"You all kept pressuring me to join your team," he contin-ued. "At first, I didn't trust any of you, but after everything we've been through." He looked at Raine, and she returned his gaze. "I would like to say we're friends." He gave her a slight smile.

Raine smiled back.

"That's why it hurt so much. But something happened to me down there. I felt this surge of power well up from within, and now I have more power than I did before." He looked at Vin. "I can now see those who are good and those who are evil. It's because of that I was able to take down The Syndicate." He nodded thoughtfully. "But also, I can see you three as well."

Lily, Vin, and Raine all perked up at this statement.

"And now I can see that you guys are genuinely good." He smiled at them. "Which is why I want to stick with you and help the queen."

"Do you mean that?" Raine asked hopefully.

Isaac nodded. "Yeah. Ubel threatened Queen Lucia tonight as well as King Roland. I want to know why."

"What? Why would he do that?" Vin asked.

"He said he coordinated the attack on Adamas," Isaac explained. "I also found that the artifact is somewhere in the forest below. Likely in another facility similar to what we found in Vaerun."

"You figured all that out by just fighting this organization?" Raine asked.

He nodded.

"And you killed Ubel, a council member," she said blankly.

"Yeah."

"I don't really know what to believe anymore," she told them as she stared into space. "We were always told that the council was here to protect us. I never would have guessed one of them would consort with demons and plan attacks on us."

"It's all true," Isaac said. "I saw the evil in Ubel. It was the worst I've seen yet."

Raine took a long drink, emptying her water glass. Vin folded his arms in thought.

There was a long pause before Isaac looked at Lily. "They found your father. He's at the castle in protective custody."

Lily perked up. "I saw it on the news. So, he's alright?"

He nodded.

She stood up and walked over to him. "You've done so much for all of us." She gave him a gentle hug. "I don't know how we can ever repay you ..."

Isaac shifted nervously. "I didn't do this for some kind of reward, you know."

She pulled away and smiled warmly, looking into his eyes. "Thank you, Isaac."

"You should go see him." He smiled back. "The guards should let you in. They might even have questions for you, so be prepared for that."

"Gonna be a long day ..." she said. "I've also called the guards about the mess upstairs."

"Oh yeah ..." He looked away in shame. "That's going to be interesting trying to explain that."

"Don't worry." She winked at him. "I'll figure it out. You just rest."

He chuckled softly and nodded.

Lily turned and looked at Raine, then back at Isaac. "Come on, Vin." She motioned toward him. "Let's go to the castle."

"Huh?" He looked at her, confused. "Me?"

"Yeah, you wanted a date, right?" She smiled flirtatiously at him.

"I don't think now is the time for..."

"What, you're gonna let me walk there all alone?" She fidgeted her fingers, pretending to be nervous.

Vin stared at her for a moment, trying to decide what to do.

"I mean, it's just going to be us, you know." She winked at him.

He jumped up and grabbed his shoes. "Well, when you put it that way." He smiled as he headed for the door.

"We'll be back later, alright?" She smiled at Raine and winked. They left the room and closed the door behind them, leaving the two of them alone.

"Well, that couldn't have been more obvious," Isaac said, glancing at Raine. "So ... how are you feeling?"

"I've felt better." She placed her empty water glass on the nightstand next to the bed. "Head is still fuzzy."

He walked over and took the glass. "I'll get more water." He walked out of the room, and after a brief moment, he returned with a full glass. "It's from the purified fountain in the hallway," he told her as he handed her the glass and sat next to her.

"Thanks." She took a drink and then looked at him. "Lily told me everything, by the way."

He nodded but didn't reply.

"She said you fought your way across the city to save me." She stared at the glass in her hand.

"She tends to exaggerate."

Raine looked at him and smiled appreciatively. "Thank you."

He looked away nervously. "I couldn't just let them take you, ya know."

"Does this mean, you forgive me?" she asked.

He sighed. "Yeah ..."

Her gaze was soft and comforting. "I never meant to hurt you. You're my friend."

"I know." He put his hand on her shoulder. "It's okay, Raine."

She looked at his injuries and messy hair. "You look exhausted."

"And you look like hell." He chuckled at her. Her hair was even messier than his, and she had bags under her eyes.

She laughed and took another drink. "It was a rough night."

"Probably shouldn't drink anymore until we get back to the castle." He smiled at her.

"Good idea," she replied.

The two of them sat for a moment in silence as Raine finished her water and set the glass on the nightstand.

"Come here. We should get some rest." She lay down on the bed and motioned to him.

Isaac gave a nervous smile and laid next to her. "It's been a good minute since I got any sleep."

"I'm not feeling rested either," she told him as she turned onto her side.

He also turned onto his side, and they stared at each other.

"I'm really glad you're here," she said. "I mean that."

He smiled again. "I'm still warming up to the place."

"Well, I'll continue to do my best to help you along the way." She snuggled into her pillow.

"I would like that," he replied, closing his eyes. "I'm so tired."

"We'll probably sleep into the evening," she said. "Hopefully no one disturbs us." She waved her hand, and the door to the room locked. "Let's just sleep and figure things out later."

"We definitely need showers." He chuckled as he felt himself falling asleep.

Raine laughed and closed her eyes. "I call first."

"Deal," Isaac replied sleepily.

The two of them fell asleep with thoughts of each other on their minds. The battles were over for now, but little did they know that a looming darkness approached.

EPILOGUE

The woman smiled at Isaac as she pushed her black hair away from her eyes. "Are you starting to understand?" she asked.

He thought for a moment before replying. "Not really."

"Is the darkness really controlling you?" She tapped her fingers on the table of the interrogation room. "After all, it's supposed to be a bad thing, right?"

"What are you talking about?" He frowned at her.

"The two times you were in danger, you called upon that power. Or perhaps it wasn't you who was in danger?" She smirked.

"You mean the demon?" he asked. "If I didn't stop it, then Ubel would have won."

She shook her head. "You misunderstand. Did you do all of this because you simply wanted to win?"

He didn't answer.

"You said you didn't want this fight, yet all you've been doing since you left the castle, from my understanding, is fight." The woman narrowed her eyes at him. "These conflicts, it seems, you've brought upon yourself."

"What?" Isaac looked at her angrily. "I didn't cause all of this!"

"Why did you help that girl? You could have just ignored her," she told him. "Not once, but twice. You even helped that girl at the inn, even though she was working for the enemy."

"Maybe I'm just a sucker for cute women," he responded dismissively.

"Or perhaps there's something you aren't telling yourself." The woman smirked. "Were you really mad at your companions, or did you force yourself to become distant out of fear?"

Isaac looked away.

"If I were to guess, you called upon the power of darkness against the eidolon out of fear of losing them, the same as why you used it to defeat that arch-demon." She smiled.

"You're wrong," he said matter-of-factly.

"Am I?" She gave him a knowing look. "Take this place, for instance." She gestured at the room. "Why a prison? You could have thought up something else."

"I didn't make this place," he told her sternly.

The woman leaned toward him and looked him straight in the eye. "Yes, you did." Her tone was serious. "Just like you made my appearance the same as hers."

"If I made this place, then why can't I leave?" he questioned.

"Because you haven't resolved the conflict in your heart," she explained. "Perhaps that is why this place is what it is. Because you feel trapped."

He scoffed. "You've got me all wrong, lady."

"You keep lying to yourself," she said, unamused. "You protected that city with no obligation. Even used the power deep within your heart to do so."

Isaac gave a chuckle and turned his head away from her.

"You hear a voice, don't you?" she asked him blankly.

He didn't reply.

"You've heard it since you got to Terra, correct?"

He glanced at her but remained silent.

"I see." She leaned back. "Do you know what that voice is?"

He shrugged.

"You will have to discover that on your own." She grinned secretively. "Perhaps it will be a clue to your deepest desires."

"Why don't you just come out and tell me?" he asked her almost demandingly.

"You aren't here to be given answers," she told him. "You must discover them for yourself. The reason you're here. The darkness in your heart. It all has a connection, but that is for you to figure out and understand." She cocked her head. "But these answers are more obvious than you realize." She laughed. "But of course, if you could see them, we wouldn't be here."

Isaac frowned at her but stayed silent.

"I'll give you a hint." She smiled mischievously. "Think about how you got here. To Terra, I mean."

"Like I said, I was pulled here against my will," he explained with a slight growl.

"Yes, yes, you did say that." She dismissed his comment. "I'm not talking about that." She lowered her gaze. "I mean *before* that."

He swallowed as his eyes met with hers. "What about it?" he asked cautiously.

"You didn't tell them about *that*." She wore a grim expression.

"You know?" His voice was quiet.

The woman nodded.

He gave a quick chuckle, however there was no amusement in it. "So what?" He shrugged defensively. "It's not like it matters."

"Yes, it does." The woman spoke sternly. "Everything that leads up to that final moment you spent on Earth matters."

He froze at her next words.

"The moment you died."

www.ingramcontent.com/pod-product-compliance
Lightning Source LLC
Chambersburg PA
CBHW011418010726
47494CB00011B/2390